A. F. SMITH

EQUINOX

EQUINOX

A Book by A. F. Smith

Copyright 2020

ISBN # 9781735141107

Book Cover by Self Pub Book Cover-Tina Pappaslee # 52264

Inside Photo by Ilya K. Purchased through Shutterstock Royalty Free stock photo ID694210762

This book is a work of fiction. References to real people, establishments or locations are intended to provide a sense of authenticity. They are used fictitiously. This story is drawn from the Author's imagination and are not to be construed to be real.

Dedication

I would like to dedicate this book to my wonderful sister, Patricia. She has been a constant source of comfort and friendship. Without her this book would have sat in notebooks forever.

I would also like to dedicate it to my Husband. His love and support are constant and very much appreciated. Thanks for being my number one fan.

Lastly, I thank my Family. This book may be a little bit wishful thinking. I appreciate and thank you all for being who you are.

Remember, change your eyes. You may be surprised at what you'll see.

XXXXXXXXXXXXXXXXXX

CONTENTS

1. 1972
2. The Meeting
3. Rayna
4. March 11 through September
5. Leanne
6. The Plan
7. The Birth
8. Hill of Tara
9. The Years Fly By
10. Ireland – Spring Equinox
11. Que Sera Sera Estates
12. Summer Solstice June 21st
13. Summer and Fall
14. Holidays and Babies15.
15. Que Sera Sera December 2025 Sean Patrick
16. O'Sullivan
17. January 2026
18. Rayna's Birth Story
19. March & April 1997 Merena and Maeve
20. Leanne January 2026
21. Leanne March 20 1997
22. Leanne 2026
23. Rayna 2026
24. Sean
25. Rayna and Leanne
26. Visit with Fairies – Sunday
27. February 2026 Meadow
28. Wedding Day March 20th Spring Equinox
29. Diedre and Bernie, 1997
30. Spring and Summer 1997
31. The Project
32. Rayna and Liam
33. The Meadow and Plan

Que-Sera-Sera, The Autumn Equinox

Prologue

Have you ever wondered if things happen for a reason? Like we are destined to live the way we end up. That no matter the choices we make, what will be, will be. Or do you believe that our choices change the destiny of our lives. I think that in this life we need to open our minds. Open them to the possibility that all is not what you see. Possibly behind the veil of our reality is something more. Maybe if we "change our eyes" we will see behind the veil. What wonders do we miss when we just go about the business of living our lives as planned?

Chapter 1: 1972

Walking through the mist, she heard a soft murmuring. Slowly, she followed the sound. Looking around, she felt confused. Where am I? she thought. Starting to talk out loud, she said "Am I dreaming?" Last she remembered was tossing and turning in her bed trying to cool down. The hot breeze blew the curtains toward the bed. As she drifted off, she thought she heard the sound of a flute.

She wore a long nightgown and her long hair was braided down her back. Looking down to her feet, she realized she was barefoot. The soft wet grass felt cool on her bare feet. The sound of the flute grew louder. As she walked on, the mist lifted, and a large tree came into view. It looked like the time of day between dawn and sunrise. Not quite dark, but no sun yet either.

Around the tree flew hundreds of what looked like butterflies. She felt compelled to walk towards them. A beautiful bench was placed in front of the tree. It was intricately carved with pictures and symbols. Sitting down, she ran her hands over the design. A group of women walked towards her from around the tree. Five slender, long haired women. The middle one had light hair down to her knees. All the women were beautiful, but she seemed special. Standing in front of the girl she asked, "May I join you?" The girl tensed a little, moving her hand to her lap. "Yes, she whispered, who are you?" The woman spoke softly. "Don't be afraid, we won't hurt you. My name is Serena. We've been waiting a long time to meet you." Serena took the girls hand. "May I?" She asked. The girl shook her head yes.

The other four women glided to the grass. Sitting cross-legged, they each took a musical instrument out. Soon the air was filled with hauntingly beautiful music. The girl was mesmerized by the sound. As she listened, the winged creatures she had earlier thought were butterflies, flew to the music. Looking closely, she thought they were more than insects but they were too fast to tell. Serena squeezed her hand. "Look at me dear", she said. Turning toward Serena, the girl pulled her eyes away from the women and dancers. Looking into Serena's eyes she asked, "why am I here?"

"One day this will all make sense" Serena whispered. "You are destined to save our worlds." "I don't understand, how could I?" the girl asked. Serena took the girls hands in hers. Looking straight into her eyes, she said, "Your life will be full of children. Some will be your own, others you will care for. You will impact many people. I have no doubt that you will help our worlds when the time comes. Now, go live your life and sometimes look for the magic. Now we will walk to the end of the meadow with you to show you the way home."

With that, the women and girl stood and started walking. The air was warm and the sun had risen. At the very edge, the five women stopped. The girl looked around. "Where is my home?" she asked. "Just follow the path through the woods" Serena said. "You'll be home before you know it." The girl smiled at the women. "Goodbye" she said. "I hope to see you again." "You will someday," the five called out. The girl started through the woods. She turned once but the women had gone.

The sun shined through her bedroom window, falling across her pillow. The kitchen sounds of breakfast being made woke her. Staring at the ceiling, she held onto the memory for just a second. From the bottom of the stairs her mom called. "Leanne, let's go, you're going to be late." Swinging her legs over the side of the bed, she answered. "Coming, be right down." That's weird she thought, looking at the bottom of her gown and feet. They both were damp and grass stained. Her mother called again. "OK" Leanne called back. "I'm up."

As she quickly brushed her teeth, she noticed glitter on her hands. By the end of the day she had forgotten the dream. Over many years she would dream it, again and again.

Chapter 2: The Meeting

It was one of those fall days. Leaves turning orange and gold. The air that day was crisp with the hint of winter to come. The dog was lying curled up on her yellow chair. She forlornly stared out the picture window. Leanne cleaned up the kitchen from the morning meal. She stared blankly out the kitchen window. Early golfers were already on the course. This annoyed her, she had hoped to take a walk with the dog there. She finished up the morning chores.

The days could be so long here she thought. Being retired didn't feel like it was all it was cracked up to be. The dog audibly sighed as she carried the laundry by the living room. She felt guilty, even the dog was depressed. She decided to go for a ride. Taking the leash, she called the dog. Rosie came running. Always ready for an adventure. She was eager to get going.

Leanne decided to go to the state park. Hopefully there would not be many dogs on the trails. Grabbing a water, energy bar and two pieces of fruit thinking ''I really want a donut and coffee.'' She stuffed them in her bag. Her car always made her happy. She called it the "Golden Engine."

Being a childcare provider for 30 years really messed with your brain she thought. Most of her thoughts played out like a children's book. Funny, happy and to the point.

The ride was short. At the park she drove around to the back. There was a picnic area and short walking trail. Rosie was excited, jumping from window to window. Her favorite place was N.H. where she was able to swim and run. Though, here she needed to be leashed, Leanne planned on letting her swim. The sky had clouded over, grey. Sweatshirt weather for sure. Getting out of the car, she opened the back hatch. There, were her jacket, snack and other "necessary" things. She always felt prepared. In her car were an extra leash (in case she found a dog), a baby car seat (don't ask), and a box of extra clothes for herself (just in case). She never needed these things but by God she would be prepared.

Her kids growing up were the ones with the plastic bags to sit on at field trips. They were always glad to have them, but scoffed at first. Rosie barked excitedly. Leanne opened her door and she bounded out. At least somebody is excited, Leanne mused. Being a work day, there were only a few cars visible. She could see a few. Two tents and a camper parked at sites nearby. It was late in the season and most campers and park users had gone back to their lives after Labor Day. Still, she figured best to hook on the leash.

Rosie pulled along smelling everything. Such a simple thing as a walk could make her day. Leanne felt guilty for not doing this more. Deep breath she thought, no negativity. Enjoy the day she told herself. Looking up, she realized the sky had cleared. Beautiful blue with the sun shining off the colorful leaves. Who could feel down on such a beautiful day? She told herself how lucky she was, nice house and family who loves her. Her husband tells her every day how much he cares. Somedays it just didn't feel enough. What was wrong with her. Stop, she screamed in her head. Enjoy this day be glad you have it!

Just then Rosie started pulling her. She nearly pulled Leanne off her feet. Someone was sitting at the picnic table at the water's edge. Rosie pulled right over to the person sitting there. She started jumping and licking. It was a young woman, long dark hair, average height. She laughed and welcomed Rosie's advances. On closer inspection, Leanne noticed she was probably in her early 20's. She was dressed in multiple layers and there was a sadness about her. "Sorry, sorry," Leanne cried out. "Rosie stop, sit down." Rosie continued to greet her new best friend. "It's OK" the women called out. "I like dogs." Rosie was acting like it was her long-lost friend. The girl/woman looked up. "Rosie, did you say Rosie?"

Their eyes met. Leanne could not believe it. "Rayna?" "Nana!" she cried. In that moment Leanne could see it in her face. The little girl she had loved all those years ago was still there. They moved to each other; Leanne wrapped her arms around her old daycare child. The years melted away. They both laughed as Rosie danced around. "I thought the dog was extra friendly. I remember when you brought her home to daycare," Rayna said.

Rayna had been one of the special ones. Over the years, caring for so many children, a pocketful stand out. The ones you really felt bad when they left you. Leanne always treated each child as equal as she could but there was no denying some were closer to her heart. Rayna was one of those. She had been a foster child living in the neighborhood. Her foster parents were nice enough. They both worked in Boston. Rayna was put in Daycare in 1998, she was a year old. She stayed in Leanne's care until 12 years old. Then had been her dogwalker for Rosie 2 years more. No wonder Rosie was so glad to see her.

Leanne stroked Rayna's face. "I would know this face anywhere," she cried. "How are you? Do you live down here? I am so sorry about the Stones." They were her foster parents and had died in a horrific New Year's Day accident two years before. "I know, I know," Rayna cried, "it's been a tough few years."

By now Leanne had large tears running down her face. "I am so glad to run into you. let's sit down and catch up. First, I have to let Rosie swim." She unhooked her leash and Rosie bound into the water. She did her usual swim about. The water had to be a bit chilly, but she enjoyed every minute of it. Rosie came up on shore shook off and lay down. The grass was soft and the sun warm. She was snoring in no time.

Leanne opened her back pack. "Are you hungry?" she asked Rayna. "Yes, I just can't believe it's you," she said nodding her head. Leanne pulled out the energy bar, water and two apples. Taking out some hand sanitizer and a small paring knife she set the items on the table. Then she pulled out a plastic tablecloth, napkins and a couple of dog biscuits. Rayna giggled. "You haven't changed at all Nana, always prepared." Leanne cut the bar in half, then handed an apple, water and half the bar to Rayna. "Wash up," she laughed. The sun warmed her back, Rayna warmed her heart.

What a special day, she thought. They chewed their bar and took turns slicing their apples. Both gazed over the water lost in thought. Rosie, sufficiently dry and warm, loped over for her biscuits. Rayna asked, "how old is she now?" Leanne answered 11 years soon. "Wow," Rayna answered. "Seems like yesterday and a million years ago, at the same time." They talked about the old Daycare kids, where they were now. They talked about Leanne's grandsons; the boys were a little younger than Rayna.

With tears in her eyes, Rayna talked about her Foster parents. They had been killed almost two years ago. It was a drunk driver on New Year's Eve. Her parents had taken an UBER and someone else slammed into them, killing all three instantly. Rayna had been away with friends. Things had gone downhill from there. Leanne hugged Rayna, "I'm so sorry," she said. "That must have been hard for you." Rayna shook her head yes. She picked up her napkin and blew her nose. 'Well it was great while it lasted." she cried. "I really miss them."

Leanne looked around. "Why are you here Rayna?" Rayna excitedly jumped up. "Oh, oh, I have to show you this, come to my site." Leanne packed up her bag and with Rosie, followed Rayna down the path. Nestled in a wooded site was a small camp. Tent, clothes line, fire pit and an older car. Rayna ran to the car. It was a 1998 Ford Mustang. The car had been well cared for. Rayna opened the trunk and rummaged around. After a few minutes she emerged with an afghan and a book. "Look Nana," she called 'I still have the blanket and goodbye book you made me."

Leanne couldn't believe it. After all these years, Rayna had held onto something she made. Every time a child moved on from Leanne's care, she would crochet a blanket. She called it a warm hug from Nana. She had even sewed in a tag saying when the children moved on. Nana would take their order. The child picked the color they wanted. The fun part was watching Nana work on the blanket at free playtime. When the child left, they got the blanket and a book of pictures. It warmed Leanne's heart to think in such a small way, these items were so special to Rayna that she had kept them.

Rayna showed Leanne around her site. She was proud of the way she kept everything organized. "Aren't you lonely?" Leanne asked. "No", Rayna replied, "there is a real camaraderie in camp sites. I will be moving on soon anyway and we often have a communal camp fire."

It was starting to get cool and Rosie was itching to explore a little more before going home. "Why don't I walk you to your car?" Rayna asked. Leanne took the leash and they started towards the parking lot. The sun was lower and there was a chill in the air. "Will you be warm enough?" Leanne asked. "Oh yes," Rayna replied. "We always have a big fire and I have a beautiful sleeping bag." "Oh, to be young again," Leanne laughed. Rayna giggled when they got to Leanne's car.

"I would have known this was yours Nana," she chuckled. "Golden Engine like Thomas." Leanne said. Rosie got a few more pats while Leanne dragged the ramp out of the back seat. "Oh", Rayna cried. "She needs a ramp?" "Yes, we're not getting any younger." Leanne answered. Rosie sprinted up the ramp and said her doggie goodbyes. Leanne shut the door and turned to Rayna. "You are just what I needed." Rayna smiled. "Me too. I will be here a while longer, will you come back?"

"Sure," Leanne answered. "I'll be back Monday. Rosie will love another adventure. Why don't I bring some sandwiches? We'll meet you at the picnic area for lunch," Leanne said. "Is there anything special you would like?" "I would love an Italian sub, chips and a diet coke." Rayna answered. "You got it." Leanne replied. Leanne reached out to give Rayna a hug goodbye. She wrapped her arms around her.

As she leaned in, she felt a kick. With her hands, on Rayna's shoulders, she stepped back. Shocked, she looked down at Rayna's tummy then up to her face. "Are you, are you pregnant?" she sputtered. Rayna stepped back. That was when Leanne noticed Rayna was wearing multiple sweatshirts. Originally, she had thought Rayna had put on a little weight. Who hadn't put on the college extra weight? Rayna turned and started walking back towards her camp site. "Will you still come with lunch?" Leanne closed her gaping mouth. "Of course!" she called out. "I'll even add a cupcake, see you Monday."

Sitting in her car, Leanne buckled up and turned the key. This day had defiantly turned out different than she thought. As she slowly drove out of the park, her mind was racing. Leanne didn't say a word to anyone in her family. She thought it best to keep her "adventure" to herself. All weekend her mind raced. Questions; How would Rayna take care of the baby? What were her plans? Could Leanne help with supplies and food? How much should she do?

Monday couldn't come soon enough. It rained all day Sunday. The men were watching their football. As long as Leanne kept them fed, they were content. Leanne went down to the basement. She still had boxes of clothes, toys and blankets from her Daycare days. She pulled out a few items and threw them in the wash. She would bring them tomorrow for Rayna.

Leanne thought about how miserable and cold it probably was at the park. She hoped Rayna was warm enough. Monday morning dawned beautifully. The sun was shining and the ground was drying quickly. In true Indian summer fashion, the temperature was rising. Leanne got her husband out the door. She jumped in the shower and dressed for the day. She found herself excited. Rosie sensed that adventures would happen. She did not let Leanne out of her sight. She finished the morning chores. She started a pot roast in the crockpot, put dishes in and turned on the dishwasher, and was headed out the door.

Rose saw her leash being taken down and jumped for joy. Leanne laughed out loud at the dog. "What, another adventure for you Rosie? Let's go for a ride," she sang out happily.

First stop was the local small market. Leanne jumped out of the car, she felt so light. She hurried into the store. At the deli she ordered two sandwiches, chips and tonic. While they were being made, she picked up some cupcakes and a few sundries for Rayna. That morning she had packed a small bag with the baby items.

It was exciting. Leanne felt so happy to be doing something. Rosie was happy to see Leanne emerge from the store. She immediately started barking and jumping around. Off they went for the short drive to the park. The weather had gotten warmer. She rolled up her sleeves and parked the car.

This time Leanne brought a small folding wagon. She put the lunch, baby things and jacket in the wagon. Rosie jumped out and they started towards the water. The sun was brilliant. The way it sparkled over the water was just like diamonds. The beautiful fall colors of the leaves were mirrored at the water's edge. Was everything really so beautiful, or was it the anticipation of the meeting Leanne wondered?

They approached the picnic area, Rosie spotted Rayna, her back was toward them as she looked at the pond. Rosie pulled on the leash. Leanne glanced around making sure no one was coming. She let Rosie off the lead. Rosie raced down to Rayna. Passing her, she ran to the water and began lapping up the cool fresh drink. Immediately, she started coughing and sputtering. Next, she was swimming in circles lapping up more water.

Rayna was startled, then burst out laughing. "Rose you're getting me soaked," she screamed. Rayna turned to Leanne still laughing. Leanne could not hide her shock. Rayna was huge. Not a little pregnant (if there were such a thing) but oh baby big. Leanne's face must have showed her shock. Rayna chuckled, "still don't have a poker face I see Nana." Leanne sputtered "It's just, it's just I didn't notice the other day. Now I wonder how could I not have noticed?" Rayna smiled, "I'm starved let's eat."

Leanne pulled herself together. She took out the tablecloth, napkins and lunch she had brought. Rayna couldn't wait. "This is great", she cried taking the first bite. "I haven't had this in a long time." They both ate in silence for a few minutes. They watched the dog. Rosie was trying to catch a fish and was quite amusing to watch. After the last bite of sandwich Leanne wiped her mouth, turned to Rayna and said, "Tell me about it". Rosie had come up to sit in the sun and gone to sleep. Rayna took a long breath and started her story.

Chapter 3: Rayna

Rayna always felt like she didn't quite belong. Growing up in Milton, MA., there was a stigma to being in foster care. Up until third grade she didn't really know that she was different.

Third grade was the turning point. If the girls weren't mean, their moms were. She didn't come from the right people. Her Foster Parents were in their late 50's. The other parents were much younger, Rayna was caught in the middle. She was still going to after school care at Nana's. Her parents had made arrangements for a late pick-up. Too late for the after-school program at the school. This gave Rayna a feeling of belonging.

When she aged out of daycare, Nana hired her to walk the new puppy, Rosie. That's why Rosie still remembered her connection to Rayna.

Rayna finished school and went off to college. State schools were free for Foster Children. When the accident happened, she only had one semester left to finish. Joe and Joan were killed on New Year's Day, 2017. They had been at a party and called for a ride home. Another car lost control. They never knew what hit them. Rayna spun out of control. The home and only family she had ever known were gone. Just like that, she was on her own.

She found out that the house was rented. She needed to have it cleaned out by March 1st. While cleaning out her foster parent's personal papers she found her file from the state. She read with trepidation.

24

*Baby Girl Found on Firehouse steps. Found April
21,1997*
*Note Enclosed: Please care for my baby. She was born
at 8:25am on April 12,1997. I tried but I have no way
to care for her Tell her I loved her very much. This is
the best thing for her.*
I will always love her. XXX.

The tears ran down Rayna's face. For the first
time she knew she had been loved by her birth mother.
She had proof in the note. The next sheet was a
document giving care of her to someone she didn't
know. Then at 5 months old, she was given to Joe and
Joan Stone. She felt cheated, how could her mom have
just left her. Why didn't the first foster family keep
her?   She cried great sobs for all the loss. She went to
the kitchen. That's where the Stones kept the liquor.
They really didn't drink much, but kept it for company,
or times like this. She poured a big splash of vodka.
Gulping it down she felt the burning sensation of it
running down her throat. What should she do? She had
never felt so alone in her life. She curled up on the
couch and went to sleep. She slept a long time and her
dreams haunted her. It was dark when she woke up.
She finished packing up the house.

Joan had recently retired. Most of the clutter
was gone. There was a box with her name on it.
Opening the lid, Rayna found mementos of her life. A
passport for Rayna Marie. A picture of an infant

wrapped in a pink blanket. Written in marker on the white bottom strip was:

Rayna Marie-birth 4-12-1997

The picture was taken with a Polaroid camera. The next picture was of Joan holding a beaming infant. She had to be about 5 months old. Turning it over Rayna read:

Mommy and Rayna Sept 5, 1997.

Mommy and baby were both smiling. The rest of the stuff was the usual papers from school. Small art projects, cards and the occasional report card. On the very bottom was a book. Rayna reached in and pulled out the book. Turning over to the front cover she smiled. This was her goodbye gift book from Daycare. Her favorite childhood book, *The Rain Babies by Laura Kraus Melmed.* Inside on the cover was written, *To Rayna, you will always be special to me. I have watched you grow into a wonderful young woman. Good luck and come visit us. Love Nana D.C.*

Tears rolled down her cheeks. She felt so alone. So much had changed. She sat down and read the story. The Rain Babies, was about an old woman who longed for a child. It was a story both Rayna and Nana had loved. Nana had bought copies of certain books. The children could pick out one when they were moving on. Rayna had picked this one. That was the end of the personal things. Her childhood so far, basically fit into one box.

It was January 21st and the semester would be starting up again. Though her heart wasn't in it, she decided to go back to school. Packing what would fit in the mustang she drove back. Joe had made sure to pay incidentals at school up front. Tuition was covered by the state. The rent was paid through June. He also had given her ten thousand dollars in an account, just in her name. Joe was a planner; he just hadn't planned to die. Rayna planned on giving the landlord notice on February 1st.Her life in Milton would be over by March1st.

She managed to catch up at school. The Professors were understanding. She went to the house one last time. Walking through the empty rooms she remembered all the fun they had. Holidays, birthdays and vacations were always celebrated. It really hit home how alone she felt. They were good parents. Wiping the last tears from her cheeks, she closed the door for the last time. Leaving the key under the mat, as instructed, she drove away.

Her roommates all wanted to keep the apartment. Rayna got a job at McDonalds and worked to pay her rent. Summer flew by. Senior year was starting in September and she wanted to finish. She did want a semester abroad. She applied for a semester in Dublin, Ireland for September 2018. This would leave her to graduate at the end of the term 2018. She was still waiting to hear if she had been accepted. The holidays were just around the corner. Rayna's roommates were planning trips home and all had invited her. This would be her first Christmas alone. She felt numb. They decorated the apartment a little. She continued to work part-time at McDonalds. They supplemented the food bill by bringing home the leftovers. Everyone loved to see her coming home with the bag. It seemed a sin to throw away the food, Rayna thought. On the last day of the Fall term Rayna had lunch at the cafeteria.

She met up with a group of students not going home for the Holidays. They were planning their vacation time. There was a group going to Punta Cana. They were to leave on Dec 27th and return January 21st. The purpose of the trip is to help build a new school. The college sponsors the trip as a way for students to give back. The nights and one weekday are free time for the students to see the sights. The rest of the time is helping build the school. Everyone was super excited, the room reverberated with the excited voices. There were two open spots. Rayna and her roommate looked at each other. At that instant she knew she was going. Rayna jumped up, "I'm in!!!" she screamed. She could not contain her excitement. "Wait, wait, wait," the group leader said, "Hold on. Hands up, do you have a passport?" Rayna had just found her passport.

Joe had decided when she was 15 to get one for her. He again liked to be prepared. He had it filled out with just the name on the picture that was found with her. It read, *Rayna Marie Birthday 4/12/97*. This was done legally and notarized. She had never gotten a chance to use it, now was that chance. The excitement was overwhelming. Signing the papers and putting down her deposit, she was exhilarating. Something new to do. She had dreaded the holiday season. Now, she would ring in the New Year with hope.

Rayna spent the next couple of days getting ready. They were given a list of supplies to bring. The children could use pencils, paper notebooks and art supplies. Rayna shopped at the dollar store and found fun things to bring. She added hair ties, elastics and coloring books for girls. Boys got small cars, toothbrushes and combs. She spent around $100.00 and was able to get lot of things. She felt so happy. The sting of the season had been taken away.

Punta Cana was beautiful. Stepping out the Airport doors, she was exhilarated. The warmth enveloped her like a warm soft blanket. The smells were incredible. Rayna felt almost giddy with excitement. The group piled into the waiting van. The drive was breathtaking. What a beautiful country, she thought. Everyone was excitedly chatting. The van was bringing them to a group of cabins outside of town. Each cabin held two beds and they were assigned a roommate. Rayna's roommate at home hadn't been able to go. She did not have her passport and there wasn't enough time to get it. She met her roommate, Cara, at the airport in Boston. She seemed nice enough and they had chatted most of the plane ride. Cara's parents had gone on a holiday cruise. Cara opted for this adventure. She was 19 and felt she could make a difference. The gravel crunched under the tires as they pulled into camp. Home for the next month almost.

The cabins were rustic. Each had a small front porch with two rocking chairs. The lodge was also the dining hall. There was a low hanging roof. Benches were built in on both sides. Four cabins lined each side. The lodge was situated in the middle. In front of the lodge was a huge fire pit. It was circled with tree trunk benches to seat at least 20 people.

Rayna could barely contain her excitement. Rushing to the van, she grabbed her luggage. Sprinting to cabin 2, she called out "Cara lets go." They had three hours before the first meeting at the lodge. Rayna opened the door and stepped in. The cabin was small, each side clearly marked. A large window set in the middle There was a screen on it, the previous tenants had "jury rigged". Rayna hoped it would keep the bugs out. It was just netting with duct tape all around, sealing the window. Two end tables and a twin bed on each side. There was one overhead light. This would be home for the next three weeks. Spinning around, Rayna took in the cabin. There were hooks for clothes and a bench on each side of the room. Rayna guessed that was where they would leave clothes and toiletries. They both needed the bathroom. The bathhouse was behind the lodge. They dropped their things and decided to find it. There were no locks on the outside of the doors. In the airport they had been instructed to carry their passports and valuables. Each student had been given an undergarment purse. They slipped their money and passports inside. They also had copied their passports and left that under their mattresses. They were instructed to be aware of their surroundings. It was as safe as any foreign country, but you needed to be careful. Stepping off the porch step, the heat and smells hit you. This was what paradise was like, Rayna thought. Warm, smelling of vegetation birds were singing and there were lots of sounds. Rayna had no idea what they were. It was awesome Rayna thought.

They checked out the rest of the camp. Circling back to cabin 2, they decided to unpack. The supply list had included a lot of "suggested" things. Rayna had opted to go comfortable. They were allowed one backpack and one carry on. Each bed was just a mattress, you provided your own bedding. Rayna chose the bed on the left. Shaking out her sheets she made up the bed. Using some of her folded clothes, she slipped the folded bundle into her pillow case. Then just used the flat sheet as a bed spread. It was hot, but not oppressive. It was close to dinner time. Rayna took her journal and went to sit on the porch. She wanted to write about the camp and her first impression of everything. Cara came bounding up the steps. "Isn't this awesome? "Wait for me while I unpack."

Rayna rocked and her thoughts went to her Foster parents. They had always talked about traveling to warm places. They had hoped to see some of the world in retirement. Never making it just didn't seem fair. Rayna swore that wouldn't happen to her. She would travel after college. There was no one to care about graduation ceremonies. No one to disappoint if you didn't walk the walk. Maybe she would just have her diploma mailed. Maybe she would start her life in Ireland after her semester there. She wanted to see some of the world. Maybe it wasn't so bad having no one. Closing her journal Rayna went back inside to get ready for dinner. Getting ready consisted of grabbing her purse and phone. The phone was her glorified camera. Cara had made up her side. They closed the door and started for the lodge. An orientation, meal and bonfire were on the agenda. Rayna was excited. This seemed like a great decision.

The lodge was packed with excited students, their voices were happy and boisterous. All in all, there were about thirty people there, though it sounded like many more. The aroma of dinner cooking reminded Rayna that it had been awhile since she last ate. She hoped the meeting was quick. Her stomach was growling. Clapping his hands, the man in charged shouted to be heard over the others. "Settle down, settle down," putting his fingers in his mouth, he got everyone's attention with a shrill whistle. Rayna and Cara found seats; the meeting started. Groups were picked quickly everyone was hungry. Assignments were handed out. Rayna and Cara were in the morning group together. Scraping chairs back, everyone hurried to the picnic like tables. This was communal living. After this meal the students would be in charge of different parts of the meal. Rayna and Cara were assigned cleanup for the first week. The food was simple but good. Covered salads were set at each place. Rolls, butter and big bowls of pasta were brought out. The protein was some kind of fish and there was a cheese plate. Fresh fruit and cookies were the dessert offerings. Drinks were lemonade and ice tea minus the ice (it was the jungle). Rayna chose the pasta, salad and dessert options. She added cheese to her salad for good measure. The food was filling and delicious.

The evening was free time. Work on the school would start the next day. Everyone not assigned went to the fire pit to socialize. Rayna was beat. She walked slowly taking in the starlit night. It was beautiful here; she felt her soul breathe. She was anxious to lie down. It had been a long day. Breakfast was at 7 AM and the van left for the school site at 8. She headed for the cabin.

The cabin was dark, she hit the switch. The stark white light filled the room. She realized either dress in the dark or put on a show. Grabbing her toiletries, she chose the bathhouse to change in. Sleeping attire consisted of tank and shorts, that were reasonable to walk around in. Arriving at the bath house Rayna had to wait in line. It seemed the others were pretty tired also. It had been a long day. She chit-chatted with the other girls, small pleasantries, until it was her turn. Back at the cabin she stretched out on her bed. She was excited about tomorrow. She felt that this would be a great adventure. She heard Cara come in at 11:00 PM. Next thing she knew the alarm was screaming.

Breakfast was good and plentiful. Fresh fruits, eggs and bread, there was hot oatmeal as well. The leader told everyone to eat up, hard work was ahead. Cleanup was quick, Rayna and Cara made the bus in plenty of time. Everyone on the bus was given a bag lunch. The days flew by. Rayna didn't know she had it in her, she had never worked harder. She felt a great sense of accomplishment. The building was really taking shape. Each night after dinner everyone gathered around the fire pit. It was mesmerizing to sit staring at the sparks rising into the night sky. Sounds of crackling wood and soft voices in conversation or song filled the air. They talked about their day. Some of the group pared off into couples and moved away out of sight. Each night Rayna stayed about an hour, just long enough to be sociable. Then back to the cabin. She cherished the solitude, writing in her journal each night about her day. She stretched out on her bed. Hands behind her head, she listened to the night sounds. Insects, small animals foraging for their dinner. Even the distant laughter around the fire pit. It lulled her to sleep and she welcomed the dark.   There were big plans for New Year's Eve. They decorated the lodge, special food and alcohol was purchased. Rayna was conflicted. She wanted to celebrate with everyone. It was just that New Year's Day would mark the one-year anniversary of her Foster parents' deaths. Rayna thought hard and decided to attend the party. She thought Joe and Joan would want her to go on with her life. Feeling bad wouldn't bring them back, she thought. Cara and some of the others proposed a masquerade ball. Everyone voted to wear masks. They picked up feathers, shells and material in town.

Work ended at 12 noon New Year's Eve, so everyone could get ready. They put up streamers, candles on the tables and then made their masks. Rayna used royal blue feathers and gold sparkles. She had taken a black tank dress for just such an occasion. They all took turns showering. There were no hair dryers, Rayna combed her long hair out. She sat in the sunshine letting it dry. The warmth of the sun felt so good she almost fell asleep. Everyone was excited there was a kind of anonymity to being in a foreign country alone. Not to mention wearing a mask. Some of the local crew were invited to the party as well That just added to the thrill. Dinner was at 6pm, then clean up. The party would start at 9pm. It was good to take her mind off the Anniversary. Rayna had fallen asleep after dinner. She woke up when Cara came in from the bath house. Rayna sat up on the edge of the bed. Cara was like Cinderella, blond hair and blue eyes and practically had little mice making her dress. Out of her back pack that morning she had taken a rolled-up dress. It was light blue and shimmery. She carried it to the showers and left it while everyone took their showers. The wrinkles had fallen out like magic. Slipping it on, she brushed her hair. She had braided it that afternoon. Shaking out the braids her hair fell in soft ripples. She wove a light blue ribbon in on one side braid. A little lipstick and eye shadow, she looked like a princess. She finished it off with a silver mask. She looked beautiful. Twirling she asked Rayna "What do you think?" "Wow!" Rayna whispered, "You look awesome."

Rayna left her dark hair in a long braid. She wrapped it around her head like a halo. She slipped into her long black dress and stepped into her sandals. The finishing touch was the feather mask. She too, looked beautiful. What was it about masks Rayna thought? The hair was the same, same body, same face but a mask just added that bit of mystery.

The night was beautifully romantic in the moonlight. The stars twinkled and the moon was full. Rayna felt both excited and melancholy. This night would really mark the end of firsts. First birthdays, first holidays and all the rest. "Hurry Rayna," Cara called, "I want to dance." Rayna picked up the pace and they entered the lodge. It really was beautiful. Soft lights, table cloths and candles gave the room a soft glow. Rayna walked over to the punch bowl. Might as well get this party started, she thought.

First a toast to the memory of Joe and Joan. She lifted her full glass. Thanks for the family, she whispered I will never forget you; I miss you both and with that she drained the glass. She poured a second glass. The music was loud. Everyone was giddy with laughter. Someone started playing the drums. The girls started dancing. The night flew by. As the night progressed, Rayna noticed most everyone was paired off slow dancing. They still wore their masks, even the guys had them. Theirs were more basic, not adorned like the women. It still gave the party an air of mystery.

A tall dark-haired man came up to Rayna. She was just finishing her fourth glass of punch. As long as she stood still, everything was fine. The punch had gone to her head though. She didn't recognize the man walking towards her. He must be a local or one of the on-site workers. He held his hand out. "You can't be alone at the stroke of midnight," he laughed. "Dance with me." As she closed her eyes and put her arms around his neck to dance, she thought, "Maybe four rum punches were a little too much." The room was turning, but if she kept her eyes open, it didn't spin. In the middle of the second song the countdown began, "10, 9, 8, 7, 6, 5, 4, 3, 2, 1… Happy New Year!!!" they shouted. Someone had brought horns and confetti. The night felt very festive. Some of the party goers took off their masks. Rayna and her partner did not. "Let's grab a last drink and go to the fire pit." he asked. Rayna agreed. She was feeling the alcohol but carried a last drink anyway.

The cool air would be welcome she thought. They held hands and walked to the fire. Others had the same idea. Some were sitting on blankets a little distance away. Others were on the log benches circling the fire pit. It was a bit crowded and noisy. Rayna's cabin wasn't too far away. The porch looked towards the fire pit. "Let's sit over on my porch." she said. They walked hand in hand over to the steps. The stars were amazing and the glow of the fire mesmerizing. Everything seemed so peaceful and magical. Her companion was funny and shared a lot of stories.

Finishing her last drink, Rayna felt a little buzzed. She did not want the night to end. This was fun, she couldn't remember the last time she felt so free. They sat on the porch steps and started kissing. Still wearing their masks, Rayna invited him into the cabin. She just wanted to lie down for a minute. They both stretched out on the bed. In the dark she told him all about her Foster Parents and why she had come. He gently held her and as she started to cry, he whispered softly how sorry he was for her loss. They made love still wearing their masks, both willing participants. Rayna fell asleep listening to some of the others around the fire. She felt tired and rolled over to face the wall. He lay beside her, snoring softly. As she drifted off to sleep, she realized she didn't even know his name. His arms were wrapped around her and she felt good falling asleep.

The next morning was not so good. Her head pounded. UGGGH!!! she moaned, pulling the covers over her head. Why did I drink so much? Bits and pieces of the night came to her. She sat up, uggh, too fast. She laid back down. Rolling on her side, looking towards Cara's bed, she looked for her friend. Cara peaked out from under her covers. "You look as bad as I feel?" she moaned. Rayna asked, "Did you see the guy I was with?" Cara groaned, sitting on the edge of her bed. "No, I didn't get back until dawn. You were sound asleep alone when I came in. Did you sleep with that guy you were dancing with?" Rayna sat up slowly, looking around the room. Her dress was on the floor and both masks were on top of it. Looking down at herself she realized she was wearing a man's T shirt. "Yup, I definitely did," she laughed. "I don't even know his name, but he was nice. I am never drinking again." "Right," Cara laughed "till next time." Rayna had no idea who he was. He wasn't one of the other students, he must have been a worker. Oh well it's a New year and a new day and we have the day off. They both took their time getting dressed and spent the day relaxing.

The rest of the time went fast. Her group ended up finishing one school. They were excited to meet the children who would attend it. The children were very appreciative of the small gifts the group brought for them. Jan 21st came too fast. The ride to the airport was bittersweet. They took a last picture in front of the van before going to the airport. Cara and Rayna sat together on the way home. Rayna finished her journal writing without ever knowing the mystery man's name.

Rayna started back at school and work right away. Punta Cana was just a fond memory; she did not keep in touch with Cara after returning back. They were friends on Facebook but that was all. Rayna had two semesters to finish. One in the U.S and one at the University College of Dublin in Ireland.

She was excited to visit Ireland. She and her roommate had done an Ancestry. Com test. Her results showed 95% of Irish descent. That was one of the reasons she had applied in Ireland. She had been accepted for last January, but with the death of her parents they gave her the option of this coming December. The funeral and packing had constituted an emergency. She felt lucky she had not lost the opportunity completely. Now she was saving as much money as she could to go. This was her time, she felt. Work and school were both important so she could achieve her dreams. As soon as she could, she bought her ticket to Dublin. December 14th of this year. That would give her time to settle in and see some sights before class started. She wanted to make as much money as she could before leaving. She printed her ticket and put it in her locked file box. She pushed it to the back of her closet and went to study.

Chapter 4: March 11 through September

Rayna was exhausted. School was easy now but working until closing was hard. She had fallen asleep a couple of times at school. After a few late-night McDonald meals, she had gotten sick in the morning. Hearing her vomiting, her roommate called through the bathroom door. 'You're not pregnant, are you?" Rayna moaned of course not, too many fries last night. "Ok, just saying," her roommate replied through the door. "You wouldn't be the first one you know." Rayna finished up, brushed her teeth and got ready for class. The thought of coffee turned her stomach. She just felt run down, maybe too many shifts at work she thought.

Everyone was planning a pub crawl on March 17th for St Patrick's Day. Wear your green and see who can drink the most, the posters screamed. Rayna had planned on wearing green. Now that Ancestry. Com had given her, the Irish heritage, she was proud too. Drinking, that was another story. She hadn't had any drinks since New Year's Eve and she didn't plan to now. Shamrock shakes from McDonalds, well that was another story. Even that made her feel queasy though. That was when a light bulb went off.

When was my last period she thought? She always kept a journal along with her weekly weight. She always noted the first day of her periods. She anxiously flipped back the pages. OMG, she thought

December 14th was the last day listed. She went through every page of January twice, then February twice. She went frantically through again, had she missed it? Nope, her last time was December 14th, then everything fell together in her mind. The night of New Years, feeling so tired, nausea, she even had gained a few pounds. She had chalked that up to all the fries. Could she really be pregnant?

As soon as work ended, she bought three pregnancy tests. As it was Friday night and everybody was out, she could have privacy. She peed on all three tests and waited. It was now 12:15 AM. Everyone would be home sooner than later. She had covered the test wands with a face cloth. She set her phone timer for the 5 minutes. She had taken a book into the bathroom. She re-read the same page 10 times before the timer went off...She sat there numb. She already knew what the tests would prove. Still, maybe it's something else, maybe cancer she thought. Not that she wanted that but it could be. Maybe she's just run down she thought. Slowly she lifted the facecloth corner. Just do it she screamed in her mind. She was standing in front of the sink. The tubes, like little soldiers, lined up on the counter. If she was pregnant, two of them would say the word *pregnant*. The other, a pink line would show if it was positive. She stared at herself in the mirror, eyes to eyes, her long wavy hair framed her face. Her face was pale, freshly scrubbed. Did it look a little fuller? "Ready," she said out loud.

Slowly, she lowered her eyes first, then her head. She saw the first one. Pink line…PREGNANT!!! The other 2 little soldiers both said *pregnant*……..

It was now March 17th and she raised her eyes, staring into her reflection. She muttered out loud, "Now I have the luck of the Irish. What am I going to do?" Wrapping all the packaging and the three tests in plastic CVS bags, she slipped them in her backpack. She would tell no one until she figured out what she wanted to do.

Rayna picked up a book at the book store. "What to Expect When Your Expecting." She decided to keep the pregnancy to herself. With luck she wouldn't be showing until summer. Doing the old-fashioned math for determining the due date she counted back, three months from her last period. So, December minus three is September. December 14 was the date add 7 days 21st. That would make the baby due date September 21st. OMG, she thought, what do I do? She had planned to camp for the summer. They had given the apartment up for July 1st. She had planned to travel and see the country. Camping at state parks and boon docking. Boon docking was just camping where you could with no facilities usually. Most of the camp sites allowed two weeks at a time. Then you had to move on. This discouraged people from just living at camp grounds. She planned on ending up at Massasoit State Park. She had procured the caretaker job. A cabin with heat and hot water was hers from September 4th to Dec 14th. She only had to check the park and maintain the facilities. She was to meet the resident caretaker in June. The cabin would be perfect. She would be camping thru September, then stay in the cabin until December. She would have the baby there, then figure out what to do.

Graduation came at the end of May. Luckily it was overcast and unseasonably cool. No one commented on her wearing a raincoat. Her roommate hadn't even noticed her weight gain. First time Moms usually didn't show much luckily. When she looked at herself, she could definitively tell.

She wasn't graduating, but she went to watch her roommate receive her diploma. Rayna still had the semester abroad to finish first. Then she planned on having her diploma mailed. The ceremony ended and everyone was invited to a party. It was a fun celebration. Rayna left for work after congratulating everyone. McDonalds was the one place people seemed to notice her weight gain. She had raised the shoulders of her uniform top to make room for her growing tummy. If anyone made a comment or raised an eyebrow, she would rub her stomach and say "I have to stop eating the fries," and laugh. It kept everyone satisfied.

They packed up the apartment. Rayna was not surprised when everything she wanted to keep fit in her Mustang. Added to that, she had taken her camping equipment from the family home. She owned a large tent, stove, sleeping bags and other camping supplies. She planned on splurging for a blow-up mattress. Rayna still had $10,000.00 and had managed to save another $5,000.00 more. She was excited for her adventure. The pregnancy, up until now, did not feel real. This past week though, she felt the first kick. Now, it felt real!!!

The book and You Tube videos had prepared her for this. The first kicks really made her start to plan. The You Tube natural birth videos talked about unassisted births. She found out she needed to pick up forms to register the birth. She planned for the baby to be born at the Massasoit State Park. She went to the town hall. She asked for four copies of birth certificate forms in case she made a mistake. The clerk, a woman in her 50's, looked over the top of her glasses and said "You do know the hospital will help right." "Yes," Rayna answered, "I just want to be prepared." She paid the fee and hurried out.

On the internet sites, they also listed the supplies that would be useful for the birth. Rayna decided to be prepared. The Dollar Store was nearby. She stopped and picked up the list of items. She bought a plastic box and filled it with everything she thought she might need. Of course, the baby needed very little. Something to clamp the cord, syringe for the airway, diapers and a blanket. Everything else was extra's. Fun to have but not needed. Rayna wanted to have a little more so off to Walmart she went. She wanted to be prepared just in case. She used an "essential list" from the internet. They included bottles and formula just in case nursing didn't go well. She would wait on those items.

The summer flew by. Rayna went from campground to campground. She bartered to get some money off the camp fees. She learned this tip on You Tube. She ran camp stores a few hours a day, cleaned restrooms at another camp. She loved all the jobs, checking people in was a favorite job. She always arrived early and picked a well-situated site. Setting up was easy. Her new tent was a far cry from the family tent of her youth. Her tent had two "rooms." The bed to the back. In the first section she set it up as the "living" area. The camaraderie of camp living did open her up to questions about the baby. She just told people her boyfriend was deployed. That kind of ended any more questions. People came and went so she felt it was a non-issue. The summer was filled with campfires, marshmallows and friendly faces. The last campsite was to be Massasoit.

Her stay in Massasoit was set up at the beginning of the summer. She hadn't mentioned the pregnancy. She hoped they would just think she was heavy. She figured they would not encourage giving birth on-site. Checking in on Labor Day weekend, she wore a long sweatshirt with pockets. It was big on her and she thought her belly was hidden. She left her hair down to give the illusion of width. Her hair was dark, curly and down to her waist. She usually braided it, but to hide her watermelon belly, this was better. She had only talked by phone to the caretaker so he had nothing to notice differently. Rayna checked in to the park on Saturday, September 1st. Every site was full for the weekend. She only had to pay until Tuesday the 4th then she would move to the cabin. Rayna kept to herself that weekend. She was extra tired and wasn't sleeping well. She could not get comfortable. Her stomach had grown considerably since summer began. By her calculations, the baby was due on the 21st. She had read that first babies were notoriously late. We will see she thought.

Every night as she walked to her tent, the night sky filled her with wonder. She hoped to see a shooting star. She would make a wish on it and hope for a healthy child. She still hadn't decided if she would keep the baby. Rayna knew what it felt to wonder. Did my mom love me? Did she try and fail to care for me? Did my father know about me? All good questions, that were unanswerable. Was the note found with me true? Did someone make it up? There were no answers. She vowed, at least she would leave a letter to explain. She thought about open adoption. Taking the baby to Ireland. It was their heritage. It all made her toss and turn all night. December 14th was the day to leave. She decided to use the wait and see method.

September 4th dawned rainy. Slipping on the sweatshirt and poncho, she drove to the cabin. Walking up the steps to the front door. Rayna felt at peace. Before she could knock, the door swung open. The caretaker greeted her with glee, "Come in, come in," he said.

Rayna stepped through the door. This would be her home until Dec 14th. Her baby would be born here. She was surprised by how warm it was. The caretaker brought her towards the kitchen. It was perfect. One big room living space to the left, wood stove and full bathroom. Rayna couldn't wait to have a private living space. The caretaker had some bad news. The floors were set to be replaced and the bathroom updated. It would not be available until Monday September 10th. She said "No problem she could camp until then". She took the keys and headed back to her site.

This was awesome Rayna thought. The caretaker had given her the schedule. She only had to keep all the restrooms clean until Columbus Day. Then the restrooms were closed and winterized except for the front gate bathrooms. They remained open until December 9th. She only had to maintain the visitor center and those two then. Rayna felt this would work out beautifully.

The caretaker stopped by on his way out that afternoon. He was on his way to Florida for the winter. "Let me know if anything happens. Here's my cell number, if all goes well call next summer." Rayna smiled, "probably not," she said laughing. "I hope to be starting a new life by then." "Okey dokey", he called, "good luck." "You too, drive safe." Rayna answered. She went back to making her list for supplies in town.

Rayna drove by the cabin on her way out. The men were already there working on it. The caretaker had said they would start right away in case winter came early. Rayna thought about that and decided to get some extra warm clothing for her and the baby.

Driving into town she passed a Salvation Army Store. They were open and she thought why not. Even if she didn't keep the baby, she could always donate back. The store was brightly lit. Florescent bulbs buzzed overhead casting a harsh light. They had all kinds of baby gear, strollers, bassinets, highchairs, every item you could need or want. Rayna decided on a hooded bassinet. Its hood was covered in lace with a ribbon strung along the edge. It came with a mattress and two sheets. It was in perfect condition. Rayna pulled it to the front of the store. Next, she went to the strollers. They had many to choose from. She needed one that could lay flat. She needed to take the baby to the bathrooms when she cleaned. She found one towards the back, only it was a two-seater. She folded the seat and it was perfect for an infant. The clerk came over. "Are you looking for a twin stroller?" she asked. "Not really." Rayna said patting her tummy. "Are you sure?" the clerk said laughing. "Yup!" Rayna replied. Then the clerk brought over a car seat. "You can click this on the front and use the back for your diaper bag. It's only $20.00. The car seat is $10.00. I'll throw in some blankets and clothes with it." Rayna couldn't resist. There was also a 25% off coupon. The bassinet, stroller, car seat and clothes came to a little less than $30. The clerk threw in a diaper bag and 6 bibs. Rayna was thrilled. Good thing the car was empty. She managed to get everything in, it wasn't easy. The seat did fold down, but still it was a tight squeeze. Next, was a stop at the supermarket.

Now that she would have a refrigerator, she could get a little more. Before she had left, she checked with the workmen. They said no problem with using the refrigerator. Rayna stopped for lunch at the D.Q. She started with a chicken sandwich, fries and a diet coke, then enjoyed a large vanilla cone. It tasted so good. She was happy driving back. She couldn't wait to unload her treasures. This made the baby even more real.

She decided to set up a post office box next time she went into town. That way when the baby was born, she could have the birth certificate sent there. That was another problem. An unassisted birth had to be proven. You needed two people to say they saw you pregnant. Otherwise crazy people could steal babies and get birth certificates naming themselves as the mother. This was a dilemma. Rayna had no prenatal care. The birth story sites she frequented said get a book. She had gone to Barnes and Noble. Everything she read seemed to imply that she was in good health.

Women had been having babies forever, how could it be that hard she thought.

So far so good. She watched every birth she found on You Tube. She was confident she would be able to do it. Would it be nice to have a partner? Of course, it would. She couldn't even remember what the father looked like. All she remembered was tall, dark hair and blue eyes. Embarrassing!

Pulling into the campground she passed many people walking their dogs. Most of the campsites were empty but day trippers and locals used the trails. Summer was over and there was a definite chill in the air. Parking next to her site, she decided to leave everything in the car. She was wiped out from all her errands. She decided a nap was in order. She had packed the cooler at the store. She wanted to make sure the workmen left for the day before going to fill the refrigerator at the cottage. Zipping the screen behind her she slipped off her shoes. Lying down on her bed she stretched out. The mound of her belly was impressive, like a giant hill. "Hello baby", she whispered; "I love you already." As she rubbed her belly, the baby seemed to kick in answer. Rayna drifted off. She dreamed of her mother. As Rayna slept, she could hear a flute in the distance. Was it in her dream or real? She was too tired to care She curled up and drifted into a deep sleep.

Laughter outside the tent woke her. There seemed to be a group at the next site. Rayna sat up.

She really needed to use the bathroom. One thing about being pregnant, she always had to pee. Sitting up, she grabbed her hooded sweatshirt. She pulled it over her protruding belly. It was the extra-large men's sweatshirt. She had bought it to fit through the pregnancy. It came down mid-thigh and with her hands in the pocket she looked either chubby or pregnant, depending on who was looking. She slipped on her shoes, unzipped the tent. Grabbing her lantern and backpack, she stepped out. It was noticeably cooler and getting dark. She walked quickly to the bathrooms.

After taking care of business, Rayna walked to the sink. Looking into the mirror as she washed her hands, she thought she still looked tired. She opened her backpack and took out her toothbrush and paste. Brushing her teeth always felt good to her. She then splashed cold water on her face and thought how nice it will be to have her own bathroom again. Brushing her hair, she pulled it back. Putting it in a long braid over her shoulder. She had taken to wearing it in some form of braid, maybe it was time for a makeover, she thought. Looking down at her clothes, most of them this last couple of months had come from Big Lots. Elastic waist pants and skirts, men's t-shirt's and of course her favorite hoodie. She was looking forward to getting back into her favorite clothes. She turned sideways and looked at her reflection. This was no basketball. This was an extra-large watermelon shape. How could anyone not know she was pregnant she wondered? Just goes to show you people see what they want to sometimes. No wonder her back hurt and she had trouble walking far. She used her cup and drank a couple of glasses of water. She was extra thirsty tonight. Checking her watch, she saw it was after six. It was kind of nice being on her own she thought. After all the years of home, school and roommates to think about. She vowed to enjoy these last few weeks. Solitude when she wanted, company when she wanted. Win, win she chuckled.

As she walked back to her site, she listened to the forest sounds. Rustling leaves seemed to follow her path. She shone her flashlight toward the sound, nothing to see. Must be a night animal foraging for food she thought. She heard the sounds of frogs croaking in the distance. It always seemed synchronized to her. Like they were calling to each other. There was a lot of water in this forest, even a lake.

Lake Rico was used for boating and fishing. It really was a beautiful spot. Some of the trees were starting to turn colors. In the dark they all looked the same, still full of leaves. Up ahead Rayna noticed what looked like moths flying around. Some had lit onto the branches. Rayna thought that strange. Why so many? She shone her flashlight, but they were just far enough to not get a good look. They seemed to be following her. She continued on and as she approached her site she stopped. All around her tent were moths and butterflies. The group at the next site had stopped to stare. "That's weird!" a girl exclaimed. "I've never seen so many butterflies at one time." Rayna stopped at their campfire. "Weird right? I felt like they were following me." "I don't know about that," the girl answered, "but it is cool." As they watched, all the winged creatures flew up and away. Their wings were beating fast. They flew in a group towards the caretaker's cabin.

Rayna looked at the group. It was two couples, probably late 20's. They had been sitting around the campfire wen Rayna showed up. "Hey, want to join us?" the blond woman asked. "We have beer, wine and juice." her partner chimed in. The other couple pulled over an extra camp chair. "We pack extra," the girl said, "So we can have company." "Half the fun of camping for us is meeting people."

The group had already had a few cocktails at this point. Rayna accepted her juice and asked the appropriate questions. They were breaking camp the next morning. Back to work, they joked. "Hope you don't mind a little noise tonight". Rayna laughed. "Just remember 10:00 PM is quiet time. I am the acting caretaker starting today." "Figures," they laughed, "We're next to you. We better start singing now." Rayna took that as her exit. "Well, I have some work to do. Thanks for the drink, enjoy your night." She slowly walked to her tent. She consciously tried not to waddle. She grabbed her computer and books from the front seat of the car. Out of the back seat she got her small cooler. She had a sub, chips, apple and container of chocolate milk. She hoped to enjoy her evening inside. It was amazing how warm a tent was, if you closed the flaps it really retained heat.

Her computer was fully charged. She tried to watch one birth each night. That, she hoped, would prepare her for the big day when the baby decided to come. She was counting on being late. It seemed most first babies were. She plugged in the head phones and watched the home birth. The key, she thought was to try to stay calm and not scream. The thought that the need to scream was even on the table put a nugget of fear into Rayna.

She could hear the couples singing old songs. They were really having a good time. She could hear the fire crackling. The smell of roasting hot dogs and marshmallows wafted her way. She decided to eat her meal. Rayna always tried to eat nicely. That was a throwback from Daycare. Nana always said a meal is better eaten with manners. Rayna took out her plastic mat, plate and napkins. She set it all out on top of her cooler. She had a turkey sub with lettuce and tomato and a bag of chips, an apple and the milk. She was pretty hungry; it had been quite a while since lunch. She turned off the computer and put it away. The warm glow of the lantern gave enough light. She ate ravenously.

The You Tube posts didn't lie, when they said

how hungry you could be. She slowed herself down after she finished the sandwich and chips. Slicing the apple, she finished the last of the meal. She certainly didn't want to go looking for the Rolaids. At least not during the meal. She cleaned up, putting the wrappers in a closed plastic box. You never left food unattended in the forest. You never knew what lived there. All campers were instructed to put trash in proper receptacles.

Rayna lay on her mattress. She needed to stretch out after her meal. The glow from the lantern just reached the bedroom area. It was just after 10 PM. She could hear the campers whispering. What she would call an Irish whisper, but they were trying. The forest sounds were somewhat quieting down. The occasional rustle, little feet skittering. It was a peaceful night. Rayna started to drift off to sleep. She thought she could hear a fluttering sound. Opening her eyes, she saw nothing. In the distance she could hear music. It sounded like a flute, magical and mystical. Did she really hear it or was it in her dream? Rolling over, Rayna saw that it was 11:30 PM. Now she had to pee again. Usually, she made one last trip to the bathroom. She had an emergency bucket if she needed it after that. Even though she felt safe camping, she was still alone. She locked the tent zipper for an added measure every night after her last trip out.

Rayna grabbed her backpack, slipped on her shoes and crawled out of the tent. As she passed the campfire next door, the girls jumped up. "We'll walk with you", they said. "Wait for us." They both ran to their tent and grabbed their toiletry bags. They walked down the path toward the facilities. The girls chattered on. "What's with all the moths?" Mary asked Rayna. "Moths?" "Ya, look up." Rayna looked up and there seemed to be about 50 moths. They were in the branches and pretty big. Some seemed the size of small birds. "Eww," her friend whispered. "I don't like moths, they're creepy." "Maybe it's just the time of year," Rayna said. "Maybe they lay eggs or something. I'm sure they won't bother us." They all used the bathroom for their nightly routine. As they walked back to their site, the moths seemed to follow. For some unknown reason they seemed to be drawn to Rayna's site. Weird Rayna thought. She fell asleep to the soft sounds of the forest.

Next thing she knew the birds were singing and the sun was coming up. Back to the bathroom she went. The rest of the sites were quiet. No moths today, she thought. Rayna decided to drive over to the cabin. She wanted to get the food into the refrigerator before the workmen showed up. She drove over to do that.

She hadn't really looked around the site. As she drove up, she really looked around. The cabin was on the right. The land was cleared out, probably about an acre. Rayna wasn't mathematically inclined so that's just what she figured. The porch faced towards an open area. Probably half way towards a large meadow, was a spring. Water was rushing over the rocks, going towards the right of the property. There was a small bridge of sorts connecting the meadow and front yard.

Rayna pulled into the designated parking area. She pulled out the cooler. Luckily there was a handle and wheels on it. She rolled it to the front door. She had a key and opened the door. Stepping inside she took in the sight of her baby's birthplace. She really felt it was perfect.

The workers had replaced some of the flooring. All the furniture was moved to the kitchen area. The wood stove was on a tiled area. It seemed perfect. Walking over to it, Rayna realized it was the kind of stove with an oven. She was determined to bake something in it. Hopefully they would only take a few days to finish. A new shower and toilet would finish the job. Rayna finished up, used the bathroom and decided to take a walk. She didn't bother locking the door. She closed it, walked down the steps and started for the stream.

Halfway there, she came upon a flagpole. It was the caretaker's duty to fly the American Flag every day. A safe distance away was a fire pit. Circling the pit were a few benches. The benches were made of a tree cut and stained. It looked unused. She continued on towards the bridge. By now the sun was shining brightly. The trees on both sides of the water were beautiful. Yellow, orange and red lined the stream. The bridge was about 10ft long. Stepping up onto it, Rayna felt nervous. Would it hold her weight? Was it rotted, she thought? Then she realized, the worst that would happen would be she'd get wet. She could deal with that. In the middle, she stopped, looking to her left. The stream seemed to come down the hill, towards the right, where the water rushed through the trees. Straight ahead, Rayna saw a meadow or field. There were three large trees practically cutting the field in half. Each tree seemed to be far enough away from each other to just touch branch to branch. There were some kind of flowers in the meadow. Rayna continued toward the field. It was turning out to be a beautiful day. She carried her backpack as always. At the edge of the meadow she decided to rest. She pulled out her flannel table cloth. Spreading it out, she slowly lowered herself to the ground. Seriously this baby must be huge. She next pulled out her banana, bottle of water and energy bar. Breakfast of champions she thought.

Slowly, she ate her breakfast. All the morning sounds of the forest were back. She stared at the three trees. One was definitely an oak. The second looked like an ash tree and the third, she thought, looked like a Hawthorn tree. Somewhere she had read that was the perfect trifecta of trees. She couldn't remember why. She pulled herself up. She actually had to kneel and get up by pulling herself on a huge boulder. I guess she should have just sat on the rock. Rayna picked up all her stuff. She folded the tablecloth and put the trash into a baggie for later. She stretched and started off toward the trees.

Moving closer, she noticed that each tree was circled by stones. No stone was smaller than 12 inches wide by 6 inches tall. Weird she thought. Then there was a huge semicircle around the entire trio. "What is this about", Rayna wondered? There was a stone bench in the center of the semicircle. Actually, right outside of the center. It was 12 ft long, with 3 flattened rocks under it. Sitting on it, if you faced the trees, you were outside the circle, but smack in the middle. Sitting with your back to the trees, you were headed downhill. Rayna sat to catch her breath again. She faced the trees. Looking closely, she noticed the moths and butterflies again. Nestled among the colored leaves were at least 100 winged creatures. Softly in the distance she could hear music again. The eerie sound of a flute or many flutes. Rayna turned towards the other side. She couldn't see where the music could be coming from.

Maybe its boon dockers, she thought. Sometimes people drove into the park and just parked. They wanted to be free to do whatever. Maybe there was someone playing music. It was getting late; the workmen should be there soon. Rayna started her walk back. Butterflies and moths flitted from tree to tree almost like they were following her. Crazy, she thought. She decided to sing to calm her thoughts. "Over the river and through the woods to baby cabin we go," She hummed the rest of the way. Up ahead the workmen had arrived.

They were very friendly, three guys in typical jeans, work shirts over t-shirts. They all looked to be 20 something. Rayna joked with them. "Hey don't eat my stuff guys!" she said. All three had dirty coolers lined up on the porch. "We have food." they laughed. "When do you think you'll be done?" Rayna asked. "Saturday," we hope. "We're waiting for the shower and toilet." "That reminds me, I've got to use the bathroom before I leave." Rayna quickly went to the bathroom. She was excited to move into this cabin. The guys turned on their radio and started to work. "Hey, have you heard any flute music?", Rayna asked them. "Ah, no, who would play that." they laughed. "Just checking," and she took the cooler and left.

She decided to drive around and see what she could. She drove all through the park. No boon dockers were visible. There were only three sites in use. The couples next to her site were packing up. She stopped to say goodbye. She went back to her tent to tidy up. She wasn't ready to move of pack everything, but she liked to neaten it up every day. In such a small area, things got cluttered quick. She waited until afternoon to clean the bathrooms. Better to do it when most people were checked out or gone.

Each day became like the day before. Rayna liked the routine of it. Wednesday, she decided to go down to the water. The plan was to move to the cabin late Monday. She was excited for the move.

Chapter 5: Leanne

Leanne was speechless. Rayna seemed naive and brave at the same time. "Show me the cabin." she asked. "Sure," Rayna answered, "but we'll have to drive". Leanne called Rose. Rose jumped in the car using her ramp. Rayna got in the front seat and showed Leanne where to go. They left Rose in the car when they got there. Rayna opened the door. They both went in. Leanne was surprised at how cute it was. The main area was finished. They were still waiting for the shower. The men would be back tomorrow to finish. Leanne could see it was perfectly suited for Rayna. She, herself, had thought about having a baby in the woods once, many years ago. This was so much better. Twenty minutes from a hospital. Food and supplies even closer.

They sat on the futon. "Tell me your plan", Leanne asked Rayna? "Well, I am going to have the baby here. I bought some supplies. I also looked up how to get a birth certificate." "How?" Leanne asked. "I need two people to swear they saw me pregnant. Then I have to fill out the forms and birth certificate. I have to go to town with everything and pay a fee. The certificates should come in two weeks."

Leanne smiled; "I think you have a good plan. I could help you with it. Show me the forms." Rayna had three of each form. "Why do you have so many Rayna?" "I wanted to be sure not to make a mistake." she replied. "When is the baby due?", Leanne asked. "I estimate around the 21st" Rayna replied. "My grandchild is due around then." Leanne replied. Her daughter had made it clear no help was needed. Leanne felt ok to offer to help Rayna. "Why don't I be on call for you. I took some courses to be a doula. I had 4 children 3 of them natural. I would feel better if you were not alone. You never know, better to be prepared." Rayna took a deep breath. "I would love that Nana. I really didn't want to be totally alone. Everyone on the internet has at least their partner with them." "I would be honored Leanne replied. Why don't I drive you back to your site? You're looking a little tired." As they walked down the steps, Rayna pointed out the moths. "They're back," she said, "isn't it weird?" Leanne couldn't believe how many there were.

She dropped Rayna off at the site. A few campers were there in nearby sites. Come on over they called. "Sorry, going to take a nap," Rayna called, "be over later." Leanne packed the lunch remnants, hugged Rayna and drove home. Rayna gave Leanne her cell number. Leanne drove down the path and noticed even more moths. She thought it kind of eerie.

She pulled into the garage, then let Rose out. Putting away the picnic stuff, she couldn't contain her excitement. Opening the inside door, she could smell the pot roast. Good thing she had thought to put the crock pot on. She had made it home just in time. After dinner, she would mention the meeting to Mr. D. First, she got her computer and watched a couple of birth videos. She wanted to be prepared. Leanne also looked up the forms. They should be notarized. Luckily, she was still a Notary. She had become one for Day Care. This would be a great thing to use it for. She had also become a justice of the peace. She hadn't had to use that yet, but you never know.

Mr. D. arrived home. He enjoyed his meal while watching the news. Leanne sat and listened to her headphones. When dinner and the news were over, Leanne paused the T.V.

"Hey, you'll never guess who I met this week?" Mr. D looked over. He could tell Leanne was excited at the news. "Hmmm, I don't know who?" "Remember that little girl, Rayna. You know, the foster child who walked Rose?" At the mention of his Princess, he turned attentive. He knew Leanne had an aversion to lying. Whether it was from all those years of child care, or life itself. He also knew she didn't mind omitting a truth if necessary. That was different. At least, in her eyes.

"Rose actually seemed to recognize her first," she said. "Then we talked and I brought lunch back a couple of times." Leanne could see his hand itching for the remote. "That's nice." he didn't ask where, so Leanne didn't elaborate. Getting up she cleared his dishes.

They watched their shows and had dessert. Leanne went to lie down at 10:00 PM. Her mind was racing. A million scenarios went through her mind. She planned a visit back to the park. She wanted to help Rayna get ready. She tossed and turned. Always a night full of dreams, she woke up often. By 5:00 AM she knew sleep was over. Grabbing her robe, she quietly left the bedroom. The dog stirred but didn't move. Making a cup of coffee, Leanne planned her day.

Rummaging through the unpacked boxes she unearthed the box marked *moms desk stuff*. She was pretty sure the notary stuff was there. She pulled it down and found everything she was looking for. A small strong box unlocked, with key inside. The contents were her Justice of the Peace Stamp, Notary Stamp, Passport, Birth and Marriage Certificates. She also found forms to fill out if she had ever gotten to marry someone and her Doula Certificate. Leanne had never actually practiced. The heart attack had come and she stopped her studies. It was one of the great regrets of her life.

Leanne had a "million bags". Mr. D constantly gave to charities. They sent stuff. Dream catchers, calendars and more bags than anyone needed. Leanne put the box in a bag. Next, she got a new notepad, again one of a million.

Leanne always gave parents notebooks. It was a good way to communicate back and forth. She grabbed one and started a list for Rayna. After it was done, they could start checking things off. Leanne was excited. Finally, something to help someone with. Finishing her coffee, she woke Mr. D and started her chores.

Leanne called Rayna's cell. Breathless, Rayna answered on the third ring. "How's it going?" Leanne asked. Rayna answered, "Well, I'm packing up the car with things I won't need the next two days. The bathroom will be usable on Wednesday the 12th", she added. "Perfect, why don't I bring lunch again today?" Rosie needs an adventure and we can make some plans". "Turkey sub please." Rayna laughed. "Great I'll be by around noon."

Leanne prepared the dinner for the family. She chopped the vegetables, added the chicken and noodles and put them all in the crock pot. She loved that thing. The house would smell great, easy prep. Off she went.

The drive was only 5 minutes from her house. It took longer to get to the campsites once inside. Rosie was hopping. It only took her a few times to be familiar with her destination. Again, they stopped at the small convenience store. The sandwiches were good there. The excitement Leanne felt was intense. She felt like Rose was acting jumpy and excited too. Driving the familiar path, Leanne really looked around.

It was a beautiful park. Once inside, you really felt in a different world. More and more of the trees had turned their beautiful colors. The sun was shining and sparkling water shone through the trees. Leanne felt the anticipation of what was coming. She didn't really know fully what to expect. It was nice to wake up and have something to look forward to, not just get through.

Leanne pulled in and parked next to the mustang. She opened the back door and Rose bounded out. It was like she was a puppy again. She raced around the site, smelling everything.

Rayna was packing things up to get ready to move over to the cabin. She had piles of clothes and supplies. There wasn't much room in the mustang for all she had. Two large plastic containers were full. The car still had all the baby supplies in it. "Why don't we drive over to the cabin?" Rayna said. "We can check on their progress. We'll take both cars. The living area is done. We can store the stuff in the corner."

"Are your forms ready to be filled out to get the birth certificate?" Leanne asked, "because I have a thought. Leanne told Rayna her idea. They could get the workmen to sign off on seeing her pregnant. Then Leanne could notarize the form. That way, whatever Rayna decided later, at least there would be a valid birth certificate. Rayna thought for a minute. "Do you think they would do it?" "Why not, their guys, they won't care," Leanne answered. "Besides I brought some extra cookies and chocolate milk to sweeten the deal. No skin off their backs." Rayna wanted to have them sign all three copies just in case. She was petrified she would screw this up. She really wanted to stay under the radar.

They loaded the cars, called Rose and drove over to the cabin. As expected, the work truck was there. The three men were sitting on the porch finishing their lunch. Rayna parked and walked, more like waddled, up to the porch. "Hey guys how's it going?" she called. "Almost ready," the "boss" replied. "You'll be able to move in by Thursday the latest. Sorry for the delay. The bathroom fixtures were special order". "No problem," Rayna replied. "We're going to start unloading a few things, is that ok? I will put them in the living room." "Sure, they'll be fine." he replied. He was a friendly guy. Tall with curly red hair, about 25 or so. Rayna took a breath.

"Hey, will you guys do me a favor?" "If we can," they laughed. Rayna unzipped her sweatshirt. "I need two witnesses to say they saw me pregnant." Looking at her large protruding stomach the work men laughed. "Is there any question?" "Well, to get a birth certificate, I need a form to send in." Clearly none of them had children. Or if they did, they didn't think about how the birth certificate was attained. At this moment Leanne brought the forms and her notary stuff. Also, the bag with the chocolate milk and cookies. "My friend will notarize the forms, if you guys fill them out." Rayna explained. Rayna insisted on all three being filled out in case she lost or destroyed one. She picked the two workers over 21.

She didn't know if it mattered but didn't want to take any chances. Leanne pulled out a notebook and her notary supplies. Each guy wrote their name, address and cell phone numbers. Then they filled out each form and Leanne notarized them. She handed out the treats.

With that done, Leanne and Rayna decided to have a picnic lunch. Leanne took out the wagon. She filled it with the lunch cooler, two folding camp chairs and Rosie's treats and Frisbee. Rayna wanted to show her the meadow. They started across the front of the cabin. Leanne hadn't seen the stream with the bridge yet.

The sun shone through the trees. Yellow, orange and red leaves fluttered down like rain. You could hear the water flowing over the rocks. Well, until Rose started splashing and carrying on. Leanne laughed. It felt good to be here. They pulled the wagon over the bridge into the meadow. Leanne stopped abruptly. To her left were the three massive trees. The meadow was full of daisies. "Wow!" Rayna said. "I don't remember those from the other day. I must have missed them." Rose was like a dog in a movie running through the flowers.

Leanne rummaged for her phone. She snapped a picture; it was so beautiful. "Let's eat over in the shade." Leanne pulled the wagon; boy was she glad to have a chair. Her days of comfortably sitting on the ground were long gone. First, she opened the chairs. She had found these on the internet. They were perfect, small enough to sling over your shoulder, but would hold up to 300 lbs. Luckily, she wasn't close to that, but better safe than sorry. She always imagined she and Mr. D would have weekend adventures. Unfortunately, most of the adventures were watched on TV. Next, she pulled out the reusable tablecloth, napkins and straws.

Rayna laughed, "Nana your still pretty prepared. I remember our trips to the park for swimming and lunch. We always were prepared for anything. Nice to see some things stay the same. What's for lunch I am starved?" "Turkey sandwiches, chips, fruit cocktail and chocolate milk for you. I get a diet coke." "Sounds good let's eat." Rayna plopped down in the chair. Leanne pushed the wagon between them and served the lunch. The shade felt good. They faced the three trees. They ate in silence for a few minutes. Looking towards the trees. Leanne remarked it was strange the way those trees are right there in the middle of a field. Why would someone circle them with stones? I wonder if it was done a long time ago or more recently. Rayna swallowed her last morsel. "Any more cookies", she asked? "I am eating for two you know." Leanne pulled another bakery bag of cookies out of her cooler. "I knew they were your favorite," she laughed. "Might as well eat them now once the baby comes, you'll be watching your figure again." "Maybe!" Rayna said smiling. She munched away. "The stones are pretty weird. In ancient times people used them to keep others away. Or to mark sacred ground. I have studied the myths and legends of North America. There were three tribes of Native Americans here in this area. Maybe it's to do with that." "Hmmm," Leanne replied. "What are you studying?" "I have finished all but one semester. My semester abroad is set for Jan 21st. I have a ticket to Dublin December 14th. Then I will have a major in English with a minor in myths and folklore of the world." "What about the baby? Are you taking him or her with you?" "I don't know. I want to get through the birth before making the decision. That's why it's important to get the birth certificates right away. I can send for a passport hopefully at the same time." "Wow, you really have a lot to plan," Leanne answered. "I will help any way I can."

Just then Rosie came bounding over. "You rest", Leanne said, "I'll throw the Frisbee a few times. Poor Rose never gets to run like this". Rayna finished the cookies. Nana made her feel like everything will be all right. She was so happy they found each other. The Frisbee flew into the semicircle. Rosie cautiously sniffed at the stones. "She must smell something", Rayna called out. Rosie sat at the stone bench and wouldn't get the Frisbee. "Ugghhh! she does this to me sometimes in NH, at the water. Fun, fun, fun. She swims for it in the water and all of a sudden she decides she's done and walks away." At least this time it's dry. Leanne stepped over the rocks. As she reached for the Frisbee, she caught something out of the corner of her eye. Rosie stood up and she sniffed the air in the direction Leanne had seen the grass move. Must be a chipmunk or something. She picked up the Frisbee, stepped back and started towards Rayna.

"Look!" Rayna called. She was pointing towards the trees behind Leanne. Leanne turned and looked up. Each tree was shimmering in the sunlight. Tons of butterfly's were flitting from branch to branch, tree to tree. It was amazing, like the butterfly tent at Disney world. All colors and sizes. It was mesmerizing. Even Rose seemed enthralled.

Far away in the distance, they heard music. It was a flute or some kind of melancholy instrument. It wasn't scary, just, I guess, mystical, Leanne thought.

She started back toward Rayna. Rose walked by her side. She kept looking up at Leanne as if to say "what the …. was that?" "Do you hear that music" Rayna asked Leanne? "Yes, what is it." Rayna shook her shoulder. "I thought someone was boon docking over there. I drove all around but found no one. Weird huh... sound does travel but I don't know. What about the butterfly's? Sometime my imagination kicks in. I have studied a lot of legends. Sometimes I think why would everybody lie?"

Leanne laughed, "I am not the one you should check with on reality. I've spent so much time reading to children all the magical books. I think in stories." They both laughed. "We certainly are a pair." They laughed again. "Let's go unpack the cars and check on the work." Leanne repacked the wagon. Rose ran ahead to get a cool drink from the stream. Rayna zipped her sweatshirt over her stomach and walked ahead. They talked about some of the favorite children's books. Nana had read two times a day in daycare. Each child picked a book to hear. Both Rayna and Leanne had loved the Rain Baby Book and Bernstein Bears. Leanne truly felt that this was meant to be. She was so happy.

As they started towards the cabin the sound of hammering met them. They quickly unloaded both cars and stashed the stuff in the corner. Rayna popped her head into the bathroom. "Any estimate on the time you'll be done?" she asked. Boss Tom put down the brush he was using. "Well, we have everything. Now it's Tuesday today. Why not plan for, oh, Thursday the 13th? We'll be finished and everything will be move in ready." "Sounds great," Rayna replied. "Let me just get a few things out of the fridge." She collected her stuff and they went back to the site.

Leanne went with Rayna to clean up the restrooms. It really wasn't that hard. Luckily most of the current guests had wiped up after themselves. They were done in no time. Rosie walked along. Even she seemed tired. Rayna was tired and decided to lie down for a while. Leanne asked if she needed anything. She would come back Thursday to help with the final move. It felt weird to just leave her there, Leanne thought. I have two bedrooms unused. Rayna was happy and wanted to do this her way. So off Leanne drove. Rayna waved, "I'll call if I need anything." Five minutes later she was pulling in the garage. Rose jumped out and went right to her yellow chair. She was snoring in no time. As dinner was cooking Leanne went down the basement to look through the day care stuff again.

She started a small pile. A couple of blankets, cloth diapers and hats. That was all she had left. Rayna would show what she had, and they could make a list. Again, she thought this is exciting. Mr. D arrived home, as usual. Leanne, again mentioned that she had lunch with Rayna. She slipped in the fact that she was pregnant into the conversation. Then, immediately talked about Rosie and playing Frisbee. As she predicted to herself, he would focus on Rose and let Rayna's baby be unmentioned. After 45 years, you had to learn something. Baby steps, Leanne thought, baby steps.

The evening progressed as usual. Dinner, the news, shows, clean kitchen, bed. Typical night except Leanne often skipped cleanup and did it in the morning. Not now. She wanted to be ready if Rayna called. Leanne knew the baby could come at any time. The best made plans of mice and men she thought.

She brought her cell into the bedroom along with the land line. That night she dreamed of Indian people and legends. An old medicine woman was trying to tell her how to deliver a baby. She also dreamed about butterflies and Leprechauns. Since her heart attack, she had been on metoprolol. This drug was known to cause hallucinations and weird dreams. She had both since starting the drug. Made for some interesting nights.

Leanne didn't want to wear out her welcome. She spent Wednesday at home and doing errands. She did the weekly shopping. While there, she added a few things for Rayna. She picked up new born diapers, wipes and ready to feed formula. Sometimes it was good to have a backup plan. Nursing moms sometimes had to supplement. She took Rose for a walk on the golf course before dinner. That way she could clean up before sitting down. She wanted to leave early Thursday to go to the park. She was leaving Rosie home this time so she wouldn't get in the way.

Thursday the 13th was forecast to be a beautiful day. She felt kind of bad leaving Rosie. She walked her before getting in the car. She had bought lunch fixings at the store yesterday, so no stopping on the way. The ride had become a routine in such a short time. She turned left into the park driving down the path. Leanne felt awesome.

Rayna was hard at work. She had taken all her stuff out of the tent. Deflated the mattress and piled everything around. Rayna wanted to fold the tent while it was still dry out. With any luck, she would not need it for a while. Leanne helped her fold it and slide it into the bag. Rayna kept her things nicely. Leanne put the seat down and they loaded both cars. Rayna was going to drive her caretaker route and meet LeAnne at the cabin.

Leanne pulled close to the steps. She realized she didn't have the key. She unloaded everything and carried it to the porch. She moved the car so Rayna could park there when she arrived. She took her cup of water out of the cup holder. She had a Disney Princess cup. Leanne really was a kid at heart. She sat on the top step looking towards the meadow. The sun was directly overhead. She took off her sweater and stretched her legs out in front of her. It was so quiet and peaceful. Nature really was beautiful. The sound of the birds, rustling of small animals, even the water made a gurgling sound. Very calming. In the distance, Leanne thought she heard music playing. That eerie flute sounds.

She turned as the crunch of Rayna's tires driving in startled her. Rayna slowly climbed out of the car. "Sorry, I forgot to give you the keys." she called. "No worries," Leanne replied, "I was enjoying the view. This is amazing." "Right"? Rayna replied.

Rayna waddled over to the steps. She had taken the sweatshirt off. With her hand rubbing her back she groaned. I'm exhausted let's have lunch first ok?" They sat on the steps and enjoyed the beautiful day. Leanne collected all the trash and they started bringing stuff in.

Rayna had a lot more than she thought. The baby equipment took up quite a bit of room. LeAnne laughed, "years ago they just used a bureau drawer for the baby."

The cabin looked great. New floor, counter and bathroom. They must have felt bad for Rayna, they even cleaned up. It wasn't big, but it had plenty of room. The couch was a futon for sleeping. There was a twin bed against the wall. Pillows lined the back. Rayna decided to keep the futon to sit on and just use the twin for sleeping. Next to the wood stove was an old rocking chair. Perfect for rocking the baby, Leanne pointed out. There was a small TV mounted on the wall. A satellite TV and also a land line for emergencies. The caretaker had given Rayna instructions on all the working's. There was even a golf cart in the shed. Most caretakers used that to do their rounds. It made it easy to bring supplies to stock the bathrooms. It really was perfect. Rayna was happy to have a real building. As fun as camping was, she was getting sick of it.

They drove the "golden engine" back over to the site. Everything left fit in the back. Then Rayna drove Leanne around showing her the care taker duties. She had a hard time fitting behind the wheel. "Are you sure you're not due until the 21st," Leanne asked. "The baby seems pretty low. It seems to have dropped this last week." "Dropped?" Rayna, turned towards Leanne. "I read about that; I think you are right It does seem lower. I sometimes feel like he/she is going to just slide out." "Wishful thinking." Leanne sighed. Back at the cabin, they unloaded the rest of the stuff. The actual camping stuff, tents and items not needed in the cabin, they put in the shed. The rest went inside.

Leanne helped set everything up. They made the bed. They went through all the baby equipment. Rayna was excited to get ready. Leanne offered to take any clothes or washing home. They decided to wash all the baby stuff. Then LeAnne took out her notebook. "Let's check off what you need for delivery." Rayna showed her a box of items. Leanne looked over everything. Looks great, you did a good job. Rayna handed her a book. "This is what I have been following. So far so good. The classic what to expect when you are expecting." "Perfect!" Leanne replied.

It was getting late. Rosie would be alone. James would have walked her, but then gone to his place. Rayna looked pretty tired. "Will you call if you need me?" Leanne asked. "Of course, I'll be fine. I am going to make some soup and watch a show." Rayna replied. Leanne hated driving in the dark. With no street lights, it would be pitch black. She took the laundry and threw it in the back. Rayna waved from the porch. Her silhouette was quite round. Leanne smiled. This is exciting she thought. It was a warm night. She rolled down the window and enjoyed the air. Without the radio on she could hear the night sounds of the forest. Somewhere far away she thought she heard the flute. Weird, where is it coming from? In the rear-view mirror, she thought she saw moths or butterflies swarming around.

As she drove up the driveway, Rosie was sitting looking out the window. As soon as she took care of the dog, she started the laundry. Leanne got some dinner and sat in her chair. This was Mr. D's night out so this was her night to watch what she wanted on TV. She decided instead to watch a few home birth videos and took notes. It was a great day.

As Nana drove away Rayna smiled. She felt so at peace. Nana had always been there. She remembered childhood, songs, stories and her first friends were all because of Nana. When she didn't fit in as a preteen, Nana had let her walk Rose. She had even gotten some babysitting jobs from Nana's clients.

She felt good. As she turned to go in the cabin, she heard music. It seemed to be coming from the meadow. She felt she should investigate as it was her job. Grabbing the lantern flashlight on the step she started across the front. The warm breeze felt good. Fireflies were flitting in the trees surrounding the stream. Another swarm of moths and butterflies danced in the air over the meadow. She stood on the bridge listening, still hearing the faint sound of the flute. Darkness was closing in quickly. Rayna didn't want to keep going. Tomorrow she would drive again over the other side of the meadow. She must have missed the boon dockers last time. It was legal to camp like that but not usual. She turned and lumbered back to the porch. A few of the moths and butterflies seemed to follow. The cabin shone like a beacon in the dark. Rayna could not wait to take a shower, eat her dinner and go to sleep. It had been a long day.

Leanne thought about how she would broach Mr. D. You didn't stay married all these years without a routine. Leanne always tried to soften any news. Good or bad you had to know your audience. Mr. D liked to relax when he got home. He wanted his dinner and time to chill.

Leanne always fed the family before sharing news. Unless there was an urgent need to know, she waited. She never understood the women who called husbands at work about trivial things. Mind you, her young marriage was before cell phones and texting. Now everyone can instantly know all kinds of things.

Leanne liked to keep Mr. D on a need to know basis. He seemed to like it that way. When he arrived home from his night out, she let him change and sit. She put the TV to mute. "Hey, remember I told you I met Rayna?" He looked at her with a kind of blank look. "You know, the old daycare kid. The one whose parents were killed." "Ya, ya right." he replied. "Well guess what?" Leanne squealed. She waited for a guess. Sometimes Mr. D was infuriating. "I don't know … what?" "She's pregnant!" Leanne whispered. "Pregnant by who?" "I'm not sure." Leanne replied. "Hmmm!" Mr. D replied, and turned the TV on. Leanne wasn't upset. Years ago, she would have been, but this is how they played the game. She expected nothing more. She would tell him just enough so that no matter the outcome, it was not a surprise to him.

Leanne's mind was racing. What would Rayna do come Dec 14th? Maybe she would stay in the US and finish her studies here. Maybe she would move in with them. There was plenty of room. Two empty bedrooms on the second floor. There were so many possibilities. Baby steps she thought. They watched a show together. Leanne got up and kissed Mr. D goodnight. That was one good thing. They always kissed good night, hello and goodbye in the morning. They did love each other.

The next morning Leanne texted Rayna. Rayna replied everything was good. She had rounds to make. It was the weekend and campers would be arriving. Leanne planned on going Saturday to help. Rosie could stay home with Mr. D, that way she could stay longer. They texted back and forth through the day. It really was a good thing. Not the same as a phone call but great for just checking in.

Leanne did Rayna's laundry and her family laundry. She took Rosie on the golf course. Mr. D always came home by 6 on Fridays. She made a fish dinner and they were in their seat's, TV on by 7 PM. They ate their dinner companionably while watching the world news. "What's up for the weekend"? she asked him. Leanne knew dam well nothing. The dreaded football had begun. This is how weekends went for Mr. D. Stay up late Fridays. Sleep till noon Saturday. Up late Saturday night. Sunday sleep late. Football the rest of the day. Leanne fed him every four hours. She joked "like a baby". She truly felt he was working every weekday and didn't blame him. This was her opportunity to help Rayna.

Leanne offered to drive along with Rayna, in case the baby came, and Rayna needed the help. She took care of Rosie, fed her, gave her the insulin shot she needs and let her out. Rosie would gladly climb into bed with Mr. D, leaving Leanne free to help Rayna.

She stopped at the coffee down the street. It was so peaceful this time of day. She got two coffees. Two chocolate milks and 2 egg sandwiches. Rounded out the order with 2 muffins for later. This was a treat and she would enjoy it. It only took 15 minutes to get to the park. Already quite a few cars were in the lot. Leanne was happy she hadn't taken Rosie. Too many dogs, she would have been very barky.

This park was so beautiful. The sun sparkled through the trees. The sky was bright blue with wispy clouds floating by. As she drove to the cabin, she caught peeks of water through the trees. That was absolutely beautiful. The water sparkled like diamonds. She turned off the radio. Opening the window, the forest sounds were musical. Birds, insects even a few fish jumping out of the water. Leanne thought how if you really listen, it almost was like another world. No wonder people found such peace in nature.

Pulling up to the cabin she noticed how homey it looked. Rayna was sitting on the porch rocker. "Good morning", she called out. "Isn't this awesome?" "It certainly is," Leanne replied. "Let's have our breakfast out here." They each ate their food and sipped their coffee. It was like being in a movie. Birds singing, small animals rustling in the leaves. You could even faintly hear the spring running over the rocks. They brought the muffins and milk in to the cabin. They both used the bathroom. Rayna laughed; some things never change. "Nana, remember you always sent us daycare kids into the bathroom before anything". "As we got older you said: Remember, always take advantage of a clean bathroom." "I never forgot that good advice. Let's take a walk to the meadow before we drive around."

They started towards the bridge. The air was warming up. In the distance Leanne thought she heard music again. "Do you hear it?" she asked Rayna. "Yes, it's coming from the other side, I think. We'll drive there after we get back. I do need to check it out. Even though they don't have to pay to boondock, they are supposed to sign in." They made it over the bridge and to the clearing in front of the three trees. "Let's sit on the stone bench," Leanne chuckled. "I'm too old and out of shape to sit on the ground. I mean I could do it but getting up would be a chore." Rayna laughed, "I would be quite a sight as well." First, they sat facing the trees. Looking up, they noticed at least a hundred butterflies. It was quite beautiful. "What do you think that is all about?" Leanne asked. "I've never seen so many in nature." Rayna shook her head. "Me either. I have studied a lot of myths and legends though. There are even these trees that have magical stories about them. Native Americans believe in Pukwudgie."

"There were said to be magical little people of the forest. Of course, there is the fairy folklore. Some people believe in them but they are quite elusive. They were regarded with suspicion by us, much larger humans. The belief was very superstitious. More and more people began believing these little people had magical characteristics. Legends say they retreated to the woodlands to live a secretive life." "Wow," Leanne answered. "You really know your folklore and legends. That would be so cool if it were true though, right?"

Rayna smiled, "sometimes just believing makes it true. Take these trees. Three trees with stone circles. Who did that? Then the semi-circle and this bench. Weird right? I think it was done many years ago. Maybe hundreds. Someone believed this was a special place. Fairies for instance are said to pick their spot for its beauty deep in the forest. Maybe they picked this place before the cabin was built. Enchanted creatures are said to be safe there. Now if we walked to the top of the hill, what would we see?" Leanne stood up. "Let's do it."

They both lumbered up the hill. Past the trees to the top. "Are you all right Leanne?" Leanne was walking backward huffing and puffing. "I think so what about you?" "I'm good." Rayna huffed, but she too turned around and walked the rest of the way backwards. Reaching the top, they both stopped putting their hands on their knees. Going down will be

a lot easier, they laughed. It took a good five minutes
to catch their breath. Standing up they looked forward.
In the distance they could see Lake Rico to their left,
forest on the right with the stream running through.
Beyond that, the cabin's chimney. The sky was bright
with many clouds. The trees were really magnificent. It
was like being in a beautiful painting. "Wow!" they
both said at the same time, just wow.
This is amazing. Just then the swarm of butterflies
flew in to the air. It seemed like a thousand, but in
reality, probably at least 100. They flew straight up,
then flitted to the left and disappeared into the forest.
"Weird right?" Rayna said.

They took a better look at the trees from this
side. Again, there was a stone wall surrounding them.
This was a circle. There was a stone bench in the
middle directly under the middle tree. The stones
circled about three feet out. They walked down to them
and sat down. Now they were facing up the hill.
Leanne had carried her backpack. She pulled two
bottles of water out. Handing one to Rayna she said. "I
try always to be prepared" gulping down the water.
Rayna laughed "I needed that Nana. I was about to go
to the spring for a drink. That hill was tough." "It sure
was." Leanne drank her water. "Tell me more about the
fairy legends. I find it somewhat fascinating and
believable." "Well they are said to have been pagans
and worshiped pagan deities. They were in union with
nature and possessed keen psychic senses." Rayna
continued about the Algonquian Native Americans
folklore. She talked about persons of the wilderness.
"They were said to be knee high or smaller. They were
mischievous but were said to also help a neighbor.
Makes you wonder, doesn't it, maybe there is truth to

some of it?" Maybe we don't see what we don't believe in." Leanne mused. They sat in the quiet for a few more minutes.

Leanne stood up. "Well we better get back. I need to use the bathroom again." "Me too." Rayna laughed. "Being pregnant is hard." Leanne helped Rayna up. As they went through the stones Leanne stopped. She pointed to a second circle in the middle of the stones. "That's weird too don't you think?" Rayna looked where she was pointing. In the center of the circle was a second circle. Much smaller stones. The rocks were maybe 2 inches by 2 inches tall. Each one was very light. Growing between the stones/rocks were mushrooms. Each mushroom was a color. All the colors of a rainbow. "Weird!" Leanne whispered. "I didn't notice those while we were sitting there." "Me either," Rayna whispered back. "Another myth is that a magic fairy circle is ringed in rainbow colored mushrooms. The fairies must know you believe in them before they show themselves." Just then the butterflies were back. They flit all around the two women. Leanne looked at Rayna. Rayna looked at Leanne. Their eyes were huge and they both said "I think I believe". "This is magical." "Let's go and check the sites." Rayna said. They slowly waked back down the hill. They were quiet, lost in their own thoughts.

At the bottom of the hill they paused and looked back. The butterflies were back in the trees. The sun was shining overhead and it had warmed up considerably. Both Rayna and Leanne took off their sweatshirts. "I don't know about you Rayna, but I feel like we are in a fairy tale." I like it." she laughed.

Over the bridge and across the front yard, they both walked briskly. Well, as briskly as an overweight 60 something woman and an almost 9-month pregnant young woman could. They washed their faces, used the bathroom and took the keys for the golf cart. Leanne took her small cooler out of the car. She had added ice at home. She took a couple of waters, their chocolate milk and the muffins. "Let's have a picnic snack after rounds." she said.

Rayna drove. First, they checked all the paid sites. Then the bathrooms. In the back of the golf cart they carried toilet paper, paper towels and Clorox wipes. They cleaned up and drove on. The park was hopping. It was at least 75 degrees and everyone wanted a walk in the woods. Children rode bikes, skated or ran ahead of their parents. Some carried plastic bags and were picking up pretty leaves. Rayna drove slowly. She wore her ranger /caretaker vest and a baseball hat. This gave her a look of somewhat authority. At this point the most she had to say was please keep your dog leashed. In crowded areas, it was, make sure you pick up your dog's waste to a few owners.

They drove the whole perimeter. As they got to the right side of the meadow area, she slowed down. "This is where we thought the music was coming from right? Keep your eye out for the boondockers". Leanne knew that boondocker was a person who camped without a site. It was allowed in a lot of state parks and people liked to be away from other campers. Up ahead and through the trees Leanne spotted a few tents. "There they are." she quietly said. They got the golf cart as close as they could. Rayna got out, grabbed the keys and her clip board. They could hear laughter coming from the camp. As they walked through the trees and the group turned towards them.

Sitting around a campfire were about 10 women. They looked to be in their 30's and 40's. They were laughing and talking. "Hello", Rayna called out. "I am the park caretaker." One woman walked over to them. "Hey come sit down, you look ready to pop." They brought out two camp chairs. Leanne and Rayna sat.

Rayna explained the rules. Though they didn't need a site they did have to register. They could only stay up to 14 days in each state park at a time. They needed to use safe fire making. They needed to clean up their trash.

"Welcome, welcome" the woman said. "I'm Sherrie, this is, ah, my women's group. We are here for the fall equinox. Every year our group comes for two weeks. Some stay the whole time, others go home during the week and come back. We bring tents and food and enjoy a man free, child free time. Is that a problem?" "No, no," Rayna replied, "could you just fill out this registration?" handing her the form and clipboard. Sherrie looked it over "No problem, give me a minute." While Sherrie filled out the form another woman came over.

"Welcome, my name is Maya. How far along are you?" "Due the end of the month." Rayna replied. "Exciting", Maya smiled. "A few of us have our infants here." That's when Leanne and Rayna noticed a few babies. They were strapped to their moms and either eating or sleeping. Maya laughed, "Our rule is no walkies, no talkies this week. We leave the older kids at home. This is our time to bond with our sisters and infants." "That's great," Leanne smiled. "What a wonderful idea." They were invited to stay for food but begged off. "Nice to meet you all, have fun." Getting back in the golf cart they turned to each other and said. "That was cool." The rest of the ride was uneventful.

"What did they mean celebrating the equinox?" Leanne asked Rayna. "Well, legend has it that the Mabon-Autumn Equinox; it's the time when day and night are the same length. A time of balance if you will. The focus is often on the second harvest. Getting ready for winter. Many cultures from pagans to ancient Greeks celebrated the Equinox." "You are a wealth of information." Leanne laughed.

"Yup, my education isn't totally a waste." Leanne looked at Rayna. "What do you mean waste? Did you decide not to finish?" "Well, I don't know now with the baby and all." "You could just finish here in the US." Leanne answered. "I was so looking forward to Ireland. So much of my plans included that. I won the scholarship. I already postponed once. Besides I'm not sure if I'm keeping the baby." Rayna started to cry.

"Pull over, Leanne said, "talk to me." "I feel so bad, but I want this baby to have a good life. I'm not ready. I want to travel. I want to get a teaching job. I want the baby to know I loved him or her. I don't want to repeat my life. I'm really not sure what to do," she put her head down on the steering wheel and sobbed. "Seeing those earthy, crunchy moms," she hiccupped, "I'm not even sure I want to nurse the baby."

Leanne rubbed her back. "Calm down it's alright. All these feelings are natural. Everyone is different. As long as the baby is cared for, they will survive."

"I even thought about open adoption for the baby. That way I could be in control and see them. Maybe even share them on weekends. You know like divorce." "Well I don't know how good that would be for the baby. It might be confusing. Then what happens if the adoptive parents go to court to change the agreement. I don't think I would pick that. Calm down now let's think about this."

Rayna stopped crying. Leanne handed her a tissue. She wiped her eyes and blew her nose. "It's just so much," she sighed. "I miss my foster mom. I'm so glad I found you Nana." Leanne smiled. "We'll figure it out. Let's stop at the next picnic area for our muffin. You'll feel better after some chocolate milk."

Rayna started up the cart and they continued through the forest. Up ahead was a beautiful spot. In the sun at the side of the lake, they parked and walked over. Leanne carried the cooler. Taking a table cloth out of her backpack she set out their snack. Along with the muffins and milk she had a bag of grapes and 2 bananas. Rayna had calmed down and was enjoying the view. Sitting across from each other they watched the water. A small child was fishing with what looked like his grandfather. His squeals of delight filled the air. Fish jumped almost taunting them. The child splashed and frolicked in the sun.

Leanne's mind was racing. She wanted to offer to care for Rayna's baby until she could herself. Maybe in the grandmother capacity. Many mothers left babies with relatives for many reasons. She couldn't offer without Mr. D's approval. It wouldn't be fair to do that without him on board. She had no doubt she could convince him. She wouldn't bring it up to Rayna until she got the ok. Leanne could hardly contain her excitement. They finished up and started back to the cabin.

Rayna was exhausted. Between the meadow, driving and the emotion of the day, she was beat. "I need a long nap." she said. Leanne laughed, "You certainly do. You look beat. Do you have something for supper?" "Yes, I'm having spaghetti & meat sauce." Rayna smiled. "That was always your daycare favorite," Leanne smiled. "Enjoy. Call if you need anything. Why don't I pick you up at 2 PM tomorrow? We'll go to lunch. Then Walmart for anything else you need baby or otherwise." "It's a date." Rayna laughed.

Rayna stretched out on the bed. She pulled her afghan (the one Nana had made so long ago) up over her. She fell asleep almost instantly. The sounds of the forest whispering in her mind. She dreamed of her foster parents. Joe and Joan were happy in the dream. They told her they were at peace and watching over her. In the dream they told her to not be afraid. Everything will work out. They smiled. Just then there was a loud noise. Rayna startled awake. What was that? She sat up and listened, nothing. Funny she thought, it must have been in her dream. Her dream came back to her. It reminded her of her loss. But also reassured her.

The cabin was dark and she had to pee. Slowly she made her way to the bathroom. Looking in the mirror as she washed up, she thought, I'm looking pretty tired still. Pregnancy glow my butt. Putting the water on to boil, she took out the pasta. She had bought a 5 lb. bag of meatballs. She took four out. She liked meat sauce, but wanted the ease of frozen. She crumbled the meatballs added sauce and simmered on the stove top. Pasta ready, with sauce and grated cheese, she dished out a good size portion. Poured a tall glass of milk and carried it to the futon.

Turning the TV on, she watched some old comedies. Her dinner was delicious and she thoroughly enjoyed it. She washed the dishes and decided on a shower. Pjs were her favorite outfit of late. She couldn't wait. She put a couple of logs on the fire. She wanted the room to be toasty.

Rayna enjoyed her shower. She washed her hair and braided it wet. Toweling off she opened the door to let the steam out. The fire had really warmed up the room. Almost too warm. It was almost 11 PM. Rayna was already exhausted again. The baby felt like it was doing acrobatics in there. She made a cup of tea to have with a few cookies. Putting the TV back on she watched the news to hear the weather. More for the company of voices. She could just google the weather tomorrow. The room was definitely warm. Maybe I should have only put one piece of wood on it, she thought. Putting her snack on the coffee table she went to open the door.

She stepped on to the porch and looked at the stars. The sky here was so beautiful. A million stars and the moon were close to full. As she turned to go inside, she heard music coming from the meadow area. This time it was a flute and the beat of a drum. She listened for a minute and then chanting started. Women's voices could be heard clearly. It was very calming and almost magical.

If she wasn't so tired, she would walk over. Not tonight, she said out loud as she closed the door. She drank her tea, ate her cookies and peed again. Locking the door, she shut everything but off but one night-light. Laying down, she just used the sheet to cover up. It was still pretty hot but comfortable. Staring up at the night sky, she could still hear the music and chanting. She wondered how long they would be there. It was after midnight when she fell asleep.

In her dreams, she was in the meadow. The women from the camp were singing and dancing in the moon light. They didn't see her come across the bridge. As she walked towards the trees, she was distracted by movement behind them. She decided to walk or rather float. That is what it felt like, floating. As she rounded the first tree, she looked down. The mushroom circle was glowing. In the center were butterflies. Rayna thought that weird. She knelt down. Peering closer she saw not butterflies, but fairies. Small little women with butterfly wings.

She was startled and sat back on her haunches. They flew clockwise over the circle of mushrooms. They were of different colors. Their wings were beautiful, spotted and speckled, with shimmering flecks. Rayna whispered "How can you be here"? One fairy flew over to her. Her wings were yellow and silver. "You can see us because you believe in us. We are nature spirits and because you believe, you will see us." "Well, I definitely see you," Rayna whispered. "I am dreaming though right?" The fairy whispered "yes." "Remember, legend says if you sit under a full moon in a grove that has ash, oak and thorn trees, Fae (fairy) will appear." She giggled and the six fairies flew away. Rayna slept peacefully until morning.

Leanne decided to bring dinner home. She stopped for pizza. They hadn't done takeout in a while. Mr. D ate out more than she did. He was excited when she arrived with the hot pies. Rosie was happy she was back, the men often forgot to feed her dinner, but gave her lots of treats.

She poured a couple of diet cokes and plated the pizza. Sitting in her chair she muted the TV. "So how was your day?" she asked. Mr. D was in his usual weekend attire. Sweatpants and sport shirt. Patriots, Red Sox, sometimes Celtics. Usually he saved them for St. Patrick's Day. He replied, "Watched TV and looked at the computer, what about you, did you have fun?" "Yes, I helped Rayna settle in and we drove around the park in a golf cart. Sound fun? We met this group of women boon docking." "What's that boon docking?" "Leanne explained it in as few words as possible. "Camping off the grid". "Hmmmm," he chewed. "The women were there for the next two weekends. They are celebrating Mabon – the Autumn Equinox". Leanne could tell her talking window was closing. Mr. D was already looking at what to watch next. Leanne brought him another piece of pizza, now was her chance.

Leanne took a deep breath. "Remember I told you Rayna was pregnant." Mr. D put the control down and looked over. "Ya?" "What would you think of me taking care of the baby for a while?" Now she had his attention. "Why," he asked? "Well she's young and doesn't know what she wants." Leanne replied. "She's hoping to go to school and finish her degree. That would be best," Leanne continued, "Then she could support them both. "That's true," Mr. D agreed. "It would be better if she finished. "Would you really want to care for babies again? You are retired you know. We're having another grandchild soon."

"Well our grandchild has two parents. Our daughter wants to stay home and she wants to do it alone. As for being retired, I would do the usual things, laundry, dinner, eat. Just with a baby. It might be nice." Mr. D continued to chew his pizza. "I'm OK with it, if that's what you want to do." Leanne didn't realize she had been holding her breath. She took a sip of her drink and said, "I think it will be nice. It's nice to help someone who needs it." "Very true, very true." Mr. D replied, want to watch a movie?"

Leanne was screaming inside YES, YES, YES!!! She knew it would be a lot of work, but she missed being needed. This way Rayna could keep the baby out of the system When she wanted to be a full-time mom, the baby would be here. She couldn't wait to offer this solution to Rayna.

Sunday morning Leanne cooked a big breakfast for Mr. D. She plated it and covered it with tin foil. The men, James and Mr. D, could eat when they wanted. She made a cheese plate and the dinners. Then covered and labeled everything. The big game was on at 1:00 PM.

Every game was the "big game" but whatever. Leanne was happy to have plans for a change. She walked Rosie, fed her and drove to pick up Rayna. They would go to lunch. Then the shopping plaza. Then Walmart. It would be fun. She texted Rayna, planning to arrive at 1:00 PM.

Rayna was waiting on the porch. She looked pretty in a yellow blouse. Her hair was braided down her back. She stood up, grabbed her purse and slowly walked down the stairs.

"I did my rounds already and I'm starving. Can we go for burgers for lunch?" Leanne laughed. "I was hoping you would pick that. It's one of my favorites too." Climbing, they drove slowly out of the park. It was another beautiful warm day. Many people had come to enjoy the day. Leanne commented "I guess a lot of people don't care about football." "I know right?" Rayna laughed. It was 15 minutes to the restaurant. "Let's eat inside?" Rayna asked. "I need a bib if I eat in the car now." "I hate eating in the car." Leanne answered. They picked their meals and Leanne carried the tray to a booth in back. She was hungry too.

Over lunch, Rayna told all about her night before. The first dream. The women in the meadow and the dream about the fairies. "Wow, you dream like me on metoprolol." Leanne laughed. "I know, right?" Rayna smiled. "It seemed so real. It's true what the fairy said in the dream. Legend says if you believe, then they will show themselves to you." Leanne thought for a few minutes while chewing her burger. "It does make you wonder. Why would all these different religions, races and people claim them to be real?" "For God's sake, you will have a minor in legends and myths. Where did the ideas come from? Some must be born from truth. Wouldn't you think?" Rayna laughed, "I was thinking the same thing. There must be some truth. Some people believe there were two races. Humans and magic's. Humans got the world we live in. Magic's, Leprechaun's, fairies and elves went underground. Moving from world to world through secret doors."

They both finished eating in silence. Leanne wrapping up her papers said, "I don't doubt there is the possibility of something more, you never know." They decided on Walmart for food and baby supplies.

They both grabbed baskets in Walmart. They headed towards the baby department. "I have my list of everything I've gotten so far." "Great," Leanne answered. They chose a package of receiving blankets. Infant hats, t-shirts and cloth diapers. Leanne had already brought the used clothes back washed and folded. These additional items would suffice until the baby grew. They added two boxes of diapers, diaper cream and wipes. Next, they checked the ready-made formula bottles. Leanne was buying half the baby things. Rayna was still not sure about nursing. They figured they would be prepared. Leanne told Rayna to relax. Better to be prepared and don't need it, than to need it and not have it. They had fun. They decided to get food as well. Frozen dinners would be useful in a pinch. Babies do take a lot of time. They loaded up the cart. It was a fun outing.

Leanne helped carry everything in and put it away. They went through the supplies for the birth. They had everything they needed. At least they hoped they did. The check list was checked and checked again. "Now we need to write a plan for when you go into labor."

"I've read a lot about it. I've watched a lot of videos. It seems like it will take a while." "True, true," LeAnne replied "but let's write it down."

1. As soon as you feel pain call me.
2. Time the pains, have your notebook ready.
3. Lay out plastic where you want to lie.
4. Get comfortable. Night gown, no panties.
5. Walk around, maybe sit on the rocking chair. Cover it.
6. Get supplies laid out. Towels, scissors, birth bin.
7. Try to relax.

"As soon as you call me. I will get ready to come and stay until the baby comes. Luckily Mr. D and James are taking the dog Saturday, the 23rd to NH. They will stay about 10 days. They are closing the houses and watching football both weekends. I can stay until you feel well. I can do the care taker duties if I need to. It will all workout."

Rayna was getting a little nervous. All of a sudden this felt very real. The baby kicked as if to say, "yup it's real." "You'll be fine," Leanne smiled. "It's a lot of work but your young and we can do it together. Do you want a cup of tea?" I'll stay awhile. The men are watching football and they have food." "Sure, that would be great." Rayna answered. She put a log on the fire. Leanne put the kettle on. "Are you hungry?" "Nah, I'll just have some Graham Crackers." Leanne made the tea and set it on the coffee table.

She pulled the rocking chair over and they sat. Rayna looked worried. "I hope everything goes well." she whispered. "Don't worry, we know where the hospital is if we need it. We could always call an ambulance. I think you will do well." "I hope so Nana, it feels so real now." They talked about the birth. "Have you thought about names," Leanne asked. I'm leaning towards Joseph if it's a boy and Joannie if it's a girl." "That's so nice Rayna. They would be proud to have their grandchild named after them." "I hope so," Rayna replied. They sipped their tea in silence.

Outside they heard the music again. "Earlier than last night," Rayna said. "Want to go see what they're doing?" Leanne asked. "We could just go to the bridge and peek."

Rayna slipped on her shoes and grabbed her sweatshirt. Leanne grabbed hers. They opened the door and the music was louder. Chanting and drums along with the flute. It felt magical.

They grabbed the lantern and shut the door. They walked across the front towards the bridge. The stars were so bright and the air was cool. The moon was not quite full. It was visible in the clear sky. They crossed the bridge and looked towards the other side.

The women they had met the other day were in a circle. The leader, Maya, was speaking. The drum was a steady beat and the flute was being played by a woman with an infant strapped to her front. Maya spoke in a sing song way.

"Breathe, relax. Fully enter in to the moment. Focus your awareness inward. Think of the things you want to call forth in your life. Think of the things you are ready to let go of, to create space for your dreams. Breathe, relax, breathe, relax."

Then they started dancing. They were wearing scarfs of many colors. As they danced, they chanted – "Breathe, relax, follow your heart." The music stopped and they each stated a wish for the coming year. It was very mesmerizing. Leanne whispered to Rayna, "Let's leave. I feel like we are intruding somehow." "I do too." Rayna replied. They quietly turned and walked back to the cabin. Leanne looked at Rayna, "That was beautiful. They seemed so happy." "I know, right."

Leanne walked with Rayna into the cabin. She grabbed her purse. "Remember, call me if anything happens". "I will, don't worry." Rayna laughed.

Leanne drove home. Funny, the drive didn't seem so bad even though it was pretty dark. She felt good. Football was over and Mr. D was watching a show. "Have a good day Hon?" he asked. "Great", Leanne replied. "Dinner was good Hon, thanks."

Leanne sat down and they watched the news. Leanne told Rayna unless she needed her, she wouldn't go back until Wednesday. They would text each other each day to check in.

Rayna got ready for bed. Brushed her teeth and put a log on the fire. She stretched out and fell right to sleep. In the distance the beat of the drum and flute music continued. It felt very comforting to fall asleep to the sounds.

Soon she was back at the trees. Again, the mushrooms were glowing. The fairies flew in dance like motions. Around in clock wise motion then back the other way. They were laughing. The sound was a tinkling, high pitched sound. Rayna had never heard such sounds before. She knelt down to get closer. "You are real, aren't you", she whispered. The same fairy who spoke to her before, flew over. "If you believe, we are." "My name is Aine. I am the queen of these fairies. We've been watching you."

Rayna sat back. The baby belly was not conducive to kneeling. She cradled her belly. "Why?" "You are special to us," Aine replied. "We've heard you talk and we know you have studied our culture. There is something special about you, Rayna. All of your children will be special too." "What do you mean?" Rayna whispered. "You will see, some day when the time is right. Now enjoy your sleep, you will need strength for the birth."

The next sound Rayna heard was the rain falling on the skylight. It was not quite morning, so Rayna used the bathroom and went back to sleep. This time she had a dream-less sleep. She woke at 9:00 AM. The rain had stopped, fire had gone out, and there was a chill in the room. Rayna showered, dressed and ate some breakfast. She took the golf cart and made her rounds. The park was pretty quiet. Only a few sites were rented. She did her jobs and decided to loop around to the women's boon docking site.

There were only a few cars parked. The tents were still set up. In the middle around the camp fire, a few women sat. Rayna walked over to say hello. "We just made a pot of tea," Maya called. "Would you like some?" "Please," Rayna said sitting. "The last few weeks are tough being pregnant, aren't they?" asked Maya, while handing her a steaming cup of tea. "This smells amazing!" Rayna took a long breath. What a delightful aroma.

"I saw you guys in the meadow the other night. It looked like you were having a lot of fun." "You could have joined us," Maya answered. "We will be celebrating the full moon and Autumn Equinox next weekend. Some of the women have to go back to reality during the week. The rest of us get to stay on. We sit around the fire and enjoy each other." "Sounds like fun, Rayna said getting up. "Thanks for the tea. I have a little more to do." "Come by anytime" the women called, as she drove down the path.

As Rayna turned to drive back, she wondered about the women. What a fun camping adventure. Sharing their stories, bringing the newest members. Even dancing in the night. What a fun time.

Rayna decided to have lunch and a nap. The pregnancy was really wearing her out lately. She watched a home birth on You Tube and ate her lunch. She stretched out and pulled the afghan over her mountainous belly. The baby was certainly rolling around in there. There was barely any room she felt. She slept for a good two hours. When she woke up, it was raining again. The cabin was dark and cold. After using the bathroom, she went to the porch. The sky was dark and the wind had picked up. Rain was falling sideways. It must have been raining awhile as there were big muddy puddles in front of the cabin.

Rayna grabbed 4 pieces of wood. Carrying them in, she started the fire right away. There was a definite chill to the room she put the lamps on and made a cup of tea. First, she watched Judge Judy or as she liked to call her Jerk Judy. Then the news came on. The room had warmed up considerably. She cooked her dinner and enjoyed her home. An old movie was showing on TV. *"The Blue Lagoon"*. She made some popcorn and put her pajamas on to watch it. After an enjoyable evening she fell right to sleep. The pitter patter of the rain was her background noise. She had a great sleep.

The rest of the week was uneventful. Leanne texted every day at 1:00 PM. She was bringing lunch by on Thursday. Rosie was coming too for a change. They decided on Italian sub sandwiches. Leanne would pick up some food at the market. Rayna texted a short list.

Leanne arrived when expected. The sun was shining and it had warmed up. Rosie couldn't wait to greet Rayna. Rayna looked a little tired to Leanne. Her belly seemed lower and she was a little pale. "Hey let's have a picnic in the meadow." she called. Leanne pulled her wagon out of the back. Filling it with the small cooler and lunch items, and two chairs. She also threw her jacket and backpack in. "Let me just bring the other groceries in for you." She brought 2 bags of food into the kitchen. Put the perishables away and used the bathroom. "All set Rayna?" "I'm good." They walked down the stairs. Rosie ran ahead sniffing everything. Leanne pulled the wagon and they crossed the bridge. In the middle of the rock circle, the bench had been made into an alter or table. On it was a table cloth. Green with white and orange candles. Marigolds were potted on each side. All around the bench were colorful leaves. The leaves had been laid out in a distinct pattern. They must have been wetted down to keep them in their shape. It looked pretty cool. "This must be from the women", Leanne said. "Kind of like an alter don't you think?" "They invited us to join them." Rayna answered. "That would be interesting." Leanne replied. They spread the blanket in front of the alter. Leanne put the lunch out and they started to eat. It was good. Rayna opened her chips and chocolate milk. "I can't believe how much I like this combo Leanne. I never loved chocolate milk so much as now." Leanne laughed "That's your official craving then. I think you have a right." "I want it all the time."

They both watched Rosie. She was having a great time running all over the meadow. As they finished up Rayna told Leanne all about her dreams. It's like they were so real she explained. I can't describe the feeling. "Let's check out the mushroom circle. See if it's still there." Leanne pulled herself up on the bench edge. "I'm definitely too old to be sitting on the ground." She straightened up and chuckled. "Need a hand, your definitely too pregnant to sit on the ground." They both laughed. Leanne helped Rayna up. They packed the things back into the wagon. They walked around to the back of the trees, checking for the mushroom circle. Sure enough, it was still there. They looked all around, no fairies. Then they looked up in the tree branches and there were the butterflies. All different colors and sizes.

Each one seemed to be decorated uniquely. Some were spotted, some striped. The wings of some were iridescent. It was beautiful. The sun was shining just right to make them feel magical. Rosie barked breaking the spell. For whatever reason, she would not pass through this stone circle. She sat and then lay down in the sun watching. "It's so weird, I really feel like they are fairies." "Could be," Leanne whispered, "Who are we to say all those myths and legends are not based on fact." "Exactly," Rayna whispered back. "I have an idea. When I studied fairies one of the stories was," Rayna stopped. "Let me get this right" she continued whispering. She thought to herself in case they are real. "The legend or story goes – if a mortal makes a wash of marigold water, rubs it around the eyes. sits under a full moon in a grove of ash, oak and thorn, fae will appear." "Interesting," Leanne whispered back. "I'll try it, will you?" "What can it hurt," Rayna answered. "Hey, there is a marigold plant near the alter. Let's take one flower bud and we can make the water. It will be a full moon on the weekend."

The butterflies flitted all around. At least 20 seemed to follow them back to the cabin. Leanne emptied the wagon into the car. They sat on the top step. The sun had warmed the day. All the puddles were gone and it was peaceful and beautiful out. Do you really want to try that?" laughed Leanne. "Sure, what's it going to hurt." Rayna answered back.

They talked about Leanne's daughter. She was due to have her baby any day. She had her husband with her. Leanne was to visit on the weekend. Sitting next to each other on the steps, Leanne turned. "Rayna have you decided what you want to do?" "Rayna thought, she took a deep breath. "Well, I really want to finish my degree. I would like to go to Ireland as planned." "You can do that," Leanne answered. "Do you want to take the baby with you?" "I think it might be too hard," Rayna cried. "I really don't want to give up the baby, I don't know what to do." Rayna cried softly. Leanne put her arm around her. "I have an idea." she said softy. Rayna looked up, took a tissue blowing her nose and said, "Tell me".

Chapter Six: The Plan

"Well," Leanne started. "What if I take care of the baby while you finish school in Ireland? I will care for your baby." "What do you mean Nana?" "Well, you can give me custody, like if I were the grandmother, "Nana." "Lots of Grandmother's care for their Grandchildren. When you're ready to come home, you get your baby back." Rayna looked at Nana. "Are you serious, you would do that for me? What about Mr. D. What would he think?" "Well I already asked him and he is fine with it." "The tricky part is keeping you out of the system." "What do you mean Nana?" "Well, we don't want to go to court if we can help it. As soon as you're in the system, you have a hard time getting out." "That's true, I'm still in the system as I was a foster child." Rayna said. "Right, so I think I have found a way around it."

"It is a little shady," Leanne replied. "What is it?" "Well, I think when you fill out the birth certificate you need a father." "But I don't know him, remember Nana?" "Right, well I thought why not put my James as the father." "What? won't that be wrong?" "Well yes, but that way I would be the Grandmother." Leanne explained. "Do you think he would go along with it?" "Hmmm", Leanne paused. "I wasn't planning on telling him about it. He never has to know. When you come back, you'll take the baby back and live your life. You can write a letter saying we made it up. Then we will have it notarized and keep it safe. If we ever need it, then we have it. In the meantime, you can leave the baby with me. Go finish school, come back and get a job and be on your own. I'll always welcome the baby as a Grandchild." "Very interesting," Rayna replied. "Let me think about it." "Just don't take too long." Leanne replied. "You need to send the birth certificate right away. You will need a passport and a pediatrician." Rayna smiled; this could work.

They sat in silence a few more minutes. Both lost in their own thoughts. Standing up, Leanne smiled. "Don't worry, everything will work out. You think about it. Remember to text if anything happens. I hope to see my newest Grandchild. Saturday. Mr. D and James are taking Rosie up to NH for two weeks. I can stay whenever you need me." Leanne gave Rayna a big hug. "Don't worry, it will all work out."

"Thank you so much Nana, I love you." Rayna hugged her back. Leanne smiled all the way home. When she got home there was a message, she was a "Nana" again. A new baby grandchild a granddaughter. Mother and baby were doing well. Life was good Leanne thought.

The next few days flew by. Leanne was getting some things for her new granddaughter, Nora. She also had to send food, medicine and supplies with the men for their trip. She kept her phone charged and ready in case Rayna called. They texted each other daily. Everything was status quo. Saturday, Leanne was thrilled to meet the new baby. Daughter and her husband had everything under control. The baby was perfect. They only visited for a short while. Then the men and Rose were on their way.

Leanne was excited. She packed a bag in case Rayna called. She went over her notes on birth and baby care. Double checked the supplies she wanted. She planned on bringing her laptop just in case. Also, the birthing kit she had put together. Food and drinks were last on her list. She had a special tea to help during labor for Rayna. Leanne thought she was ready. She took her shower and got ready for an early night. Texting both Rayna and her daughter, she got the "all's well" from both. Bringing both the landline and the cell phone into her bedroom, she went to sleep.

Rayna wasn't sure if she should call Nana. Her back had been bothering her all day. It wasn't like pain that you could time. Just an ache all day. She went about her day as usual but just slower. For dinner she had a can of soup and some saltines. She figured she would put some wood on the fire and get ready for bed.

Rayna fell asleep very quickly. In her dream she was back in the meadow. Her hair was flowing down her back. Her eyes were ringed in marigold water. Slowly, she floated through the forest. She lowered herself to the ground next to the mushroom ring, just like before. The small creatures were dancing around the circle. Rayna could see them perfectly. They were truly beautiful. Again, the fairy, Aine, flew to her. "You've come back Rayna." She smiled. "I see you truly believe." Rayna nodded, "Yes," she whispered. "I do. I do believe." Aine smiled. "I see you will give birth soon. You are special and all your children will be too. You've been marked by the fairies and are a true believer." More of the fairies came to Rayna's side. "You will have a difficult journey ahead. Would you like some magic to help with the birth?" Rayna whispered "What do you mean?" "Well, we can sprinkle you with fairy dust." "Why?" Rayna asked. "It won't take away all the pain, but the birth labor will be short." "YES, I WOULD... like the dust that is, as long as it won't hurt my child." "Your birth will go smoothly. We will watch over you. Let us start the rites of birth" and with that, all the fairies started whirling around.

As they whirled, some of the iridescent sparkles fell from their wings. The sparkles rained down on Rayna. More and more butterfly like creatures appeared. It was a world, full with wings. Their little voices would canter. Rayna couldn't make out the words. She felt at peace. All of a sudden Rayna opened her eyes. She was lying in bed. The room had grown cold and the fire was almost out. She sat up looking around. She spoke to herself. Was that a dream or real? Putting her feet on the floor to go for wood and use the bathroom, Rayna looked at her feet. They were covered in mud. Her arms and legs sparkled, like she had used lotion with glitter. She touched the sparkles. They weren't ordinary glitter. This is weird. She threw a couple of logs on the fire going into the bathroom. She looked at herself in the mirror. Her eyes were ringed in gold. "What the heck"? she said aloud. This is so weird.

She washed her feet and braided her hair. Tea sounded good. She was awake now. Might as well eat something. Her back was still bothering her, but not too bad. She watched a couple of birth videos until she was sleepy again. Her mind kept going back to the fairies... did she sleep walk she wondered? She lay down again for a couple of hours before dawn.

Sunday, the morning sky was a beautiful pink and red. The old saying red sky in morning, sailors take warning, popped into her head. What actually does that mean she thought? The weather man had forecast a warm day. Rayna decided to shower and wear a long dress. She wanted to get her work out of the way. Her back was still bothering her in an ache kind of way. She stripped down and was amazed that the sparkles were everywhere. So strange. It didn't take long for her to do the rounds.

Luckily the bathrooms only needed a quick once over. Leanne was coming around 3 PM. She planned on staying a few days. Tomorrow they would go to town for more supplies. Leanne drove in at 3 PM, right on the dot. Rayna was sitting on the porch rocking. She had poured two teas and waited for Leanne to sit down. "How was your night?" Leanne asked. Rayna said, "You're not going to believe this." She recounted the "dream" then added the fact of the glitter like substance and the marigold water around her eyes. Leanne shook her head. "Are you kidding me?" "Nope, I'm serious. I was covered in sparkles. My feet were muddy and I had marigold water around my eyes. I kid you not Nana." "Well, maybe we should try again tonight. The moon will be almost full." "Legend did say, if we sit in the grove under a full moon, the fairy will appear." "The women should be in the field. We could watch them as well". "Sounds good to me," Leanne answered. "I am on vacation, sort of."

On a more serious note, did you think more about my idea?" Rayna shook her head yes. "I think we can try it Nana. Tell me again how we can make it work?" "Well, you will fill James Doherty in as the father. That makes me the Grandmother. When we see the pediatrician, you can sign off on me bringing the baby. You will write two letters. One telling the authorities James is not the father. One telling your child that you plan on coming back. Also, that I am their adopted Nana. We will notarize the letters. We will get copies of the birth certificate. You keep one and one with letters for the child. The child will never know because you'll come back and start your life." Rayna nodded. "It really is a good plan Nana. What about Mr. D? Are you sure he will be on board?" "Yes, we will keep the baby downstairs with us for as long as needed. We could even use the office for a baby room. We do have two empty bedrooms upstairs. He'll be fine with it." Rayna thought about it. It could work. "Would you Skype while I'm away?" "Twice a week if you want. The baby, I'm sorry to say, won't even know. You'll be back by June, right?" Leanne asked. "That is the plan," Rayna answered. "I'm in."

Rayna stood up she put both hands behind her. "My back has been killing me." she sighed. "Really" Leanne looked over. "Are you in labor?" "I don't think so. Just a sore back. This baby feels low and huge." "You are pretty big," Leanne smiled. "Any pain at all? Any blood or water?" "Nothing but continuous backache." Rayna sighed. Leanne said, "Let's go inside and I'll make us an early dinner. I think I'll eat light tonight. Soup and grilled cheese sound good to you?" "Yes very." answered Rayna. They went inside and Rayna put a log on the fire. "Cozy!" Leanne said smiling. They ate, lost in their own thoughts.

Leanne was excited. The thought of seeing real fairies thrilled her. They put the marigold in a glass of water before dinner. They planned on circling their eyes with that water. Better to try and have it not been real, than to not believe at all. There had to be something to this.

Rayna rested after dinner. Leanne used her computer and put an old movie on. They planned on going to the meadow around 10:30 PM. Rayna woke at

9. She rolled off the bed and padded into the bathroom. Calling Leanne a few minutes later, "Not to be gross," she said, "but what is this?" She put her hand out and showed LeAnne. "Hmmm, that's the mucous plug Rayna." Rayna turned pale and sat down on the toilet. She looked up at Leanne. "This is it? I am having the baby?" she questioned. Leanne squeezed her shoulder. "It could be awhile honey. Did your water break?" "Definitely not." Rayna replied. "Well put a pad on and we'll get ready to go to the meadow. It is good to move around. Any pains?" "No, just the back ache." Rayna replied. "Well, let's get this show on the road," Leanne answered. "I'll get everything ready just in case."

Leanne shut the door. She could barely contain both her excitement and terror. She had helped her younger daughter give birth. She had four children but always there were medical people to step in if needed. She heard the shower running. Carefully, she started to lay out what they would need. It wasn't long before Rayna was out. She looked a little pale and scared. Leanne did her best to reassure her.

Outside, the first sounds of music wafted in. Drums beating, and the whimsical sound of the flute. They pulled on their sweatshirts. Just before leaving, they took some of the marigold water. Each of them used a finger to spread it around their eyes. Leanne looked at Rayna. They burst out laughing. "You ready for this?" they both said in unison. "Yes," Leanne whispered. "The next 24 hours are going to be awesome." "I'm a little scared", Rayna answered, Leanne hugged her. "You will do great. I just know it."

Slowly they made their way to the meadow. "I think labor is starting." Rayna whispered. "What do you feel?" "Cramping a little, I think," Rayna whispered. Leanne looked at her watch. "We'll time them. Do you want to go back?" Rayna shook her head. "No, let's go, just walk slow. I feel like the baby is going to just fall out." "Okee-dokey" Leanne whispered back.

At the end of the bridge they could see the women. They were as they were before, only everyone had white on. Each woman was wearing a dress or pants and white tops. They each held a scarf in each hand. The scarfs were all fall colors. The music was louder. They danced to the beat of the drum. Chanting as they whirled. It was mesmerizing. The giant yellow orb of the moon hung in the sky. Many sparkling stars shone around it. It was a beautiful sight. Between the women, and the night sky, it took their breath away.

Leanne had carried her backpack. She had her phone, blanket and ever-present snacks. She also carried a small notebook and pen. Rayna grimaced, another pain. Leanne wrote down the time. "They are pretty far apart," she whispered. "Let's go around back to the mushroom circle." The butterflies were back. They spread out the blanket and lowered themselves to the ground. Rayna sat with her legs straight out. Leanne did the same. The mushroom circle was glowing. Butterflies lit on each one. Rayna pointed and whispered to Leanne. "That's the one from my dream." Just then the fairy butterflies flew to them. One of them landed at their feet. "Ah, I see you've come to see us." she said in a very soft voice. "Leanne and Rayna turned to each other. "It worked," they whispered, "they are real." "Of course, we are real." The fairy flew straight up. She was eye level. Leanne could see her beautiful face and iridescent wings. She had long dark hair, gray or blond streaks wove through it. "I am Aine, queen of the fairies."

More fairies flew to join in. They circled the humans. They flew around for a short time. Rayna let out a gasp. All the fairies stopped and landed. Aine came over, "I see you will give birth soon. Your birth is a special one. Would you like us to dull the pain?" Rayna turned to LeAnne. "Should I?" she asked now. Leanne had given birth 4 times. She had three by natural birth and it hurt. You never remembered the pain until the next child was on its way. "Is it safe?" she asked the fairy. "Of course, it will still hurt, just not as much." Leanne looked at Rayna. "I say go for it." Rayna thought for a minute. "I'm in", she laughed. "I'm already scared." Aine smiled, she clapped her tiny hands. With that all the fairies, there had to be a hundred or so, began flying clockwise around them. The music on the other side became louder. The beat of the drum. The flute, chanting and singing. The two women realized, not only were human women singing. The fairy women were also singing. It was truly magical.

After what felt like hours but actually was only 4 minutes, they all stopped. Aine flew over to them. She flew at eye level. "You will have a magical birth Rayna. The birth will happen before midnight tomorrow. We have sprinkled you with fairy dust to help with the pain." With that all the fairies flew away. Leanne and Rayna were left all alone. "Oh my God did that just happen?" Leanne whispered. "I think so." Rayna whispered back. Looking down, they were both covered in a shiny sprinkling of dust. They each lumbered to a standing position. Leanne grabbed their things. "Damn, I wish I had taken a picture," she whispered. "No one will ever believe this."

Slowly they walked back. The women in the meadow were still dancing. Some sat on blankets eating and drinking. They had put a ring of candles around their site. The two musicians played on.

Rayna had two more pains on the way to the cabin. "How bad are they?" Leanne asked. "Well, they are getting worse since we started back." "This is it," Leanne exclaimed. "Let's have a baby." It was close to 2 am when they got back to the cabin. Leanne rushed to get everything ready. She covered the bed. Laid out all the equipment, brought wood in and put a couple of pots on to boil. She felt scared and excited at the same time. She pulled the bassinet over closer to the fire. "Just imagine there will be a baby in there before long." "I can't wait," Rayna murmured. "Let's hope the fairy magic helps." "It will I'm sure," Leanne answered. "You'll do great. Why not try to rest a bit. It will take a while for a first-time baby." Rayna stretched out on the bed. Leanne lay on the futon. They left a few night lights on. Neither slept, both lay there lost in their own thoughts.

By 7 AM, it was very evident no one was sleeping. "How about a little breakfast?" Leanne asked Rayna. Do you feel like you can eat?" "Tea and toast please." Rayna replied. "How's the pain going?" "Well it's about every 30 minutes, but not too bad yet." "I'll do the rounds early for you", Leanne offered. I don't feel comfortable leaving you for long. "Sounds good", Rayna answered. "I'll do some walking and rocking. I read that helps labor along."

Leanne took a quick shower. Rayna didn't want to wash the dust off just in case. She just braided her hair and put on a large t-shirt. The cabin was quite warm and she felt comfortable. Leanne grabbed the golf cart keys and her phone. "Call me if you need to. I'll be quick." She drove the loop. Checked the bathrooms and was back in 45 minutes. Rayna was on the rocking chair rubbing her tummy with her eyes closed. "That was a long one Leanne, it's going to be today for sure." Leanne decided to drag one of the outdoor rockers in. "How about a movie to take your mind off the labor. I brought *What about Bob?* and *Overboard."* "Tough choices," Rayna laughed "let's start with *What about Bob?"* They both enjoyed the movie.

Leanne made a light lunch. Tea and turkey sandwich and apple sauce. Rayna needed to keep her strength up for the birth. Still, the water hadn't broken. Rayna thought maybe she missed it. "Well we will see, let's just time the contractions".

Leanne prayed everything would go well. So far Rayna seemed quite in control. Contractions caused discomfort but didn't seem as excruciating as Leanne remembered. She kept the scissors and string in the boiling water. She gathered the clean towels and facecloths for washing up and drying the baby. She even had a scale to weigh the baby. Everything was ready. By eight o'clock things turned more intense.

Chapter 7: The Birth

Rayna's contractions were five minutes apart consistently for two hours. She used the bathroom one more time. "Wow," she said holding the bottom of her belly. "I'm ready. I think the dust is helping." "Could be," Leanne answered, if not for real the placebo effect was helping. "I think I need to push." Rayna whispered. They had soft music playing. The room was well lit but not too bright. Leanne helped Rayna settle on the bed. She took off her shirt leaving on only her sport bra. Leanne had pillows behind her back. She pulled a towel over her middle for privacy. Not that giving birth was private, but it wasn't time yet. The towel would be there to wrap the baby.

Rayna started pushing at 9:30 PM. With each contraction the baby's head was visible. Leanne had her put her hands behind her knees. "Ok Rayna, when you need to push, bear down while pulling your legs toward you." "Ok", Rayna whispered. "Here it comes." "Take a big breath" Leanne said. "Listen to me, now push, push, push, ok pant, pant, pant, push again, it's almost here. I can see it," Leanne was excited, she could see the baby's hair. "You got it Rayna, push, push." The head slipped out. "Pant, pant", something was wrong. LeAnne put her hands under the baby. Just then Rayna gave a cry and out slipped the baby. It was the most amazing thing; the baby was completely covered in the amniotic sack. For a minute Leanne froze, what is this, she thought. Rayna sat further up, peering down. "Why isn't it crying?" she cried. Leanne took a finger and broke the sack. The baby unfolded like a flower opening. The water came gushing out and the baby stretched its little arms. Leanne pulled the rest of the membrane away. She swept the mouth picked the baby up and checked for the sex. "It's a girl!" she whispered. She pulled the baby the rest of the way out. Rayna was crying. "Is she ok Nana?" Nana started wiping the mucus off of the baby. The baby howled in protest. She had a head of black, curly hair. She seemed small but perfect. She handed her to Rayna wrapped in the towel. "What was that around her, Nana?" Rayna asked. "I read about it," Nana replied. "It's called caulbearer, or born with a veil. It's very rare." Rayna kissed her baby. "She's beautiful isn't she Nana". "I should say so," Nana replied. "Hold her tight while I clean up a little".

"Nana will you sing to her with me." "What do you want to sing?" "You are my Sunshine." Leanne always sang that song to any baby she cared for, hers or daycare. Rayna sang softly and Leanne joined in. She went to get the scissors and string for the umbilical cord. Rayna stopped singing. "I think I have to push again Nana." "What? it must just be the placenta." Leanne answered. "That's normal. Let me cut the cord." Rayna handed the baby to Leanne. Bearing down she started panting. "This doesn't feel right Nana." Nana cut the cord and wrapped the baby in the towel. She quickly pulled the bassinet closer so she could keep an eye on the baby. Rayna pushed again. LeAnne grabbed another towel and a chux. She thought that the placenta would be wrapped and buried outside. Leanne felt Rayna's stomach. It still seemed pretty hard. Just then Rayna pushed, holding legs back. There between her legs looked like another baby. LeAnne looked up at Rayna. "I think there is another one." "What do you mean," Rayna panted. "Twins" Leanne whispered. "Push". Just the head slid out. This baby too was covered in the sack. What are the odds LeAnne thought? It wasn't quite as surprising as only moments before she had broken a sack. Again, she poked a hole. The baby was identical to the other. Dark hair, solemn eyes. Leanne used the blue bulb to clean out the mouth. "Is it a baby?" Rayna asked quietly. Leanne looked up, tears streaming down her face. "Rayna you also have a son." With that she lifted him up and placed him on her chest.

"Oh my god, two babies." Rayna cried. "How? What? Oh my God"!!! The baby solemnly looked up at his mother. Leanne massaged Rayna's stomach. Now it seemed quite soft and empty. She freshened Rayna up and went to the bassinet. The little girl was quietly watching. Leanne wrapped her in the towel and brought her to her mother. She lay the baby next to her brother. "Happy Mother's Day Rayna. They seem perfect. Let me cover you all with a blanket while I clean this up."

Leanne saved the caul, and put the placentas in a covered pail. They had planned on planting something on them. She hurried over to the new family. "Ok, let me cut his cord now." She had thrown the scissors and string back in the boiling water to sterilize them. "How do you feel Rayna?" Leanne asked. "Shocked but ok." Rayna replied, with her arms full of babies.

Leanne took the boy first. She weighed him with her luggage scale 5 lbs. 2oz. He was 18 inches long. They were born at 10:15 and 10:45. She dressed him in a t-shirt, diaper and hat. Next, she wrapped him in a blanket. She lay him in the bassinet. Now the girl.

She weighed in at 5lbs even and 18 inches long. She dressed her the same. She put the yellow hat on her. She lay the baby next to her brother. As if on cue, they turned their little heads and looked at each other. She rolled the bassinet over to the bed. Rayna looked in. "I can't believe it." she whispered.   "Me either." LeAnne whispered back.

"How do you feel?" Leanne asked. "Well, tired I guess but hungry and dirty too." "Do you feel up to having a shower?" "I really do." Rayna replied. "Ok, let's get you into the bathroom."

Leanne helped Rayna up and slowly, they went to the bathroom. "Ok sit there on the toilet for a minute." LeAnne said. She quickly rolled up the soiled bedding. Thank goodness for flannel backed table cloths she thought. She grabbed some clean clothes for Rayna and brought them to her. "Take this ibuprofen and a quick shower. Leave the door open just in case. I'll make some soup and tea."

Leanne put the kettle on, started the soup and put some cookies out. She added a few pieces of wood to the fire. Wouldn't want the twins to get cold, she thought. Twins, OMG, I just delivered twins. She walked over to the bassinet. Both babies turned as she leaned in. They were beautiful. Their dark eyes looked up at her. They seemed so content. When Rayna came out of the bathroom, she was radiant. She had braided her hair and slipped into a button-down night gown. She walked slowly over to the bassinet. Tears fell slowly down her cheeks. "Nana, I never could have done it without you," she sighed. "They are beautiful, aren't they?" "Gorgeous, thank you for sharing this with me." Nana answered. "I wouldn't have missed it for the world." The babies drifted off to sleep. Leanne and Rayna had their meal set on the coffee table, in sight of the two new additions

Almost on cue the twins started stirring as they finished their meal. Rayna had decided to both bottle and breast feed. She lifted the girl and put her to her breast. The baby ate hungrily. Nana changed the boy and then switched babies. As she changed the little girl she asked "Have you picked the full names yet Rayna?" "I'm giving them Joseph and Joannie after my foster parents. I haven't picked middle names yet." Leanne smiled "That is wonderful. I know they really loved you." "Joey and Joannie." Rayna whispered to the baby. They each held a baby and rocked them to sleep. Rayna looked at Leanne, "Isn't this wild. Can you believe this night?" Just then, they noticed that it was raining. They could still see the full moon through the skylight. Hearing the rain on the roof, they both said at the same time "moon showers". They looked up at each other. "Moon Babies." "I'm not going out there," they laughed.

Leanne changed the babies and lay them down again. They both fit in the bassinet. She cleaned up from their meal. Turned off the light, and put a log on the fire. Everyone went to sleep and didn't wake for 4 hours.

Opening her eyes, Leanne looked over at Rayna. She was glowing. One of the babies was nursing. Leanne smiled, "You've taken to nursing very well Rayna, haven't you?" "They seem to latch on well," Rayna replied. "Though I'm worried they will drop too much weight. I think I want to supplement right away. What do you think Nana?" Leanne replied, "We could offer the 2-ounce bottles after each feeding after you nurse. Then I'll burp and give the bottle. That way they'll keep their weight. Once the milk comes in you can reassess." "Sounds good Nana."

Leanne pulled the other chair closer. "Can I pick up the other baby?" "Sure, you don't have to ask." Rayna replied. Leanne scooped the baby up. "They really are beautiful aren't they!" she exclaimed. "Yes, truly." Rayna answered. They rocked the babies. Leanne turned, "Are we going to talk about the meadow." Rayna looked, "You mean the women or the fairies." "Well, both I guess," Leanne chortled. "Mostly the fairies. We can't tell anyone what we saw. They'll think we are crazy." "Are we?" Rayna asked? "I don't know", Leanne answered. "Sure, seemed real to me." "To me too." Rayna replied. They continued to rock and then Leanne said, "Let's not mention it. Ok?" "I think that's best." said Rayna.

The babies were fed, changed and back in the bassinet. The women had their eggs, toast, sausages and coffee. It was delicious. Leanne decided to send a text to Mr. D. It read; babies born. Twins, a boy and a girl. All is well. He didn't reply, it was early. "Let's get the birth certificates filled out,", Rayna said. "Good thing I got extra's." "It sure was." They filled them out and planned on visiting town hall on Wednesday the 26th.

They did fill in James W Doherty as the father. Rayna did write the letters telling the truth just in case.

The rest of the day was spent resting and feeding and caring for the babies. They were the best babies Nana had ever cared for. They ate, slept and slept some more. Leanne sent a text to her daughter. Baby Nora was home and doing well. She declined any help; her husband was with her. Leanne couldn't wait for the three babies to meet. That would be fun.

After lunch, Leanne took the golf cart to the boon dockers. They greeted her with smiles. "Is the baby here" they asked? "Yes", Leanne called "She had twins, a boy and a girl. Momma and babies are doing well." "We thought we heard a cry," they laughed. Tonight, is the official Mabon ritual Autumn Equinox. Come by for a moon welcoming. Its good luck for the babies." "I will tell Rayna" Leanne answered. "I love how you all dance in the moonlight. We saw you the other night, very magical." "Every year we come, join us any time." Maya offered. "Thank you," Leanne answered. "I better get back." She took out her notebook. "How long are you staying?" "We're all leaving on Wednesday." Maya said. "It's been a wonderful festival this year." Leanne marked it off. "Safe home if I don't see you. It was nice meeting you all." She drove back to the cabin. Just then a text came in from Mr. D.

You must be in your glory with twin's lol. Have fun. Talk to you soon.

He was a man of few words she'll give him that. When Leanne got back everyone was napping. She sat down and put her computer on. Before long she was asleep too.

Leanne woke up to Rayna singing. Each baby was nestled in her arms. Leanne grabbed her phone and took some pictures. They were a beautiful sight. She went to the kitchen next. They had skipped lunch. She made tea and a couple of English muffins. Then she put chicken, potatoes and stuffing in the oven. "You'll need to keep your strength up Rayna, we'll eat in an hour." They enjoyed the tea. Each fed a baby, then changed them and rocked them again. It was amazing how little they cried. Leanne gave Rayna the low down of the caretaker job. She extended the invitation from the women. "I don't know, would it be too cold for them. What do you think?" she asked. "Well, let's wait and see. We'll eat and care for the babies then decide. No worries." Leanne replied.

Dinner was delicious. They both were very hungry. Leanne added gravy, corn and cranberry sauce and warm rolls. They both ate two servings. Rayna laughed, "I haven't had this good of a meal in ages." "Thanks." Leanne replied. "It is good, isn't it?" Around 9 PM the music started again. The night was warmer than usual and the babies were fed and changed by 10 pm. The moon was shining in the skylight. Both babies slept peacefully. "Let's go." Rayna said. "We'll just walk over and show them off." "Ok by me!" Leanne said. "We have extra warm blankets in the box." They got ready. Each woman carried a baby nestled in her arms.

Leanne felt such comfort. They walked slowly to the bridge. A few butterflies had started to follow them. They decided to first stop behind the trees. They didn't want the other women to see the mushroom circle, in fear they would ultimately destroy it. As they turned the corner of the trees, Queen Aine flew over. "Ah, I see you have given birth. Hopefully our magic helped." "Yes," Rayna answered. "It was very quick." "We stopped to thank you for your help." Leanne added. "These are very special children. I know they are caulbearer. They were born behind the veil, weren't they?" Rayna and Leanne looked at each other. Turning back to the fairy they said "How do you know that?" Queen Aine smiled, "I know they will be very good. It is a good omen, a sign of luck and greatness. They may have psychic gifts. I will send a spirit to guide them. We call it Fylgia. Welcome the spirit and it will keep your babies safe." Rayna nodded, "I will," she replied. "Thank you."

Rayna remembered in her studies; the myths of fairy legends told of the fact that no gift from a fairy was free. That every transaction is an exchange and it's never one sided. Rayna felt a little scared. On the other side of the trees, the chanting grew louder. Leanne decided to say good bye before the babies got too cold. Queen Aine flew first to Joseph then to Joannie. She lit on their hat and said a blessing. Then all the fairies flew around whispering their names.

All at once, they flew straight up to the trees. Rayna and Leanne looked at the babies. Each solemn face was wide eyed. There was a sprinkling of fairy dust all around. Goodbye the women whispered, thank you. Slowly they went to the other side of the meadow.

The ritual was well underway. Drums beat and the eerie music of the flutes was beautiful. Two women played the flutes and two others used the bongos. They all chanted a song it was beautiful.

We dance, in the moonlight
Under the starry sky
We dance. We dance.
The moon goddess in our hearts.

The women looked beautiful in the moonlight. All shapes and sizes. For the first time in a long time Leanne didn't even think of how she looked. They both swayed to the music. The songs continued.

Moon goddess moon whisper your secrets
Share your light
Moon goddess moon, shining so bright.

It was truly wonderful. The women turned and saw Rayna and Leanne. They gathered around oohing and aahing. Marveling at the new little lives brought forth. Maya hurried over. "Would you like a moon welcoming of the babies?" she asked Rayna. Rayna nodded her head, "Yes." "Great!" Maya smiled.

Maya placed her hands on each baby. The chanting of all the women started.

Welcome to your brand-new world baby.
Welcome to our universe.
Were so glad you are here!

Each woman brought a leaf for each child. They made a wish and tossed the leaf into the moonlight. Then they joined hands and circled the babies.

Rayna and Leanne, may you be blessed. May wisdom dwell within you. May you create peace. They repeated it 3 times.

They finished up with:

Moon Goddess moon whisper your secrets.
Moon Goddess moon
Shinning so high
Share your light
We dance beneath you
Share what you know
The circle of love surrounds these children.

The drums continued and the women danced all around the babies. It was very moving and Rayna felt tears running down her cheeks. Looking at Leanne, she saw the same thing managed to affect them both. When the dancing ended, Maya invited, "Have a glass of juice with us." She offered them a plastic cup. They both drank greedily. Thanking Maya and the group they said their goodbyes. "Come back next year." the women called. "The babies won't quite be walkie talkies." They laughed. "Maybe, thank you." Rayna replied.

Leanne and Rayna started back to the cabin. That was interesting to say the least. The babies were wide awake and staring up at the sky. "They can't see that can they?" Rayna asked. "I'm not sure," Leanne answered. "Wouldn't surprise me though. Nothing would surprise me right now."

Back at the cabin they fed, changed and put the babies down in the bassinet. Rayna showered while Leanne read a little. Then they put a log on the fire and went to sleep. They were beat. They fed the babies without talking during the night. Nurse, bottle, diaper, bed!

Wednesday dawned a cool crisp day. They started the day with showers and breakfast. Now that there were two babies, they already needed to do laundry and get more supplies. Leanne listed their chores. Bury the placentas. Do the rounds, and caretaker duties. Walmart and laundry and most importantly, they had to go to the town hall and turn in the paperwork for birth certificates. "Oh no," Rayna called, "we only have one car seat. It was required that the clerk at the town hall had to see the babies." "No worries," Leanne answered. "I have one in the van. I always carry it just in case. You never know when you'll need it." Rayna laughed, "Like the dog leash?" "Yes, you never know. Look, we need one now." "That's true!" Rayna replied. Leanne brought the second one in. They put the babies in sleepers, wrapping blankets around them. They were adorable.

Leanne had been in touch with her daughter. Nora was doing great. She needed nothing.

They loaded the car and off they went. Everything went smoothly. The town clerk cooed and awed over the twins. Rayna ended up naming them Joseph James Doherty and Joannie Marie Doherty. They did list James W. as the father. Leanne got to be the proud Nana. Unassisted births needed witnesses. They had Leanne and had asked Maya to sign off on knowing Rayna. That and the workmen's forms was all it took. It would take two weeks to get back the certificates. Rayna was thrilled. Next Leanne took Rayna to her house. It was the first time Rayna was seeing it. She was impressed. Leanne ran upstairs and threw the laundry in. Rayna didn't do the stairs; she was feeling a little pain from the birth. They both thought better of it. Rayna loved the house. Leanne showed her the office that was where she might possibly put the babies if they didn't sleep well in her room. Rayna loved the brightness of everything. Leanne switched the laundry. They fed and changed the babies then off to shop.

They bought outfits, diapers, formula and new bottles. They picked up food for the rest of the week. They were driving back to get the laundry and stopped for burgers. We deserve a treat they both said. Rayna stayed in the car. Leanne got the laundry. They were driving back in the park 15 minutes later. It was getting dark and the cabin was pitch black. Leanne got out first. Taking the key, she opened the door and turned on the inside light. Then carried the laundry into the cabin.

Heading back to the car she heard something in the corner of the porch. It sounded like a whimper. "Stay in the car." Leanne called to Rayna. Rayna rolled down the window. "What's the matter?" Leanne put her hand up. She switched the porch light on. There under the second rocker was a small animal. It was dark in the shadow so Leanne carefully bent down and peered in under the chair. Looking up at her were the most solemn eyes. "I think it's a dog." Leanne called to Rayna. "A dog, here? Why?" Leanne motioned to the dog talking in a sing song way. "It's ok you can come out. Did someone leave you?" The pup slowly crawled out from under the rocker. It licked Leanne's hand and sniffed around. Rayna got out of the car. "Whose is it?" she called out. "I don't know?" Leanne answered. "He thinks he's mine, shall we bring him or her and the babies in?" Rayna opened the back door taking Joey in. Leanne put the pup in the cabin and got Joanie. Then Leanne brought all their purchases, the laundry and supplies into the cabin. The dog went immediately to the bassinet and lay down under it.

"Whose dog is it I wonder?" Leanne questioned out loud. "No collar or tags." "Do you think someone just left him here?" Rayna asked. "Could be, let's use Rosie's bowl and offer him water." Leanne went to the cupboard. She had left food and bowls in case she stayed long with Rose. The pup scampered out from under the bassinet. He was hungry and thirsty. Leanne next ran out to the car. She returned with the collar and leash she always carried. "You never know when

you'll find a puppy. See, you thought I was crazy."
"You are a little crazy." Rayna smiled. "But prepared."
He ate like he was starving. He was a small, white, short haired pup. On both sides he had black and brown markings. More on each side of his flank. He looked pretty young. Maybe a few months old. His cutest feature was he had huge paws. "Look at those paws!" Rayna exclaimed. "Doesn't it mean the dog will be big?" "I think so." Leanne answered. Just then the babies started stirring. Immediately the pup came running. He looked from one woman to the other as if to say "Do something, they need you." Leanne laughed. "I guess he is their protector." As soon as both babies were being cared for, the pup went back to his spot under the bassinet.

Rayna and Leanne rocked and talked as they fed the babies. Rayna first nursing and then Leanne topping each child off with the formula. The plan was to get their weight up before going to the pediatrician. They hoped the birth certificates would arrive soon.

As most new Mothers do, Rayna wanted to talk about the birth. Every mom usually relives the labor and delivery. "I can't believe they both were born as caulbearers." Rayna had looked it up that morning. It was very rare to be completely in the sack. She found an article that claimed the children would/could be psychic. They are said to have special sensitivities and be able to navigate between many worlds. Also, to see the future. Caul was associated with an accompanying spirit. She shared all this information with Leanne. Leanne looked up. "I read that too, the accompanying spirit is called Fylgia. It is said, after birth, it would manifest as an animal, object or person." They both turned and looked at the dog. He almost seemed to understand their conversation. He backed up once and put his chin on his front paws. Leanne and Rayna turned to each another and burst out laughing. "We are losing it!" Leanne exclaimed. "Oh, this is weirder than fairies, calls, dancing in the moonlight. Now a dog. Interesting that you draw the line at Fylgia." Rayna laughed. "I wouldn't be surprised at anything right now." Leanne said grinning.

They settled the babies in and then Leanne took the dog out for a quick walk. It was still a beautiful night. Stars twinkled and the moon cast a brightness on the ground. Wait until Mr. D hears we found a dog Leanne chuckled to herself. Twins and a dog. We'll decide what to do about him tomorrow she thought.

The twins were down for a while. The women decided to have a cup of tea and snack. They unwound on the futon with an old movie on. The room was toasty warm. They were keeping it warm for the babies. After the movie ended, they went to bed. The dog never left the babies bassinet.

The women fell into a routine quickly. Babies, dog, shower breakfast. Then Leanne did the caretaker duties while Rayna stayed at the cabin. When she returned, she walked the dog.

They had found a rope for Rayna to tie him up outside when Leanne was not there. So far, he didn't seem to want to be too far from the babies. Afternoons were the same. The women enjoyed each other's company. They weighed the babies and both had kept their birth weight. The formula was the key. Rayna felt good nursing and each baby got ample holding from both women.

The week flew by. Leanne text or called Mr. D every day. The men seemed to be enjoying their time being men. Rosie, of course, was loving her NH adventures. Leanne did tell him about the puppy. He laughed and said "I always knew you'd find a dog. Dog and Twins. Are you ever going home?" "Of course!" Leanne replied.

The dog was great... kind of like a living alarm system. Twice this week campers had driven up to the cabin. The dog had run to the door and barked to alert the women. He then spent most of the day under or near the babies. After the dog had been there for a week, Rayna sighed. "I guess we should name him. I'll at least keep him until December." Leanne looked up, "Are you still planning on Ireland?" she asked. Rayna looked over, "If you will still care for the babies, I am she replied."

Leanne was secretly thrilled. Her whole life she had wanted twins. As a young girl she had cared for two sets. Then in daycare she had two sets. She was a little worried about what Mr. D would say, but she wouldn't let on to Rayna. "Of course, I am still in. If Rosie can get along with the pup, I'll take him too. Its only 6 months. Then you'll be back ready to start your life." "Oh my god Nana, I was so scared to ask you. When we saw twins, I thought my chances were over." "We'll make it work." Leanne replied. "The babies will be almost 3 months old when you go. It will work you'll see." "Well we better name the dog then," Rayna said. "I think I will name him FY, short for Fylgia. He really seems like a spirit animal to me." she added. "What do you think Leanne?" "A good strong name," Leanne replied. "I like it." She bent down and called to the pup
"Here FY come." The dog immediately came lumbering over. "FY it is." laughed Leanne.

The week flew by. Mr. D was due home Oct 8th. It had been a busy weekend at the park. Rayna took the stroller and walked the babies to check the loop. The bathrooms were easily cleaned. The babies lay happily in the stroller looking all around. She tied FY to the handle and he was perfect. If anyone got too close to the stroller, he warned them with a growl. He truly was their protector. Rayna insisted on doing the job herself. She knew Leanne was due home Monday night. She would miss the camaraderie they shared. It had been a wonderful couple of weeks. Sunday, Leanne took all the laundry and a list of the supplies needed.

She wanted to get Rayna situated so she didn't have to go out alone yet. Two babies and a dog were a lot. Leanne threw laundry in at home. She went shopping for her own house and for Rayna. Picked the laundry up and picked up Chinese food and an ice-cream cake to celebrate. The babies had done well on rounds. FY had been quiet, unless anyone tried to touch the babies. Everyone loves babies. Leanne had brought one of Rosie's extra beds for FY. She planned on taking the towel he had been sleeping on. She thought if they got used to each other's smells they would feel familiar. Time would tell. After feeding and caring for babies and the dog, Nana and Rayna filled their plates. It was a nice celebration. Leanne felt like it was the end of a great vacation. Her last night staying over. Just before bed, after the last feeding, they enjoyed the ice-cream cake. It was delicious. FY had a nice Soup bone treat. As they both settled down, Leanne reminded Rayna, "Remember, it is going to be hard alone. You can stay at night with us. Then drive back to do your caretaker duties." Rayna answered, "I know, thank you, but I think I'll be alright until December." "Awesome!" Leanne replied.

Monday dawned absolutely beautiful. Clear blue cloudless sky. Cool, but with the promise of it warming. You could hear all the forest sounds, birds were chirping. It was like a Disney movie Leanne thought. The babies were happy and content. They had started looking around more. They reached for each other while in the bassinet. FY liked to lick their fingers if given the chance. After breakfast everyone walked the loop.

Leanne helped with the cleaning. Already Rayna had a system. Leanne felt confident it would work out. She was sad that this part was over. She was looking forward to seeing Mr. D, James and of course Rosie, but still… twins…. After the dinner time feeding. Leanne and Rayna shared the leftover food from last night. The men wouldn't be back until 1 PM. Leanne helped clean up. She took FY for a walk. Then packed her stuff into the van.

The babies were two weeks old already. Hopefully, the birth certificates would arrive sometime this week. Rayna had used Leanne's address so they wouldn't be lost. Leanne kissed everyone goodbye. She hugged Rayna and Rayna whispered "Thank you Nana, I couldn't have done it without you." Leanne sniffled, "Your welcome, but don't sell yourself short honey. You did all the work. I just caught them. I love you. Call if you need me." Out the door she went. As she went down the stairs, she heard FY give a little whimper.

Mr. D and James arrived home with much fanfare. Coolers, dirty clothes, dog supplies and dog. They could wreck a room in a minute. Leanne gave them both a big hug and a kiss. "Miss us honey?" Mr. D laughed looking at the mess. "Sort of." Leanne answered. She pulled out her phone and showed him pictures of Joey, Joannie and FY. "Cute kids." he said. Within the hour, he was in his seat relaxing.

The next day Leanne went to visit her newest grandchild. Little Nora was beautiful. She seemed huge to Leanne who was used to the tiny twins. She didn't mention the babies, she just enjoyed the visit. Leanne thought no sense getting her children involved in the decision making of her life. The visit went well. Her daughter seemed to be handling motherhood very well.

Leanne text back and forth with Rayna. Everything seemed fine. On Friday the birth certificates arrived. She texts she would come Saturday morning to visit and bring them.
Leanne felt a little bad for allowing James to be named as the father. She rationalized it to herself:

1. *He'll never know.*
2. *He can prove he isn't.*
3. *Rayna will leave a letter with copies.*

It was the only way she could be named grandmother, without going to court, she thought. Well what's done is done.

Saturday Leanne got up early leaving her clothes in a pile. She grabbed them on the way out of her room. Rosie came with her. She showered and dressed. She took Rose for a walk. She wasn't ready yet to have her meet FY. Rosie had never been great with other dogs. Meeting the babies and FY, Leanne thought, would be too volatile. Besides, Mr. D was home. She was just going for a couple of hours. Mr. D and Rosie would be fine. They would take Rose for a walk later.

Driving into the forest Leanne noticed all the bare trees. Almost like overnight all the leaves were gone. It was sunny but a definite chill in the air. She had picked up some groceries for Rayna. More formula and diapers too. Parking beside the cabin she got out of the van. Even in late fall it was a beautiful spot. Just then FY came bounding down the steps. "Hello there!" Leanne called. "Your excited to see me? You must know I have treats." FY sat right down, almost in anticipation. Laughing, Leanne grabbed a biscuit for him. "There you go." she said, handing it to him.

Rayna was at the door holding Joey. "Good morning!" she called, "Great to see you. We missed you." Leanne followed them inside. "I missed you guys too." She went right over to where little Joannie lay. She was wide awake. Picking her up Leanne hugged her. "They are precious you know." They caught up on the week. Leanne told about her Granddaughter Nora, and showed Rayna her picture. It will be cute to see them together Rayna said.

They took the babies and dog for a walk after looking over the birth certificate. Everything was good. Leanne weighed each baby and they were both over 6lbs. Rayna decided to call the doctor to have them seen. That would be next week. The plan was for Leanne to go with them. Rayna would sign off on having Leanne bring them while she "worked ". Everything was falling into place. Right after the 2 pm feeding, Leanne took her leave. She and Mr. D were going to take Rosie to the canal for a walk. They would get dinner in Plymouth. "Text or call if you need anything." Leanne said as she drove away. "Bye!" Rayna waved.

As Mr. D and Leanne walked the canal, she told him about the birth. Of course, she left out fairy talk, and women dancing in the moonlight. She did tell him about the caul and how each baby was encased. Then she shared about finding FY. "That's a weird name for a dog." he said. Leanne just looked at him. "Well Rayna does study myths and legends it's from one of those." "Interesting!" he answered. Leanne thought to herself, "hmmmm, need to know basis sir." They had a great fish dinner on the Plymouth water front. Over dinner she asked "You still OK with me watching the babies for Rayna?" "Why wouldn't I be?" he said munching on a French fry. "No reason, I guess because there is two of them now. "If you want to, then go ahead." he replied, Leanne took her phone and showed him both Nora and the twins. They had a nice time.

The week went well. The doctor's office was no problem. Rayna signed a form saying Leanne could bring them for emergencies or regular appointments. They even gave us one to use at hospitals. They were up to 6.2 lbs. at the Doctors office. "Whatever you're doing is working." the nurse said.
Everything seemed to be moving along. Rayna still planned on leaving Dec. 14th. Leanne still planned on caring for the children.

They decided to have the dogs meet. Leanne brought Rosie to the park. This time she parked at the bathroom area. Rayna was going to walk with the stroller and FY. Leanne walked Rose around. Then she spotted Rayna on her way. FY was on the right side of the stroller. Watching them approach Leanne realized how big he was already. He was only a little smaller than Rose now. When Rose saw Rayna, she started her jumping. Rayna parked the stroller leaving FY still tied. She knelt down patting Rosie. Then she stood up, took the leash and brought Rose to the other side of the stroller. "Rosie meet FY!!!"

Rosie growled a little, FY just stared. "FY meet Rosie." Rayna whispered. "See the babies, Rose?" she whispered again. Rose sniffed the stroller, she sniffed FY. He stood quite nicely, never snapping or growling. Rosie turned back to Leanne as if to say "fine, I'm OK." Leanne took the leash and they all walked the loop. Back at the cabin, both dogs were let off lead. They raced around barking and playing. The women sat on the steps, each with a baby. They turned to each other and said "I guess the dogs get along." Leanne laughed, "I'm in. Good thing Mr. D likes dogs now." It was a good visit. They cared for the babies. The dogs lay together watching.

The weeks flew by. The routine was Monday, Wednesday, Friday, Leanne took Rosie to the cabin. She cared for the babies, Rayna went to do her rounds and cleaning. They had a nice lunch together. The dogs frolicked in the front area. Then lay watching. FY was bigger than Rosie now. He was a big lovable pup. Rosie was quite taken with him. She lay watching right alongside FY.

Rayna planned on attending the Thanksgiving feast at Leanne's. She was looking forward to meeting everyone again. Growing up in a day care home, you do meet the other children. Leanne was excited for her grandchildren to meet the babies. Especially Nora, as she was only days older. Leanne did tell Rayna not to mention Ireland. She explained it was on a need to know basis and her family didn't need to know yet. Rayna understood, don't lie just don't offer the info.

Thanksgiving was a gorgeous crisp day. Everyone was arriving at 1 PM. Leanne made sure the tables were set and the food was ready and she also made sure there were places for the babies to roll around and also for the three dogs, Rosie, FY, and Teddy. Teddy was her Daughter and Nora's dog. She had not met FY yet. Teddy was used to other dogs though and Leanne didn't think there would be a problem.

Leanne felt nervous. She hoped all the babies would be happy. She really didn't want her family to know about the arrangement yet. Let them meet and then see where it goes. She didn't see them that much except birthdays and holidays. Christmas would be the first time they were back with the twins here. It would be fine, she hoped.

Leanne's daughter and Rayna enjoyed each other. The babies were wonderful. All three had bottles so the other women enjoyed feeding them. It was a wonderful dinner. Couldn't have gone better. Even the dogs got along. Leanne felt it was a great success. She was so relieved. She felt like she had been holding her breath all day. At the end of the day Mr. D and Leanne sat in their seats. "Weren't the babies awesome?" Leanne asked him. "They really were." Mr. D replied. I loved seeing Nora and the twins rolling around on the blanket. And FY", he continued, "What an awesome dog." Leanne smiled, "Then you wouldn't mind us caring for them?" "Not at all." Mr. D answered. "Perfect!" Leanne replied.

Leanne drove to the park on Monday after Thanksgiving. Though they did text daily, she didn't like to bother Rayna with phone calls. It truly was a different time. People today seemed bothered by having to actually talk in real time. Texting gave the option of reading your thoughts. So, you could change it before sending. It was a whole different world.

Driving into the parking area the tires crunched. No one was in the park today. It felt cold and desolate. There was definitely a winter feel to the air. Leanne got out and opened the door for Rosie. She bounded out and ran all around the front area.

Soon Rayna opened the door and FY flew down the stairs. They had become quite good friends. They chased each other all around while Leanne unpacked the car. Rayna stood in the door frame. "It's freezing come on in." Both dogs bounded up the stairs rushing into the cabin. Leanne laughed, "Hey don't knock me down!" she cried. The cabin was so comfy. Joey and Joannie lay on a blanket in front of the stove. They kicked their little feet and cooed. They both had a lot of dark hair and dark eyes. They were really beautiful children. Leanne leaned over them. "Hey babies", she cooed, Nana's here. Solemnly, they looked up then both smiled. Nana did her baby talk and both babies seemed to answer. It was adorable. FY and Rosie planted themselves in front of the front door. They each had a bone to chew and were quite content.

Rayna made them a cup of tea. She put the bottles to warm for the babies. She had stopped nursing every feeding. She just nursed them first thing in the morning and lastly at night. It was working nicely. They were growing fast. "Thanksgiving was great." Rayna said. "I really enjoyed meeting everybody again. Little Nora was so cute. Boy she was quite a bit bigger than the twins. Everyone was so nice." she added. "They loved you too." Leanne replied. "It was fun. I'm glad to be invited to your family Nana." "I was happy to have you there too." said Leanne. They enjoyed their tea and watched the babies. The dogs had lay down a little closer. The babies reached out to touch them. Leanne grabbed her phone and took some pictures.

Finishing her tea, Leanne put the cup down. The babies were content, not ready to eat yet. Leanne looked at Rayna and said. "It's December 1st on Saturday, what are your plans?" Rayna put her cup down. She looked at the babies and then back to Leanne. "If you're still willing, I want to try. I feel like I will resent the children if I don't. I know that's not fair to them but I will. I think if we Skype and text daily, it's not much different than if I worked every day. If I worked every day what would I see them, maybe 2 hours daily? This way you as Nana will give them love. They'll still know me from the videos, hear my voice. Then when I finish in June, I can get a teaching job nearby here. You always said as long as a baby feels loved they would be ok. You are great, your family is great Mr. D seemed nice and fine with both the kids and the dog. Even little Nora would be a great friend for them. You and your daughter could go on outings together". Help each other out. You're used to multiple children. I feel like this a win-win. I can come back. I could finish here. It's just that the scholarship is for Ireland. There are a lot of myths and legends that started there. Are you still on-board Nana"? she asked. "Absolutely!" Leanne answered.

"Let's make a list after we feed these little "monkeys." she laughed. Leanne took Joannie and Rayna took Joey. They drank down 6 oz. each. After

two good burps. clean diapers and rocked they took their nap. They were still in the bassinet but it was a little cramped. Soon they would move to a bigger crib. The question was would they sleep apart or together. Rayna got her notebook. Starting a list, they figured everything they would need to do. On Rayna's list was a picture of them with Santa. She did not want to miss their first Christmas celebration. Leanne was putting her tree up that weekend. "Why not get stockings, a gift and outfits. We can do a whole little photo shoot. Their babies, they don't know what day it is." Leanne added. "Santa is already at the mall too."
The paperwork, birth certificates, and passports, they were still waiting for. Rayna had gone to the post office and filled out passports just in case. They were waiting for them to arrive.

The letters to the children and James were there, along with papers from Rayna's own birth. Leanne was keeping Rayna's things at her house. They would store everything in the basement. That way Rayna wouldn't pay for storage. Her car, she planned on selling on craigslist. She would put the money away. When she got back to the States, she would buy a bigger car. A mustang really wasn't great for two car seats a big dog and all the paraphernalia having two infants curtails. She had already gotten some questions about the car.

Everything else seemed to be moving right along. "I think it will work fine." Leanne smiled. "You can always come home early. I have two rooms you could stay with us until you get a job." "Thank you so much Nana," Rayna said, "This means so much to me." "Your children will have a Nana and a Grandfather for as long as you want. Forever if that's what you want. You are part of my family now Rayna. I love all of you." "Thank you." Rayna whispered.

Leanne left before dark. Rosie was happy to climb up the ramp into the back seat. Thoughts were swirling around in Leanne's mind. She started getting ready for the babies. She brought up a pack and play from the old day care equipment. She set it up in her corner of the room. She set a second one up in the living room. The swing and seats were already out for Nora so no notice there. They were still pretty little so they didn't need much. Rayna had the car seats and stroller. The bassinet would also work for a while. Mr. D noticed none of these items. Leanne put the Christmas tree up and started decorating. She wanted to be as ready as she could be. Once the twins arrived, she wouldn't be out shopping much.

She was scared that maybe it would be too much. She was willing to try though. She didn't voice any concerns to Rayna. Leanne really wanted to give her the chance. The family birthday party was set for Dec 9, a Sunday. Leanne hoped no one would ask too many questions. Hopefully Mr. D wouldn't mention Leanne caring for the twins. The party went great. Everyone was busy discussing Christmas plans and celebrations no one asked about the twins except in passing. It was a great day. Less than a week to Twin Day.

Rayna made lists upon lists. She packed up all the clothes she wouldn't need. She had a box to donate and items the twins already grew out of. She was so happy to fit into her old pre pregnancy clothes. She wanted a carry on and backpack to travel with. She would take a camera, phone and computer. The baby's passports were due this week. She would feel better when everything was done. She wanted to be sure Nana could care for the kids legally as their Nana. She had an appointment for FY on Wednesday. Nana was coming to care for the babies. Rayna would do her errands and take the dog to the Vet. She wanted everything done. License for the dog, she hoped was the last thing.

Leanne arrived at the cabin at 9:30 AM. She wanted to give Rayna plenty of time. Rayna helped feed and change the babies before leaving. This was her last time to shop before getting on the plane. She was gone from 10 AM to 4 PM. Leanne truly enjoyed Joey and Joannie.

They were the best babies. They truly hardly ever cried. They would solemnly look at you, but mostly cooed and "talked". Out of all the infants she had cared for, they seemed pretty "easy". I can do this, Leanne thought. The afternoon flew by. Just about 4 pm Rayna came flying in. She was talking excitedly. FY went right to the babies as if checking on them. Rayna showed off all her purchases. Outfits for Christmas for the babies. Toys and stockings to hang. She even had stocking things for Leanne to put up on Christmas Eve. Leanne showed her the passports had come. Everything was falling into place.

The plan was to have a mini Christmas on the morning of the 14th. Then, Rayna would be picked up to go to the airport by 2 PM. Tomorrow was pictures with Santa. Rayna was bringing stuff to Nana's, then they would leave the dogs home. Nana would drive to the mall for the Santa picture. Someone was buying the Mustang on Friday morning. They were paying $2,000 dollars cash and picking it up in Nana's driveway. If it falls through, the car will be parked there. Everything seemed well planned. Rayna and Leanne both hoped nothing could go wrong. Rayna was leaving $3,000.00 dollars to cover formula and clothing/diapers. She authorized Leanne to use some or all of the car money too, if she needed it. She still had money in the bank. Rayna had added Leanne's name to her account just in case. They thought they had covered all the bases. Both were happy and scared at the same time.

The visit to the mall went well. They actually ran into Leanne's daughters. They were in line waiting to get a picture with Santa too. They all got their individual pictures. Then Leanne asked if all the children could do one picture. Even her oldest grandson went along. Leanne got a picture of all her grandkids sitting on Santa's lap. It made her heart sing. It was a great surprise meeting.

The morning of the 14th dawned crisp and cold. The sky was clear with wispy clouds. Rayna took one last picture of the cabin. Then shut the door. Locking it for the last time. She felt sad. This was where she had become a mother. This was where she had felt a purpose bigger than herself. This was where she truly had become a believer in other worlds. The babies were in the car. Rayna took one last look around. She needed to double check that all was locked up. The winter caretaker was checking in on Saturday. She wanted everything right.

As she rounded the porch, a swarm of butterflies appeared. Rayna was dumbfounded. It's way too cold she thought. This can't be possible. Just then eight of the group flew down to the porch. "Have you forgotten us already Rayna?" "There before her was the fairy Queen Aine, she was as beautiful as ever.

As before, she spoke in a soft voice. "I have been watching you. Your children are beautiful. Do you know they are special? Caulbearers have special powers," she continued. "They are psychic and can see the future. They must be protected." Just then FY stuck his head out of the car. Queen Aine turned and looked at him. He just stared at her. "I see FY found you. He is their spirit animal. As long as he is alive, he will protect your children." Rayna whispered "protect from what?" "Sometimes worlds collide and your children are valuable in all worlds. FY will protect them. "Queen Aine continued, "My world is in danger. We need you to take a message to my father, Egobail. He is a High Fairy King in Ireland." "Where? How? Why?" Rayna sputtered. Queen Aine continued, "You owe the fairy, Rayna. We helped you with the birth of your children. Remember the fairy dust. That helped you have a quick birth. Now we need a favor in return." "Ok" whispered Rayna. "Good," Queen Aine said. "Here is a message." At that four fairies flew over. Between them they carried a cylinder. Rayna held out her hand. The cylinder was placed in her palm. It looked like an intricate lipstick tube. The outside was silver and there were flowers, birds and fairies carved in it. One side could be turned, Rayna opened it, out slid a rolled-up paper. There was a wax seal of rose holding it together. "Do not open it." Aine said. "Take it to Ireland. On the first day of Spring, March 20th, go to the Hill of Tara in County Meath. There will be a tree, like our trees. The tree will be circled in stone as well. Find the ring of mushrooms. They will be in the stone circle. Place the tube in the middle of the ring. When you have done that leave the area. Do not look back." Rayna shook her head yes. "I will do as you ask." she sighed. Queen Aine and the other fairies circled Rayna as she walked to the car. Then they flew in a clockwise circle chanting. FY watched them with interest. Just before flying away the fairies sprinkled Rayna and the car with fairy dust. "Good luck Rayna, may the gods be with you." With that they were gone. Rayna placed the lipstick like tube in their backpack. She would do this to appease the fairy Queen Aine. FY gave a sharp bark. They drove away slowly.

Leanne met them at the door. She had Christmas music playing. Rayna brought the twins in and they put the kids in the living room. FY and Rosie kept guard. Leanne and Rayna emptied the car. Then they fed the babies and took pictures under the tree. The car was sold and Rayna put the money in an envelope. All the important info was in a locked box. They added the money for food and supplies. Leanne put it in her closet.

They had a nice day. Rayna was a little nervous. Leanne asked her if she had changed her mind. Rayna shook her head no. She didn't want to tell Leanne about the fairies. She didn't want her to worry. They really hadn't spoken that much about the night the twins were born. It was almost like a dream.   Finally, Rayna's ride came. She kissed the twins good bye. Leanne gave her a hug. "Don't worry, I'll take good care of them. Text when you want, we'll Skype at 12 PM our time 5 PM Ireland time. First Skype is set for Sunday the 16th." Rayna wiped the tears from her face. Patted FY and left. Leanne called out, "Safe travels, remember you can always come back." She stood at the window and watched the car drive away.

Turning around Leanne looked down at the babies. Both seemed to be watching her. The dogs gave a whimper. Leanne spent the next couple of hours settling everyone in. Mr. D arrived at the usual time. His dinner was made and the babies were happy.

After they finished eating Leanne told Mr. D about the arrangement. Mr. D was rather surprised. "Rayna went where?" he asked. "Ireland. I told you she was going to school." Leanne explained. "We're keeping these babies?" Mr. D asked. "Well not keeping," Leanne continued. "I told you I was taking care of them. Actually, I asked you." she finished. "The dog too?" at mention of his name, FY perked up. "Yes, this is not news!" Leanne exclaimed. Then she relented. "I didn't actually tell you they were staying over, did I?" "No, you did not." he replied. "Does it matter?" Mr. D looked at the babies. They couldn't have been more adorable. The dog lay quietly at his feet. It was like Leanne had planned the scene. Mr. D shook his head. "How long?" he asked. "Well could be until the end of May." "What, are you kidding me?" "Not really." Leanne answered sheepishly. "I hope you know what you've gotten into?" he laughed. "My dinner better be ready on time." He was only half kidding. "Do you want to hold Joey?" she asked. There they sat, each holding a baby with two dogs at their feet. Leanne smiled to herself. This is awesome, she thought.

The whole family gathered at Christmas. Nora and the twins were the hit of the day. The three were actually dressed alike. Lots of pictures were taken. Leanne's family were surprised at the situation. As the babies were good no one made much of a fuss. When asked, Leanne was vague about when their mom was coming back. The three dogs were great together. At 2 PM everyone Skyped with Rayna. She had a few friends say hello as well. It put everyone's mind at ease. It was a great day.

After Christmas, Leanne's day fell into a busy routine. The babies ate then happily sat in their seats while Leanne got Mr. D out to work. Then they took their morning nap in the living room. So far, they still shared the pack and play. They fussed when they were apart very long. Then Leanne got herself ready for the day. She often prepared dinner for the crock pot. The babies were bathed and dressed for the day. Out for fresh air with the dogs. Lunch, naps and afternoon outing or walk. Twice a week they saw Nora. Sometimes at Leanne's, sometimes a field trip. It was a busy happy time.

Mr. D didn't seem to mind at all. James was starting to interact with Joey and Joannie too. He always stopped down to say hello. He walked FY along with Rosie every evening.
James also started to stop in on Saturdays. His friend Marie visited every Saturday. They hung out often going out for dinner. February, they started interacting a little with the dogs. They took them for walks. Then they would stay and play with the babies. James also helped with the Skype and took movies of the twins to send. Time was flying, Leanne didn't regret taking them for a minute. They went to the Doctor appointments without any problem. Everything was moving along.

On March 17th Rayna Skyped a happy St Patrick's Day. She was planning on a party that night. Then a short trip to County Meath. She mentioned she had to be there for the first day of spring March 20th.

Leanne dressed the twins in green. Even the dogs had shamrock kerchiefs around their necks. It was a festive sight. Leanne took pictures and sent them to Rayna. Nora joined the group. The girls had green bows around their heads and little Joey wore a green scaly cap. Rayna loved it.

It was Leanne's birthday on the first day of spring. The family had come for St Patrick's Day. They had corn beef and cabbage and a giant cake. It was the perfect day. James had invited Marie and they both held a baby. Leanne took lots of pictures. On her birthday, Leanne's daughter brought Nora and they drove to the zoo. The air was warm, at least at 2pm. The three car seats just fit in the van.

They left the dogs home together. It was a beautiful day. All three children seemed to enjoy the outing. Leanne especially did. Rayna had texted Happy Birthday very early. She mentioned she had an errand in County Meath at the Hill of Tara. Leanne's daughter took a picture of Leanne sitting with all three babies at the zoo. Rayna "liked" it. "Have a great birthday Nana." were the last words from Rayna. The babies slept all the way home. Mother and daughter enjoyed the ride home. They talked about all the things caretakers of infants talk about.

Leanne was happy. Mr. D brought dinner home that night. After the babies went down, they enjoyed a nice meal. It was the best birthday in a long time.

The next few days were busy. The twins had a checkup and shopping had to be done. Leanne texted Rayna every day, as usual but got no answer. She chalked it up to Rayna being busy. Leanne knew she had a lot of work to finish. By Saturday Leanne was getting a little worried. It wasn't like Rayna to not answer texts. She would at least answer at the end of the day. She set up the room to Skype on Sunday. Joey and Joannie were in their saucers. They loved to jump and spin in them. First Leanne took a movie, then set up the computer to Skype. Usually Rayna was waiting for them. Not this time. By 5:30 PM Ireland time, she still had not checked in. Leanne started feeding Joannie, leaving the screen open. Then she fed Joey. Still no Rayna. This was totally out of character. Leanne had a bad feeling. By 1:30 AM she had been waiting for an hour and a half. Both babies were rubbing their eyes. She decided to leave the "window" open but put them to sleep. Leanne texted Rayna but no reply. Now she was really worried. She decided to wait until Monday to contact the college. Maybe she was away from electricity or busy with new friends. Who Knew? Leanne was very uneasy. It was not like Rayna to not answer.

Leanne still had no word from Rayna by noon her time. That made it 5 PM Ireland time. She had been busy all day caring for the babies. For the first time since she cared for them, they were fussy. Even FY seemed out of sorts. He whimpered and whined on and off throughout the day. Leanne had a bad feeling about this. She contacted Rayna's roommate. Rayna had left the number just in case. The roommate hadn't seen Rayna since St. Patrick's Day. She wasn't worried because Rayna mentioned the trip to Hill of Tara. The roommate thought it had to-do with the myth and legend class. Leanne thanked her and asked her to text if Rayna showed up.

When Mr. D came in, Leanne shared her concerns. "I wouldn't worry." he said. "She probably got lucky." "I know she would still contact us." Leanne replied. "She missed the Skype on Sunday." "That is concerning." he said. "I'm sure she's fine. What's for dinner?" Leanne fed everyone and got the babies to bed. She didn't sleep well at all that night. The babies were also restless. They fussed unusually into the night. Leanne ended up sitting with them in the living room.

At 2 AM, there was a noise from the computer. She opened the window and there was a woman on screen. "Hello, hello, anybody there?" Leanne ran over and clicked on. Trying not to wake the babies she answered "Yes, I'm here." Sitting on Rayna's bed was a beautiful woman. Her hair was red curls all over. Beautiful green eyes stared out of the screen. "Hi, I'm Orla," she said with the musical brogue of Ireland. "Are you Leanne?" "Yes," Leanne answered. "Why are you on Rayna's computer?" Orla answered "I'm looking for her. She hasn't come back from the weekend. She missed work and class. I don't know what to do. She's not answering her phone." Leanne sat closer, "Do you know where she was last?" "She was going on a field trip. I thought," Orla answered. "I haven't seen her since St. Patrick's Day. I had a lot to drink and I left without her." Orla finished. "Well can you go to the school office and report her missing this morning?" Leanne asked. "Find out if they have heard from her. Will you please call or Skype with any news, ok?" Leanne asked. "Yes, I will. I will text you if I hear anything." Leanne nodded "I will do the same. I'm sure she is just taking a break. She'll be back soon." "I hope so." Orla replied. She signed off the computer. Leanne definitely was not going to sleep anytime soon. At that, Joannie started to fuss. Leanne warmed a bottle and rocked her back to sleep.

151

The next day Leanne contacted the school. She spoke to the Dean. He assured her that the authorities had been called. Rayna was officially a missing person. There was a real possibility that foul play was involved. They may send local detectives to question Leanne and her family. Especially the babies' Father. The Babies' Father!!! Oh No!!!

Leanne was sick with worry. She was going to have to tell James about the deception. First, she had to tell Mr. D that night after dinner (because she never gave bad news before dinner)

Leanne told Mr. D how they had made the birth certificate and named James as the father. She told him it's on paper only. That Rayna had written a letter to both James and the children explaining the truth. She explained that it was the only way to keep the kids out of the system. We were the grandparents legally. It did hurt that he was holding Joey at the time. He solemnly was staring at Mr. D with his big brown eyes. He was holding on to Mr. D's finger as well. Mr. D looked down then over at Leanne holding Joannie. "It will work out," he smiled. "You know you have to tell James." "I know, will you watch the babies? I will go for a walk with the dogs and James. It's always better to walk and talk."

"Hey James?" Leanne, called upstairs. Will you walk the dogs with me? I have to tell you something."

Leanne took Rosie's leash. James took FY and they started down the driveway. "James, I have to tell you something." Leanne started. "Ok," James replied, "What?" "Well, you know how Rayna is missing?"," Yes", James answered. "Well, before she left, we needed to fill out the birth certificates." "OK?" James replied questioningly. "Well, Rayna didn't know the father." "I know." James answered. "Well, so that I could be the named grandmother," Leanne let the sentence sink in. "Yaaa?" James stopped walking. He turned to Leanne, one look at her face and he knew what was coming. "Well… well, we put your name down." James walked in silence. Leanne let it sink in. "If I was the grandmother, then I would have custody. We didn't think you would have to know. We figured when she came back, we could change it or say nothing." James turned to her. "I understand Mom but that's not right." "I know, I know. Rayna wrote a letter and we notarized it saying it wasn't true. She also wrote a letter to the babies saying it wasn't true. We thought we covered all the bases. We weren't trying to hurt you. Only keep the babies out of foster care if something happened."

At the mention of foster care, James softened. He loved the babies too and wouldn't want them in foster care. "OK, if anyone asks, I'll agree," he said, "but you owe me big time Ma." "Thank you, James, you are truly helping keep the babies safe. We won't tell the rest of the family. It's only on paper." They walked back toward the house, both lost in their own thoughts.

Mr. D was happily bouncing a baby on his knee. Leanne gave the OK sign and he said nothing. Sometimes it must be nice to be a guy Leanne thought. That was that.

The local police did call by the next day. They questioned us all together. We told them what we knew and they said they would let us know if they heard anything.'

The Irish Police had no leads. On the fourth day they found her phone. It was at the Hill of Tara in

County Meath. Nothing but the phone and her jacket. They were found under a tree folded neatly. No other sign.

Leanne took some of Rayna's money from the joint checking account and hired a private investigator. He found nothing else. No one had heard or seen her since she left to visit the Hill of Tara on March 20th. Cold trail, nothing.

Easter week, her roommate packed up her personal belongings. She was going to wait another month to ship them in case Rayna showed back up. The police entertained that she had met someone and taken off with them, maybe gone to England or Spain. But her passport hadn't been found or used, so that seemed unlikely.

Leanne was heartbroken. If not for the babies, she would go and look for herself. Truly, she knew it would not be good to leave them.

They heard nothing more. Days, went by, then weeks. In June, a package arrived with Rayna's things. The private investigator had collected and insured the items. Everything seemed to be there, even her money. Leanne went through it all multiple times. Even reading her journal. The only entry that raised an eyebrow was March 20 – Hill of Tara – leave note. "What could that mean?" "Leave note." What note she thought. There were no answers she could figure out. At the bottom of the package was her passport.

Joey and Joannie were 9 months old now. They were beautiful children with their dark curly hair, big brown eyes and fair skin. Little Nora also had brown hair and big brown eyes. People mistook them for triplets often. They were all crawling. The dogs kept them contained. The three amigos, we joked, seemed to really enjoy each other. The summer went quickly and still no word about Rayna. We took the twins to NH and they loved the water. The rest of the family joined us, not asking if we were keeping the twins. James enjoyed the kids the same as before. We never discussed the birth certificate again that summer. We still Skyped, or rather blogged, to have memories for Rayna. James often took the footage.

The babies were all having their birthdays in September. Nora had her party first. Then the twins had theirs, they all looked so cute pushing their cars. Leanne felt so bad that Rayna was missing out. She could not imagine what had happened. She knew Rayna would not have left.

Chapter 8: Hill of Tara

St. Patrick's Day was so much fun. Dublin was hopping, all the bars were full. Everyone was laughing and dancing. Rayna met Sean at the second bar. They had a great time and went home together. Rayna's phone had died so she left it in her pocket. On March 20th she would go to the Hill of Tara as Queen Aine had asked. She carried the cylinder with her in her small bag. She would go and leave it as instructed. Then she would have paid the fairies back and be done with it all. It was very interesting studying about such things when you had actually seen them.

She said her good bye to Sean and made her way to the Hill of Tara. It was a big place. How would she ever find the right spot she thought. She followed the other tourists. There seemed to only be one group. Up the hill they went. Rayna figured that would be the best place to scope out the fairy tree. At the very top, Rayna couldn't believe how beautiful it was. As far as the eye could see there were green hills and valleys. To the left of where they were standing, at the bottom of a hill, Rayna spotted a large tree. "What is that she pointed?" The tree was covered in ribbons and trinkets. The guide said, "That is the fairy tree. People come from miles away to hang wishes on it. Legend has it, that fairies live nearby." Rayna nodded. After the tour she would look there. If there was a rock circle with mushrooms, she will find it. Walking over to the tree, Rayna could almost feel the magic. The day had warmed up considerably, and for once no Irish rain. "Who knew Nana." she whispered out loud.

Everyone must have gone into town for lunch. Rayna was quite alone. She climbed over the fence. There were all kinds of things hung on the tree. She slowly walked around the trunk.

There were stones around the base, at least 5 ft. around. In the middle was the mushroom circle. She leaned down, taking her jacket off. She laid it on the fence. She used a nearby stick to dig a small hole. She carefully placed the cylinder into it. She whispered "This is for King Egobail from Queen Aine." Standing up, she moved to pick up her jacket. She leaned on the tree and before she knew what was happening, she was falling into a large dark hole. The tree trunk had opened up like a trap door. Rayna fell head over heels into a dark cavern. As she passed out, she thought of Joey and Joannie.

Chapter 9: The Years Fly By

Leanne never stopped hoping Rayna would come back. The twins grew like weeds. It wasn't long until they were walking and talking. The second summer, Leanne and her daughter taught the three to swim. They all love the water. Teddy and FY acted like swim instructors. Both dogs swam with the children. Rosie lay watching from the side. They called her the life guard. It was a good life. As the twins grew, James took more interest in them. He and his friend Marie spent many Saturday mornings playing with them. James and Leanne never mentioned the birth certificates. No need to at least until the twins needed to start school. Leanne and James continued to film /blog each week for Rayna. They kept it private but every week there was a video diary made.

The Twins and Nora all started school at the same time. Nora went to a school in the next town. Every week Nora got to stay for a sleep over. The kids all slept upstairs. Nana played a movie and Grandfather watched it with them. It was a wonderful life. The twins seemed to have lived up to their special abilities.

Leanne's Daughter and Nora were leaving one day. Joey and Joannie started crying. "No, you can't, something bad will happen." Joannie cried. Leanne tried to calm them down. They just became agitated. "No, no, no they cried." Leanne's daughter stayed a while longer. Then packed up to leave. Twenty minutes later the phone rang. Leanne answered. "Thank God we stayed longer," her daughter said. There was a huge tractor trailer crash. We just missed it."

Then, one morning, they both started crying for "Uncle" James. "Get him Nana." they cried. Nana told them he was sleeping. "Nana you need to wake him up," Joey cried. Nana went upstairs. James was unresponsive. The heater was malfunctioning and carbon monoxide seeped into his room. He would have died. Leanne knew then that the children were very special. Caulbearers are known to be psychic, she knew. These things were proving it.

Not two months later, they were very insistent. "Nora's Daddy stay home." they cried. "What do you mean?" Leanne asked – "Gunshot" – Joey cried. Leanne knew her Son in Law was in Law Enforcement and carried a gun. She called her daughter and warned her. "Call him and explain." Leanne pleaded. "I will," her daughter promised. Three hours later he was able to avoid a shooting. Leanne knew it was very real.

When the children started crying for their MOM, Leanne listened. "We need to save her," Joannie cried. "Where she is, she can't get out," said Joey, looking up with tears rolling down his face. "She's lost in the other world and they are going to keep her." "Yes," Joannie shook her head. "We need to save Mommy!"

Chapter 10: Ireland---Spring Equinox 2025

"Don't cry little one, "Queen Aine said. She was dressed in a flowing white gown. Her hair was long and flowing. She had a beautiful smile. "I know you can help her, sit down. I will tell you how." Queen Aine waited for the children to sit, Leanne sat over on the wall, both dogs sat attentively watching. Aine repeated what she had said earlier.

"I asked your mother, Rayna, to deliver a message to my father. He is the King of the Fairies in Ireland. I told her where to go. She was supposed to leave a note then go away. Something must have happened. If she was brought into the land of fairies, then it's very hard to leave on your own. There is usually a guard at the secret entrance to our other world. Humans are not often invited to our world. They are notorious for ruining things. They find it too beautiful not to share. Then, other humans will come and destroy what we have. There are strict rules about this. Rayna should have left the note. However, she may have accidently fallen through the portal to the other world."

"Will we be able to save her?" the children whispered. "Well, I hope so," Queen Aine answered. "I will write you a letter for my father. Then you will have to deliver the letter in person, with some special gifts. Just you three will travel to the special entrance. Tell no one where it is." "Nana, Nana, can we do it?" The children were very serious. "Can we go to Ireland to get mommy?" Leanne looked from one sad face to the other. "Well, I will talk to Grandfather, and if he agrees, I will take you. You are right. We have to try and save her. We will have to make plans. I will talk to Grandfather tonight when you are in bed. Tomorrow, if he agrees, I will look at flights and hotels. We do have to try and save her."

Darkness had fallen. It was the shortest day of the year December 21st Winter Solstice. The temperature had dropped as well. Luckily, Leanne always had a flashlight and two small lights for the children. "Well, we better get going before its pitch black out here. Grandfather will get worried if we are out to late." Queen Aine put her tiny hands, first on Joannie, then on Joey. "Don't worry we will make a plan. If your mom can be saved, we will do it together." She sprinkled a little fairy dust over them. She did the same to Leanne and both dogs. "This will keep you all safe. We will meet here again on New Year's Day and make the plans."

"Yes," Leanne agreed, "thank you. Now we really need to go. I don't drive very well in the dark." "No worries, "Queen Aine smiled. "We will show you the way."

With that, Queen Aine made a signal and the air was full of wings. It was hard to tell if they were all fairies or some moths mixed in. They lit the way across the field and to the car. The dogs were mesmerized as the children were. They scampered to the car and waited for the ramp to be lowered. The children smiled and waved at the flying group. "Thank you, thank you," they sang.

Leanne buckled up the children, then her own seatbelt. Lowering her window, she turned to see Queen Aine perched on the sill. Whispering, Queen Aine said, "Rayna needs to be rescued on the date of the day she went missing. Each day in fairy land equals 7 years in human life. So, we need to find her on the date of her disappearance. "Before midnight?" Leanne asked. "Yes, "Queen Aine continued, "she will feel only one day has passed, not almost 7 years. It will be a shock to her." "We'll take that into consideration while making our plans," Leanne answered. "Thank you Queen Aine, I will come alone on New Year's Day. We will make our plans then. With that, Aine blew the children a kiss and flew away.

"We couldn't hear Nana, is everything ok," they asked. "We will see," Nana replied. She backed up and pulled onto the road. Each side of the road was flanked by soft white light. Almost like a thousand fireflies. They continued to light the way out of the forest. Making it to the gate, all the creatures flew away together. It was almost like they were never there. Both dogs gave a final bark and laid back down.

The children talked to each other quietly in the back seat. Leanne was lost in thought. As she pulled into the driveway, she reminded the children not to say anything at dinner. "What's the family rule?" she asked. "Eat first then tell news!" they chimed in. "Right, except this time we say nothing. I tell Grandfather first. We don't tell him about Queen Aine being a fairy. Some people don't believe, so we don't lie but we don't share either." "Right Nana." "Now, out you go. Wash up and set the table."

Both dogs and kids clamored out of the car. Leanne's mind was a million miles away. How will I make this work she thought? Dinner was made quickly and Grandfather returned home from work. These days, he only worked a couple of days a week. Mostly to spend time with his youngest son who worked with him. Now that the twins were here, everyone ate at the table. Usually, it was lively, but tonight the children were a little subdued. They still chatted about their day. They told Grandfather about the trip to the park.

"Nana, you cook out today?" he asked. "Sure, just like old times," she replied. Leanne and her best friend from childhood would take their children for fall and winter cookouts. They went to Houghton's Pond in the Blue Hills back then. "It was fun." she added. "Rosie and Fye loved it."

"You're a nut!" he laughed. "It was fun Grandfather" both kids said. "Good, good, did Nora go too?" he asked. "No," Leanne answered. "We went on a whim. Next time we'll plan better.

"Grandfather, there's no school for a whole week," the children cried, "Movies, movies, movies!" they pleaded. "Ok, what do you want to see first?" Grandfather asked laughing. "Peter Pan," Joey shouted. "Ok, you guys get your pjs on and we'll watch it together. OK Nana?" Mr. D asked. "If they promise to go right to sleep after."

The kids brought their dishes to the sink. "Need any other help Nana?" Joannie asked. "No, go ahead honey, put your clothes in the hamper." Up the stairs they scrambled. Watching them leave, Nana thought out loud, "oh to be young again."

Turning to Grandfather she asked, "did you have enough to eat?" "Very good," he replied. "We'll have dessert in the living room." Leanne was happy that she had the bigger house. The children took up space and with Christmas in four days there was lots to do. "Is everybody coming for Christmas Day?" Mr. D asked. "Yes," Leanne answered. "They will all be here at some point." Leanne smiled.

Their family had multiplied. Their youngest son and his wife had welcomed a new baby in July. They had twins Brian and Bethy, who were born April 23, 2022. This past summer, they welcomed little Jack William, on July 18, 2024. Then, there was Nora, 6 years old like Joey and Joannie. Nora had a little brother, Charles Irving, born June 4th 2022. Of course, there were the oldest grandchildren, Isaac 23 and Tyler 21. Both had great jobs and were seeing nice girls. It would be a full house that's for sure. That made nine grandchildren and with the adults, we were nineteen altogether. The dining room sat eighteen people not including highchairs. Every family was bringing some food. It would surely be a nice day. Mr. D was happy about that.

Leanne said, "after the kids go to bed, I have something to talk to you about." "Everything alright?" he asked. "Yes," "we'll talk later. I will clean up. Why don't you turn the tree on for the kids? I will bring dessert in soon. The dogs waited patiently for their dinner. Leanne fed them and cleaned up. The movie was playing in the living room. She got cookies and hot chocolate for all three and placed them on a tray and carried it in. "Thanks Nana," all three chimed.

Leanne got out her computer. She found a blank notebook and started listing what she needed to know. When had Rayna gone to the tree? She rummaged through a box of papers. The box had been sent home after Rayna's room was cleaned out. Was the journal still there? Yes, Leanne grabbed it out of the box. She quickly turned the pages. There on the March calendar listed under March 17th was Pub crawl. 'I think I have met the man of my dreams. Sean!!!' Rayna had written and had drawn four hearts after the entry. Next, was written 'March 20th, the first day of spring, Fairy tree excursion.' That was the last entry. There it was in black and white. They needed to be there March 20th before midnight at the fairy tree.

Back and forth Leanne paced the kitchen, what to do, what to do! Should she risk it and tell Mr. D about "the magic"? How could she make him understand otherwise? This could not be spun like other things. It involved Ireland for God's sake. Leanne wouldn't lie, she always tried to tell the truth or tell nothing. It wasn't really lying if you just didn't share everything, though right? What to do? There was no way around it. She would have to tell him all of it. Then she would go anyway, but truthfully.

The movie was over. Joey and Joannie brought the dishes in. "All done Nana." "Great, kiss Grandfather goodnight and run upstairs. Brush your teeth and pick a short story each. I will be right up to read." Leanne stuck her head around the corner. "Don't start another movie, we have to talk sir. I will be down in about 15 minutes." "Okey-doke!" Mr. D answered.

Joey and Joannie were in the second bedroom. Twin beds up against one wall. They had picked out comforters themselves. There were plenty of toys and stuffed animals in the room. Framed over their bureau was a poster size picture. The picture was Rayna holding each baby with a Santa hat at Christmas 2018. Every night, they said goodnight Momma, we love you, come home soon. It broke Leanne's heart. "We picked our books Nana." She took both books. Joannie's was the *Rain Babies*. It was her Moms copy. Joey had picked *King Puck*. It too, was a Daycare book. Their cousin Tyler had loved it as a child at

Nana's Daycare. It was about a goat, and his wish to talk, by fairies in Ireland. Hmmm… Leanne smiled; I'm seeing a hint here. She finished the bedtime routine with a song and a kiss goodnight. "You are my sunshine" was always their song pick. Nana had been singing that daily for a long time. "Now, stay in bed past 7 am tomorrow, no school." "Love you Nana," they whispered.

Leanne was anxious about talking to Mr. D about it all, but now was the time. Going into the Great-room, Leanne sat on her chair. She muted the tv. "OK Mr. D, I want you to listen to me all the way through. This is going to sound a little crazy, but it's all true." Mr. D had a concerned look on his face. "What do you mean," he asked? Leanne took a deep breath and started her tale.

"Well, I told you how I helped Rayna deliver the babies. He nodded. "We all know the story." Leanne shook her head, "no not all of it." He sat up more attentively, "what do you mean," he asked? "Ok, just listen until the end, then I will try to answer your questions."

"Before the babies came, we saw lots of moths and butterflies flying around. Then, when visiting the meadow, we found a mushroom ring. Legend has it that a multi colored mushroom circle is where fairies have danced." His eyebrows raised and a smirk was on his face. Leanne paused in the story.

"You know how Rayna was studying myths and legends?" "Right?" he answered. "Well, it was just like in the books. We saw the moths turn into fairies. She took a deep breath and looked at Mr. D." "You're joking right?" he asked. Leanne shook her head no. "Did you eat the mushrooms?" he asked seriously.

"No, we did not," she protested. "If you believe, they will show themselves to you, Leanne said. "No, really," Mr. D continued, "you're pulling my chain now." Leanne held her hand up. "Wait until the end of the story, please, just listen."

Leanne continued, "I really met the Fairy Queen, Aine. She sprinkled us with fairy dust. She asked Rayna to deliver a letter to her father. He is King Egobail, King of the Irish Fairies. He lives under the Hill of Tara, in Ireland." Leanne felt that it was best to just tell enough, but not so much that he would have her committed, if they even did that anymore. "That is why Rayna was visiting that site in Ireland. She went to deliver that message to King Egobail. Something, then, must have gone wrong.

Mr. D interrupted. "Why are you telling me this story now?" "She has been missing since 2019, almost 7 years." "Well," Leanne answered, "I told you how the children were "special". They can sense things and they know things we don't. Remember, their birth story about caulbearers? It's not a myth. The children have been concerned for their mom. They say she is in trouble. I hate to doubt them. They have been right before, you know that."

Mr. D nodded, He knew they had saved more than one family member over the years. "I know they are special," he added. "Well, I thought it would be good to take them to the cabin area and meadow. You know, children typically believe in magical beings. Santa, Easter bunnies and all that. I hoped the fairies would appear. I did not tell them that. I didn't want to put it in their minds." Leanne continued.

Mr. D took a long drink of water. "Are you telling me the kids saw these fairies too?" he asked. Leanne nodded. "Yes, they did. Queen Aine appeared and both children spoke to her. They told her their mom needed help." "Are you kidding me!!?" Mr. D choked. "Really, the kids saw this Faerie ring. They spoke to a fairy." His face showed shock. "Did you put this in their heads Leanne?" "No, no, I never said a word. Wait until I finish the story, ok?"

Nodding, Mr. D took another sip of water. Leanne continued, "Queen Aine told the children about the message Rayna had delivered. Rayna must have fallen through a portal or something, to the other world. She may have been taken by the guards at the entrance." "No, seriously, your making all this up, aren't you?" Mr. D said. "You can't possibly believe Rayna is in some other world after all these years?" "I believe that she is trying her hardest to come back," Leanne said. "When we were leaving the park, Queen Aine and the other fairies lit the way for us. Then, Queen Aine told me to come back on New Year's Day for news of Rayna. She whispered to me that one day in our world, equals seven years in the other world. We need to find her by March 20th, the day of the Spring Equinox. If we don't, every day more will be more years."

Leanne took a long drink of her water. Mr. D looked a shade paler and took a drink to. "Are you really serious Leanne?" he asked dumbfounded. "Do you really believe all this, or are you messing with me 'cause it's not funny anymore?" Leanne got up and sat next to him on the couch.

"This is why I never mentioned this before. I knew you would have a hard time believing." "Well, yes, it does sound nuts. Most people would think you need medication." "I know, but try to understand," Leanne said. "The children and I have really seen the fairies. Rayna did also. Look at the facts. Rayna studied the legends and myths of many countries. I never told the children, but they feel she needs help."

"Well, what do you want to do?" Mr. D asked. "I want to take a trip to Ireland," Leanne answered. "Either I will take the children alone or you could come too. We could make a vacation of it. Your Birthday and mine are close. February and March. We could go for three weeks. One week before the Equinox, the week of the Equinox and the week after. If we find Rayna, that will give us time to prepare her for what she's missed."

Mr. D sat and thought about what his wife had said. It sounds absolutely crazy. Yes, lots of things are unexplained but Fairies? "Let me think about it for a minute," he said smiling. Leanne handed him a notepad. On it was written:

1. *Fairies, myths.*
2. *Caulbearers.*
3. *Hill of Tara.*

"Why don't you google these three things? I will get us a snack. Then we will decide, we need to decide by the 23rd. I will need to book flights and hotels."

Mr. D took the notepad. "OK, I want ice

cream," he added. Leanne laughed, "Alright!" she answered. Fy and Rosie were both at the door wanting to go out. After letting them out the back door, she got the snack ready. Not "too" bad she thought. Hopefully, the "white coats" won't come for her.

She let the dogs back in and joined Mr. D in the Great Room. They sat together watching a Christmas movie, both lost in thought, both had their computers open. He was looking up his three things. She was on looking at flights and hotels. They went to bed that night with much on their minds. The next morning, Mr. D called Leanne into the bedroom. "OK, let's do it. I always wanted to see some of Ireland anyway. I'll be 70 and you'll be 71. If not now, we probably never will. We need to take the chance. If we do find Rayna, the children will be so happy. If we can't find her, at least we tried. "I am so happy," Leanne said and hugged him. This can be our present to each other for Christmas and Birthdays." Mr. D laughed, "Good," he replied, "I'm glad I haven't gone to CVS yet." "Well, no need now! your covered with this trip!" Leanne said, smiling while shaking her head.

Mr. D took her hands in his. "Now, I don't think you should share the fairy part with anyone. Not everyone will believe you. No need to sound crazy. You know how you hate it when we call you "crazy lady!" I'll tell Joey and Joannie that we'll go to where their Mom was last seen. I'll tell them not to share the fairy story yet." "Good, good, I think that will be best," Mr. D said.

Christmas was an excellent day. Everyone was

there. Babies, toddlers, big kids and adults all had a great day. Leanne's sister and family stopped by that night. Everyone played *Family Feud* and had a great time. Their youngest son's family stayed the night, so they could enjoy everyone. All the youngest kids slept in the playroom. Sleeping bags were everywhere. Leanne was reminded of her Christmases as a young mother. Kids sleeping over so parents could relax with a drink, or just enjoy each other longer than a minute. The day after Christmas, a large brunch was served. Then everyone bundled up and took a walk, even the three dogs, Ted, Rose and Fy. Leanne hated to see the holiday end.

Everyone was shocked that Leanne had planned the trip to Ireland in the spring. Why not wait until summer? they asked. "Well, it's more crowded and we don't want to wait that long," Leanne answered. Joey and Joannie were beside themselves with excitement. They had all their cousins join them on the video to their mom. The adult children shook their heads. More than one thought it wasn't right to keep their hopes up. Leanne always thought it didn't hurt. What was wrong with giving them hope?

Mr. D and Leanne enjoyed their family more than you can know. Babies to rock, littles to read stories to. Then there were the three amigos, Nora, Joey and Joannie. The older grandsons and their uncles were in the living room with Grandfather watching football. He never missed a Patriots game. It was a wonderful time. Leanne put everything on hold for the holiday.

When it was over and everyone had gone, Leanne made the reservations. The flight was to be on AERLINGUS, leaving March 7th, a Thursday, at 4pm. They decided on a hotel in Dublin. They would sight see and then they would take a trip to County Meath where the Hill of Tara was located. They planned on touring the south the first week. Then, depending how things turned out after the 20th, the North. They would book the tours when they arrived. Everything was coming together. Now, the anticipation waiting to go would be hard for the children.

New Year's Day dawned quite nice and sunny. Teddie was staying the week. Leanne's oldest daughter was vacationing at Disney and Universal this week. Leanne decided to bring the three dogs to the park. Her car was almost 10 years old now, but still ran well. It was great for ferrying the kids and the dogs. She took the car seats out and lay down the back seat. Teddie was getting pretty old as well. She was younger than Rosie, but for some reason, Rosie seemed a little spryer. The vet couldn't figure it out. Leanne set up the ramp and the dogs climbed in. She jumped in the front seat and drove to the park.

The kids had gone to see the new super hero movie with Grandfather. The dogs were excited to go on an adventure. Leanne turned down the tree lined path towards the cabin. It was cold, but no snow had fallen. Winter was late arriving, thankfully. She parked as usual in the cabin driveway. The car bounced with the excited pups. Leanne looked all around, no one was near. She took the leashes but let the dogs jump and run. They made a b-line to the stream. Water cold and fresh, rolled over the rocks and under the foot bridge. After a cool drink, into the meadow they ran. They chased each other like young puppies.

Leanne walked to the tree and rock wall. She sat on the wall watching the dogs. They raced back and forth chasing each other. Leanne smiled at their exuberance, it felt good to sit in the sun. The perfect winter day, blue sky, sunshine and happy dogs. Just then she noticed a cloud of what looked like moths and butterflies flying over the meadow. Their white and multicolored wings beat in a beautiful flutter. It was too cold for normal insects. This had to be the fairies arriving. Leanne glanced towards the dogs. All three sat watching.

The insects flew to the tree and lit on the branches. Looking closely, you could see that they were not truly insects. They were small beings, human like with wings. They almost seemed to change as Leanne looked at them. One flew to Leanne. "Nice to see you again," she sang. "I'm glad you came. I have news."

Queen Aine told Leanne that indeed Rayna had been unwittingly captured by the guards. As she did not have the note-letter on her, they took her into custody. Rayna explained the mix up to the guards but they kept her locked up until they found the letter. "Remember Leanne," Aine continued, "its only been one day in the other world." Leanne shook her head; "Do you mean, she thinks its March 20th ,2019?" Yes," Aine replied. "She will only have lived one day. If you can go and get her out by midnight, March 20th in this, our year 2025, she'll meet her children now, in our time." "Tell me what to do," Leanne said. "I will give you another letter to my father, King Egobail. I will also send my daughter Deanna with you." "How can I take a faerie?" Leanne asked. "Magic of course," Queen Aine answered. "Have Joannie take a few toys in her carry on. Deanna will look like a doll to non-believers. When you go to Hill of Tara, she will help you."

All three dogs were sitting on the ground watching the exchange. Queen Aine looked at them. "They're getting old, aren't they?" she said. Leanne looked down, "Yes, the vet can't figure why Rosie is still here." "Fairy dust," Queen Aine replied. Leanne looked at her quizzically. "What do you mean," she asked? "Well, way back when the twins were born, you all were dusted remember?" "I do remember. You took the blanket from Fy it had been dusted Is that why I feel well enough to care for the twins?" Nodding, Queen Aine continued, "We can't turn back time but we can help with getting older. Just like our world is seven times slower than this world. We age a lot slower. I can sprinkle all of you again. It will buy you and the dogs some more time here. Not forever, but some, baring accidents." "Could you give me some for my husband?" Leanne asked. "For you, yes, just sprinkle it on him at night. It should help with his aches and pains going forward." Queen Aine flew over to the mushroom circle. Under one, she picked up a tiny jar. The jar was the size of a thimble. "This should do it," she smiled handing it to Leanne. "Sprinkle it top to bottom." Then, she and the others flew around the dogs sprinkling them with dust. "Remember, this won't last forever, but it will give them more years. They will also feel better, more puppy like." "Awesome!" Leanne whispered.

When finished, Queen Aine flew back to her. "When do you leave for Ireland?" she asked. "We are leaving March 7th." "There's no need for you to come back here, we know where you live." Leanne smiled, "I thought you might," she said. "We keep our eyes on you. We have a tree on the golf course. I will bring you the letter, and Deanna that morning, "Queen Aine said. The dogs took a last runaround as the beings flew away. Leanne sat with the jar of fairy dust, hoping it would work for Mr. D. Leanne's mind raced as she drove home. It's true, she thought, she did feel better. She was able to take care of the twins and Mr. D. She had actually ridden a bike with them a few times. She definitely did feel better. There was no doubt about Rosie. She still ran around with Fy. It would be awesome if it helped Mr. D and Teddie. Queen Aine said it wouldn't turn back time, but it could ease some further aging. She would sprinkle Mr. D tonight after he fell asleep.

That night, Leanne got up to use the bathroom. Taking the small bottle, she sprinkled it from head to toe. For a split second, the dust sparkled, then faded after a few minutes. Mr. D snored away, none the wiser. Leanne giggled to herself as she lay back down. Time will tell, she whispered to herself out loud.

Teddie was like a young pup the next morning. She was racing around the house. Mr. D called out, "What's got into Ted?" he asked. "I don't know," she answered from the kitchen. "She does love rugs". "She's not limping at all!" Mr. D said, coming into the kitchen. "Well," Leanne answered, "she did drink from the spring at the meadow. Maybe it's the fountain of youth. Want to go for a drink?" "I just might," Mr. D added, as Teddie flew by again. "Who wants pancakes and bacon?" Leanne called. They grabbed their plates and went to the table.

On the second morning after the sprinkling, Mr. D woke up with much less noise. Moaning and groaning was a morning ritual. Hopefully, he would notice a difference soon, Leanne thought. The next week, Mr. D said to her "Hey, you know, I think those pills you gave me are working." Leanne had forgotten about the hemp pills. She had bought them for Christmas, hoping it would help him with the pain. "Awesome, keep taking them," she said with a smile.

Mr. D's Birthday came in February. All the family met for a special 70th birthday party. Gifts were geared to the trip. The kids all commented on how much better he seemed to be getting around. "Hemp pills," he told them; "your mother got them for me." Leanne was happy he was feeling better. He still used the cane, but he seemed to be in much less pain.

March 7th came quick. Queen Aine had said she would be there before they left. Finishing up a list of "things to do while I'm gone" for James, Leanne looked out to a yard full of butterflies and moths. She went out to the yard, and met Queen Aine. Deanna was with her. "This is my daughter, Leanne." Deanna was smaller than Queen Aine. She had long red curls cascading down her back. She had the most beautiful emerald green eyes, her eyelashes dark auburn. She wore a short green sparkly dress. Her wings looked like gossamer and shimmered green and orange. She had the tiniest cloth shoes on. She did look like a toy, Leanne thought. Leanne had a small mesh bag. The bottom was padded plastic. There were two dolls that resembled Deanna. Leanne asked Queen Aine if this would be alright.

"That will be fine," Queen Aine answered, "just perfect." She took out a tube, like the one she had given Rayna. "This is the letter for my father, King Egobail. Do not, under any circumstance, go into the other world without it. Deanna will make sure you get back." Leanne answered, "We will do our best to bring Rayna with us. The drive to Logan Airport wasn't bad. The children were so excited. "I know we will find her." Joannie chirped. Leanne carried a letter from James. As their named father, he had to give permission to the Grandparents to take them out of the country. Leanne had also found Rayna's passport. It had been sent home in the box of belongings from Dublin College. James stayed home to care for the dogs.

Arriving at the Aer Lingus counter, they checked two suitcases. Then, they headed toward the gate with their carry-on bags. Joannie kept her toy bag out and carefully carried the dolls. Though Queen Aine had assured them Deanna would be fine, Joannie felt better doing it this way. Boarding wasn't until later, so they got lunch and settled in to wait. Mr. D seemed excited too, he had always wanted to visit Ireland. Since sprinkled with the Fairy dust, he was in a lot less pain. Leanne was thrilled. More than once, he praised her for the hemp pills. She took a few pictures of everyone for her scrapbook. She wanted this trip documented. Hopefully, it would be a successful mission. Even though Rayna missed the twin's baby and toddler years, they still had childhood left.

They finally boarded and settled in for the long flight. They touched down at 5:15 AM Friday morning. With the luggage collected, they hired a car to take them to their hotel. Leaving their bags at guest services, they went out to explore. Joannie carried her doll bag along.

Leanne had everything all planned out. They ate breakfast and then went to the college. The children wanted to see where their mother had last spent time. Next stop the Dublin Zoo. It was damp and cool. They had planned for this so they weren't bothered. Mr. D was able to rent a scooter, so Joannie put the dolls in the basket. It was a wonderful morning. It felt good to stretch their legs after the long plane ride. Their last stop before leaving was the butterfly house. Mr. D was able to drive right in with the scooter. As they rounded the first trail, a multitude of insects surrounded the group. Joannie and Joey were very excited. At first Mr. D was a little taken back. Leanne looked at the children. "Do you see what I see?" she whispered.

They nodded and all three smiled as one creature lit on Leanne's shoulder. It was a tiny fairy of course. Only believers could see her. She whispered, "We've been waiting for you. Safe travels, keep our princess safe." Then they all flew up to the top of the enclosure. Mr. D laughed, "that was weird," he said. They finished up the morning and headed back to the hotel.

The Hotel served lunch at the pool area. They spent the rest of the afternoon there. Leanne and Mr. D planned the next day while the children swam and played. The dolls sat in the middle of the table. Leanne felt it was best to keep them/her in sight. They planned the next day's activities.   The week and a half flew by. Mr. D really felt better. He was able to do so much more than usual. Deanna had flown away from the hotel garden the first night. She left the letter with Leanne. The letter was in the lipstick like cylinder. Leanne locked it in the room safe with their valuables.

The morning of March 20 dawned warm and spring like. It was not only the first day of spring, but Leanne's 71st Birthday. She hoped by the end of the day they would have Rayna back. The sun was shining and there wasn't a cloud in the sky. Leanne had not fallen asleep until late into the night. Between the excitement of hoping to find Rayna, or the possible dread of not finding her and disappointing the children, how could she sleep? Also, there was the fear that Rayna would not be able to accept the lost years. She had missed their early childhood and nothing could change that.   Leanne sat the children down. She told them about the difference in time. They were smart and accepted the facts. "Nana, remember we have our videos," they said in unison, "She'll watch them and know us." Leanne put her arms around them. "She might be sad though. We might have to give her some space to get used to the idea. I know she will be so happy to meet you both, that's for sure. You are wonderful children."

They packed up what they needed for the trip to the Hill of Tara. The last items came out of the safe. A copy of Leanne's passport and the cylinder.

The hotel ran a shuttle to the area. Evidently it was a very popular spot for both tourists and the locals. Many people celebrated the Spring Equinox. There would be a fair like festival until 5 PM. The plan was to enjoy the fair, then go to the tree at 6 PM and rescue Rayna by midnight.

The Hill of Tara was hopping. Vendors lined the bottom of the hill. You could buy all kinds of food and crafts. The food smells wafted through the air making their mouths water. Mr. D was hungry (big surprise), he went off on his own to scope out the offerings. They met up at the concessions and everyone got something.

Leanne was too nervous to eat. She just had a tall ice tea. They finished up and stopped at the flower stall. The children wanted to leave some at the fairy tree. From across the field the tree sparkled in the sunset. The sky looked like cotton candy. "Red sky at night sailors delight," the children whispered. "That's a good sign, right Nana?"

People came from all over to hang trinkets and

ribbons in the branches. The children could hardly contain their excitement. Leanne could almost feel the energy in the air. Mr. D was nervous, he wanted to believe. He walked beside Leanne with his cane. "I brought a blanket and folding stool in the backpack," Leanne told them. She kissed them all goodbye. She strapped her pocket book around her shoulders. Inside, was her I.D, and the letter for King Egobail.

Leanne slowly walked around the fence that circled the tree. The tree was huge. No one was around at this point except her family. There was still music coming from the festival and it carried on the evening air. "Be safe Nana, bring her back," the children called out. "I'll try my best, love you guys," she answered. Mr. D knew the plan was, that if she wasn't back in an hour, he was to leave. He would bring the children back to the hotel to wait. He hoped he wouldn't have to do that.

Deanna had explained that King Egobail might be able to use his power to help them. He could let them leave right away. They would be in the time that Leanne was in now. If he waited until the next day, the children would not be there. They would have passed through more time. Leanne was nervous. "Please, please, let this work," she mumbled under her breath.

She circled the tree, turning back one last time, she waved to her family. She lay her hands in the middle of the trunk. There was an indent, almost like a door. Gently she pressed forward. In the next instant, she was inside. She hadn't realized her eyes were closed tight and she was barely breathing.

When she opened her eyes, she was in a wondrous world. Flowers bloomed everywhere and the air was heavy with the scent. Lilacs and roses were growing everywhere. It was bright and beautiful. Coming towards her were a group of… what were they? she thought. Leanne took a deep breath and willed herself to calm down. Reaching into her purse she pulled out the tube. Holding it in the palm of her hand, it gave her strength. The group of beings were getting closer. Leanne stepped forward to meet them.

They looked human like. Well, in body and face, she thought. They were all about 4 ft tall or shorter. Each very unique. Three females flanked by two male beings. The women looked like beautiful creatures. All had long hair and petite bodies. The most beautiful thing about them were their wings. Gossamer wings came down to the back of their knees. The wings shimmered in the light. It was mesmerizing. Just as she was a few feet away from them, Deanna stepped forward to greet her.

Deanna was close to 4 ft tall. Leanne stuttered, "How is this you?" she asked. "Here we are much bigger than in your world," Deanna said. "We need to be inconspicuous in your world. People can't know about our world. The humans would destroy all this. We only show ourselves to people we can trust from your world." One of the male creatures stepped forward. "We understand you have something for the King." Leanne swallowed, "Yes, is Rayna here?" "Give us the letter, then we'll take you to her." "No, Leanne shook her head, no, I'll see her first. Deanna, will you take me to Rayna and then to the King?" asked Leanne. Deanna walked with Leanne. "I will take you to her." Leanne noticed as they followed the group, that each fairies' wings were different shades of color. They sparkled in the light. Even their skin had a shimmer to it. They seemed to float along rather than walk. Leanne tried to take in all the sights. She wanted to remember as much as she could. The twins would have all kinds of questions.

They walked quite a way before they saw houses. The houses were like fairy houses that people put in their gardens. Bigger than in Leanne's world but small compared to human houses. The houses were thatched cottage style, painted in pastel colors. Tiny children flew around. Their laughter was like a tinkling bell. Leanne wished she could take pictures. The children would love to see this. Mr. D would surely believe then. Leanne was having a hard time herself. Deanna was talking and asking questions of the others. They finally arrived at what looked like a castle.

There were guards standing in front of a large gate. Deanna whispered to the guard, he smiled and stepped aside opening the gate. "Welcome," he said, "enjoy your visit."

Deanna ran ahead. "Grandfather I am here," she called out. A larger man figure came down the stairs. He was as tall as Leanne. His wings were magnificent. Much larger than the others. They beat softly as he walked towards Leanne. His hair was shoulder length, curly and shimmering. He also had a beard. His eyes twinkled as he hugged Deanna close. "My Deanna, dear granddaughter. How is your mother?" "Good, good, she sends her love," Deanna answered. Stepping back Deanna brought Leanne forward. "Grandfather, this is Leanne. She means us no harm. The Queen has entrusted her to bring me and a message to you." King Egobail stepped forward and shook Leanne's hand. "I thank you for bringing her safely to me. May I have the letter please," he said extending his hand. Leanne handed him the silver tube. The King opened the cylinder and read the letter. "Did you read this Leanne?" he asked. "No!" was her reply. "I was told to just bring it to you." I am here to bring Rayna home, is she here?"

King Egobail called to the others, "Go get the woman. She is in the castle." "Is she being held against her will?" Leanne asked angrily. "No, of course not," the King answered. "She was brought to me by the guards. When she fell through the portal, we needed to be careful. We don't want to be discovered by your people. There are many types of fairies. Gnomes, elves, trolls and even leprechauns. We all live, mostly peacefully together. Rayna was first taken by the trolls who were on duty at the portal that day. She claimed to have fallen in after burying the cylinder for me." King Egobail added "Had she been brought to me immediately; this all could have been avoided. Trolls will be trolls. They took their time. The letter was exactly where she said. By then it was past midnight. If you don't go back before midnight of the equinox, you lose 7 years in your world." Leanne glanced at her watch. It had already been two hours. She wanted to get back to Mr. D and the children sooner rather than later. It had to be dark on The Hill of Tara. She had left the backpack with a lantern and snacks but she wanted desperately to get back. She certainly couldn't afford to age 7 years. It was her 71st birthday.

"King Egobail," Leanne started. "I really need to get back. I have Rayna's children waiting. If we don't leave by midnight, she will lose more time. They were only 3 months old when she left. Now they are almost 7. Please help us leave." With that, Rayna came running down the steps. "Nana, Nana is that you?" Oh my God I can't believe it. You came for me, how are the babies?" she asked.

Rayna had not changed at all. For her it felt like barely 24 hours. She stopped and looked at Nana. Are you ok, how did you get here?" Leanne hugged her. "I am so glad to see you," she said, while tears swam in her eyes. She stepped back and wiped her eyes. I am so happy to have found you. King Egobail then took Rayna's hands in his. "Rayna," he started, "I know you feel like it's been just one day." "Right," Rayna said, "I fell through the tree by accident, the trolls took me to the council. Then they brought me to you and you said I could leave right?" "Rayna, Leanne has come a long way to find you. You need to listen carefully; we will talk on our way."

A carriage pulled up to them. It was pulled by two large horses. Both Leanne and Rayna felt like they were getting into Cinderella's coach. The King got in first, then the women were helped up. They sat next to each other across from the King. "We need to talk as we head to the portal." Rayna looked from one to the other. Something is wrong she thought. Leanne couldn't have gotten here so quickly.

"Rayna," the King started, "There is no easy way to tell you this. You will go back to your world tonight. Our worlds are on different time lines. One day here is equal to 7 years in your world. He paused to let that sink in. Rayna took a big breath. "What do you mean?" she asked him. King Egobail repeated himself. "One day here is 7 in your world. You have been gone almost 7 years. Rayna 's face drained of all color. "Do you mean my children are almost 7 years old?" King Egobail and Leanne both nodded. "Today, I am 71 years old," Leanne added. It is March 20th ,2025.

Rayna started to cry, "I missed their childhood." Rayna put her head in her hands and sobbed. "Are they still with you, Nana?" she whimpered. Leanne took Rayna's face in her hands. She looked her straight in the eyes. "Of course, they are, they are beautiful children. They are smart, kind and happy. Every week they have continued to blog for you. They are waiting at the tree for us. They knew you were in trouble and got us to come for you."

"We have arrived," the King announced. The horses pulled up to a large door. The door was at least 7 feet tall and guarded by two Leprechauns this time. King Egobail stepped out first. Giving Leanne his hand he helped her down. "You have been very brave. Deanna tells me you were very careful bringing her to me. For your kindness, I will dust you with Fairy dust.

You will not lose any more time. Also, because it is the Spring Equinox, you will go back to your time." Then he helped Rayna down. "I can't change the time for you. I can offer you this. Should you have any other children, they will be magical." At that, the door swung open. Stepping inside, they climbed a stairway straight up. "Follow to the top and push the door open," the guard instructed. Step out quickly, it will only open for one minute. Good luck, safe journey" he added.

Seven years, seven years, mumbled Rayna as they walked up. They reached the top and caught their breath. Rayna seemed fine, except for the tears streaming down her face. Leanne however needed a minute to catch her breath. She felt every one of her 71 years right now. It took a few minutes for her heart to stop racing. Leanne pulled Rayna close. "We can't change the past, only the future. Dry your eyes, blow your nose, and get ready to meet your wonderful children. Ok, try not to be shocked... ready??? Rayna nodded. "We have one minute, kind of like the Day-care fire drills," Rayna said. "Yes," that's right. One two three, push!"

The door swung open. It was pretty dark outside. Stepping out, Rayna looked toward the meadow. There were the children. Tall, beautiful children. They squealed and ran to her. "Mommy, mommy," they cried. "We knew you would come out." Leanne walked behind them. Just then the air was full of butterflies. The creatures flew all around them. Leanne looked toward Mr. D. She mouthed I told you.

Just then one creature flew down to Leanne. It was Deanna. "Thank you for bringing me here safely. In appreciation, and in honor of your Birthday, we got you a lotto ticket. I have a feeling it will be lucky." Then she sprinkled all of them with fairy dust. She flew over to Mr. D and sprinkled him as well. "Until we meet again," she sang flying away. The rest of the insects followed. They lit in the branches of the tree. Mr. D hugged Rayna and Leanne. "I am shocked," he whispered in Leanne's ear. "I never thought you could pull this off. Let's go get something to eat." Leanne slipped the ticket into her purse. They called for a car and went to the hotel.

The children talked nonstop to Rayna. She seemed to be in shock. Leanne was a little nervous that she would not adjust easily. Joey filled Rayna in on school, his friends and Fy. Joannie was a little more subdued and just held her mother's hand. Mr. D had been very quiet on the way back to the hotel. He kept glancing at Leanne. "I can't believe this; I was sure you were crazy." He just shook his head mumbling. They didn't want to say too much in the car. The driver was chatting on about the area and they chose to listen. Soon enough, they pulled up to the hotel. Mr. D paid the driver and in they went.

They decided to just eat in the Hotel. Joey and Joannie chatted on the way. Rayna was pale and quiet. Leanne was worried. They were seated at a large table over to the side. There were a few other families seated as well as a lively bar. The children were so excited. Rayna sat between the two, across from Leanne and

Mr. D. Leanne couldn't believe how happy the sight made her. The meal was delicious They were finishing up when Rayna asked what about school and my things? Leanne put her hand over Rayna's and said, "Let's finish up here and when the children go to sleep, I will fill you in." "That sounds good," Rayna said smiling. Just then a waiter brought a Birthday cake over to the table. Sitting it down in front of Leanne, they all sang to her. She was shocked that Mr. D had planned this. As Leanne blew out the candles, she knew this would be a great year. Everyone had a piece of cake and they wrapped up the rest. The meal lasted two hours. The children were getting sleepy. Mr. D paid the bill and they headed upstairs.

They had reserved adjoining rooms. Rayna would stay with the children. Leanne had brought some clothes and toiletries for Rayna. They could shop tomorrow. The children were sharing a bed. Rayna tucked them in and kissed them good night. "Will you be here in the morning Mama?" Joannie asked. Rayna bent down and kissed them both again. "I will do my best to always be with you. I love you both so much. I am so happy to be with you now. Close your eyes, we've had a long day. Sweet dreams babies of mine." Rayna moved into Leanne's room. She sat down with a sigh. "I really can't believe those are my children," she whispered. "I missed it all." Tears rolled down her cheeks. "I never should have left them," Rayna sobbed. Leanne moved to sit next to her. She draped her arm around Rayna's shoulder. "Honey, you had no way of knowing," she said softly "If it wasn't for the children, I wouldn't have come." Leanne handed Rayna a tissue. "Now wipe your eyes, we have planning to do. Rayna blew her nose and washed her face "Ok I am ready."

Leanne got the backpack with Rayna's papers in it. She had taken her passport, driver's license and some pictures she had printed from Rayna's phone. She also had brought her phone. "How did you know where to look for me, Nana?" Rayna asked. "Well," Leanne said, "I looked in your journal. The last entry was about The Hill of Tara. You also mentioned going there on the Spring Solstice. So, I started there. It was the children who insisted you needed help. I took them to the meadow and they met Queen Aine, she helped us. They are special children. More than once they have saved the family. They seem to be growing into their caulbearers gifts." Rayna smiled, "We knew it right? I can't thank you enough for caring for them," she continued. "You went above and beyond." Leanne smiled, "We have loved them like our own. They are our own." Mr. D piped up, "Me too, I think they made us younger." "I am very grateful, overwhelmed, but so happy to be here."

Mr. D turned the TV on of course while Leanne and Rayna talked about everything. "Just think your body is six and a half years younger than the rest of us," Leanne said. "No wonder the Fairies look so great," Rayna added. They talked into the night. We bought a ticket back home for you, Leanne said. "How did you know you would find me?" "The children insisted, and frankly, they don't insist unless they're right," Leanne said. "I would rather have canceled it, then not be able to take you home." Leanne choked on a sob, "I thought you were lost forever," she whispered. "I am so happy," Leanne cried. Mr. D looked over, "Funny way to show "happy" honey," he said. "I know," Leanne said blowing her nose. "Let's get some rest, we have a lot to do tomorrow," she added. Rayna stood and hugged Leanne. "I can't thank you enough. See you in the morning," Rayna said, closing the door between rooms.

Leanne lay awake wondering how they would pull this off. Rayna had been missing for almost 7 years. How could they explain where she'd been? She fell asleep around 4 am still with no answers.

The children woke up at 7am, too excited to stay in bed. They decided to order room service, to let the adults adjust. Rayna wasn't sure how getting back to the States would work. She knew Leanne had the passport, but was it expired? She imagined there had to have been an investigation into her disappearance. Wouldn't that set of some red flags? She couldn't eat much worrying about it. After breakfast they sent the kids to get ready for the day. The adults had to figure out a plan.

Just then there was a sharp knock on the door. Rayna turned to Leanne. "Are you expecting anyone?" she asked. Leanne shook her head no. The knock came again. Leanne opened the door and there stood a small distinguished looking man. His hair was white under his scaly cap. He wore a suit and carried a briefcase. "Can I help you?" she asked. He looked up with the most beautiful green eyes she had ever seen. "K. Egobail sent me. I can help you." With the mention of K. Egobail, Leanne opened the door wide. As he passed, he handed her his card. The lettering was gold. K. Egobail Enterprises, Adere, Limerick. The second line read, Seamus O'Malley, The Fixer.

Leanne followed him into the room. "Mr. O'Malley, this is my husband Bill. I am Leanne and this is Rayna and the children, Joey and Joannie." Seamus smiled at each in turn. "Well, it's nice to meet everyone," he said smiling. I hope I can help you get home safely. "Would you like a cup of tea Mr. O'Malley; we were just finishing breakfast." "I would love a cup, if it's not too much trouble," Mr. O'Malley said, "but please call me Seamus, Mrs."

Leanne poured the cup and offered the plate of scones. "I could use a little sustenance," he chuckled. Mr. D poured another cup of coffee and settled down to listen. Leanne took a sip of water, swallowing she asked, "Why are you here Seamus?" "Well, the way I see it, Rayna needs a way to get home. You don't want the authorities asking too much and neither do we." Seamus looked from one to the other and said, "Some of us pass back and forth. We are able to live in both worlds as we say. We own land, have money, and have our people helping those who help us." Opening his briefcase, he pulled out a large manila envelope.

In the envelope were documents stating that Rayna had lived in Adere, Limerick these past 6 plus years. The papers stated she had turned up March 21,2019. She called herself Nancy O'Grady. She was bleeding from a head wound. No one questioned her. The local Doctor treated her. She lived in one of the cottages owned by K. Egobail Enterprises, working for the company as a housekeeper. She fell, injuring her head this week. When she regained consciousness, she remembered her real name. The official Doctor's report was included.

Next, he pulled out a passport. The old one had expired. Leanne had brought the old one but hadn't figured out how to get a new one. Now, she didn't have to get one. The new passport was dated from when the old one expired. "How can this work?" asked Rayna. "They won't believe this. I've been in this country illegally for 6 years." Seamus smiled, "You'd be surprised what a little Fairy dust can do. I will be your ambassador. I can get you on the plane. The custom officials will except this passport. The authorities will except the story of your lost years. We hope in return you will not share this story with anyone. We do not want people digging up fields and areas where they think we are."

"We won't," Leanne and Rayna said at the same time. "Me neither," Mr. D agreed. "I just want to get everyone home safe and sound." Leanne poured more tea for Seamus. "Why are you helping us Seamus?" she asked? "Has this happened to others? Have others lost 7 years too?" Seamus nodded, "Yes, but most times they want to stay. Our world is beautiful. You only saw a tiny part. We live longer, are happier on the whole, and go between worlds to help both. We are helping you for a few reasons. Rayna fell in while delivering the first letter. You came to save her and reunite her with her children. Lastly, you brought Deanna, the princess safely to the King. Neither of you exposed the site in Massasoit. You didn't get the authorities involved in this visit. You all proved to be trustworthy and King Egobail wants to repay your kindness. He hopes you will do him one last favor. Would you bring this letter back to Queen Aine?" He took a small tube from the envelope. "You just have to bury it in the middle of the mushroom circle in the meadow."

Seamus stood up, "I will let you get ready for the day. I will be back with a limo to take you to Limerick. We will visit the village of Adere. Rayna, you will have to be familiar in case your questioned. We will also go to Dublin College for your transcripts. We will let them know you are safe." He turned with a grin. "Good thing you studied the myths and legends of Ireland. Your kind of living one yourself Lass." He chuckled and opened the door. "I'll be back at 2 PM" and with that he was out the door.

The three adults looked at each other. "Is this for real?" Mr. D asked. The new passport looked identical to the first. "I feel like we're in a movie," Rayna said. Mr. D added, "I will believe anything now. I feel like this is all a dream. Well one of Nana's dreams, actually." "This is so over the top, I would not have dreamed it, Leanne said. Getting up, Mr. D grabbed his cane. "I'll go get ready. I almost feel like I don't need this cane anymore," he said, putting it on his shoulder. Leanne said "keep it anyway."

Rayna helped Leanne stack the dishes. "What do you think about all this?" she asked Leanne. "I know it's hard to believe, but what do we have to lose," Leanne replied. "Who would believe any of this right?" Rayna added. "I will go get ready," Leanne said. "We will shop and take the kids to the park," she added.

Joey and Joannie were lying on the bed. They were dressed and watching TV. Both were anxious to go exploring with Rayna. Coming into the room, Rayna stopped to take it all in. These were really her babies. Children now. She sat on the bed. "I am so sorry," she started to say. "I wish I never came here; I've missed so much time. "No Mama," they said sitting up. "We taped everything for you. First, Uncle James and Nana, then we learned how. You are going to love it." "I know," Rayna answered, "I look forward to watching it with you. I will get dressed, and we will all go out," she added.

Everyone was ready by 10:30, even Mr. D. They walked around town. Rayna popped into a clothing store called *Carousel*. She found some unique clothes. She bought a couple of outfits and accessories for the trip back. The store was close to a small park. Grandfather offered to watch the children play. He found a bench to sit on. The kids really needed time to run off some energy. Leanne and Rayna picked up lunch and carried it to the park. It was a rare warm sunny day for March. The children finished quickly and ran off. They had made some new friends. Rayna watched them play. "I just can't get over it Nana," she said. "I missed it all so far and so fast, what was I thinking?" she asked. "I know," Leanne said, "it is hard. If not for them at this age though, we wouldn't have found you. Let's concentrate on getting home. We have until next Thursday to pull it off."

As promised, Seamus O'Malley was waiting in a black limo. The children were excited. They had never been in a limousine before and couldn't wait. The driver opened the door, Leanne climbed in first. Rayna and the children followed with Mr. D behind. Lastly, Seamus climbed in, the driver shut the door, and they were on their way.

It was huge inside. There were refreshments for everyone. Mr. O'Malley spoke to the children. "Did you have fun at the park?" he asked. "Yes, we made three new friends," the twins said. "Well, well you must be very friendly children," he said chuckling. "Help yourself to some treats," he added. "Can we?" the twins turned to Rayna. "Yes," Rayna said smiling, it was nice to be asked. Both children shook Mr. O'Malley's hand. "Thank you, sir, it's nice to meet you." Rayna smiled, even though she had not taught them, she felt proud. They all settled in for the drive.

The scenery was beautiful. Blue sky, rolling hills, farms and animals with mountains in the distance. The children were mesmerized. Seamus took out some papers. "We need to keep the story straight. Rayna was injured and had amnesia. She thought her name was Nancy O Grady. She got a job and tried to write in her spare time. Short and sweet. This will be accepted with a little magic." He winked at them. The limo slowed down and pulled into a driveway.

A row of thatched cottages lined the road. At the end of the road was a sign, K. Egobail Enterprise. A large barn was in front of them. Leanne asked, "What is this place?" Seamus answered, "It's our store room. Items come here and then are shipped to our customers." "What items?" Leanne asked. "This and that," he answered, "We sell lots of different things. No worries it's all legal like. Would the "wee ones" like to visit our playground?" "Yes," they shouted. Mr. D offered to watch them.

Leanne and Rayna were taken to one of the cottages. The cottage they entered was set up for communal living. Four bedrooms with a main shared kitchen. "This is where, if asked, you'll say you lived." Seamus told Rayna. "Look around, be a little familiar with it. They took some pictures with their cell phones. Soon it was time to go. Rayna ran to get Mr. D and the children. The limo pulled up and they all climbed in.

When everyone was comfortable and had a snack, Mr. O'Malley went over the plan. The college was next on the route. The college desk was run by a student. Rayna explained that she wanted her transcript from the winter term 2019. The girl pulled it up, printed it and handed it to Rayna. No questions were asked. "That was easy," Rayna said, walking out.

The plan was for Seamus to pick them up each day. They would sight see and be dropped back. Dropping them off, Leanne was the last one out of the limo. She turned and said, "Thank you so much Seamus, you have been a tremendous help." "It's been my pleasure, Leanne," he said. "You have a wonderful family." Leanne smiled, "I am very lucky, that's for sure." As she turned to leave, Seamus called out, "Did you check the ticket?" Leanne turned back, "You mean the plane tickets?" she asked. "No, the ticket Deanna gave you the other night," Seamus said. Leanne had just slipped the ticket into her purse. She had totally forgotten about it. She found it tucked in the zippered compartment. She pulled it out showing it. Seamus smiled and said, "I'd check that against tonight's National Lottery if I were you." Leanne looked from the ticket to Seamus. "Are you kidding me?" she asked. "Ah Mrs., I will never tell," he laughed. Check it out in the morning," and he drove away. Carefully, Leanne returned the ticket to her bag. This could be interesting, she thought.

Everyone was hungry, so they walked to the corner pub. The bar was hopping, they were lucky to get a table. They all ordered fish and chips with tall glasses of ice tea. It was delicious. The music started just as they finished. Joannie and Joey jumped right up with the other children. A woman was teaching them some Irish steps. The look of them would make you think they were Irish born. Joannie's long dark braid flew from right to left as she counted 1, 2, 3, 4, 5, 6, 7, 1, 2, 3, 1, 2, 3. Joey, with his curly mop, danced right along with her. They made a beautiful sight. There was clapping and tapping from most of the patrons. It was a wonderful night. Rayna beamed with happiness. They walked back to the hotel at 9:00 pm to get the children to bed.

Rayna came back to Leanne's room after tucking the children in bed. They called for room service and ordered tea and dessert. "This has been the best day I can remember, excluding the day they were born of course," Rayna whispered. "I really can't thank you both enough she continued. You have treated them as your own all these years." Leanne and Mr. D nodded, "We hope you will stay with us until you decide what to do," they said. "Thank you, I will," Rayna said hugging them both.

Leanne decided to get the lotto ticket out. "Look, she said showing Mr. D. "Where did that come from," he asked. "Deanna gave it to me the other night," Leanne said. Seamus reminded me this afternoon." Leanne read the ticket, Date March 23, 2025 drawing at 8:45 pm. "Well, it's too late to watch it live." "Maybe we could pull it up on our phone," Mr. D suggested. "Give me a minute." He pulled up the lotto page. The number was posted. Leanne did not think they could win, but magic was behind them. Mr. D asked for a paper and pen. He wrote down the number. He actually had to wipe the sweat off his hands and head. "Ok Leanne," he said read out the numbers. Leanne took a sip of water. "OK, here goes," she giggled.

The first number is 3, 19, 21, 29, 31, 35, and bonus number 22. Mr. D's face drained of all color, "Are you kidding?" he croaked. "Read them again Leanne, no joking." "I'm not," she answered. "Ready, the first number is 3, 19, 21, 29, 31, 35, and bonus number is 22. "OH MY GOD!" he yelled, "WE

WON!!! WE WON!!!" "Oh my God." He was pale as a ghost. "No, now you are kidding me?" Leanne said, her hand shaking. "Rayna, you read them," Leanne said, taking the phone from Mr. D. "We won, we won," he was mumbling. "Rayna, here's the ticket, go!" Leanne said. Rayna read out loud "3, 19, 21, 29, 31, 35, and bonus 22". Rayna looked up at Leanne. Leanne read the numbers on Mr. D's phone, "We really are the winners. What is the jackpot Rayna?" Leanne asked. Rayna took the phone. "The jackpot is 18.9 million-euro pounds," Rayna answered. "What is that in American dollars?" Leanne asked. Mr. D took the phone. "To put it into American Dollars, it comes out to $21,233,569.26 or roughly 21 million dollars." "Oh my God, 21 million dollars." Mr. D came over to Leanne and said "Sign the back now Leanne, before anything happens to it. Then put it in the envelope with the passports. We will lock it up until Seamus comes." Leanne did just that. "I can't believe it," they all said looking at each other. They were all in a state of shock. None of the adults slept much that night. Each one lay there lost in their own thoughts.

Finally, at 4:00 AM, Leanne and Mr. D got up. They sat together in the sitting area of their room. Mr. D was a great business man. He had already estimated the taxes. "Taxes are about a third, so that would leave us about $14 million dollars. Leanne, we can help the kids, Rayna, the Grandchildren. I am stunned," he whispered. "I think when Seamus comes back, we should get a lawyer. It sure was a golden ticket, right?" "Yes," whispered Leanne, "now let's go back to bed," she added.

At 7:00 AM, breakfast arrived. Everyone ate in there pj's. Rayna came in the room rubbing her eyes. "Was it a dream Nana?" she asked. "What was a dream?" both children asked. Rayna looked at Mr. D and Leanne "Should we tell them?" she asked. They both nodded yes. Rayna looked at the children and said, "You can't tell anyone, promise?" "We promise," both children said at once, "what is it." "Well Nana 's birthday ticket won the lotto." "What's that?" they asked. "It's a lot of money," Mr. D answered. Everyone ate, lost in their own thoughts. The knock on the door was expected.

Leanne opened the door; Seamus came in with a jaunty step. With a twinkle in his eye he said, "I see you checked the ticket. You are all white as ghosts." "Won't this bring to much attention to us?" Leanne asked. "Ah, you've done nothing wrong, Mrs. It will be fine," he smiled. "You all get dressed and we will tour around. We can't go to lotto headquarters until Monday." Turning to Leanne he asked, "is the ticket safe? Did you sign the back?" "Yes, to both," Leanne answered. "Then go get dressed. I will meet you all downstairs in an hour," he said.

They had a wonderful day sightseeing all over Dublin. Dropping them off, Seamus told them he would hire a lawyer. He was picking them up tomorrow, Monday, at 12:30 PM to take them to the Lotto headquarters.

Seamus arrived promptly at 12:30. "Ready to be rich?" he said smiling. They all answered "Yes we are." They were driven to the National Lottery, Abby St. Lower Dublin. As they pulled up, Leanne checked her purse for the fifth time. The ticket was safe and sound. "Relax," Mr. D said "You'll have a heart attack." "I know, I know," Leanne whispered. "I just can't believe this."

The limo driver opened the door and everyone stepped out. The children clung to Rayna. Mr. D and Leanne held hands. Seamus brought up the rear, Talking by phone to a lawyer. They entered the building and were shown into a big room. White leather couches sat facing each other. The coffee table was littered with books and brochures about buying cars and private islands. They were shown a video where Craig Doyle explained the information. You do not have to go public; you will wait a few days for the money and make sure to sign the ticket. Also, you may want a lawyer, he added.   They decided to stay anonymous. Leanne was the owner and the money would be given to her. They didn't want too much attention around Rayna. They hoped to get it by Thursday, when they were set to leave. They were issued a fake check for photo purposes. They took a few pictures and left. The lawyer would contact them tomorrow. Leanne turned to Seamus. "Why?" she asked. "Just the luck of the Irish I guess, Happy Birthday Leanne." The ride back to the hotel was exciting. Everyone had ideas.

The rest of the week was a blur. They bought souvenirs for everyone. It was fun not really worrying about cost. Wednesday the check had not come through as yet. Seamus assured them by the time they landed in the U.S., the money would be in their account. They trusted him and were fine with that. He was riding with them to the airport. They left generous tips for the hotel workers and left the hotel. Seamus went over the plan. "Be matter of fact," he told Rayna. "You have done nothing wrong. If anyone starts questioning you aggressively, take a pinch of this fairy dust," he said. "Sprinkle a tiny bit, they won't see it," he added. "It will work. I will give you all a last sprinkle before you get out. He raised his hand and blew fairy dust in the air. "That should do it," he said. "You'll all feel like a million bucks, or should I say $14 million." Leanne took the fairy dust cylinder and letter tube. She slipped them into her purse. "Thank you so much Seamus, you have been very kind to us. We will not share your secrets." She gave him a big hug. "I know you won't Mrs." Seamus said hugging her back. Mr. D shook his hand. "Thank you for everything, I'll never forget this trip." Rayna was next. She hugged him. "Thank you for all you've done." The twins hugged him tight. "We loved everything, especially getting mom back. Thank you to the moon and back," they added. Seamus smiled, "Thank you all," he said with a little bow. Good bye, God speed.

They had no trouble with the tickets, passports or immigration. Everything went smoothly. Leanne took no chances and wiped a bit of dust on everyone's passports. No problem on either side of the Ocean.

The plane landed safely, late afternoon. They

had decided under the circumstances to hire a limo. As they were waiting for their baggage, the Lawyer sent a text that the money was in their bank. "OMG," Leanne whispered, "we are rich."

The limo was waiting and they excitedly climbed in for the ride home. Rayna breathed a sigh of relief as they pulled away from the curb. "Wow that was intense," she said. "I was so afraid they would stop us." Uncle James was waiting with both dogs as they pulled up to the house. Mr. D tipped the limo driver and everyone got out. Fy ran towards Rayna, it was like those videos where the soldier comes home. He was so excited to see her. Rosie ran to Mr. D; she too was very excited.

They hadn't told anyone that Rayna was found, nor that they had won lotto. Leanne and Mr. D had an appointment with a Lawyer tomorrow. Rayna was the big news now. The dogs took their turns greeting everyone. James helped bring in the luggage. He could not believe they found Rayna. Joey and Joannie laughed excitedly, "See Uncle James, we told you we would find her." James smiled, "You were right. I didn't believe it." The children grabbed their back packs. "Come see our room, Mummy." James watched them pull Rayna in. Turning to his parents he said, "I am shocked, how did you do it?" "Never under-estimate your mother," Mr. D said going into the house, Rosie at his side. He plopped himself down and said "hey what's for supper?" James laughed saying, "Some things never change!"

They sent out for dinner and sat in the living

room. The children insisted on showing Rayna the first two videos. James gave the low down on everyone. Nora couldn't wait to come visit, he told them. Leanne planned a lunch on Friday with her. The kids had picked out a special Irish doll for her. They couldn't wait for her to meet their mom. "James, don't share this yet but something exciting happened in Ireland." "What, more than finding Rayna?" he asked.

"Yes," Leanne said smiling, we won the lotto." "What, you won, how much," he asked. "A lot," answered Leanne. "We're seeing a lawyer tomorrow." "Unbelievable," he murmured cleaning up the dishes.

Chapter 11: Que Sera Sera Estates

It was a whirlwind week. The lawyer sent them to the tax man. They set aside one third for taxes. Saw a financial adviser, and then they had some fun. They bought new cars for James and Rayna. Leanne and Mr. D would upgrade theirs. They were conservative, no car more than $35,000. The family was all getting together on Sunday. Everyone was excited. Leanne had told them to bring a "wish" list. Leanne didn't want the money to cause problems. She and Mr. D had to be careful.

On Saturday morning, a registered letter arrived for Leanne. Turning it over, she first noticed the seal. The seal was a golden foil circle with K. Egobail Enterprises. The second line read Dublin, Ireland. Weird, she thought. Taking out the cover letter she read.

Dear Leanne,

We at K. Egobail Enterprises thought you may be interested in this property. Located near your present home, bordered by conservation land. Thirty acres of land are included. This is a new development with a mixture of private homes. A four-unit condo building is also on the site. Each home is on a one-acre lot. There are two pools, playground and main building with a function hall. One of the pools is indoors. There is a small maintenance building with caretakers. Next to the entrance, is a community garden. There are also chickens and goats housed there.

We here at K. Egobail Enterprises thought your family might be interested in purchasing this property. We have included a map for your viewing. We are offering you this property for $2.2 million dollars. K. Egobail Enterprises will pay all taxes and town fees in return for a small office on site. You may pick the last four house styles. If interested, call the number at the bottom of this letter. We look forward to hearing from you.

Sincerely,

Seamus O Malley
K. Egobail Enterprises
Dublin, Ireland.

P.S:
The property has a private beach on Lake Nico. Large dock and boat house included. Wooded drive from Estate to lake.

If interested in viewing call 555-604-7865.

      The map was folded and Rayna opened it up. The community was called Que Sera Sera Estates. There was a gate to drive through. To the right was the Amenity Building. The homes started just past that. In the middle of the property was a stone walled garden

with benches and a tiny pond. To the left of the gate
were the caretakers building and community farm area.
Six homes were built already. Also, four-unit condo
building with underground parking. Four cleared house
lots were ready to go.

Leanne could not believe it. How wonderful
would it be to have her family all together? The Taxes
would be paid by the company. No one would carry a
mortgage. Leanne handed the letter to Mr. D. He read
it then reread it. Looking up he muttered, "are you
kidding me?" "This would be unbelievable," he added,
"just like a resort." "Do you think the family would
want to?" Leanne asked? "I don't know," he replied,
"but I want to see it. You call the number, I'll get
ready," he said.

Leanne called the number on the letter. A
woman answered, "K. Egobail Enterprises, how may I
help you?" Leanne explained the reason for the call.
Kathleen O'Brien agreed to meet them at 1:30 PM that
afternoon. Leanne wrote down the address and hung
up. She could hardly contain her excitement. Rayna
had taken the kids and Fy for a ride. She did not want
to get the kids hopes up if it wasn't going to happen.
Mr. D wanted to take Rosie, so they got her into the
old Escape. Plugging the address into the phone they
realized the Estate was only three miles away.

The road to the property was very rural. They
passed only two houses, then the tree lined street led to
the property. The property was enclosed by a beautiful
brick wall. There was wrought iron fencing for added
height. The gate was at least 20 feet wide. Large stone

columns flanked each side with huge stone planters filled with greenery. Around each planter were crocuses trying to push through the soil. The right side had a sign which read; Que Sera Sera Estates Est: 2025 on the bottom, K. Egobail Enterprises est:2008. As they pulled up to the gate, it swung open. To the right was a small parking area.

Standing in front of the Amenities building was a woman. She waved and smiled as Leanne climbed out of the car. Rosie jumped down and all three walked to meet Kathleen. Leanne shook her hand and introduced Mr. D and Rose. The property was gorgeous. Leanne could not believe how beautiful it all was. Kathleen showed them everything, starting with the community building. It had an indoor pool, showers and game room. A large function room that could fit 100 people was on the second floor. Best of all there were both stairs and an elevator. They rode up to see the view. The room was wonderful with huge windows looking out over the woods. In the distance, you could see the lake. This was too good to be true, Leanne thought. It did look like a resort. "Who cares for all this," she asked Kathleen. "The company does," Kathleen replied at no cost to you. We have a full maintenance staff. "What does the company get out of it?" Leanne asked? "Good question," Kathleen answered.

"The company uses the far-left corner of the property. There is a paved driveway gated off from the Estates. We have two buildings there with about six workers. The first is training for our main business.

The second is a kennel for dogs. We breed and sell Irish wolf hounds and Glen of Imaal terriers. When we finish here, I'll drive you by."

Though it was the end of winter, spring had sprung. Leanne thought the house she and Mr. D would have was amazing. Exactly what they needed, even a covered walkway to the hall. Each house was perfect for their family. Almost as if they had chosen them. They were built for privacy but included covered front porches for socializing. The beach area was secluded and gated off for safety. They ended the tour with the company buildings. They had a separate entrance and their own parking lot.

Kathleen gave them brochures and order forms. They could keep the furnishings, order new or bring their own. It was all included in the one price. They shook Kathleen's hand and thanked her for her time. Mr. D was totally shocked. "Do you think the kids will want to?" he asked?" "They'd be crazy not to," Leanne answered. They drove back home in silence each lost in thought.

Rayna and the kids were still out when they returned home. Rosie was exhausted and went right to sleep. Leanne spread out all the information on the dining room table. They had a poster size map of the Estate. They took a pencil and "assigned'' the homes.

They, of course, took the cottage. Condos were next. They put their Grandson's in 2 of them. The oldest Grandson in one and the younger one in the adjoining condo. Next they chose the ranch for James. It was a little big, but he (and we) would love the sound proof music room. Next to James, their youngest son and his family. They would fit that house perfectly. Five bedrooms and playrooms on both basement and first floor. Next to them would be Nora, Charlie and their parents in a four bedroom, with finished basement and three baths, perfect. Rayna's house would be next. That way the best friends were next to each other. Lastly was their second oldest daughter and husband's home. A large ranch with a five-car attached garage. Over the garage was a two-room studio. It included a kitchenette and bath. Four more house lots were cleared and landscaped. Each of the homes were decorated beautifully, move in ready, if they wanted.

Kathleen had also offered to rent the three home owners homes. They had three families arriving from Ireland in September. The company would pay $3,000 a month rent. There would be a one-year contract/lease on each. If the Estates didn't work out, those families could move back. If they did work out, they could always sell the existing homes. It all seemed like a win, win Mr. D thought.

Mr. D wanted to take the Grandsons to buy cars. Leanne wanted to get the little Grandchildren new bikes. They would check with the parents first and then let the kids pick them on line. It would be so much fun. They were both giddy.

Everyone arrived at 2 PM on Sunday. It was like Christmas morning; you could feel the excitement. Leanne had moved the brochures and map to the living room. They were on a folding banquet table covered with a sheet and an old easel. She planned it all as she always had done. Her M.O. was always feed them first, then discuss business. She could barely contain her excitement.

Rayna was catching up on some of the videos with the twins. The adults were anxious for the party to start. It was a pizza party, with ice cream and cake for dessert. Leanne was so nervous; she could barely eat. Instead, she held each Grandchild that would let her. That way the parents could eat in peace. Everyone was excited to see Rayna. They had decided to keep to the "official" story. The big talk was on the lotto winning. The adults felt funny making a wish list. Leanne assured them it would be fun. Leanne pulled aside her second daughter and said "Dad wants to buy the boys a car, would that be ok?" "Sure, why not, it's up to you," she said. After the meal, Leanne set the children up with a movie. *The Rescuers*, an old Disney classic, was the pick. Leanne told the adults to get a coffee and sit in the living room.

She felt apprehensive. What if they didn't want to try it.? She wanted to play it "cool", and not let on how happy it would make her.

Twelve adults all talking made quite a racket. Leanne walked to the table in the corner. "I want everyone to listen while I explain, no questions until I finish," she said. We have been offered a wonderful opportunity. I am excited to tell you all about it (so much for keeping her cool).

Leanne started her speech. She explained the offer. She and Mr. D would buy the Estates under a family trust. Each family would own their own home. They could keep the furnishings, order new furniture or take their own. It would be their choice. "Your Dad and I toured the property and loved it. Let me show you a map." With that, she "unveiled" the map with a flourish. She taped it to the easel so everyone could see it. She even had a pointer to show each unit.

Everyone was quiet as she gave her presentation. "Are you kidding me?" James called out. "Nope," replied Leanne. Then, she took the pointer. "This is where we figured each family would live and why. It truly feels like it was made for our family. Leanne handed each family the brochure for the home best suited for them. They all sat with their mouths open, kind of in shock. "How can we afford this?" James asked looking at his brochure? Leanne answered, "You'll only be responsible for heat and electricity. K. Egobail Enterprises will pay the taxes, maintenance, and upkeep. They will even cover the homeowner's insurance." "Why will they do that?" Leanne's youngest son asked. "Well, they have two businesses on the property. I imagine its tax deductible for them. We checked with the Lawyer and he saw no red flags."

"Why don't you guys talk among yourselves. We will sit with the children. Can they have a treat?" Leanne asked. All parents said ok, but be reasonable. Leanne turned to leave; I almost forgot; the company has three families coming from Ireland in September. They would be interested in renting our homes for a year. That would give you a trial year. They have offered to pay $3,000.00 in monthly rent to each of us and they would pay the utilities.

After the movie ended, Leanne, Mr. D, and all the children went to the living room. It wasn't unanimous yet. There were two hold outs. "No worries," Leanne said. "Let's decide not to commit until we all see it on Saturday. Everyone, pack your lunch, bring swimsuits and we'll spend the afternoon there. Kind of like a resort day." "Yes, that sounds great," they all agreed.

"Ok, now what about the wish lists?" Mr. D called out. "I & TY, what do you say we pick you guys out some cars? Up to $25,000.00 and your first year's auto insurance included," Grandfather shouted. "OMG!" they jumped up and hugged Grandfather tightly. "Thank you, thank you," they said, "That is awesome! "Let's check some out on the computer." Grandfather pulled up a local Dealer.

Leanne called the other grandchildren into the room. Let's order some new wheels for you kids too," she called out. The adult parents were still busy talking with each other and looking at the brochures. It was an exhausting but exciting day for everyone. The older three children had school the next day. Their parents started packing things up. They all had plenty to think about as they went home that night. It would be a long week, Leanne thought to herself.

Grandfather made plans with the Grandsons. They were to meet at the Car Dealers on Tuesday. They were very excited and so was he.

Rayna walked the dogs and sent the children to

get ready for bed. She sat down with Mr. D and Leanne. "Thank you so much for including me in your family," she said. Taking her hand, Leanne squeezed it. "We are all family. We love you and the children, don't we, Mr. D?" she said. "That's right, we are family," he replied. Leanne finished with "I hope this works out." "Me too," Rayna added.

The week passed quickly. Mr. D went to look at cars and they chose reasonably. Leanne fielded calls all week from her children. It seemed like they would give it a try. Everyone agreed to meet at the Estates on Saturday.

Saturday morning, April 12th dawned sunny and warm. Everyone agreed to meet at 11 AM. The plan was to tour the compound and then have a picnic.

It was Rayna's birthday. Mr. D and Leanne took their car with Rosie. James and Rayna drove separately. Each family brought their own picnic lunch, although Leanne had enough for all of them. Driving down the road, the sun shone through the trees. The buds were just growing and crocuses bloomed. As they arrived at the gate, butterflies filled the air. Glancing over to Leanne, Mr. D said, "what's this all about?" "Hmmmm, just hatched I guess," Leanne commented. She carried the Fairy Dust cylinder in her bag for luck. Secretly, she wanted credit for not sprinkling it on the brochures. After parking the car, they let Rosie out. They were the first to arrive. Kathleen was there waiting for them.

Shaking their hands Kathleen asked, "Is everyone on board?" "Well," Leanne said, "I hope they will be by the end of today." Kathleen smiled and said, "We had three litters of puppies today." "We'll show them last, to seal the deal," Leanne said laughing. "Mr. D," Kathleen added, "I had maintenance bring out a scooter for you." They sat on a bench chatting while waiting for everyone.

Soon, excited voices filled the air. Both children and adults. The babies were in strollers and the big kids ran on the sidewalk from house to house. Every yard was explored. Each family was thrilled with their assigned house. No one had any complaints. It was a bit of a walk to the kennels. They passed the garden, chicken coop and goat pens. Mr. D was glad to have the use of the scooter. Finally, they were all at the kennels. A worker took three at a time to see the new pups. Three litters, two were Irish Wolf Hounds, and one terrier litter. The pups were curled up with their moms. Smiling to herself, Leanne thought "If this doesn't seal the deal, I don't know what will."

Back at the "clubhouse", they spread out their picnics. Everyone talked excitedly, they sat at picnic tables and enjoyed their lunch. After lunch Leanne and Mr. D watched the children play. The parents had a meeting inside.

A short time later they came out. "We would love to try this," James said as spokesman. "Thanks Mom and Dad for the opportunity. Kathleen stood and said, "that is exciting news. Why don't you take a pad of paper and a pen? Go through your house and decide what you want to keep. Meet back here in an hour and we'll see where we are at. Sound good?" she asked.

Leanne and Mr. D stayed with the children. The kids were safe at the playground. Rocking a baby, Leanne looked at them and whispered, "Just what I had hoped." "No really?" Mr. D said sarcastically.

Everyone was back on time. Each family was excitedly talking to each other. They gathered up their children and said goodbye. "We'll set a date by the weekend," Leanne told everyone.

Leanne and Mr. D put their house on the market the next day. They had an offer by the weekend. Their two daughters decided on the rental plan. After a year they would re-evaluate. Their youngest son and family were renting and gave notice for June 1st. Everyone agreed that would be the big moving weekend. Packing started almost immediately. They all donated a lot of things to charities. They wanted to choose carefully what to take. Leanne even decided to donate all her clothes. She wanted a fresh start with new clothes that fit. Mr. D followed suit. Rayna was helping the children choose what to take. They wanted everything to come with them. They were especially excited that Nora would be next door.

Even the dogs knew something was up. Fy paced from upstairs to down. He followed everyone to the door. Rosie had aged this spring. She would be 18 in the fall. She strategically lay and watched the packing. Sprinkling a little dust from the Fairy cylinder, Leanne hoped it would help. There wasn't much dust left and she wanted to sprinkle a tiny bit at each house. Just for good measure.

Watching the last of the videos of the kids

Rayna packed them up. She had been feeling a little unwell these last two weeks. She had been sick these last three mornings. At first, she chalked it up to all the excitement. This week, she said to herself, if I didn't know better, I would think I was pregnant. Then she started feeling nauseated at dinner. She decided to get a pregnancy test after dinner. CVS had many brands of tests. She couldn't decide which so she chose three different brands. She also picked up deodorant, sunblock and a treat for the kids. Otherwise, they would be bugging her to see what she had. Joannie had already been acting a little strange. Rayna had chalked it up to the move, now she wondered.

When everyone had settled in for the night, she took the tests. She was just as nervous as before. She covered them with a face cloth and set her phone timer. She sat on the closed toilet. Then she picked up her checklist for the move. Mentally, she checked off all the reasons for "not pregnant." First, she hadn't slept with anyone for more than 6 years. Second, she hadn't been with anyone since coming back. Third, you would think she would know if anything happened in the other world.

The phone alarm startled her from her thoughts. Taking the facecloth off she slowly looked down. "OMG," putting her hand over her own mouth she mumbled "How can this be?" There in front of her eyes were three positive pregnancy tests. She looked up and staring back from the mirror was her pale shocked face. It wasn't as scary as the first time. She did have family and would be in a beautiful home soon. Still, she screamed in her mind, "OMG, how is this possible."

Rayna gathered the tests and packaging. She bundled up the trash to take out. As she walked by the children's room, Joannie called out, "Mama, you're having a baby, right?" she whispered.

Rayna quietly went to the bed and knelt down. "What do you mean sweetheart?" she asked. Joannie sat up and looked her mother in the eyes. She softly said, "We were waiting for you to know." From the darkness Joey said, "We knew for a while." Rayna stood up, putting her finger across her lips, "shhhh," she whispered. "It's our secret for now, ok. Let's wait to tell everyone It will be a nice surprise when we move." They both nodded solemnly. "We won't tell." Rayna turned to go, "now go to sleep guys its late," she said. "Mama, one more thing? Joannie whispered. "Yes?" Rayna tuned back, "what is it?" "Mama, there's more than one." "What?" she choked out. "Ya," Joey added, "there is more than one baby growing in your tummy." "More to love," Rayna answered and left the room. "Love you guys, go to sleep," she called back quietly.

Rayna nearly fell on the floor. What, how could they know that? She had heard the stories from Leanne about them "knowing things." She just never thought about it. They were just so little when she left. It was a beautiful night, she decided to take Fy for a walk. She needed to wrap her head around this. Fy, always eager, came running. Walking out the door, Rayna looked at the night sky. There were a million stars in the sky and the moon shown down brightly. Rayna walked to the back of the property. She felt a calmness come over her. This was going to be a good thing she felt. She had family, money and a new home. Life was good. She had only slept with one person since the twins. That was St Patrick's Day, March 17th 2019. That would make this the longest pregnancy in history. Luckily, no one would believe it. Now, she had proof that your body aged slower in the other world. "Luck of the Irish strikes again," she laughed out loud. They turned and started back. She remembered the man's name was Sean and he lived in Dublin. She wasn't sure if she remembered his last name. She laughed again. If he was the one, and he had to be, she would be three months along when they moved to the Estates. Both Rayna and Fy went right to bed.

Rayna decided to concentrate on packing and moving. Everyone now had keys to their new homes. The official move in was still June 1st. Joey and Joannie chose separate rooms for the first time. Rayna took them to pick out bedding and posters. Fy even got a new bed.

Rosie was failing, at 17 years old she slept a lot. Leanne feared the move was going to be too much for her. She had been using the Fairy dust weekly, but it didn't seem to be helping much anymore. Mr. D was beside himself. Leanne took Rose to the vet. After careful examination, the vet shook her head. "There is not much we can do. It's already a miracle that she made it to 17. Why not take her home, see how she does with the move? Any problems bring her back,"

she added. "She will let you know when it's time."
"Wiping the tears from her eyes, Leanne helped Rosie into the car. Mr. D met them at the door. "What did they say?" he asked. "She said it's a matter of time." Rosie made it to her bed and flopped down. She was snoring immediately. Leanne had hoped to let her swim at the new place.

Saturday, May 31st dawned beautiful, warm and sunny. The moving truck was due at 10:00 AM. Even though most of the furniture was being donated, they still needed a truck. James had heavy music equipment. Rayna had the items that had been stored since her disappearance. There was also all the kid's things and books. The truck was loaded until it was full and driven to the new houses. The dogs were loaded into cars and off they went. They were the first three families to move into the new compound.

Leanne and Mr. D pulled in first. Leanne showed the men where to put everything. The Estates seemed to be even more beautiful. Flowers were everywhere. Mature flowering bushes and potted boxes strategically placed. All the houses were moved in by 1 PM. Mr. D tipped the movers, and they settled down for lunch. The three families had lunch at the cottage. Marie had joined James and they stayed to help open boxes. The kids ran and played. There was a gate into the playground and they were able to go back and forth. At 3 pm everyone decided to go to their own homes. Fy and Rosie had been enjoying the warm patio. Fy was reluctant to leave Rosie, he gave her a few extra licks. The kids rode their bikes back home.

Fy turned and gave a final bark to Rosie. James and Marie walked to his house to start setting up the music room. After putting the pizza away Leanne grabbed the leash. She probably didn't need it. "Hey, sir?" she asked Mr. D. "Want to take Rosie for a swim? "Sure, I'll take the scooter if you don't mind," he answered. Leanne put a towel and backpack in the basket. Off they went. The first walk in the new neighborhood.

Rosie walked pretty slow, but so did Leanne. The pathway through the woods to the water was well landscaped. The scooter rode over the path well. In the clearing, there were eight picnic tables, two grills and a fire pit. The water sparkled like diamonds in the sun. Rosie ran to the water's edge, she walked in swimming and lapping up the cool fresh water. She seemed so happy swimming in her circle. Just like when she was a puppy. Leanne took a Frisbee out of her backpack. Turning to Mr. D she asked, "Want to throw her a few for old times?" Getting off the scooter, Mr. D made it to the water's edge. Rosie came jumping up, just like when she was young. She gave her hop; Mr. D threw the Frisbee and she raced in and brought it back. She swam out five times. She was slower, but made it. She quit and lay down in the warm sun. Leanne took out bottles of water for them and they sat looking out over the water.

"Isn't it amazing?" Leanne asked. "I can't wait until everyone is settled in. I really think this will be great for our family." "Mr. D nodded. "So do I. It will be wonderful watching them grow up together." They sat holding hands in silence for a few minutes. "Well, we better get back," Leanne said, grabbing the trash. Turning, she called to Rose, "Rosie come on bubba", time to go." Rosie didn't move. "Come on Rosie," Mr. D called, "time to go Frisbee," he called. Leanne ran over to where Rosie lay, tears stream ed down her face. "I think she's gone," she whispered. Mr. D looked from Leanne to Rose and back. He hobbled over to where Rose lay, she looked so peaceful. He lowered to the ground, gently patting her. He sobbed. Leanne also knelt down. She put her arms around her husband. They cried together. They knelt there for some time.

Suddenly, Leanne felt a light wind. Wiping her eyes on her sleeve, she looked up. All around them were butterflies, moths and looking closely, Fairies. She nudged Mr. D. He to, wiped his eyes and taking a hanky out of his pocket blew his nose. Leanne hobbled to her feet and put her hand out to Mr. D. She passed him his cane and helped him up. All around them were the fluttering of wings. Faster and faster they flew. Suddenly, they parted over Rosie's body. There standing next to Rose was Aine.

Aine, Queen of the Fairies, flew up to them. "We're so sorry for your loss Leanne. I can see how much you loved and cared for your pet. Mr. D, it's nice to meet you. I'm so sorry. Mr. D nodded, he was in shock. We have prepared a resting spot for your pet. Leanne nodded, "OK, show us please." Aine floated about three feet off the ground. It's toward the right, through the woods." She pointed, Leanne saw for the first time, a path going into the woods. "You go," Mr.

D said. "I'll stay with Rosie." Leanne kissed him and pushed the scooter close to Rose. "Sit here a minute, we'll be right back," Leanne said. She followed Aine and the other Fairies into the woods. About 100 feet in, there was a clearing. In the middle, was a huge oak tree. A wooden bench was built around the massive trunk. Someone had varnished the wood; it was smooth as glass. In front of that was a stone circle. The circle was at least 18 ft wide. Daises grew between each stone. In the middle was a ring of colored mushrooms. To the right of the stone circle was another circle. In the middle of that one, was a deep hole. A bench sat just behind the hole. Aine flew to the bench, "Leanne, you can lay Rose to rest here," she said. It will be a wonderful place to visit and remember her. Leanne thought it was perfect. Hopefully Mr. D would too. Now, to get Rosie here. She could call James and Marie, but she didn't want to taint move in day. "Aine, how will I get her here she asked?" "We will help you," Aine said.

Leanne gently lifted Rose onto a towel. Mr. D got on his scooter. "We could put her on my lap," he whispered. Aine flew forward, "We will help," she said. In a matter of minutes, the towel holding Rosie was lifted. Fairies, butterflies and moths swirled around and as if by magic, Rosie seemed to float in the air. It was almost like Rosie was the princess, carried to her final resting place. The Fairies and butterflies hovered over the hole. Gently, they lowered Rosie into the spot. Mr. D was able to walk to the area. He sat on the bench and watched. Leanne had a second towel.

She carefully spread it over the body. She then sat next to Mr. D. There were many winged creatures and Fairies hovering. Each brought a flower dropping it into the grave. They covered the grave completely. Resting against the tree was a shovel. Aine flew over, "do you want to fill it in?" she asked. "Yes, we will do it," Leanne answered. She and Mr. D took turns. "Goodbye old girl, old friend," she whispered. Mr. D cried as he said goodbye. Aine flew to the bench, she too had tears in her eyes. "It's always hard to say good bye," she said "You were all good companions. We will make sure nothing disturbs her. With that, off they flew. Mr. D and Leanne stayed a little longer, lost in their own thoughts. "We better go soon, its getting dark," Leanne said. They made it home without the others seeing them. It was a sad night. The first night with no dog, no kids or grandchildren. They went to bed early and both dreamed of Rosie.

Sunday, the first morning in the new house dawned early. After a restless night, Leanne got up early. Making a pot of coffee, she thought about Rosie as she looked out the window. Coffee ready she brought a muffin and fruit cup out to the front porch. The children were already riding their bikes. They called out, "Hi Nana". Fy came lumbering over to the gate. He whimpered and Leanne opened the gate. He sighed and followed her to the porch. He lay down with a whimper almost as if he knew and missed his old friend. Patting him on the head comforted Leanne. Nora and her family were moving in later that morning. She dreaded telling them. Teddy had been a puppy with Rosie. Just then Joey and Joannie rode by. "Nana," they called, "Mummy is making us bacon and pancakes." At the word bacon, Fy stood, licked Leanne's hand and waited to be let out. With a small bark, he raced after the kids. "See you later," Nana called after them. Leanne went in to make Mr. D his breakfast.

At 2:00 PM, two more moving trucks pulled into the Estates. One stopped at Nora's, the other Leanne's sons house. Leanne and Mr. D watched the activities from the front porch. Rayna had taken all the children to her house. Then they walked up to Nana's. The children clamored with excitement. "Come to the playground Nana, watch us play." "Sure, I'll be right over," Nana said, "can't wait."

Sending a text to all adults, Leanne let them know about Rose. It was not her preferred method, but soon the kids would notice. The text read, "Family, we have sad news. Yesterday, after a swim and Frisbee play, our Rosie passed away. Grandfather and I are very sad, but she did have a long life. We will let you each tell your children. Immediately, there were condolences sent back. Walking into the playground, Leanne locked eyes with Rayna. Rayna mouthed "sorry." The children were so excited "look at me, look at me," they each called. Laughing, Leanne called out, "I am watching everyone." Just what I needed, Leanne said picking up the youngest Grandchild. Just then Grandfather rode up on the scooter." "Can we have a ride," the three oldest asked. He pulled a helmet out of the basket," "whose first?" he asked. The kids had so much fun. Nana sat with the babies, while the others got rides. No one noticed the missing dog.

The last ones to move in were her second daughter and family. They were scheduled for next week. The children all went in for dinner at 5:00 PM. Mr. D and Leanne went in to eat as well. They sat at the table looking out into the yard. "I sure do miss her," Mr. D said. "I would like to put a plaque on the spot, what do you think?" "That's a great idea," Leanne answered, "we could have a memory party. It might be good for the kids and us," she added. "Let's do it on June 21st, the summer solstice," she added.

It was settled, they would have a cookout at the water's edge, then go to the woods to say goodbye.

The rest of the family moved in the following weekend. The Grandsons were thrilled with their condo's. Like an adjoining hotel room, they had the option of separate space or open to share. They had always enjoyed each other's company, this was a win, win for them. After unpacking their things, they came over to Nana's. They sat with Grandfather and Nana and had an ice tea. They knew about Rosie and had stories to share. It really solidified to Nana how great this was. Their Mom and Stepfather were moving in as well. Their Mom couldn't wait to start planting in the community garden.

Mr. D still liked to sleep later than most. Leanne got up at 7am. Enjoying coffee on the front porch, she decided to take a walk. This was a new beginning, she told herself. Standing up, she grabbed a light jacket and started around the neighborhood. She took a left and walked toward the clubhouse. The air was cool, with a promise of heat later. Birds flew from branch to branch in the trees lining the street. As she passed each house, she could hear her family starting their day. She decided to walk to the water before starting home. The path was well landscaped and the walking made easy. From the shore, she spotted her second daughter and husband kayaking. The sun sparkled all around their boats.

A fine mist rose from the water. Their picnic breakfast was sitting on one of the tables. It made Leanne ridiculously happy to see them already enjoying this beautiful place. So as not to intrude, Leanne turned and walked into the forest. The clearing was just up ahead. Magically, flowers were already growing around the Rosie's grave. Leanne sat and thought about Rosie. She would tell Mr. D how beautiful it looked in the morning. She walked back to the water's edge. Just then a mother duck and her 10 babies swam by. The kids will love this, she thought. She turned and started to head back. As she walked towards home, the rest of the families could be heard starting their day. The oldest three Grandchildren would finish up at their schools this week. Then, in September, they would all attend the same school. James was not up yet. He, like his Dad, was a night owl. The condos were next, and it sounded like they were starting their day too. Once home, Leanne enjoyed a second cup of coffee, waving as the kids went off to school.

The parents had decided to tell their own children about Rosie. They collectively decided against a "memory party". On the 21st they decided to have a Summer Solstice Party. They would light wish lanterns and send them over the water. They would cookout and enjoy a bonfire.

It was warming up nicely and Mr. D enjoyed his breakfast on the porch. It was very peaceful. They sat companionably. After a while, Mr. D stood up saying "I think I'll ride over to the maintenance building." They may have something to make Rosie's plaque." "Good," Leanne said, "I'll clean up and walk over and meet you." The scooter was housed in a shed next to the porch. He rode towards the building, as Leanne smiled watching. Already, he was moving around more here, she thought, and it was only the first week.

As she was cleaning the kitchen, she heard the door. "Knock, knock," Rayna called out, "anybody home?" "Come on in," Leanne called out. Coming into the kitchen Rayna, walked to the window, so cute. "Would you like a cup of tea?" Leanne asked. "No thanks, water please. I have something to tell you." Rayna added. Let's sit outside OK?" asked Leanne. They took their waters and went to the patio. They fixed the umbrella and settled down.

"Where is Mr. D?" Rayna asked. Leanne told her about the marker. "That's a nice idea, good for him." "The Estates was such a great idea wasn't it? The kids love having everyone here." "Ok, let's stop avoiding the subject here," Leanne said. "What do you have to tell me?" "You're not going to believe it,"

Rayna said. "Hmmm," Leanne said putting her finger on her chin. "Let me guess, you're pregnant?"

Rayna stood up, "how could you guess that?" she asked. "I've been away almost 7 years and only home 3 months." "Well," Leanne asked, "am I right?" Rayna sat back down. "Unbelievably, yes you are." "Well," Leanne added, "you have looked a little peaked lately." "Well three tests and my psychic children tell me I am," she said. "All I can figure out, is March 17th was my lucky day. Luck of the Irish I guess .... again. I am not even sure of the fathers last name," Rayna continued. "It was over 6 years ago." "Longest pregnancy ever," Leanne giggled. Rayna glared at her, "it's not funny Nana!" "I know honey," Leanne got up putting her arms around her. "We'll help you anyway we can. You know I love babies. Will you see a Doctor this time?" she asked. "Yes, well I wanted to tell you before Joey and Joannie did. They also informed me that there is more than one baby. Again!" Rayna added. Leanne choked on her water. "Seriously?" she asked. "I will go to the appointment with you if you want," Leanne said. Rayna stood up. "I better go let Fy out and make the appointment. I'll text you the time. Let's keep it a secret until it's confirmed," added Rayna. "If it's alright, I'll just tell Mr. D," Leanne said. "Sure, that's fine, he needs some good news," Rayna said.

Arriving at the maintenance building, Leanne found Mr. D in an animated conversation. Turning, he said, "we found the perfect piece of wood." He put it in the basket. "Let's go for a stroll," Leanne said.

Leaving the building, they went left. Not wanting to set a precedent, they decided not to visit anyone. If anyone was out, they waved and called out "good morning "and walked on by. At the path to the beach they decided to go to the water's edge. They took in the beauty of the spot again. The water lapped against the shore. In the distance they could just make out the boats. Leanne took two bottles of water and two bars, out of her backpack. They enjoyed their snacks, quietly lost in their own thoughts. As they finished, Leanne turned to Mr. D. "Guess what?" she asked. Looking up he said, "I don't know, what?". Leanne smiled and said, "Rayna's pregnant."

"What, how?" Mr. D asked. Leanne raised an eyebrow. "You do know how that works, right?" she laughed. "I do remember," he said. "I just haven't seen her with anyone." "It seems her body only aged 3 months, not 6 years." Leanne said. "She was with someone on March 17th 2019." "She's not telling a Doctor that is she? They will commit her!" he added. "Guess what else," Leanne asked. "I have no idea," Mr. D answered. "Should I be afraid to hear it?" "Joey and Joannie say there is more than one baby." "Holy smoke!" Mr. D laughed. "Right up your alley." She asked us to keep it a secret until the Doctor confirms it." Leanne added. "Sounds like a plan," Mr. D said, motioning zipping his lips. "Ready to ride back? I still have unpacking to do." Leanne said.

Later that day, Rayna text the Doctor's appointment. "Tomorrow, their fitting me in at 11AM." Leanne answered back, "I will be ready by 10 AM."

The next morning Leanne was ready and waiting. Mr. D was working on Rosie's plaque. Rayna was prompt and off they went. Rayna chatted nervously as they rode along. "The children all want to go swimming at the pond today. Then, to the swimming pool," she added. "They're cooking up all kinds of summer plans," Leanne added. This really is awesome, they both said. Leanne said, "Even better than I hoped. I and Ty stopped by after work. The middles ride their bikes by and I give them ice pops. The littles are at the playground most every afternoon. It really feels magical," she added. The GPS lady broke the spell. "You have reached your destination," she said.

They entered the Doctors office. Many women in different stages of pregnancy filled each chair. Rayna was given forms to fill out. It wasn't long until she was called. Leanne accompanied Rayna to the room. They nervously waited for the Doctor. A tall, willowy women breezed in to the exam room. "Hello, I'm Doctor Mary Mahoney," she shook Rayna's hand. "Why are you here?" she asked. "Well, I took 3 pregnancy tests and all were positive," Rayna said. "Ok, let's examine you. Please lie down." After the exam Dr. Mary said, "Well your definitely pregnant. According to your dates, I would say your due in December. I would like to do an ultrasound to confirm the date. You can go now, right across the hall." The nurse handed Rayna a second gown. "Use this like a robe, we'll go right there."

Rayna climbed up on the table. The Tech

squirted the cold jelly on her stomach. The Tech moved a wand back and forth, a heartbeat could be heard. Rayna and Leanne stared at the screen listening. Let me get the Doctor she said picking up the phone. Rayna turned towards Leanne. "Do you see what I see?" Leanne just nodded, her eyes on the screen. The Doctor breezed into the room. "Let's see what we have here… All right now, this is pretty exciting," she said. "Brace yourself Rayna. Look here. This is Baby A. Over here is Baby B and this over here? That, is Babies C & D. You are expecting quads…. All the heartbeats sound great."

Rayna's mouth dropped open. She looked up at Leanne. She had paled considerably. The Tech brought over a chair. Rayna smiled and said, "Well, this should be interesting. "Quads!!!" Rayna whispered. "I can't believe this. Joey and Joannie were right. This will be quite the news to share with the family."

Rayna was totally self-absorbed as they walked to the car. "Do you want me to drive?" Leanne asked. "No, No I'm ok," Rayna answered. Let's just sit for a minute." Leanne took two waters and two bars out and they snacked while sitting. It was already around 1pm. Mr. D was on twin duty. He would watch for the twins and keep them at our house until they returned. They finished up and got ready to go, turning towards each other they burst out laughing. "OMG!!! QUADS!!!?" they said in unison.

Leanne giggled, "I won't lie, I am pretty excited. Of course, I don't have to carry them or birth them, so there's that." "I am pretty excited myself, Rayna said.

"I did miss an awful lot of the twin's infant months."

Rayna parked at her house. She let Fy out and packed up the swim gear for the twins. It was too late for the pond, so they went right to the pool. Nora's mom and brother were already there. Leanne's Daughter-in-law showed up with her children. Nora and the twins ran ahead. Leanne begged off after greeting everyone, she wanted the young mothers to bond themselves. They didn't always want a mother or mother -in -law hanging around.

Back at the house, Leanne and Mr. D had an ice-tea on the porch. "Everything go ok?" Mr. D asked when they were alone. "Definitely pregnant!" Leanne said giggling.

They talked about the party for Summer Solstice. They wanted a full day of fun. Everyone was packing a picnic for the beginning of the day. Then dinner was a catered cowboy picnic. Fried chicken, steak, hotdogs and burgers, beans and potato salad. This was to happen around the pool area. Then, at just about 9 PM, they would line the sidewalk with paper lanterns. The lanterns would go into the beach. At water's edge each person would write a message on a lantern. Then, the lanterns would be lit and sent over the water. They were both looking forward to it.

Just then their Grandsons showed up. They had a drink and talked for a bit. They were on their way to their Moms for dinner. They cleaned up and went inside. Mr. D looked over at Rosie's bed. "I sure do miss our girl, don't you honey?" "Yes, I do," Leanne answered. Mr. D put the news on and Leanne made dinner.

Chapter 12: Summer Solstice – June 21st

The day of the Summer Solstice dawned with a brilliant sunrise. The weather was predicted to be perfect. Preparations for the big party had been underway all week. The middles had all finished school on Friday. They looked forward to the easy days of summer.

The adults had voted to have this first party to residents and significant others only, in order to enjoy each other and their family. After this, anyone could entertain however they wanted. They wanted this first celebration to be special.

Leanne took her usual morning walk. Mr. D had finished his plaque. He was quite proud of the finished product. Leanne was happy he had enjoyed working on it. It was a labor of love. As Leanne got to the top of the street, she saw the dog walker. There had been new litters at the beginning of May. The wolf hounds were huge for seven weeks old. The terriers were tiny in comparison. The breeder put all the pups in a fenced in area with their moms. "Good morning," Leanne called out, stopping for a minute to admire the pups. The breeder smiled, "They sure are cute aren't," they she said. "How many pups are here?" Leanne asked. "Well, we have two litters of each breed. I try to get them out each day. Bring the children by anytime. We like to socialize the pups before they are adopted." "Will do," Leanne said smiling at the little balls of fur. "Enjoy your day," she said walking on ahead.

Every home was preparing for the fun day. The Festivities would start at 10 AM. The boat race was first, frog catching for the kids, then a picnic lunch at the beach. The littles needed rest time, the plaque placing was scheduled at 1:30 PM, then nap time. Everyone would go to the outdoor pool area around 4pm. The day progressed as planned. The boat race was won by Leanne's youngest son in the adult division. Nora won in the children' s division. Every child found a frog and released it unharmed. The mother duck even made an appearance at lunch. The day warmed up beautifully. Swimming was enjoyable. The adults mostly stood or sat around watching and chatting. The oldest Grandsons took their girlfriends on a kayak ride. Right before leaving for family rest time, they walked into the clearing. All around Rosie's grave were wildflowers. "Wow, they grew fast," Leanne thought. Mr. D placed the plaque in the center. The Grandchildren each put a 'biscuit' for Rosie, in a pile. As they lay the biscuit down, each said, "you were a good old pup". The adults had a tear in their eye. Each child seemed more matter of fact. Just the way Leanne had hoped. Not too much sadness, but respectful of the circumstance. Fy lay down next to Teddie in solemn tribute. Then everyone took a break.

Leanne and Mr. D both lay down and rested. The caterer was due at 4 PM. "It's kind of great not having to cook," Leanne said, "so relaxing."

At 4 PM, they met at the pool area. The children were raring to go. The littles had slept, the middles had chilled with a movie. Even the parents looked rested. The 2-4 break had been a good idea. The food spread was wonderful. There were many Delicious choices. Leanne called the group to silence. "Everyone, may I have your attention," she called out. Everyone stopped talking.

"I just want to thank everyone for giving this arrangement a chance," she began. This has been such a fun and wonderful day. Seeing everyone laughing, talking and playing together makes it all worth it. We still have a wonderful dinner and evening festivities to enjoy. I hope you left room." Some of the adults groaned. "We also have an announcement to make. Rayna do you want to come up here?" Leanne asked. Rayna smiled, she had decided to share both the pregnancy and the multiple news. She had told the twins earlier; they had kept the secret.

Rayna walked over and stood next to Leanne. She began, "First, I want to thank everyone for making me part of your family. I know you all accepted my children, treating them like your own family while I was not able to be here. I am truly grateful," she added. She looked at James and Marie. "You James, stepped up, when you didn't have to. I am eternally grateful. Marie, you spent many weekends helping with my children, thank you. Thank you both," she continued. "A special thank you to Nora's parents. You welcomed Joey and Joannie into your lives. I, of course, thank Nana and Grandfather for opening their hearts and home and never giving up on me. Now for my big news," Rayna continued. I went to the Doctors yesterday; I am expecting again. "More than one baby, Mommy," Joannie called out. Rayna smiled and said, "Yes, more than one." "How many?" Nora called out. Rayna held up 4 fingers. "Are you kidding us?" called out Mr. D. Leanne and Rayna burst out laughing. "The Quads are due in December," Rayna answered. I guess I'm going to need some help," she said. Everyone was talking excitably. "That's the news," Leanne said, now let's all move towards dinner."

They all filled their plates and for dessert there was a special cake. *Welcome longest day of the year* was written on it. After dinner, the children played. There were relay races, bubbles and just running around. At 8:30 PM, the oldest Grandsons and their girlfriends helped the middles. They lined the walkway with paper lanterns all the way to the water. The families filed down to launch the flying lanterns. Down at the picnic tables everyone used a marker. They wrote a dream or wish on the lantern. Then, when everybody was finished, James and the two oldest Grandsons lit the wick. Each person's lantern floated up into the sky. It was a mesmerizing sight. Twenty lanterns drifted across the lake. The middles started singing, "This little light of mine." Everybody joined in singing. At that moment, the air was full of butterflies, fireflies and moths. They flit from tree to tree. The final lantern flew out over the water and with that the insects seemed to circle around the little group. No one seemed afraid or upset by this, it was mesmerizing. Off into the forest the flying insects went. Rayna, Leanne, Mr. D, and the twins knew it was more than butterflies. The others just thought it was strange. Fy and Teddie never even barked. They led the way out of the forest. As each family reached their home, they said goodbye. The Grandsons had stayed back to take care of the lanterns. The caterers had cleaned up and left the leftovers in the clubhouse kitchen. A perfect ending to a perfect day. Mr. D and Leanne had a cold drink on the front porch before heading off to bed.

Chapter 13: Summer and Fall

The official start to summer was always July 4th. It was no different at the Estates. This year, each family hosted their own party. They had voted to run it like a block party. The kids decorated their bikes for a parade. There was face painting and games. Some families cooked out, some just picnicked.

Every summer Wednesday evening, Leanne offered the parents a break. She watched the children at the playground from 4 to 7 PM. She fed them a picnic dinner and had them ready for bed at pick-up. Mr. D and Leanne enjoyed the time alone with all the littles, middles and even on occasion, the oldest Grandchildren. The oldest would sometimes stop by to rile everyone up, then they would leave when it got crazy. Leanne loved it all.

The summer passed quickly. Each month Rayna grew bigger and bigger. The Doctor was happy with her progress, but some days she was quite tired. In August they found out there were two sacks. Each held two babies. She was having two girls and two boys. Everyone wanted to play the name game. Rayna put her foot down and told Joey and Joannie, she would choose the names. "We'll probably guess them anyway," Joannie said.

In early August a litter of Glenn of Imaal terriers was born. It was a large litter of eight pups. The littlest female had been born with a twisted double paw. This ruined its chances for selling or breeding. Mr. D had taken to stopping at the kennels weekly. He and the middles (Joey, Joannie and Nora) played with the little pups. One night sitting on the front porch Mr. D asked Leanne, "how would you feel about adopting the little runt? I call her Lulu," he said. "Really?" Leanne asked. "You want to start over with another pup? It was so hard when Rosie passed," she added. "I know, I know, but I miss the company," Mr. D said. "Let's think on it," Leanne answered. The next morning, Leanne stopped on her morning walk. Walking into the kennel she called out, "hello, good morning, ok to visit?" "Sure, come on in," the breeder called out. Looking up, she asked "how can I help you?" I came to meet Lulu," Leanne explained. "I wondered when he'd send you," the breeder said smiling. The breeder lifted up the cutest pup. She was tiny, shaggy and her little tongue licked away at Leanne's hand. "Watch out, the breeder said, "you're not going to want to leave her." Leanne had to agree, she was pretty cute. "What's wrong with her?" Leanne asked. "She just has a twisted paw. She still can walk, but not breed or show. They can't leave for another 3 or 4 weeks so think about it." the breeder said." Putting the pup down with its mother, Leanne had a feeling.

That morning when Mr. D was having his breakfast, Leanne brought up her visit to the kennel. Sitting down to drink her ice tea she said, "Well, I stopped by to meet Lulu this morning. I can see why you want the pup," she said with a smile. "I know right?" Mr. D answered. "She is cute," they both said at the same time. "I'm just not sure," Leanne continued. "I always felt Rosie would be our last." They looked over to the playground area. Some of the Grandchildren were playing on the swings. "It's going to be lonely when their all back in school," Mr. D said. "I thought it would be fun to have a pup again."

"Alright," Leanne answered." We'll go over after breakfast and tell the breeder." "Excellent!" Mr. D said happily. He finished his drink and went to get ready. Later that morning, they put their claim in for Lulu. They would bring her home, just as the kids started back to school.

The rest of the summer flew by. Rayna was doing well. Some of the Grandchildren started school. The bus picked them up at the Estate gates. There had been no interaction with Fairies since the night of the Summer Solstice party. Rayna was feeling very vulnerable. The twins were turning 7 soon and she was single, expecting Quads. After the kids got off to school, Rayna stopped at Leanne's.

"What's up honey, you look upset." "Just out of sorts," Rayna answered. "Can I do all this?" she patted her tummy. "We'll help," Leanne answered, "don't worry." Want to take a ride over to the cabin?" asked Rayna, "for old time sake," she added. "Sure, I 'll pack a picnic lunch," Leanne answered. We'll leave at 11:00 PM, OK?" Getting up, Rayna left to let Fy out. As she walked home, she thought about her writing. Her novel was almost finished. She had written about a magical land and the people who lived there. She felt confident that there was no chance of exposing her Fairy friends. Still, maybe a visit to the meadow was warranted. Arriving at the park felt like old times. They had taken Fy and Teddie for the ride. They drove around to the cabin. The currant caretaker was out front. "Can I help you?" he asked looking up. "Would you mind if we parked here?" Rayna asked. He took one look at her belly and said, "Sure, just don't block me in." They let Fy and Teddie out, Leanne grabbed the lunch. Fy and Teddie galloped ahead over the bridge and toward the meadow. The leaves were just starting to turn, the sun warmed them. In the distance they heard the sound of a flute. "Wow, just like last time," they said looking at each other.

They decided to sit on the stone wall. It was already getting hard for Rayna to get down on the ground. She was getting to look like she wouldn't make it three more months. She was already as big as she had been when she delivered the twins.

They sat and ate their sandwiches. The music floated over the meadow; the dogs chased each other frolicking. "Do you think it's the Mabon Ceremony Rayna asked?" "Well, they did say they came every year." Leanne answered. "I never thought to come back, we could drive over if you want," she said. Rayna thought for a minute, then said "it's still hard to get used to, the fact that it's not last year." Leanne smiled and put her hand on Rayna's. They might be some of the same people but it was seven years ago. Won't know if we don't go," she added. They sat in silence watching Fy and Teddie. They were chasing butterflies. Just as they got close, one would sit on their head or tail. Getting up from the wall Rayna walked around the tree. As Leanne came around the tree, there was the Fairy circle ringed in the multicolored mushrooms and in the tree were many butterflies. Just then, Aine appeared in the center of the ring.

"Hello, she said smiling, nice to see you both." Rayna and Leanne smiled back, "nice to see you as well." Aine continued, "we've been watching over you. The family seems happy in your new home." Turning to Rayna she said, "I see new arrivals are expected soon". Rayna nodded her head, "Yes, four new babies." "The twins will be seven soon," Aine continued. "The age of reason. They are destined to do great things for our worlds you know," she said. "What do you mean?" Rayna asked. Aine just smiled, "You will see, she said. "Would you like a blessing for your babies?" Rayna nodded, "Yes, please." Aine flew over to them and with a whistle, she called others. The beat of their wings caused a chill over Rayna. Then, each Fairy smiled and sprinkled a little dust. Lastly Aine handed her the now familiar flask. "Sprinkle a little on your tummy the night of each full moon until their birth," she said. "Thank you," Rayna whispered. Aine smiled and said, "You and your children are very special to our worlds." With that all the butterflies flew away. Rayna turned to Leanne. "What do you think she meant," she asked. "Time will tell," Leanne answered. "We better get back, the children will be home soon," she added.

They called for Teddie and Fy who came bounding across the meadow. Leanne picked up the lunch remnants. "Do you think they know about my book?" Rayna asked. "Could be," Leanne replied, "they always seem to know about everything." They quietly walked towards the cabin and the waiting car. They could still hear the sound of the flute playing.

Mr. D met them when they got back. He had made a nest for Lulu in his scooter basket. Fy and Teddie gave a sniff of approval and off they went. Mr. D took off to meet the bus and show off Lulu.

The three middles shared a birthday month. Nora, Joey and Joannie decided on a joint party. Each invited two friends from school. Add that to their cousins and it was quite a party. Rayna couldn't help noticing that a lot of butterflies were around. That night tucking the children in Joannie started crying.

Mom we can't go to school tomorrow she sobbed. "Honey, honey you're just tired, it will be fine," Rayna said. "No," Joannie said, "bad things are going to happen." Joannie sat up and Rayna sat next to her. "Tell me what you mean," Rayna asked. "A bad person is going to bring a gun," Joannie whispered. Now, Rayna had heard about Joannie's warnings while she was away. She wanted to do the right thing. Do you know who it is?" Rayna asked her. Joannie shook her head. "He is wearing a mask and a long coat. He has a machine gun under the coat and a bag. It's going to be bad mommy," she sobbed. "We need to stop him." "Ok, ok," Rayna said. "Let me call Nora's daddy and see what he thinks." "Rayna left the room and called over to Nora's Dad. She explained the situation and he walked right over. Nora's Dad took this quite seriously. He remembered his own close call. Joannie had saved him that day and he had no doubt something might happen. Sitting on the end of her bed he said, "tell me what you feel Joannie." Joannie reiterated the story. Nora's dad stood up, "let's keep them home tomorrow," he said to Rayna. I will contact the police, just to be safe. Rayna kissed Joey and Joannie good night. "You did good," she said. "Nora's dad will look into it."

The police were skeptical. They thought it was just the imagination of a child. Nora's Dad was able to convince them to plant a dozen plainclothes police in and around the school. Not wanting to alarm parents or students, they quietly sat in wait. The school was locked down at 9:00 AM. At 9:25, a beat-up Chevy Malibu pulled into the parking lot. The driver parked towards the woods at the back of the parking lot. He was wearing camouflage clothing with a cap on his head. He looked around and not seeing the officers, got out of the car. Pulling a bag out of the back seat, he slung a gun over his shoulder. With quiet determination, he purposefully walked toward the front door. All the officers were on alert. They couldn't believe the tip was right. Reaching the front door of the school, the gunman pulled the hat over his face. Only his eyes were visible. He swung the gun up, and pointed it at the door. He managed to get one round off when he was tackled from behind. "Get down," the officer yelled. "Drop the weapon, hands behind your head." They disarmed him and marched him to a cruiser. Thank God, not a single casualty that morning. The crisis was averted. In his pocket was a kill wish list. The last line said KILL MYSELF.

By 10:30 AM, news trucks and parents had swarmed the school. Everyone had heard of the little girl who had foreseen the future and changed it. The Estate had hired security in case her name got out. Joannie was happy they had listened.

That night was the night of the Autumn Equinox. The twins begged to go see it and the "dancing ladies". They had heard about it many times. It was part of their "birth story". They knew the ladies would be in the meadow. Under the circumstances, Leanne and Rayna decided to take them. They felt a little mystery and excitement would heal the horror of the last few days. Nora was allowed to go as well. At 6:30 PM, they drove to the state park. Rayna remembered where the boon dockers had set up camp. They had packed flashlights, snacks and blankets.

They drove to the right of the meadow. Sure enough, there was a camp set up. They got out of the car and walked over. They were greeted cheerfully by a small group of women. The women sat around a large bon fire. There were a few nursing mothers and some children listening to stories. Rayna recognized Maya from before. "I remember you," Maya said smiling, "and these must be your babies, almost grown up." "That's right," Rayna said smiling, they just turned seven, and this is their cousin Nora." The three children all smiled and said hello. "Nice to meet you," Maya said. "What can I do for you?" Maya asked. "Oh nothing," Leanne replied. "The children have heard so many times about their birth. They wanted to meet some of the women who gave them the blessing that night." "Ah yes, it was a special night wasn't it. We are just about to have our first dance. Would you like to join?" All three nodded solemnly. Leanne said, "I think I'll watch.

She was offered a chair next to a nursing mom. The women joined hands, someone started playing the flute. Each child shyly stepped forward. Rayna held Joannie and Nora's hands. Joey held Joannie's other hand. The women began singing to the moon. "Moon sister moon whisper your secrets. Moon sister, moon shine down upon me." They circled around the camp fire, repeating the verse. Then everyone stopped and each person talked about what they wanted to call forth in their lives.

Rayna wished for a happy, healthy family. The twins asked that the babies be well, and Nora hoped her family would stay happy. Everyone had a positive thought. It was a magical night. After the dance, refreshments were passed around. Leanne's group chose apple cider. The fire cast a warm glow over the group. Soon it was time to go. Thanking everyone, their flashlights led the way out. The sleepy children nodded off on the short trip home.

Fall passed quickly for Rayna. She submitted her finished book to a publishing house at the end of October. None too soon she felt. The babies would arrive soon. She was having a much harder time moving around. Now that the book was done, she had time to get baby things in order. The men in the family came to put the cribs together. The women threw a baby shower. It was an exciting time. As instructed, she had sprinkled a little Fairy dust on each full moon. If nothing else it gave her piece of mind.

Chapter 14: Holidays and Babies

Thanksgiving was held at the "clubhouse". Each family invited whomever they wanted. It was totally catered and they just had to give a count on the Monday before. The children decorated each table. Families each brought favorite desserts if they wanted. It was a perfect day. Rayna was treated like a queen. The twins waited on her so she didn't have to move too much. There was music and dancing to round out the night.

Anxiously awaiting the quads arrival, Rayna prepared for Christmas. Just to be safe she had all the gifts bought and wrapped. All the decorations, including the tree, were put up on Thanksgiving weekend. This was her first real Christmas with the kids and she couldn't wait.

On Wednesday, December 4th, while tucking Joannie and Joey into bed, Joannie whispered "the babies are coming". "Yes, pretty soon," Rayna whispered back. "Nope, tonight!" Joannie whispered back. Rayna had no indication of this, but knowing her daughter, she said, "We'll see now go to sleep." Joannie smiled and said, "love you mommy."

At 2:00 AM, Rayna woke with her first labor pain. Her first thought was "why do I ever doubt, Joannie knows." Taking the Fairy dust cylinder, she sprinkled a little on her belly. "Can't hurt," she thought. She lay awake timing the contractions until dawn. At 6 AM, she text Leanne. "Babies on their way," it read. Leanne answered right away, "be there soon". The twins were up, dressed and ready for school when

Leanne knocked. "This is so exciting Nana, we can't wait," they squealed. Mr. D was staying with the children until the bus came. Leanne would drive Rayna to the hospital. Kissing the children goodbye, Rayna got a little teary eyed. Joannie gave her a hug and said, "they're going to be fine Mommy, we'll meet them after school." This calmed Rayna down; she knew her daughter. She had been right every time so far. With a deep breath, Rayna hugged and kissed both children goodbye. "Love you both, see you later," she said. The excitement was felt by everyone. Leanne grabbed the suitcase and off they went.

At 2:30 PM the first infant arrived. The complete birthing process took only 40 minutes. The boys came first weighing in at 6.2 and 6.3 lbs. Then the girls at 5.1 and 5.2. All were healthy, and sent to regular nursery.

Rayna had not totally decided on the names yet. They went to the nursery. Their cribs were labeled Baby A, B, C, and D Stone. By the time the twins arrived, they were named. She decided on James and Sean for the boys and Patricia and Annie for the girls. The twins were so excited to meet their siblings that evening. They were set to go home on Saturday December 7th. Rayna nursed and bottle fed each baby. By Saturday, everyone on the Estates had signed up to help Rayna the first week's home. They even hired a Doula for the night shift. Everything went pretty smoothly. The twins were a big help. School was closed on Friday the 20th for the Holiday break. Rayna was ready for the holidays and so they spent time caring and cuddling the new babies. There were many visitors who came to help. Dinner was brought over each night. Rayna felt so lucky to be part of the family.

On December 22, the first day of winter, the family sat down for dinner. Having fed and changed the babies and put them in their swings, they sat down to eat. Christmas music played in the background. Rayna had just served the entree when the doorbell rang. Standing, she brushed her hair back with her hands. "Who could this be?" she said out loud. Walking to the door, she felt butterflies in her stomach. She looked back at the twins. Joannie had a small smile on her face. "Open it Mama," she said. Just then there was a soft knock. "Coming," Rayna called out. She flipped the porch light on, and opened the door. Standing on the porch was a tall man. He was at least 6 ft. He had a cap on his head and about twenty butterflies were circling. "Hello," he stammered. "My name is Sean Patrick O'Sullivan." "I am looking for Rayna. I met her St Patrick's Day, 2019. He tried to brush away the butterflies. Nervously he said, "I have no idea what's up with these butterflies. They have followed me through the Estates." "I am Rayna," she said. "I can't believe I finally found you," he whispered. Rayna looked up and realized who he was. Standing in front of her was Sean from the St Patrick's night. This was the father to her babies. All at once the color drained from her face. "Who is it?" Joey called out. Rayna snapped out of it and welcomed him in. "Come in and meet the family," she said smiling. Sean stepped through the door. Rayna introduced him to the twins. "This is someone I knew in Ireland children. Say hello."

He stayed long enough to make sure it was really Rayna, his Rayna. "May I come back tomorrow," he asked. I need to check into my apartment." "Sure, I will see you then, Rayna said.

As she closed the front door behind him, she thought, "this is going to get interesting."

Chapter 15: Que Sera Sera
December 2025
Sean Patrick O'Sullivan

Rayna opened the front door. Standing there, again, is the father of her new born quads.

Sean stands quite tall, and with the porch light behind him, looks rather celestial. Rayna stutters, "ah, ah, ah, hello!" Sean looks down at her and says, "I never stopped hoping that I would find you." Rayna steps aside. "Would you like to come in?" she asks. Sean steps in. From the other room, Joannie whispers, "I knew he would come back." Sean follows Rayna to where the children are sitting. Joannie and Joey look up and smile. "Hi," they say. "Hello again," Sean says. He turns to the row of swings. "Who are these little leprechauns?" "They are our babies," Joannie and Joey say at the same time. "All of them?" he says turning toward Rayna. "Yes, they are all mine," she says laughing. "Wow," Sean says, "what are their names?" "They are Sean, James, Patricia and Annie," Rayna said. "Would you like a drink? Tea or coffee? We are kind of on borrowed time, they'll be waking up soon." Coffee would be great," Sean said.

Rayna poured a cup of coffee, and set out some cookies. Carrying the tray, she sent the twins to get ready for bed. "I never stopped hoping I would find you," Sean said again. "When you disappeared, the police questioned me. I had no idea what had happened to you. I looked for you for many months," he added. "Then I took a job with K Egobail Enterprises. I saw your picture in the company newsletter. There was a story about Leanne and the lotto. They mentioned you as the reason she had come to Ireland. The picture was of you all with the check. Then it mentioned the Estates and our facility here. I asked to be transferred here to see for myself if it really was you."

"It's me alright," Rayna said, "and it's a long story." Just then the babies started fussing. "Would you like help feeding them?" Sean asked. "I have plenty of experience." Rayna raised an eyebrow, "hmmm," she said, "I never turn down help these days. I will get the bottles." After two hours, all the babies were fed, changed, burped and tucked into their bassinets for a while. Sean smiled and looked at Rayna. "That was intense!" he chuckled. "You better get out of here before we have to start all over again," she said. "Good point," Sean said. "I do have to unpack. I'm staying at the K Egobail Enterprises apartments for the next 6 months at least. Can I see you again?" he asked. "Yes," Rayna replied. "We do have a lot to discuss." "Great, I will stop by in a few days," Sean said, putting on his coat.

He left, giving Rayna a warm hug. "I'm so happy I found you safe and sound," he whispered. Rayna softly closed the door. Turning, she spied Joannie and Joey sitting on the top step. "Come kiss us good night, Mumma," Joannie whispered. "I will be right there, brush your teeth guys." She checked on the babies and grabbed the monitor.

As she tucked her in, Joannie looked Rayna in the eye. "He's the babies' father, isn't he Mumma?" she whispered. Rayna sighed, "yes honey, but he doesn't know it. He thinks he hasn't been with me for 7 years. The other world is hard to explain to non-believers. We need to take our time. Can you keep it a secret?" Rayna asked. "Yes Mumma, but he will need to know someday." "Let's see how it all works out," Rayna said, kissing her on the head. "Go to sleep now. Love you." Then, she kissed Joey good night. Rayna put her pj's on and went back downstairs. She prepared the bottles for the night and then lay down. What a crazy night, she thought, as she drifted to sleep. What next?

Sean walked slowly to his apartment. It really was her he thought. He had looked everywhere for her and spent lonely nights wondering what could have happened to her.

The days flew by. Feeding and caring for 6 children was a huge job. Christmas morning was delightful. It was like the babies knew it was a special day. Joannie and Joey were delighted with their gifts. They had picked out a small gift for the babies. Breakfast was muffins, fruit and hard-boiled eggs. Christmas dinner was planned at the amenity building. It was a catered meal for the whole family, and any guests they invited. The family had extended the invitation to any workers who were alone this Christmas. That included Sean. He had accepted the invite. Rayna was looking forward to some adult conversation.

Joannie and Joey begged to visit Nora and her family. They were excited to see what Santa had brought their cousins. Nora's mom had given the ok and off they went.   Rayna enjoyed a cup of coffee and a minute to herself. The Quads were all sleeping and she was on borrowed time. She took the coffee and baby monitor upstairs to shower. Rayna still had some weight to lose, but she chose a comfortable long red velvet dress. Not wasting any time, she quickly showered, fixed her hair and put on makeup. Looking in the mirror, she thought she looked pretty good. Hopefully Sean would think so. She had that butterfly feeling in her stomach since his visit. She hoped they would make a connection again. It felt like months to her since their St Patrick's Day. She felt that it was a good sign that he had looked for her. Time will tell she thought.

Just then the babies started to stir. Her plan was to feed and dress them for the dinner out. She threw her robe over her dress, that way, if the babies spit up, she had a chance of staying clean. She grabbed the Christmas outfits and quickly went to start the feed. Two hours later, they were fed and dressed and napping in the quad stroller. The twins were back from Nora's and changed into their party outfits. Everyone looked beautiful. Rayna took pictures before they left the house.

She packed extra bottles, outfits, diapers and the gifts to exchange. They decided to pull the wagon and use the large basket for everything. The stroller pushed right out the side door, down only one small step. The quads were comfy in their fleece lined bundles.

It was a refreshing walk to the amenity building. Every house was decorated, and music could be heard from the party. The night stars sparkled and there was a hint of snow in the air. Joannie and Joey were so excited. They looked forward to the games and seeing everyone. They each were allowed to bring one gift for show and tell. All the children were running around the playground as they walked up. "Mumma can we go play," they asked excitedly? "Yes, but first bring the wagon in," Rayna answered. They pulled the wagon in the handicapped door, then waited for Rayna to push the stroller through. Take your gloves and be careful Rayna called after them. "We will, we will," they yelled back. They were gone in a flash.

The cool air had put the babies to sleep. Rayna pushed them to a corner of the room, close to the door, so they wouldn't overheat. She quickly took off her coat and went to greet the family. With 4 infants, you never knew when time would be up. She first greeted Leanne and Mr. D. "Merry Christmas!" she called. Mr. D had Lulu in his lap. She had a Santa scarf on. "Very cute!" Rayna said laughing. "How was your day?" "Wonderful," Leanne answered. "It is so nice to see everyone. There are drinks, food and sweets over there, if your starving. How are the babies?" "Keeping me busy, that's for sure, I think I will grab something while they sleep. Be right back."

Rayna loaded up her plate and grabbed a diet coke. She brought some treats for the table as well. Eating her snacks, she filled Leanne and Mr. D in on the Sean situation. "I look forward to meeting him," Mr. D said. "Me too!" Leanne added smiling. Lulu barked. Rayna actually got to finish her food before the babies stirred. The big kids were called to come in for the festivities to start. It had been a genius idea to have them running and playing outside. To children, nothing is as exciting as being outside in the dark on swings. Their cheeks were rosy and they were all mellowed out. A huge ham, turkey and roast beef dinner was being served in the dining room. First, each child was able to show and tell what gift they had brought. Then, there was a story and sing along. The quads were waking up so Rayna opened their blankets and rolled them into the dining room.

The tables were set up like a wedding, seating for 10 at each table. The parents had decided to let the cousins sit together at child size tables. They were behind the parents with some child friendly foods offered in addition to the main meals. There was a separate table for the Egobail workers. Sean had not arrived yet. Rayna felt like a teenager waiting for her crush to show up. She had warmed the babies' bottles and propped them so all could eat at once. It was unrealistic to think they would not have propped bottles. She did pick each one up to burp and they all could see her. Just as she finished burping the fourth baby, Rayna felt the hair on her arms raise. She turned around and there was Sean.

He was talking to a co-worker and sat nearby. The food was delicious, and there was plenty of it. It was a Christmas miracle because the babies were content and she was able to actually enjoy her meal.

The party activities were in full swing. Karaoke was first. Each family sang a Christmas song, then they opened it to any songs. Mr. D was convinced to sing House of the Rising Son with his two sons. Rayna thought they were pretty good.   James and Marie sang a duet about star crossed lovers, then the cousins all sang a couple of silly Christmas songs.

Everyone was enjoying the night. The two oldest Grandsons and their dates started to play some dancing music. The dance floor was packed. The quads needed changing, so Rayna pushed them out to the hallway for a little privacy. Bending over the second baby, Rayna heard a voice behind her.

"Need some help?" he asked. Rayna straightened up and turned. Sean was smiling, that smile she remembered. "Why yes, I could use some help," she said smiling. "I am at your service, what can I do?" Sean said. "Well first, throw these away," Rayna said, handing him the dirty diapers. "Then ask the kitchen to put these bottles in the crock pot." "Done and done," Sean answered. Off he went.

Rayna waited in the hallway for Sean to return. They entered the dining room together. All the dinner dishes were cleared and desserts, coffee and hot chocolate laid out for everyone. "I would like to introduce you to Leanne and Mr. D," Rayna said. "Let's sit back over there." The babies were quite content. The music and low lighting seemed to mesmerize them. Rayna introduced Sean as someone she met and dated in Dublin. He shook everyone's hand and asked if he could get coffee and dessert for anyone. Mr. D asked for some and Rayna and Sean went to fetch dessert for the table.

"They seem nice," Sean said. "They have truly saved my life," answered Rayna. "I don't know what I would have done without them." "This has been a wonderful Christmas," Sean answered. "Thank you so much for inviting us. It can be lonely at Holiday times without family close by." "Yes," Rayna answered, "holidays are special when family is near."

They chose a little of everything and carried cups of coffee over as well. The karaoke was a huge hit again and the children were getting tired. Rayna called out for Joannie and Joey. "Have your dessert and wrap it up," she said. We will be leaving at 10 PM." The twins knew better than to argue. It had been a long day, they were tired. Just then the babies started fussing to be fed. Leanne went and got the bottles. Each adult, Mr. D, Sean, Leanne and Rayna, gathered a baby up and started to feed them. Rayna smiled as

Nora's Mom snapped some pictures. It was quite a night. She felt so blessed. As usual the "Irish Goodbye" took a good hour. It was closer to eleven when they actually walked out the door. Sean had offered to walk them home. Rayna was glad for the company. The twins walked ahead pulling the wagon with gifts and treats inside it. They pushed it right inside and Rayna pushed the stroller in as well. The babies were sleeping, Rayna loosened their blankets. The twins went right upstairs after hugging Sean goodbye. Joannie whispered in his ear, "I always knew you would find us. I am glad you did." She gave him a hug and ran upstairs. Sean turned to Rayna, "she's a funny little thing". "She surely is, she knows things I don't," Rayna said smiling. "Well, I better let you get them tucked in before the next feed," Sean said. Can we see each other again Rayna?" he asked. "I would truly love that," Rayna answered. "Why don't I bring dinner Thursday, any requests?" Sean asked. "Anything I don't have to cook is good with me," Rayna said laughing. "Good, see you at 6 PM. Sean hugged Rayna good night. "Thanks for a wonderful Christmas," he whispered.

Closing the door softly, Sean took a deep breath. The air was crisp and there were a million stars in the sky. He couldn't remember a time he felt so happy. Seeing Rayna and her children just felt so right. As he walked the long way around the neighborhood, each home shone warmly into the night. As he walked up to the beach entrance, he noticed all the moths. They were sitting in the trees on each side of the path. "That's weird," he thought, doesn't seem warm enough for moths. He walked on to the apartment thinking of Rayna.

Leanne arrived at 10 AM to help Rayna feed and bathe the babies. She brought a French toast casserole, fruit bowl and sandwiches for lunch. The twins ran to greet her. "Nana, come see what we got for Christmas." Leanne went into the living room. Joannie and Joey showed her all their toys. "Wow, what lucky children," Leanne said, "everything looks so fun."

Just then Nora showed up to play. "Everyone, have some breakfast first," Leanne said. They sat at the table and Leanne served some French toast, fruit and chocolate milk. Even Rayna had some. Just as they finished the babies started calling for their bottles. Rayna and Leanne started with the boys and then the girls. The older children went out to play, it was cold, but not wet. They wanted to see what the other cousins got for Christmas.

Bath time for the babies took almost two hours. Rayna ran to take a quick shower while Leanne held down the fort. Leanne loaded the dishwasher, started a laundry and folded the clean clothes. Each child had a hamper and basket. That made it easier to sort. Thirty minutes later, Rayna appeared fresh faced and clean. "Thank you so much Nana, I really enjoyed that," she said. LeAnne poured them a cup of coffee, put Christmas cookies, napkins and the fruit on the table.

"Ok, spill it," Leanne said. "What?" Rayna said laughing. "I don't know what you're talking about." "I want to know all about Sean," Leanne said. "He is the father, right?" Leanne asked. "Well, he is the only person I have slept with since the twins' father. How am I going to convince him that a night 7 years ago produced quadruplet babies?" "Time will tell." Leanne added, "he seemed pretty smitten with you." "I felt it too," Rayna added. "He is genuinely nice. He's bringing dinner Thursday and he was a big help with the babies. Joannie did freak him out a little. She told him she knew he would find us." "She does have a way with words," Leanne said laughing.

Just then the babies started waking up. They popped the bottles in the crock pot and started changing them. They lay the four infants on the floor. They talked and played with them. Leanne sat on the couch while Rayna sat on the floor. Already they were showing their distinct personalities. It was amazing to watch them interact with each other.

Nora's mom texted to ask if the twins could stay for lunch. They were having pizza delivered for all the cousins. Rayna texted back, asking that they come home by 6 PM. Nora's mom agreed. Leanne took a sandwich out for Rayna and put the rest away for dinner. "Now you don't have to worry about dinner," she said.

They started feeding the littles, talking all the while. After feeding, changing and getting them to sleep, Leanne brought the laundry up to the bedrooms. She switched the loads and fixed the couch for Rayna to nap. "Sleep when you can Rayna you never know what's next," Leanne added. Call if you need anything." Closing the door softly, Leanne walked home to get lunch for MR. D.

Thursday arrived with a snow storm expected. The forecast was for it to start after rush hour and continue into the night. The expected snowfall was 6 to 12 inches. Sean had texted early that he was still bringing dinner. At exactly 6 pm he arrived with a large box. The smell wafting out was mouthwatering. Sean put the box down then went back out for a second box.

The babies were content and the twins had set the table. Sean first took a beautiful bouquet of roses out of the box. They were already in a large vase. "For mom," he said smiling. Then came a small box of chocolates each for Joannie and Joey. "These are for later," he said, handing them to each child. Next a salad, bread, and a large container of spaghetti and meatballs, Lasagna and Chicken Marsala. Last came an ice cream cake in a freezer bag. This, he handed to Joey. "Please put this in the freezer for later," he asked. "This is a lot of food," Rayna said, eyeing the platters. "Leftovers are good, right?" "They sure are," Rayna said laughing. "Well," Sean said, "I figured you could use a few meals. You are a busy woman." "Yes," Rayna said, "kind of like the woman who lived in the shoe. Let's eat, I am starving," Rayna added.

They all sat down and dug into the delicious food. The quads gave them a good hour to enjoy the meal. The twins had lots of questions for Sean. They wanted to know all about his childhood and family. Finally, Rayna told them to stop asking so many questions. "It's alright," Sean said, "I don't mind. "Can we watch some tv and have our ice cream cake," the twins asked. "Sure, clean your dishes first and not too loud. Let's let the babies sleep a little longer," Rayna added.

Sean started cleaning up. "Let me help. We'll have a cup of coffee with our dessert before we feed the babies." "Thank you so much. It's nice to have an adult here for dinner, especially when he brought the dinner," she laughed. Sean went back to the box and pulled out one last container. "Cheesecake with fresh strawberries madam?" he said, putting it down on the table. "Oh, how decadent!" Rayna said. They loaded the dishwasher, popped the bottles in the crock pot, and carried their coffee back to the table.

"That was so nice of you Sean. Why, after so long do you still care? We really only knew each other such a short time." "I really can't explain it," Sean said. "I haven't been with anyone since that night. I looked for you for a long time. I went back to the school and talked to your roommate. It was like you just vanished. When I saw your picture in the newsletter, I couldn't believe my eyes. I had to see for myself if you were really the girl I remembered." "Am I?" Rayna asked. "Yes, and more, I love everything about you. I love your children, your family, and mostly, I want to really get to know you."

Then the babies woke up and the night was full of feedings, diapers, and rocking of beautiful little children. They made quite a team. Sean seemed to really enjoy the time spent. The twins came running in excited. "It's snowing!" they squealed. They ran to the window, pulling the curtain aside. The snow was coming down hard. The ground was already covered and visibility was poor. "Well, I guess I better get back to the apartment," Sean said. "Will you be alright here alone?" he said turning to Rayna. "Well I'm hardly alone," Rayna said laughing. "You know what I mean," Sean said. "I do." Rayna answered "Just messing with you. We have a generator, flashlights and lanterns in every room. We'll be fine. Are you prepared at your place?" "Yes, I think so," Sean answered. He bundled up and gave everyone a hug goodbye. Rayna walked him outside. On the porch, he turned to her. "May I kiss you he asked? "Yes," Rayna whispered back; I have wanted to all night."

He took her in his arms and slowly kissed her. It was just as she remembered. It felt so right. Just then he chuckled. "Hmmm, someone is watching us." Rayna turned just in time to see the curtain drop. From the other side of the door they heard giggling and then the sound of little feet running up the stairs. "May I bring dinner back on Saturday? You better go get those monkeys in bed, maybe you'll have a minute to yourself," he added. "Thanks for everything," Rayna said hugging him. "I look forward to Saturday." Closing the door softly, she leaned against it for a minute. Maybe this could work she thought. She started up the stairs to get the twins tucked in.

The snow continued for the rest of the night. Waking up Friday morning, it was a winter wonderland outside. The weather station had been predicting at least a foot of snow. The consensus was that there was at least a foot already on the ground. It continued to fall at two inches an hour. Joannie and Joey were thrilled. They couldn't wait to get out to play. Rayna was worried that if it continued, they would run out of formula before she could get out or order more. She turned the tv on to the news and kept it on. The twins were allowed to get ready to go out to play.

The grounds keepers had so far kept up with the storm. The street and driveways were kept plowed. Nora had called to have the twins come to play. The cousins all wanted to make a fort and everyone was home so the uncles were going to help them. Even the two oldest cousins were still around so they were joining in the fun. They were barely gone a minute when there was a knock at the door.

Opening the door Rayna laughed out loud. There stood Sean covered from head to toe in snow.

"What happened to you?" Rayna asked. "The kids got me with their snowballs," Sean answered. "I was not prepared," he said smiling. "I thought I might try getting to the store," Sean said, do you need anything?" Rayna handed him her list off the fridge. "Really, the only important thing is the formula," Rayna said handing the paper over with a $100-dollar bill. "Would you stop at Leanne's as well?" she asked. "Sure, no problem. I will be back as soon as I can." Sean answered. "Thank you, be safe," Rayna said smiling as she closed the door.

Rayna felt so lucky to have Sean in her life. She had a good feeling about this relationship. Leaning against the closed door she wondered if the time was coming to tell Sean her story. Grabbing the baby monitor, she ran to take a quick shower. She wanted to shower and apply some makeup before Sean came back. The twins were with other adults and the babies were down for at least an hour. Rayna dreamily ran upstairs to look presentable for Sean's return.

She had the quick shower down pat. In less than 45 minutes, she was clean, dry and put on a little makeup. The "yoga" pants and a long sleeve t shirt were her everyday uniform. With 4 littles, comfort came first. There was a lot of time spent bending and sitting on the floor. Just as she swept her hair up in a pony tail, the first little cries came over the monitor. "Times up," she laughed out loud. She called out to the babies and hurried down to attend to them.

The next 2 hours flew by with singing, rocking, feeding and playing. Uncle M was cooking out hot dogs for all the cousins for lunch. He and the oldest cousins had a bon fire and they were feeding the children under the covered pavilion. They were set to come home at 2 PM. The weather station said this could continue for another day or more. Rayna was glad Sean had gone out. None of them would starve, there were plenty of provisions, but it was good to stock up on the extra formula. She would make a note of the fact that the weather station was predicting a snowy winter.

Sean arrived back just as Joannie and Joey were stripping off their snow clothes. Everyone shook off. Rayna hung all the coats and wet things on coat hooks. Sean helped put the store items away. The babies were cooing in their swings and the twins ran up to get comfy dry clothes on. Rayna put a pot of coffee on for Sean and herself. Sean pulled out a large bag filled with containers. "I thought you might like a prepared meal just in case," he said. "Wonderful, I was just going to do soup and grilled cheese for us, that's great," Rayna answered. "The roads aren't great and the weather stations are predicting another storm so I thought it would be used," Sean replied. "Stay for dinner and a movie if you like," Rayna replied. "Though the babies make it hard to see anything in its entirety." "I would love to," Sean replied.

The babies cooperated and the twins, Sean and Rayna, enjoyed the movie. Just as it ended, the babies started asking for their bottles. Sean offered his help and Joannie and Joey ran to get ready for bed. An hour later everyone was tucked in. Sean had read the twins a bedtime story, and the quads were all asleep. Rayna picked up the living room and put on a pot for hot chocolate.

Sean entered the kitchen and put his arms around her. Kissing her neck, he whispered, "I am really falling for you." She turned around and put her arms around his neck. Kissing him, she replied," "first we need to talk". "Would you like hot chocolate or something stronger?" she asked. "I feel like I should say stronger, but I really want cookies and marshmallows, he said. "Hot chocolate it is," Rayna said laughing. "You can always have a drink later; you might need it." Sean watched her intently as she served the snack. "You really are beautiful," he said smiling. "I feel like I've known you for years," he said.

Rayna sat down across from him. "Before we go any further, I need to tell you about myself and how I ended here. Can you listen and not jump to conclusions until I finish?" Sean took a big bite of his cookie, then a sip of hot chocolate. "Sure, I can listen, but no matter what you say, I am not going anywhere. I am falling in love with you and your children". "We will see," Rayna said. "Ok, bear with me, I will start at the beginning."

Rayna took a deep breath. She told him a quick synopsis of the time before the twins. The meeting of their father and finding out she was pregnant. Then, she started the story of meeting Leanne and having the twins in the caretaker cabin. Sean interrupted her. "I know a little about that, remember you told me you had babies when we met." "Right," Rayna continued, "but I left a lot out." "I am not going to judge you or anything," Sean started to say. Rayna interrupted, "Sean, you need to just listen, then when I finish, we'll talk. OK?" "Right, right," he answered.

"Sean, do you believe in magic or other worlds?" Rayna asked. "Well I don't, "NOT" believe and I do have an open mind. I am Irish after all." Rayna laughed. "True, true, there is that. Ok, well, after Leanne and I started meeting, we noticed a strange phenomenon. We started to see a lot of moths. First, it was weird. We thought it was a warm night or just something in the forest. Then, it felt like they were following us. Lighting the way or attracted to us for some reason. One night, I dreamed of a fairy circle. It was a ring of colored mushrooms and there were moths flying around it. Only, on closer inspection, they were actually small creatures. The Fairy who spoke to me called herself Aine, Queen of the Fairies. She told me that I was special and all my children would be too. Now, at that time I thought there was only one baby, so it didn't make sense. The next day I went about the day as usual. Leanne and I went to the tree in the meadow. The mushroom circle was behind the tree. We checked it out and there were tons of butterflies in the tree. Then I remembered the legend or story about how mortals can see them. You take a marigold flower and mix it with water. Next, you spread it around your eyes. Then, you sit under a full moon in a grove of ash, oak and thorn trees. Fairies will appear the legend claims. So, we did it and the fairies did show themselves. The twins were a surprise and the birth went well. When I decided to leave the children, it would only have been for 6 months. I had planned on coming back with a degree and chance to support my children. Just before leaving, Aine came to me with a request. She asked me to deliver a message to the King of the Fairies, King Egobail. That was where I went after our night together."

Taking a big breath Rayna continued. "Now, this is the hard part, Sean. Somehow, I fell into the other world. I was stuck in there for 7 years. In their world, time passes differently than ours." Sean looked confused. "What do you mean?" he asked. "Well, one day in their world is 7 years in ours. So, I fell into that world on March 20th at the Hill of Tara right after our St Patrick's Day celebration. This past March my family saved me. To me and my body, it was only day later. To all of you it was 7 years. So, I missed the twins first 6 years, but, if I had spent just one day more there, they would have been 14 years old, so I feel lucky."

Sean's face had paled. He looked Rayna straight in the eyes. "What are you telling me Rayna?" "Well," Rayna stammered, "I have only been with two men in my life. The father of Joey and Joannie and the father of the quads." Sean stood up, pushing his chair back. "Are you telling me those babies are mine?" Rayna stood up as well. Sean was as pale as a ghost. She walked toward him and taking his hands in hers she looked into his eyes. "Sean, they are your biological children, I won't deny it." With that, Sean turned and walked away. "I need some time to digest this." Grabbing his coat, he quietly left the house.

Rayna cleared off the table, popped the bottles in the crock pot and got ready for the next feed. She really didn't blame Sean, that was a lot to take in. At midnight, all the infants had been rocked, fed, changed and tucked in for the night. Wearily, Rayna climbed the stairs slipped into her nightgown and lay down. Sleep did not come quickly. Her mind was racing. What would Sean do, was her last thought before falling into a restless sleep.

Sean walked briskly around the Estates. How could this be, he thought. How could she be pregnant for all those years? How could the babies be his? Why should he believe her? Is she crazy? In his heart he did believe her, just holding those babies he felt a connection. He truly had loved her all this time. He wanted to be the father. How could he make it right? He would go back to Ireland and talk to his parents. They would know what to do. He went to the apartment and made his plan.

Chapter 16: January 2026

A full week went by. The twins had gone back to school. The days melted into each other. Leanne came by every morning to help Rayna start the babies' day. They rocked and dressed and fed the Quads. Each baby was developing their own personality. Mr. D brought Lulu by to play with Fy. The babies were now 6 weeks old. Rayna had not heard a word from Sean since telling him he was a father. Leanne tried to reassure her he just needed time. It was a lot to take in. One thing to be a father, another thing to be a father of Quads, supposedly conceived 7 years ago. Leanne added, "It is pretty unbelievable, you know?" "I know, I know," Rayna replied. "I really miss him though." "Give him a little more time, he'll come around, I bet," Leanne said. They finished up the morning routine. Leanne helped put them down for a nap and went home to make lunch for Mr. D. Rayna took a quick shower, planning what she would say to Sean if he came back. The days did pass quickly in a blur of children. Luckily, there was still a freezer full of dinners the family had sent over.

On Monday of the next week, Rayna received a text from Sean. It read, *Coming back from Ireland. Would like to see you Friday this week. Will bring dinner for the twins and us if you'll let me. I am sorry for my absence, will explain.*

Rayna's heart leapt. She really wasn't sure she would ever hear from him again. Not wanting to seem too eager, she texted back. OK see you then. Then, she got on with her day.

Tuesday, the children got off to school. Leanne showed up as usual to help. Noticing her subdued demeanor, Leanne offered Rayna an afternoon out. "Honey," she said, "you look like you need a break." Rayna smiled through tears. "No, I'm ok," she sniffled. "Really, could have fooled me," Leanne said hugging Rayna. "Really, Mr. D and I can hold down the fort. I would love to spend some alone time with these munchkins," Leanne added, leaning over to tickle little Jimmy. The girls were already wrapped up and falling asleep, music playing in the background. Little Sean was snuggled in Rayna's arms finishing his bottle. Leanne finished changing Jimmy, swaddled him and lay him down. "Here, I'll call Mr. D, he will be over soon, you grab your keys and go," Leanne said.

Rayna felt bad, but she really did need a few hours away. She was so torn about Sean. What would he say on Friday? It was driving her crazy and the children took up so much of her time. A complete thought was hard to follow, while dealing with six children. She wouldn't change it, but a few hours sounded decadent. Leanne actually looked excited at the prospect of caring for them. Just then Mr. D showed up. He carried a large bag of food. "Brought what you asked for Leanne," he whispered. "Awesome," Leanne said. Turning to Rayna, "chop chop! off you go. I will make spaghetti for dinner. Be home by 6:00 PM." Rayna kissed them both and taking her keys left closing the door softly.

She hadn't even known how much she needed this. Sitting in the car, she had no clue where to go. How lame can I be, she said to herself. Just drive. Coffee she thought. I will start there. The drive out of the Estates felt exhilarating. The sun shone brilliantly on the snow. The plows had done a great job and driving was a breeze. The temperature was forecast to hit almost 50 degrees. A great day for a ride. What was it about New England and ice coffee? Rayna took a long sip. It was absolutely ridiculous how free she felt. I guess I needed this more than I thought.

On a whim, Rayna decided to drive through the State Park. She knew they would have plowed at least to the cabin. As she drove through the park, the beauty still took her breath away. The cabin was closed up for the winter. The driveway had been plowed, so she left her coffee and decided to walk through the meadow.

The memories of the twin's birth came flooding into her thoughts. The beauty and thrill of becoming a mom was so ingrained in her. The Quads birth was beautiful, but not quite the same. She would never forget the kindness of Leanne and her family had shone her. It almost made up for missing her Foster parents, not to mention the pain of never knowing her birth parents. Even now, she wondered if she would ever know why. Shaking her head, she said out loud, "don't ruin the day Rayna, it is what it is."

At that, she looked up and noticed all the butterflies following and leading her. Confident that she was alone, she called out. "Hello Queen Aine and friends, hope your well." She crossed the bridge and walked through the meadow. The sun had melted a lot of the snow, so it was easy walking. Making it to the tree, she brushed a little snow off the rock wall. Sitting down, she took in a cool breath. Many insects lit on the branches of the tree. Listening carefully, she heard music wafting on the wind. Turning back to the tree, Queen Aine appeared next to her. "Rayna, how nice to see you," she said. Aine continued, "you look well, how are the babies and twins?" "Everyone is great," Rayna answered. "They keep me busy, that's for sure. How is the Fairy world these days?" Rayna asked. Queen Aine looked up at Rayna. "There is trouble brewing and you and your children are just who we need," Rayna asked, "why us?" "I'll tell you Rayna," whispered Queen Aine. First, a little magic to warm us," and, with a snap of her tiny fingers, the air was full of fairies and fairy dust. Rayna's mouth dropped open. After her trip through the tree in Ireland, nothing, she thought would surprise her. This however was surprising.

Chapter 17: Rayna's Birth Story

"I need you to listen without interruption," Aine began. Rayna nodded, looking around she took note of the clearing. They no longer seemed to be under the tree. There was a tent erected around them. Rounded frame with a tall pole in the center. A warm fire burned in the middle, and they sat on comfortable chairs.

Glancing to her left Rayna saw Aine was no longer tiny. She appeared to be human size, just short. Trying not to panic, she took a deep breath. "Here," Aine said, handing her a mug. Lifting the mug close to her face, Rayna sniffed it. "Don't worry," Aine chuckled. "It's not going to hurt you. Rayna took a small sip. "Mmmm, delicious," she said, swallowing half. "Are you ready to hear the story of your birth Rayna?" "Yes," Rayna smiled, "I have been ready for my whole life," she whispered.

Queen Aine started her story. "As you know Rayna, time is different in the other world. According to Einstein's principle of general relativity, time is relative, which is to say, that it varies based on situational circumstances. Einstein's work showed that time varies based on velocity, energy and mass or gravity. As you found out, this world is different than the other."

"Many years ago, all of us lived on your earth. Fairy folk and the magical beings stayed mostly in the woods, mountains and away from the humans. As humans evolved, they became distrustful of magic and the spiritual beings. Many of our kind were killed or taken from our families. Fairies and the magical beings, elves and trolls, banded together in an Alliance. They chose to make their homes underground and even underwater when able. All the things Einstein theorized, were proved to be true. Time was different. Our worlds grew apart. Though we could pass to and from each other's worlds, there were consequences. Fairies were often not strong enough for childbirth. Often, pregnancies didn't last until birth. Often, when they did last, the child would be born deformed or stunted. Many didn't live at all."

"Some in our world, decided to steal or ''borrow" humans. They would entice new mothers and midwives, who were then forced to be servants to Queens, and tend to Fairy children. Then there were the human men. Handsome, young men were said to be at risk of capture. They were taken to become lovers of the female fairies. One theory was humans were thought to be a stronger healthier race. They tried to enhance their bloodline by breeding with humans. Not all Fairy clans encouraged this practice, but some went even further.

Aine looked at Rayna. "Are you following me so far Dear?" Nodding her head, Rayna said, "I think so, but what has this to do with me Aine?" "I am getting there, you will see. Have you ever heard of a changeling Rayna?" asked Aine. "Well, a changeling is a child believed to be secretly substituted by Fairies, for a parent's real child in infancy. The faerie folk spirit the human baby away to live in the Faerie Realm. They leave a sickly baby in its place. Now, many of us do not condone such a practice. If found out, the Council will force the Fairy to leave their borrow or home, and give the baby back, although to be successful, specific spells and rituals need to be performed. Because of these indiscretions, our bloodlines are mixed. Between the men for breeding and the stolen babies, many Fairies have human blood. Along with that, there is a movement to join our worlds again."

"When you returned from Ireland, Leanne delivered a letter from my father, King Egobail. The letter read that I was to tell you of your heritage, that you were to be told of your family's part in saving our worlds."

"Rayna was confused. "What do you mean, my family's part? I don't even know who my Parents were. You know I was a foster child. I am just a single mom with six children."

"You Rayna, are the Granddaughter of my twin sister Maeve. We were inseparable. We grew up in the Fairy realm where you fell in at the Hill of Tara. "Are you kidding me Aine?" Queen Aine smiled. A radiant smile. "Oh, I have waited so long to tell you. I have watched over you your whole life. I would fly and sit in the tree outside your window. I followed you to school and college and always kept tabs on you."

"Your Mom's name was Merena, and your Father's name was Derek. Your Father was a human, who also fell into our realm at the Hill of Tara. "It must be a family thing," Rayna said with a nervous giggle. "Well, it was love at first sight. Your mom stumbled across him. He was sitting, rubbing his head and looking around in disbelief. She helped him and being young and full of romantic thoughts, decided to hide him. She didn't want the older Fairies to see him. He was very handsome. They would want him for themselves. Every night, she would bring him food and take him on adventures. She told him he couldn't go back to his world. She was young and it was a game. Soon, they were in love and one thing led to another, she was expecting you. When the adults found out, she was in a lot of trouble."

"My sister Maeve was very angry and threatened to send him away alone. As you know, many human years had passed in the time they had been courting. He loved her, and wanted her to marry him. The King was furious. Maeve and I had been told many times. If a human fell into out realm, we were to send him back or at the least bring him to father. Merena had been taught the same. She was lucky that the King was her Grandfather."

"He decided to send them to America. Merena and Derek were given the choice to live in our realm in Ireland, or relocate to America and live in the human world. Maeve was devastated when Merena chose America. Derek missed his family and thought they would have a better life here, even though it had been many years since he had seen his family, he wanted his wife and child to meet them."

"A huge wedding was thrown. King Egobail spared nothing. Food, drink, and every creature of the realm were invited. Everyone dressed beautifully. Maeve and I were dressed in light blue shimmering gowns. We each wore a crown of sapphires and pearls. Our wings were set off with tiny stones that matched the crown we wore. We looked lovely, we were told, but nothing compared to your mother."

"Your mother Merena, was absolutely stunning. Her dark hair was piled in curls on top of her head. A ring of Daisies encircled her curls. Silver threads sparkled and had been woven through each curl. They cascaded down her back. Her dress was full and also shimmered as she walked. It was a white gossamer fabric with daisies embroidered around the bodice and hem. Her wings, she had played down. As she was marrying a human, she wanted less to notice. She carried a huge bouquet of all summer flowers. She really seemed happy. Your father was tall, dark and very handsome. He seemed a little nervous, especially around your Grandfather, the King. The ceremony was beautiful. There wasn't a dry eye there. The wedding went into the night as weddings are oft to do. It got a little out of hand."

"Some of the male Fairies were jealous of Derek. They had many drinks and were not thinking right. As the couple were leaving the party, a group followed them into the night. They watched where the couple were spending the night. They went back to the party and drank some more. No one is really sure exactly what happened, but your Father was mortally wounded that night. Seeing what had been done, your mother took her bags and got on a ship to America."

Rayna was stunned. "He never met me?" Tears ran down her face. She must have felt so alone. I know how that feels. Whispering to herself. "Derek, my Father's name was Derek, and my mother was Merena. Thank you Queen Aine, but what happened to her? What happened to my Mother? Why didn't she keep me? I have so many questions. You are the first real relative beside my children that I have ever known. Thank you, no matter what I know I was conceived in love." "You're welcome, now do you want to know the rest? Well, the rest until now?" "Yes, yes, I do, Rayna said, wiping her eyes and blowing her nose.

"We still need your help," Queen Aine added. "You and your children can save the Realm. We have tracked both your mother and my sister to the underworld in New Hampshire. Our scouts have tracked them to an area near Pillsbury State Park. We have a picture of your parents wedding day. The other picture was taken in 1997. Rayna took both pictures. She looked at them and said, "we will help however we can. Tell me when and how." "Go back home now. I will contact you soon." Standing up, Rayna hugged Aine. "Thank you so much. We will contact you soon," Aine hugged her back. "I had to wait until you were ready. I'm sorry it took so long. Clutching the photos, Rayna left the meadow. Dusk settled over the forest. The warmth of the day had passed. She hurried across the snowy grass which crunched under her feet. At the bridge she turned to look back and all that was there was the usual tree and stones. The tent had disappeared. Hurriedly, she crossed the stream heading to her car. She climbed into the car hoping it wasn't too late. Both her ice coffee and phone were sitting in the console. Carefully, she slid the pictures behind the phone, turned the key and started the car. The time was 4:45 PM. She felt like it should be midnight. Taking a minute to warm the car up, she sipped her coffee. She looked at the photos again. Her mother was clearly pregnant in the 1997 photo. In the more recent photo, she hadn't changed that much. Maybe living in the fairy world really did pay off. Sliding the photos back, she drove home.

The children met her at the door. They were excited to share their day. "Mummy, we had so much fun. Grandfather let us watch a movie and Nana let us make cupcakes for dessert." The house smelled wonderful. The babies were all awake, happily swinging. The table was set, and dinner ready. Looking

to Leanne, Rayna smiled saying, "You're hired."
Leanne laughed. "Mr. D helped a lot and so did Joey
and Joannie. It was a team effort. Did you enjoy your
time away? "It was very interesting that's for sure. I'll
share later. Let's eat, I'm starving."

The dinner was wonderful. After dessert, the
children kissed Grandfather goodnight. They were off
to shower and get ready for bed. Mr. D took Lulu
home. Leanne stayed to help feed the babies and talk
with Rayna.

"Ok, spill it," Leanne said as they sat feeding
the boys. "You are not going to believe this," Rayna
whispered. "Oh, let me be the judge of that honey,"
Leanne laughed. Rayna told of the meeting with Aine.
The wedding, and the coming to America. She told
how her parents met, and the fateful wedding night. All
of it. Leanne listened with rapt attention. Then Rayna
got to the part about the pictures. Leanne's mouth
gaped open. Lifting little Sean to her shoulder, she
puttered "are you kidding me? You have pictures?
Where are they? How could you not have started with
that? Your killing me Rayna!" She put little Sean down
and took Jimmy. "I'll burp him. Go get the pictures,"
she said.

Rayna stood up laughing. "Ok, ok, I'm going."
Leanne continued to mumble to herself. "There are
pictures and you don't start there, what the heck."
Rayna hurried back. Leanne lay Jimmy next to Sean.
The babies were quite content and Rayna sat down
next to Leanne. She handed the first photo to Leanne.
It was the wedding photo. "They were a beautiful
couple, weren't they?" Rayna whispered. "Very
handsome," Leanne answered. "How sad." Then,
Rayna handed her the second picture. It was both

Merena and Maeve. There clearly was a resemblance to Rayna. Leanne stared at the photo for a good two minutes. Her face drained of all color. Rayna looked from photo to Leanne and back. "Are you ok Nana?" she asked? Stuttering, Leanne looked up and whispered, "I have met these women Rayna." "What do you mean Nana?"

"It was March of 1997. Before you were born. These two women stopped by. They said they were interviewing for Daycare in the area. They were clearly from out of town and I felt bad turning them away. I gave them some info, and told them to come back at 5:30 PM. They seemed very nervous. They were new in town.

The younger woman was very pregnant. We chatted and I showed them around. They seemed very interested. The next evening the younger woman stopped by. She handed me a manila envelope. She had started to fill out the forms and enclosed a white business size envelope along with the paperwork. She started to cry. I sat her down with a glass of water. She told me she had to leave suddenly and if any one came asking about them would I say nothing. I assured her, that her secret was safe with me. She seemed to believe me and she took out the white envelope. She said "In here is an important message. Only after 25 years can this be opened. Can I entrust it to you? Why me? I asked her. How will I know it's the right person? No need to worry Leanne, she said, drying her eyes. They may never come. You will know when the time is right. Then, she passed the envelope to me. On it was written March 20 ,1997-March 20, 2027 Spring Equinox. Turning over the envelope, the flap was sealed with a wax flower. Just below the seal was printed, do not open before March 20, 2022. I slid the envelope into the larger manila one. She thanked me profusely, dried her eyes, used the bathroom and left. I hugged her at the door and wished her good luck. I never heard from her again."

Rayna's mouth hung open in disbelief. "Are you telling me you met, not only my Mother, but Grandmother as well? Leanne looked at the photos again nodding her head. "I'm pretty sure." "Do you still have the letter?" Leanne looked up at Rayna. "Hmmm, I believe I do.

Leanne left and quickly walked home. She ran into the house and right to the basement. There, she had left the unpacked boxes from the move. She rummaged around until she found the one marked *DAYCARE LETTERS AND MEMENTOS*. Pulling open the top, she took out the first few items. On the bottom was the white binder. Over the years she had saved the letters and thank you cards from parents and children. Originally, she used them as recommendation letters. Now, they were there to prove she had made a difference. She went right to the back of the binder. There were multiple yellowing envelopes. Nestled in the middle, was the one she was looking for. She grabbed it, peaked inside, there was the white envelope. She hurried up the stairs calling out to Mr. D, she said, "I'll be back." "Bring cake," he replied.

She hurried back to Rayna's, careful not to slip on the walkway. She lay the envelope on the kitchen table, hung up her coat and hurried to help with the babies. Rayna had finished with Tricia and was just burping Annie. "Ready for diapers?" Leanne said picking up Jimmy. "Yep, did you find it?" Rayna asked. "You know I did. I hardly ever throw things away,"

Leanne answered. Let's get these leprechauns into bed, the big ones too. Then we can open it. What do you think Rayna?" "Sounds good, lets hustle," Rayna answered.

Leanne took care of the babies. Rayna got the twins into bed. They got one story each and ran down to kiss Nana goodnight first. They made a good team and were done in no time. Sitting at the kitchen table, Rayna picked up the manila envelope.

She slid out the contents onto the table. There were three sheets of printed forms and the one white envelope in front of them. They were almost afraid to touch them. Rayna turned the larger, now empty envelope over in her hand. "Well there is no writing on it, no name or anything." She peered inside and convinced that it was empty and no use, set it down. They both picked up one of the forms. Only a few lines had been filled in. The last form was the same. Nothing that would help them. The white envelope, now yellowed with age, was the final item. Picking it up, Rayna turned it over, the seal clearly had never been broken. The writing was clear under the seal. Do not open before 2022. Looking at Leanne she said, "wow you're good. I think I would have looked." "Well, don't think too highly of me. I probably just forgot about it. It was a pretty busy time. Out of sight, out of mind you know?" "Why do you think the dates are written like that?" Rayna asked. "We won't know if we do not open it," Leanne said. "Well, I guess you are right." Rayna slid a butter knife under the envelope flap, breaking the seal. Her hands shook a little as she slipped the two-page letter out. She smoothed out the paper. Leanne moved closer, and they both started reading.

Dated March 20, 1997

My Dearest child/children,
If you are reading this letter you know who I am. Our
worlds must truly be in trouble. You and your children
are the hope for our future. There is a map on the next
page showing you the way. Please follow carefully, we
have already lost so much.

Your Loving Mother Merena and Grandmother Maeve.

"What do you think this means Nana," Rayna asked looking from the letter to Leanne. "I think we are going to find out very soon," Leanne answered.

Solstice-Equinox

Destiny

Some people believe Destiny is determined at birth. They might think there is a grand plan and we unconsciously just follow along. Others may believe choice is what matters. We have a choice in how we will approach or deal with fate. Webster's Dictionary defines fate as:

1. Power supposedly making events inevitable.

2. Ones lot in life.

3. Outcome.

4. Death.

I believe Destiny is a path. We choose which way to follow. Right, left, straight ahead or just live your life at the crossroad? Look for the magic. Try to make your life count. Stand up for those who matter to you. Take the road you think will be the best for you.

Chapter 18: March & April 1997
Merena and Maeve

They were able to stay undetected on arriving in the states. Heading for just south of Boston, they checked into a small hotel. So far, they had not been found. A white van had followed them around Milton as they tried to find a small apartment. Though Merena had given up her birthright to marry, she would have protection from the Fairies. Merena had fallen in love with a human. She had been Destined to be a Queen like her sister Aine. On his death she fled Ireland.

Her mother Maeve accompanied her and planned on staying until the birth of her Grandchild. Rumor had it that those responsible for her husband's death wanted his child. Merena knew she could not keep her baby unless she could disappear. That was looking very unlikely. It seemed they no sooner got somewhere, that the "others" showed up. They needed to trust someone.

There were many people who helped those transfer from one world to the other undetected. For some reason this baby was marked as special.

Visiting the Daycare home had felt promising; however, they had been followed. The van drove slowly by as they left the provider, Leanne.

Quickly, they drove the rental to their hotel. They were careful not to be followed. They hunkered down for the next 3 weeks. While resting they devised a plan. At the front desk, they asked if they could leave the car rental keys. They took a cab to the airport.

Once there, they took a shuttle bus to a different

rental and rented a small SUV. Their plan was to drive north towards Washington N.H. The State Park in that town was a doorway to the other world. Merena planned on settling down with her baby and Maeve planned on going back to her people. She wanted to make sure her daughter and grandchild were safe first. Driving for two hours, it was dark when they drove through the town. Snow covered the whole town. Though the roads were clear, the forest and trees had at least 6 inches or more of new snow.

Merena had complained of a backache as they started out. At the rest area, she definitively knew she was in labor. Needing to find a place for the night, they drove around the lake. At the top of the hill sat a small white home. No sign of occupants, they got out. As with many places, the keys were found quickly. Pushing the door open, they brought in their suitcases. Merena was sure the baby would come soon. Maeve settled her in and decided to get some needed supplies at the small store nearby. Merena tried to protect the furnishings as best she could. She would leave $500.00 cash and a note. Money was not the problem. She wrote the note and found an envelope to put it in.

She searched for an appropriate book. Scanning the bookshelves, she found a book, *Country Chronicle,* by Gladys Taber. "Perfect!" she said out loud. "This looks well read. The owner will surely find the envelope." She slipped the note and money inside.

The note read:

April 11 1997

Dear Owner

Please accept this money. We needed a safe place to have our baby. We let ourselves in, hopefully this will cover any cleaning or damage.

Sincerely,
Merena

P.S,

You may want to stop leaving the keys so accessible.
M.

Taking the book, she looked around. Not wanting to leave it for just anyone, she slid it back into the book shelf. Clearly, it was a favorite, and she hoped the owner would find the note inside.

Maeve did not return as expected. Merena was sure the baby was coming. Slipping off her pants and laying a plastic tablecloth on the guest bed she got things ready. They had string, scissors a couple of hats, diapers and 2 blankets. Turning the heater on, she doubled over in pain. "Mom," she cried out, "I need you." Luckily her body knew what to do. The urge to push was strong. Bearing down, she felt the head coming. She let out an ungodly roar and with that the baby slid out. Taking a deep breath, she lifted the baby towards her chest. Checking the sex, she was happy to see she had a son. The cord was tied off and scissors ready to cut between. The next pain enveloped her body. Laying the baby beside her she bore down. She was ready for the afterbirth. Instead there was another baby. Shocked, she automatically lifted the child. It was a girl. "I have twins," she thought.

Where was her mother? She tied this baby's cord and wrapped her in a blanket. She lay them side by side. They turned their heads toward each other and laid quietly. She had a feeling that she carried twins, that's why there were two of everything. They did run in the family and she had wanted to be prepared.

Merena cleaned up and got rid of the soiled tablecloth. She found some wash cloths and wet them. She took her time cleaning off and dressing the babies. Taking a bureau draw, she padded it with towels and a sheet. She nursed each one, then lay them down to clean herself up. "Where was her mother," she thought. It had been hours since she left. Merena lay down next to the babies and fell asleep. She woke to the hungry cries of her son. Lifting him to her, she nursed him. He was a beautiful child. Just the hint of dark hair and a round chubby face. He nursed heartily. She changed him and then nursed his sister. The sun was rising and Maeve had not returned. She put a kettle on and found some teabags and crackers in a tin. Sipping the tea, she tried to make a plan. She got dressed and went into the basement. There was an old sled. She pulled it around front and into the house. If she wrapped them well, she could get the babies to the store at least. Then maybe get a bus back to Boston.

She decided to wait one more day. She thought that would give her a little more time to heal. It was a long walk and pulling the sled would be difficult. She found a couple of cans of soup to go with the crackers

and rested nursing the twins throughout the day.
Darkness fell early and still no sign of Maeve. She
plugged an old tv in for company and fell asleep with
the babies.

Around 9:30 she heard the sound of a car door.
Peeking out the window she saw her mother start down
the path. She carried a bag. Merena opened the door.
"I've been so worried," she cried. Maeve pushed
through the door. "I'm so sorry. They found me," she
said. "The babies are here mom," Merena whispered.
"Babies?" Maeve went over to the makeshift bed.
Tears swam in her eyes. "Twins, you have twins."
Merena nodded. "Yes, a son and daughter." "They are
beautiful," Maeve whispered. "We need to get out of
here and soon," Maeve said. "First, I brought food."

Maeve told her all about the town. "I knew they
had found us as soon as I entered the store. They were
sitting at the counter eating. Four men. Outside was a
van like the one we had seen in Milton near the
Daycare. I bought some items and asked about
Newport. The clerk gave me directions and I left. I
drove towards Newport and the men came running out
to follow me. I didn't want to lead them here so I kept
going. I switched cars there and circled back. I'm sorry
I wasn't here to help you. What a surprise, twins. We
need a plan, and we are going to have to separate."

They finished the food. Maeve took two bottles,
formula and diapers out of the bag. "I wasn't sure if
we would need these but thought it better to be
prepared and not need them." Taking the pad of paper,
she wrote the babies, birth-dates and time of birth.
Baby boy born April 12 1997 at 8:15 AM. Birthmark
left sole of foot. Baby girl born April 12 1997 at 8:25
AM. Birthmark right sole of foot. She copied for

herself as well. At 4am they packed up and drove away. The plan was to stop at the rest area and split up. Then meet somewhere else. Merena took the baby girl and Maeve would take the boy. Merena nursed both babies. Taking the girl, she looked for a sympathetic woman to hitch a ride. She waved as she passed her mother's car. Two weeks later, the baby was found on the firehouse steps. Included was a letter, as well as the birth statistic.

Chapter 19: Leanne January 2026

Leanne started for home. It was already dark and cold. Pulling her jacket tightly around her, she walked quickly. Something nagged at her. She had left Rayna with the letter from her Mother. Rayna was reading and rereading the letter over and over. Hugging her, Leanne had whispered, "It will all work out you'll see." Looking up, Rayna said, "I know Nana, it's just so hard to believe."

The door opened just as she reached it home. Mr. D stood in the doorway. "I was getting worried," he said. Leanne stepped, in closing the door quickly. "Lulu been out lately?" she asked. At the mention of her name, the little pup came skidding around the corner. Mr. D handed the leash to Leanne. "Would you mind?" he asked.   Buckling the leash onto her collar, Leanne stepped back out. Calling over her shoulder she said, "put the kettle on, I have news." Around the neighborhood they walked.

Lulu smelling every spot she could. Leanne trying to remember everything about that night.

Chapter 20: Leanne, March 20 1997

The children had just settled down to sleep when there was a knock on the door. Leanne quietly opened the inside door. There standing just outside were two women. One was clearly very pregnant. The other looked like her mother. Opening the outside door, Leanne smiled and said, "can I help you?" "We are sorry to just show up," the younger, pregnant woman started. "We hoped to ask you about childcare." She patted her tummy and smiled. "This is my mom, Maeve, and I am Merena." "I am sorry," Leanne said, "I have six children sleeping here. I usually conduct interviews in the evening." "We are sorry to intrude," Maeve said. Her brogue was very distracting to Leanne. It reminded her of her relatives. "Well why don't I give you the paperwork to go over. Then, if you like, you can come back for a proper interview." "That sounds good," Merena answered. "Could we come back this evening? We are only in the area today." "Ok," Leanne answered. "Let me get it." Quietly, she went into her computer cabinet and pulled out the registration packet. Handing the envelope to Merena, she said, "how about stopping back at six PM. I can give you a quick tour and interview." "Thank you so much," they whispered, leaving quietly.

The day continued as usual for Leanne. The children woke happy, hungry and ready to play. Five o'clock came fast. Rushing upstairs after the last client left, Leanne brushed her teeth and changed her shirt. It was her birthday and the family were going out to dinner at 7 PM. At exactly 6 PM, the doorbell rang.

Standing there were both women. Opening the door Leanne noticed they seemed nervous. "Hello," she said smiling, "welcome!" Stepping through the door, Maeve glanced back, closing it quickly. A quick tour, and they all convened at the kitchen table. Merena put the envelope down. "You have a lovely home Leanne." "Thank you, now have you any questions?" "Well," Merena started, "I am not sure this will work out. I have filled the paperwork as best I can. We are new to your country and I am not sure how to answer a lot of the questions." Patting the envelope, she smiled a watery smile at Leanne. "It's alright, we have time. No worries." She patted her on the hand. "When are you due?" "Not for weeks, I see a new Doctor next week. He will estimate the due date." "Ok, well how's this. I will give you my information again. Then, call me when the baby comes and we can figure out from there. Sound good?" Feeling drawn to these women, Leanne offered a cup of tea. They refused saying they really needed to get going. They were staying not far away, at a hotel and were looking for an apartment nearby.

"I have a big favor to ask you," Merena said. "What is it?" Leanne asked. "Well," Merena said tapping the envelope, "I have enclosed two sealed letters in here. Would you keep them for me? Someday, someone will come and ask about us. Then you can give it to them." Leanne looked at the women. Merena had tears streaming down her face. "You can give them to the recipient yourself honey." "Just in case anything goes wrong," Merena cried. "Well, of course I will do that for you. I am sure everything will be fine though." "We knew you were the right person to ask," Maeve said, "thank you." They got up to leave and

Leanne saw them to the door. "Let me know when the baby comes," she said. "We will try," and then Maeve hugged Leanne saying, "you are special. Have a wonderful birthday." Closing the door, Leanne waved and thought, how did they know it was her birthday? She hurried into the kitchen. Cleaned up and put the envelope in the file box. She never saw those women again, until that picture today.

Chapter 21: Leanne 2026

Lulu had finished her walk. They rounded the corner for home. It had been pleasantly cold and Leanne warmed up walking. It was a nice night in the Estates. She had noted everyone was safely home. Having the family in one neighborhood had been a great idea. She still couldn't believe that she had won the lotto just last year on her birthday. Just then it dawned on her. Wait, Merena had said there were two letters. They had only found one. She walked a little quicker the rest of the way home.

Peering out the door, Mr. D looked worried. "That was a long walk, I thought you were hurt or something." Leanne laughed, "Miss Lulu had big ideas." Handing the leash to him, she shrugged out of her jacket. Her slippers were waiting for her and she could smell her favorite tea. "You're not going to believe this," she said sitting down across from Mr. D. "Believe what?" Mr. D asked, "not more babies I hope." "I can see why you would guess that but no. Twins and a set of quads is quite enough for now. I think Rayna would run away." "Now, you have my attention," Mr. D said, sipping his hot cocoa.

"Well, Rayna just found out who her birth mother is." "What?" "How?" "Well this is the unbelievable part." Leanne said. "Rayna's mom was a fairy and her Dad a human." "Huh?" "How could you possibly know this?" Mr. D said, spilling some of his cocoa. "Well, she talked with Aine, Queen of the Fairies today. She has a picture of both of her parents and her Grandmother. The strangest thing is I met them. Well, not the father, but the Grandmother and Mother." "How?" "When?" "That's not possible," Mr. D sputtered. Leanne told him about the meeting, and the letters. "Did they ever come back or call?" he asked. "Nope, I never heard from them again," Leanne answered. "I totally forgot all about it. You know my record keeping wasn't that good. I stuck the manila envelope away and never thought about it again. That is until today when Rayna showed me their picture. I have to go look for the second letter. It must have fallen out of the envelope." "Wow, this is kind of exciting," Mr. D said, sipping the last of his drink. "You're like a real Nancy Drew detective Leanne," he chortled. "Very funny," she said laughing. "I got Rayna back didn't I." "Yes, yes you did and you got me to see the magic. Never a dull moment. Now, go look for the other letter." "I almost forgot the letter included a map. Something about Pillsbury State Park." "In Washington N.H.?" Mr. D asked. "Pretty sure," Leanne replied.

Going right to the box, Leanne started emptying it out. There were lots of letters and pictures from her daycare years. As always, once you start looking, it takes forever. She started reading the notes from parents. It made her feel good that she had made a difference in people's lives. There was a whole binder of parent recommendations. The parents that year had nominated Leanne for the Provider Of The Year Award. She had won, and had to give a speech. Old clients showed up as well as current clients. Even some of her family attended. It was nice to look back on that day. Already an hour had passed. Leanne put the letters and pictures aside. She dumped out the box onto the table. There at the very bottom, stuck under the flap, was an envelope. This has got to be it, she thought. She pulled it out and sure enough, it matched the first one. Turning it over, she noticed the wax seal. It was identical to the other letter. She quickly put all the items back in the box, closed it, and put it away. She then took it into the den and showed Mr. D.

He took the letter from her. In the right-hand corner was written, ***The Key***. He turned it over noting the seal. Then he felt through the sealed letter. "There is defiantly a key of some kind in here," he said, looking at Leanne. "Are you going to open it?" Shaking her head, "No," Leanne answered, "I think Rayna should." Mr. D handed the envelope back to her. "I will go with you. I want to see this for myself. Why don't we go tomorrow morning after the twins leave for school?" Leanne agreed. Then they settled down to watch some TV.

Chapter 22: Rayna 2026

The evening dragged by for Rayna. The babies were out of sorts for some reason. She would no sooner get one settled down then another needed comforting. Then, not to mention, Joannie had come down stairs at least three times. Finally, Rayna said, "One more time and no play date with Nora tomorrow!" "Mom," Joannie pleaded. "I just want to help them." "Who? help who?" "I don't know," Joannie said. She was close to tears. "It's like a dark veil and I can't tell who it is." "Honey, maybe it's just a dream this time. It might not be real. Try to get some sleep. We'll figure it out later." Joannie hugged her mom. Whispering in her ear, she said, "it is real Mumma, you'll see." "Love you honey, try to sleep." Joannie walked slowly back to bed. "Love you too," she mumbled, closing her eyes, still rocking little Annie, Rayna mulled over the letter.

Dated March 20,1997

My Dearest child/children,
If you are reading this letter, you know who I am. Our worlds must truly be in trouble. You and your children are the hope for our future. There is a map on the next page showing you the way. Please follow it carefully. We have already lost so much.

Your Loving Mother Merena and Grandmother Maeve.

Rayna wouldn't believe this if she hadn't been lost in the Fairy world. How crazy does it all sound, she thought? People get committed to institutions for believing this stuff. Annie had finally settled down. All four babies were content and sleeping. Rayna quietly left the room. Sitting back at the table, she studied the map.

The map showed Pillsbury State Park in N.H. Leanne and Mr. D owned property near there. Rayna had never been there. Though they had driven past the park, they told her it had been years since they had actually gone into it and walked around. Small world, she thought. Folding the map and letter, she slipped them back in the envelope. Enough for today the babies would be up again she needed some rest.

Rayna woke up with a start. Rolling over, she read the clock. 7:30 AM. The twins needed to be up and getting ready for school. Why had the babies not demanded breakfast? Picking up the monitor, she checked on them. Sean was sitting in the rocker, feeding one of the babies. Jumping out of bed, Rayna grabbed a robe and hurried to the babies' room, passing Joannie and Joey's rooms on the way.

Both rooms were empty and the beds were made. Rounding the corner towards the babies' room, she stopped short. Sean had started to sing to the babies. His voice was low and strong. It made her love him a little more. She stood in the doorway for a minute, taking in the sight. Sean sat in the rocker with one infant. All around him were the other three babies in their bouncy seats. All four babies looked raptly up at Sean. It really was a sight.

Rayna cleared her throat. "Hello!" she said quietly so as not to frighten the babies. "What's going on here?" "Well," Sean started, "I knocked and Joannie and Joey let me in. They said you were up late with the babies, so I thought I would help." "Why didn't I hear you over the monitor?" Rayna asked. "Joannie snuck into your room and turned the sound off. They are down eating breakfast, getting ready for school. Go check on them and have a minute to yourself. I have these leprechauns under control, right guys?" he said to the babies. "Don't have to tell me twice," Rayna said, turning for the kitchen.

Joey and Joannie looked up when Rayna walked into the kitchen. They had just finished pancakes with fresh strawberries and whipped cream. "Are you mad Mumma?" Joannie asked. "No, but next time wake me up when someone knocks. Also, no turning off the baby monitor again." "Ok Mom, but you were so tired we wanted to give you a treat." "I appreciate it guys, but I am the Mom so wake me, OK?" "Yup, we understand," they said in unison. "Now run and brush your teeth. Fy will walk you to the bus." The children ran for the stairs. Fy waited at the door. Nora's Dad always waited till they got on the bus, but the kids liked to think Fy protected them. After they boarded the bus, Fy would walk back home barking to be let back in. Then, he would lay near the babies until just before the bus arrived back home. He was a wonderful protector.

Rayna thought back to the day he had arrived. The twins had just been born in the cabin. They were a rare birth as both had been born "under a veil", Meaning their amniotic sacks were intact at birth. Leanne had to cut them open after birth. Caulbarers were said to possess special sensitivities to navigate between many worlds and be able to see the future.

Caulbarers were associated with an accompanying spirit, "Fylgia," which after birth would manifest as an animal, object or person. Fy had shown up the week of their birth. He protected them ever since.

The children hurried in, kissed Rayna goodbye, and ran out the door. Standing at the window, Rayna sipped her coffee, watching the three racing off to Nora's, then off to the bus. She thought to herself how nice it was to have a partner here, even if it was only for this morning. She decided to try and get a quick shower in before relieving Sean.

She showered and dressed quickly. As she braided her still damp hair, she heard one of the babies. She made her bed by throwing the covers up over it, then quickly went to the children. The fussing was somewhat under control, but Sean was changing a very messy diaper. "I'll take over," Rayna said standing next to Sean. "I can manage" Sean answered gagging. Rayna nudged him aside. She grabbed the wipes, clean diaper and an outfit. She was finished before Sean made it back from washing his hands. "That was intense," he laughed, "but I could do it." "Sure, you could, but would there be puke?" "Possibly," Sean laughed. "Here, buckle him into his seat and hand me your name sake." Sean took the baby and buckled him. Rayna got supplies ready for the three remaining. Fifteen minutes later and they were done. "Thanks for getting everyone up this morning," she said, lowering herself to the floor.

All four infants stared and smiled up at her. Sean smiled too. "I enjoyed helping. Joannie said she knew I was coming. Joey just nodded solemnly. They loved the pancakes, though." "MMMMMM pancakes," Rayna said, "are there any left?" "Of course! I made a double batch before coming and brought them hot," Sean answered. I wasn't sure if you would let me in, so I figured you would at least take food." "Let's take the babies down. I usually carry one at a time in their seats." Rayna picked up Tricia and carried her down. Sean followed with James, then they went back for Annie and Sean. "Wow!" Sean said, "so this is how you get your cardio in. The babies were content to sit and play. The adults poured coffee and plated some pancakes. "These are really good," Rayna said, finishing her third helping. "Delicious." "Why, thank you," Sean answered. "I do know how to cook a little." Just then Rayna's phone beeped. Leanne sent a text saying,

I found the second letter. Do you want me to bring it with lunch? Sure, how about 1:00 PM, Rayna text back. *The babies might be napping then.* Leanne sent a thumbs up emoji.

"What's that all about?" Sean asked. Rayna told him all about the Fairies, her Mother and Father and Grandmother. She told him about Leanne and her meeting with them. Lastly, about the letter she had and the one Leanne would bring. Sean just stared at her. "Here, I thought I was the one pressing thing. Next to your children of course. No wonder your exhausted." "Sean, what are your intentions?" Rayna asked. "Why did you fly back to Ireland? Why are you not rushing to work?

Chapter 23: Sean

(On the night Rayna told him the news)

He ran from her home. Walking around the Estates, the conversation replayed over and over in his head. Fairies, other-world, sleeping with someone 7 years ago and having babies now? What the heck, is she crazy? Then, he thought about the children. He did feel a connection. It had been strange; they met that St Patrick's Day in 2019. Sure, the parties had been wild. They had really connected. Love at first sight. Just like in Fairy Tales. It kind of felt right, but he didn't want to be a chump.

He decided to go home and discuss it with his parents. They would help him decide what to do. He made the reservations before he could change his mind. Then, he talked to work about a vacation. They were very understanding. He promised to be back by the next week. He was on the plane the next morning.

The flight touched down on Irish soil at 5 AM Ireland time. Sean went through customs quickly, as he had only a carry-on. He had decided to stay with his parents, but rent a car. They expected him for lunch at 1 PM. On the way over, he made a plan to visit the Hill of Tara in County Meath. That is where Rayna claimed to have been lost those 7 years. He put the address into his GPS and started out. For a minute, he forgot which side to drive on. No wonder there were accidents when Americans drove here. Just outside of Dublin, he stopped for a tea and pastry. He sat in the car and enjoyed his breakfast. It was a damp, blustery day. The sun had barely risen. He cranked up the heat and was glad for it. At 9 AM he was in County Meath.

Now to find this tree, he thought. As he rounded the bend, he saw the hill. There was a parking lot and gift shop not yet opened. He pulled in and parked, facing the grass area. Grabbing his jacket, phone, keys and gloves, he stepped out into the raw day.

He spotted the tree immediately. It was hard to miss. There were all kinds of ribbons and trinkets adorning the branches. He wondered how the ribbons got tied up so high. Did people actually climb up to hang them? The closer he got, he noticed not only ribbons and trinkets but Butterflies and moths. There had to be hundreds of them. He stopped in his tracks. Do I really want to find out this is true he thought? She had told him about this. He walked closer and noted the tree was ringed with stones and inside that circle was a mushroom ring. On closer inspection, he noted the mushrooms were multi colored as well. So far it all checked out. His heart quickened as the butterflies flew around the tree. It was almost like they knew who he was or had been waiting for him. He slowly walked around the tree He didn't dare lean against the tree. He certainly did not want to test that theory. Just as he stopped, a butterfly lit on his shoulder. He froze and turned his head toward the creature. It was definitely a creature with human qualities. A small doll like being. "Hello," she whispered, "you must be Sean." Sean sunk right to the ground. The fairy lit next to him. "Don't be afraid Sean, I won't hurt you." Sean smiled. I guess she was telling the truth, he chuckled to himself. "How are Rayna and Leanne?" "I am Deanna. Leanne helped get me here from America. She is the reason Rayna was able to get out of our world." "Leanne is good and Rayna is happy and a new mother to Quadruplets." "How can I help you Sean?" "Well, I guess you already have! It's all true. Now, I get to tell my parents that they have four new grand babies." "Would you like a little help?" Deanna asked. "I will take any help I can get," Sean said.

Deanna pulled out a cylinder. It was silver and the size of a lipstick. "Here is some fairy dust. Sprinkle a little on the door step before you go in. It will help them believe." Taking the cylinder, Sean turned it over. "This is beautiful. Do you think it will work?" "It should. If not, wait and sprinkle a bit on yourself and hug them. That should do it."

Standing up, Sean brushed his pants off. "Well that's that, I guess. I better go. Thanks for the help." "Tell Leanne and Rayna hello for me," Deanna said in her tinkling voice.   As Sean walked away, the sound of bells could be heard. He stopped twice on the way to his Parents. Once, for some sweets and once for some liquid courage. He didn't usually drink, but this felt needed. He pulled up at just 1 PM. He discreetly sprinkled a little dust on the door step. He had decided not to share the complete story. He thought it best to just talk about this year, not 7 years ago. Baby steps, he thought. Just as he put the cylinder back in his pocket the door flew open.

His mother stood barely 5 ft tall. She wore a long dress and her hair was short and styled. She wasn't heavy, nor thin. She was just right. "Sean!" she squealed, "I missed you, what a wonderful surprise." She hustled him into the house. His Dad sat at the kitchen table. He stood when Sean came in. He was as tall as Sean, with silver gray hair. He needed a haircut but was still handsome in a distinguished way. He hugged Sean and slapped his back. "Good to see you lad, what's the big occasion?" "What, can't a guy fly home to see his parents?" Sean said laughing. "Well, of course he can, but Skyping would have been cheaper." "True, true, but you can't touch him," his mom said. "Let's eat, I am starved," Dad said sitting. "Your mother has been planning this since you called."

The meal was delicious. All Sean's favorites had been prepared. "Mom, we can't possibly eat all this for lunch," Sean said. "Hey, speak for yourself," his Dad answered. "She never feeds me this much." Sean laughed. His Mom said, "you're fed plenty Dad."

They discussed the family gossip over lunch. When they were sufficiently stuffed, his Mom made tea and plated the sweets. They sat around the table waiting for Sean to tell them why he had come. "Well, I guess you wondering why I'm really here?" His mom took a long sip of tea, finished her treat and said, "Yes, tell us Sean." Here goes nothing Sean thought.

"Remember how I pined for that girl some years ago?" "Yes," his Mother answered. "You turned lots of nice girls away since then." "Right, I knew she was special and wanted to find her. Well, I did find her. She had been here all along. She had amnesia." "Are you kidding me Sean?" said his Dad. He had decided to go with the P.C. version rather than the F.W. (Fairy World) version. "She was nearby all this time in Adere, Limerick. She was injured on March 21 2019 and went by a different name. That's why I couldn't find her all that time. This sounds like a novella or soap opera, I know, but there must be truth in some of those stories, right?"

Now he needed to lie. They would never believe the "Fairy" story. "Well, we reconnected last March. I didn't say anything because she was leaving for the states. I was starting my new job with Egobail Enterprises and we didn't want to ruin it for each other." "So, what changed?" his Mom asked. "Well, I am at the facility in Massachusetts and I ran into her there. She actually lives at the Que Sera Sera Estates where I work. Her whole adopted family lives there. They own every house. It's a great family." "Ok, but what has this to do with us? What would warrant a trip home that you had to see us in person?" All of a sudden, his Mothers face paled. "Are you, is she in the family way Sean?" Sean swallowed and then took another sip of water. "AAH, you could say that Mom." "What? What?" she put her hand over her mouth. "Relax Mom," Sean said. "Just tell us son," his Father said, "it's ok." "Well, congratulations, you are Grandparents," Sean answered. "What, she already had the baby?" his Mom squeaked. "Yes, well, we were together back in March Mom." "What is it?" she squealed. She stood up. She was shaking with excitement. "Well, you may want to sit back down Mom." "Why, what did she have?" "Both," Sean said.

His Mother squealed in delight clapping her hands. "Twins? A boy and a girl! I'm so excited," she turned to hug her husband. Sean just stood there. His Dad taking note of his demeanor, tried to calm his wife. This was easier said than done. She was crazed. "We need to go there. I have two Grandchildren, a boy and a girl. They'll call me Grammy." "Mom, Mom, calm down, stop and relax. She stopped and looked at him. "What's the matter Sean?" "Mom, Dad, they're not twins." "Oh," his Mom sighed. "You said one of each?" "No Mom, you asked what the baby was and I said both." "Right, twins," his mother clapped again. "Mom, not twins. Quads!"

"What?" all color left her face. His Dad stood up. "There are two of each." "What?" His Mother could not comprehend this. "Mom, there are 4 babies. Two girls and two boys." His mother looked at him. "Four babies?" and she sunk to the floor. Sean rushed to her. She was out cold. His father slowly wet a tea towel and gently put it on his wife's face. "Are you sure son?" "Positive Dad, you have two grandsons. Sean and James, and two granddaughters, Annie and Patricia." "Holy smoke son, this is quite a surprise." "To me too Dad. She never told me she was expecting." His Mother started to come around. She opened her eyes. "Why am I on the floor?" "Mom, you fainted," Sean said. "Was it a dream?" she asked. "What honey?" his father asked. "Are we grandparents?" they both nodded their heads yes. "Is it twins?" "No," both Sean and his dad said. "More?" she asked. "Yup, two of each. Annie, Patricia James and Sean. They are almost 2 months old."

They helped her up off the floor and sat her in her chair. "Would you like to see a picture?" "Yes!" she whispered. Sean took out his phone and pulled the picture up. It was the Christmas photo. Next was one just taken last week. Both parents burst into tears. "They look like you did," his Mom wiped her eyes. "I can't wait to meet them." "Oh Mom, they will love you." He figured he would throw caution to the wind and said, "she also has twins that are seven years old." For a minute, he thought his mother was going down again, but she just smiled. "Tell me all about it," she said.

They were very excited to hear all about the Grandchildren. Feeling a little guilty for not telling the whole truth, Sean answered all their questions. Another meal was shared and Sean left to drive to an old friend's house.

Bernie barely waited until Sean was out the door. Picking up the telephone (landline no less) she rang her best friend Dierdre. "You're not going to believe this," she said as soon as Dierdre picked up. "I just saw Sean leave your house," Dierdre said. "What's the story?" Bernie could barely contain her excitement. "I am a Grandmother," she blurted out. "What? How?" Dierdre stuttered. "I'll be right over," she hung up the phone and ran out the door.

They lived just three doors from each other. Bursting through Bernie's gate, she walked quickly to the door. Big Sean opened it and said, "what took you so long?" "Is it true?" she asked him. "Yup, is Danny boy around? We'll be at the pub." With that he walked down the stairs. As he reached the gate, he heard the squealing from inside. He couldn't help feeling excited for Bernie and of course himself. They had longed for Grandchildren to spoil. Figures they live in the States, he thought. Danny met him, slapping him on the shoulder, he cried, "Welcome to the club Sean." They started towards the pub.

Sean pulled up in front of his friend's house, barely making it to the door before it smashed open. There stood Liam with a baby in one arm. A toddler girl hung on his leg. "Well, look who's here!" Liam shouted. "Uncle Sean did you bring us anything?" four-year-old young Liam asked. "Of course, I did," Sean said, and pulled out three little cars and candy. The children jumped up and down in delight.

Mary, Liam's wife, came around the corner. She was petite with a long blonde braid down her back. "You children better be polite to Uncle Sean." "We are," the two oldest shouted. "I hear you have big news," Mary said, hugging Sean. "I see you have news also," Sean said glancing from one to the other. "Yes, we are expecting again," Mary said, rubbing her belly. "I guess we'll be even then," Sean said. "What do you mean?" asked Liam. He had been told Sean was a father, but that was all. "Well," Sean said, sitting down. "I am the father of quads. Two boys, James and Sean, and two girls, Annie and Patricia." "Oh my God," both Mary and Liam said. "Would you like to see pictures?" "Yes!" they answered. Sean beamed with pride showing off the babies. "These are their brother and sister," he said showing a picture of the twins. "I am so happy you found them," Liam said hugging his friend.

They visited a while longer and Sean promised to skype when he went back. Driving back to his parents, he couldn't believe how happy he was.

His parents were full of plans to visit. They were thrilled to be Grandparents, wanting to meet Rayna and the babies as soon as possible. Sean had to calm them down. "I promise you will get to meet them. We just need to give Rayna time. How about I ask to skype and you can see and talk to her. We'll go out and get a new laptop tomorrow and I will set it up."

His Mom was disappointed that they couldn't fly right there. His Dad understood. "Ok son, we'll go tomorrow to buy the laptop," Big Sean said. Turning to his wife he said, ''honey why don't we pick up yarn for you". His Mom clapped and squealed. "Yes, perfect. I will start knitting right away." So, it was settled and they went shopping early. Sean set up the computer and his Mom started knitting. He had two more days to spend with his parents before flying back to see Rayna and his children.

The plane landed at Logan Airport in Boston at just after 4pm. The ride to Lakeville took over 2 hours with traffic. He went immediately to his apartment, unpacked, and began to plan his proposal.

Chapter 24: Rayna and Leanne

Knocking softly on the door, Leanne could barely contain her excitement. Shifting the bag containing lunch, she searched for her phone. Just as she located it, the door swung open. "You're not going to believe this," they said at the same time. Walking in Leanne slipped off her boots and handed Rayna the bag. They walked into the kitchen together. "Well, what happened?" Leanne asked. "Sean came by this morning," Rayna answered. He took care of all the children and let me sleep." "That was nice, did you have a talk?" Leanne asked. Taking the time to set the table, Rayna thought for a minute. "Well, I think he believes the quads are his. He told his parents and they want to skype first then visit. They are excited to be Grandparents," she added. "That's good, isn't it?" Leanne asked. "Yes, I guess," she said sitting down. "I just hoped he would want all of us." "Give it time," Leanne said. "Now, let's have lunch." They unwrapped the sandwiches and ate in silence for a minute. Reaching into her bag Leanne pulled out the letter.

"This will take your mind off Sean." "I almost forgot," Rayna said, taking the envelope. "Don't open it yet. I promised Mr. D we would let him witness it." Putting the letter back down Rayna laughed. "I wondered why there was an Italian sub still in the bag." Just then Mr. D was at the door. "Did you wait for me?" he asked. Rayna nodded her head and said "yes, of course we did." Sitting down he said, "wait no longer!" and handed the letter back.

Turning the letter over, they noted the same seal

as the first. Then, in the right-hand corner were two words, *The Key*. Getting up, Rayna brought over the manila envelope and the other letter. Opening both, she laid them side by side. The key was wrapped in tissue paper. Handing the key to Mr. D she said, "you unwrap, and check that out."

The two women took turns reading the letters. Reading out loud Rayna reread the first letter. March 20, 1997 it was dated. "Alright, that's the day you met them right Nana?" "Correct. That evening was when they asked me to keep it for them." "That makes sense. What about the fact that it's written to her child slash children? Do you think she thought it would be twins?" Rayna asked. "Maybe she would have other children," Leanne answered. "We don't know what happened to them." "True, true, she may have a bunch of children," Rayna answered. It just dawned on her that she could have half siblings somewhere. This was getting to be too much she sighed. Looking at the map, she noted Pillsbury Park was near Leanne's summer cottage.

The map showed four ponds. One was circled. May Pond seemed to be the biggest and showed what looked like Islands in the middle. There was a red circle around the biggest spot. "Looks like this is where they want us to go." Mr. D had unwrapped the key. It kind of looked like an old-fashioned brass key. It was pretty big, and looked old. "Do you think it's for a door or a lock?" Leanne asked. "I don't know," he answered, but everything will be under snow until April. That's why we close up the house and call it the frozen tundra." "What do you think it all means Rayna asked?"

Wrapping up the trash, Leanne started to clean

up. She often needed a mundane task to help her focus. Putting on the kettle, she made everyone a cup of tea. She brought brownies out of her bag and served them each one. "Perfect," Mr. D sighed. "Just what I need to think." Next, Leanne took out a notebook and pen. First, she wrote *LETTERS*. "What do we want to ask about these letters." "Well," Rayna said, her eyes filling up. "Do you mean ask Aine?" "Yes, I think we need to talk to the fairies." "Then, I want to know."

1. Do I have siblings, and if so, where?
2. Is it the twins who need to help?
3. What will happen if we don't help?
4. Will my children be in danger?
5. Is my Mother alive?

"Those are good questions Rayna. I think you need them answered before going further." Leanne said hugging her. "This is a shock to all of us." "Well, not to me," Mr. D piped up. "I think it's all exciting. Like a real-life mystery show." Leanne glared, "show some compassion Sir. This is not your usual prime directive stuff you know. It sounds dangerous," she added. Rayna smiled at him. "It is kind of thrilling, I'll give you that," she said. All three studied the map trying to figure out what it meant. From the other room came the hungry cries of infants. "Who's up for helping feed babies?" Rayna asked. They all grabbed a bottle and went to feed the babies. The afternoon flew by. Rayna put both letters in the envelope and away in the file box. Grandfather and Nana sat with the babies while Rayna took Fy to the bus stop. They made a plan to visit the meadow and fairy tree on Sunday.

Sean arrived with the promised dinner promptly at 6 PM. He brought two pizzas. One cheese and one pepperoni, a salad, bottle of champagne and a chocolate cake for dessert. He also had a dozen yellow roses and a ring in his pocket. It was Friday night, so everyone was chill and ready for the weekend. Nora had arrived to spend the night with the twins. They all wanted to sleep in the downstairs playroom in sleeping bags. They had finally decided on two parent approved movies and were allowed to eat down there. Sean set it all up while Rayna changed and settled the babies. Then he brought two candles out, threw a checkered tablecloth over the coffee table and brought their dinner in. "Wow," Rayna said smiling. "I think we need a little music." Putting the radio on, she had it tuned to soft rock and left it down low. She wanted to hear the big kids. The babies were swinging in the same room as they were sitting. Sitting down Rayna said, "this is nice. I was hoping you would still come." "Of course, I would, now eat while its semi hot."

They enjoyed their pizza and salads with diet cokes. Sean shared how excited his parents were to meet her and the babies. He told her about his Mothers reaction to multiples and how she was practically on the plane already. "They seem pretty accepting of the circumstances," Rayna said. "Well, it's a different world now. Lots of people have children alone." "I know," Rayna laughed, but six? That's a little much." "It is a lot, I'll give you that," Sean said getting up. "You relax, I'll clear the stuff up." "I think I'll run down and check on the big kids." As soon as she left, Sean set up a laptop across from where they were sitting. The babies were very content and dozing to the music. He carried in two glasses of champagne, chocolate cake and a pot of tea. His palms were sweaty and he was nervous. At the last minute, he pushed the button to record. Good or bad, he wanted footage.

Rayna came up the stairs shaking her head. "Those kids are goof balls. Their writing posters and have balloons blown up and tied on strings." "Why?" Sean said smiling. "Who knows," Rayna answered. "I asked and they said it's a celebration. I said celebrating what? They just laughed and said YOU'LL SEE!!!!!" "Funny monkeys," Sean answered. "How about dessert?" "I am going to get fat," Rayna laughed. "Pancakes with you, lunch with Leanne, pizza and all this, good grief!" She sat down and went to pour some tea. Just then, Sean cleared his throat.

"Rayna," he began, "I have spent years looking for you. Since that night so long ago, I never stopped hoping we would find each other again. When I found you last month, I still felt the same. I thought I was too late when I learned you had a family. I never dreamed that this family was part of me." He knelt on one knee and pulled a ring box out of his pocket. "Rayna Marie, will you do me the honor of being my wife? Will you marry me?" Tears rolled down Rayna's face. She held her hand over her mouth. In the background was Bruno Mars song, *Marry Me,* playing on the radio. She stood up, and taking his hand helped him up saying, "I would be honored to be your wife." He slipped the ring on her hand and kissed her. "You have made me the happiest man alive. Thank you."

Just then there was a parade in the room. The three children came marching in singing with the radio. The balloons flew behind them. The babies were mesmerized by all the hoopla and watched every move. Rayna laughed and clapped. Turning to Sean, she asked, "did you tell them?" "Nope," he shook his head. "I wasn't sure you would say yes yet." Joannie just laughed. "We already knew Mumma." Joey and Nora both laughed. "Hard to keep secrets around here." Sean went over to the laptop and stopped the recording. "Good, now I don't have to delete that footage." Everyone laughed.

The big kids admired the ring, grabbed dessert, and went back downstairs. Sean and Rayna had a glass of champagne and started feeding infants. Two hours flew by. Finishing up the last baby, Sean asked Rayna, "do you want a long engagement?" "Hmmm," Rayna said, looking at the four little babies. "I think the sooner the better. I would like a real wedding though. I intend to only do this once and I want a celebration." "What about you Sean?" she asked. "I know my parents would want to come and my best friend Liam." "Let's think on it," Rayna said. "We still have a lot to learn about each other. Tell me about your friend Liam. Do you think they will come?" "If he can get off work, I am sure he would love to meet you. We have been friends since we were in nappies. Our Mothers are best friends still." "That is a long friendship," Rayna said laughing. "We will skype with them. It's almost as good as in person. Tomorrow we'll tell your parents and Leanne and Mr. D."

They talked into the night, then Sean went back to his apartment. They had decided, even though they were parents together, they would wait until their wedding night to sleep together. Unconventional, but they both wanted it to be special. As the big kids were in the playroom, Rayna decided to sleep on the first floor with the babies. Sean had helped her settle them in before leaving. Kissing the big kids' good night,

Rayna warned them to go to sleep. "We are so excited," they whispered. "Can we be in the wedding?" "Yes, all of you." "Even Nora?" they asked. "Yup," Leanne answered. Rayna took her parents wedding picture out. She hoped she would look as pretty as her mom had. She couldn't wait to share her news.

Everyone was excited for them. Leanne and Mr. D especially. They skyped with Sean's parents and best friend, Liam. They set up a once a week schedule for both. Rayna hoped they would like her and the twins. Obviously, they loved the quads. At Rayna's suggestion, they decided to do a DNA test. She knew Sean believed her, but proof was even better. They sent the test away and waited for results.

Chapter 25: Visit with Fairies -Sunday

On Sunday, Sean offered to stay with the children. Mr. D and Uncle James were coming over for the "big game" at 1 PM. The Patriots were favored, as usual. Tom Brady, at 49 years old, was still going strong as the starting quarter back.

Leanne and Rayna left to meet at the meadow. They brought the letters and pictures in the envelope, hoping to get some information about them. Driving over to the park, they stopped at the Dunk. Hot chocolate and a donut hit the spot. Turning to Leanne, Rayna asked, "do you think I should plan a big wedding?" "I think you should do what you want," Leanne replied. "It hopefully will be your only wedding." "I know, but I do have 6 children. It seems a little wrong." "Nonsense, a wedding is a celebration of love and family. Not to mention a happy occasion. Go for it. We have the money. You could have the ceremony right at the Estates. Why not invite the family and friends from Ireland. We can put a charter together. The group could attend the ceremony and sight see for a couple of weeks. Mr. D and I will use some of the winnings to set it up."

"Would you Nana?" "I think it would be wonderful," Leanne said smiling. "Have you decided on a date yet?" she asked. "We aren't sure if we should wait on the DNA test to come back." Turning towards Rayna Leanne asked, "does it matter?" "Well, not to me. I love Sean. I am confident he loves me and all the children. I wonder if it matters to his parents." "It's really none of their business Rayna. This is between

Sean and you." "I know," Rayna replied, I just want to start on the right foot." Driving in silence, they pulled into the state park. "Well, I think you'll make a beautiful bride honey," Leanne said, patting Rayna's hand. "Now, let's try to get some answers from our friends here.

The Park was pretty much deserted. They had only seen one car in the lot. It was cold and the forecast was for snow later. The sky was overcast and heavy with precipitation. Grabbing their heavy coats, gloves and hats from the backseat, they bundled up. Parking at the caretaker cottage, they started towards the meadow. The stream sparkled with icicles and only a tiny bit of water trickled over the rocks. The bridge crackled as they made their way over. At the bottom of the meadow, towards the tree, was a couple of sets of snow shoe prints. They led to and around the tree. "That's interesting," Leanne said. "Someone's been here." "Well, people do snowshoe, sled and cross-country ski in the park," Rayna said. "I guess. I never thought about that," Leanne answered. "Do you think Aine will know we are here?" she asked. "They always seem to," Rayna answered. "Maybe they have secret cameras?" "Could be. Maybe that's how they stay untouched."

Just then, the air was filled with moths. Aine lit between them. "Good afternoon ladies," she said. "I thought you might stop by." She started a fire and the other fairies sprinkled fairy dust around the tree. Soon, they were comfortably warm. "I hear congratulations are in order Rayna," she said smiling. "Yes, I am engaged to the babies Father. You already knew that I see." "Yes," Aine replied. "We do keep our eyes on the Estates and everybody there." "All three sat on the rock wall. "Do you have something to show me," Aine asked. Pulling the envelope from her bag, Rayna answered, "yup."

First, she handed her the original letter. Aine read it and looked at the map. Then, she took the key, turning it over in her hands. "We weren't sure she had left any information. Where did these come from Rayna?" Leanne explained, "when I saw the pictures you gave Rayna last time, I recognized the women. I knew I had met them back in 1997. It was my birthday, and they stopped by to interview my Daycare. The young woman was very pregnant and they seemed nervous. I turned them away, but saw them that night. Just before leaving, the younger woman asked me to keep this envelope. She said I would know who to give it to. So, I stuck it in the Daycare Memories box and forgot about it."

Looking at Aine, Rayna asked, "what does it mean?" Aine walked towards the fire pit. It was like an optical illusion. For some reason, when the area was sprinkled with Fairy dust, she seemed larger. She was more the size of a small child, not a tiny Fairy. The same thing had happened last time. She had a stool and she sat still holding the letters.

"We don't know everything. I will tell you what I do know. Your mother and my sister were followed here by a rogue group from our world. Some of the beings want us to take back this world." "What do you mean take back?" Leanne asked. "Well, there are many theories that another race was here first. Ireland, as well as many other countries, tell tales of other races. In Ireland, one was Tuatha De Danaan. A race of tall luminous beings with a highly developed society. They are said to have lost the battle, and retreated to the underworld. Many countries have similar stories and legends," Aine said. "We don't know what is true or real. Most people wouldn't believe in Fairies, but here I am."

"Your Father had wanted to bridge our worlds. Make it a true back and forth. Opening our world to everyone. That is what got him killed." Aine continued, "when it was discovered that your Mother was with child, they sent scouts out. My sister followed to warn Merena. I have not seen her since. One of the reasons I am here is this was the last known area where they were seen." Holding the letters out, she added, "this proves they were here."

"So, you know nothing more?" Rayna asked. "Well, we know you were brought back to Massachusetts only days old. Your mother left you at the Fire Station. We are not sure why. They must have found her. Then we used magic to pick Joe and Joan Stone to care for you. I have been watching over you all these years. We even made sure Leanne cared for you. We have always been close, you just needed to see.

Rayna took back the letters. "What about this part," she said pointing to the heading. "She writes to my child -children. Do I have siblings?" "Well, Aine started, we have reason to believe you were a twin." "What?" Rayna's face paled. "A twin?" she asked. "Yes, we believe there were two babies. Your mother took you and Maeve took the other. We think they split up to throw the scout off. They were looking for two women and a baby. Not two babies and two women. We have it on good authority that Merena was captured. She was alone and would not tell where the baby was. She was captured on the border of

Massachusetts. We think she is still alive but we are not sure exactly where. The other world is vast. There are many openings and lands. Just like this world, not everywhere is easy to get to. Maeve, however, is a prisoner in Pillsbury State Park." Aine picked up the map. "May I have this copied Rayna?" "Of course, but how?" Rayna asked. "No worries, we will get it back to you. They may be held together; we are not sure. This key will get the holder into the realm." "Wait, what about the other baby?" Rayna asked. "Do I have a twin?" Aine looked at Rayna. "We are sure there was a twin boy, however we have no idea where he is. Neither Merena nor Maeve have given the information up. We only knew about you because our scout found your Mother. She hoped by giving you up, you would be spared."

"Wow," Rayna sighed. "She did love me." "She loved you more than herself, Rayna. She wouldn't give you to them and instead is a prisoner." Aine stood up. "Ok, I think you have enough to think about. Let me send out inquiries and get this map copied. Can you come back next Sunday? Hopefully, I will have more information for you." All three were quiet. Standing up, they said their goodbyes. "Thank you," Rayna said. "Please find out what you can Aine. I would love to know more." "I will try," Aine answered. "Safe home."

Quietly they walked across the meadow. Cold seemed to seep into their bones. Walking over the bridge, they stopped and turned around. Low clouds hung over the area. You could almost feel the storm coming. "That looks ominous," Leanne said glancing up. "Should we stop for groceries?" Rayna asked. "At least milk and bread," they said at the same time. It lightened the mood to joke about "storm" food.

Turning the heat on high, they waited a few minutes for the car to warm up. "You ok?" Leanne asked. "I think so, do you think my brother is out there somewhere?" "Could be, you never know," Leanne answered. They stopped on the way home for storm provisions. The proverbial milk and bread and other needed things.

The store was packed. They ordered pizzas and sent a group text inviting any one to stop over before the storm hit. Leanne wanted to be safe, so she ordered 10 large pizzas. Rayna laughed. "Are you sure Nana?" "We can always freeze them, they will not be wasted," Leanne said.

They arrived home to a house full. Rayna had offered her house, as the babies, Mr. D, and the big kids were already there. It had been awhile since everyone had been together. The whole family were there. They made it an impromptu engagement party. Everyone had an opinion on when and how the wedding should be. It took the whole" twin", lost mother thing off Rayna's mind. It had started snowing heavily by the time everyone left. Sean offered to stay through in case the power went out. Rayna agreed if he slept in the playroom on the pull-out. He thought it was pretty funny, as they already had four kids. Humoring her, he set it up. Then, they took care of the babies. She shared what they had learned today. The thought of having a twin blew her mind. In a short time, she had found out about her Parents and possibly a brother. She hoped Aine would find out more. In the meantime, she had a family to care for.

Mr. D and Leanne took LuLu for a quick walk home. Snow blew all around. Already they were having a hard time walking. The wind blew the door open as they shook off the snowy clothes. "Let's get comfortable and warm up," Mr. D said. "I'll put the kettle on. I want to tell you about our visit with Aine," Leanne called from the kitchen. Putting hot chocolate and marshmallows in the cups she waited for the kettle. "How about some cookies?" Mr. D called. "Be right in," Leanne answered.

Carefully carrying the tray, she walked around Lulu. "That dog is trying to kill me," she said. Giving Mr. D his snack, she sat next to him and filled him in on their day. "Wow," he said when she had finished her story. "That's amazing. It was kind of fate for you to have met Rayna again. Destiny even. Do you think she'll find her brother?" he asked. "I wouldn't bet against it," Leanne said. "Anything is possible." "Well, they have the same birth-date and both were probably adopted," he added. "There may not be a record though," Leanne said. "Remember, the Grandmother was trying to hide him. I always said I wouldn't let the authorities know if I found a baby. There are ways of getting birth certificates. He could be anywhere. He may not even know about the circumstances of his birth." "Well, time will tell," Mr. D said, taking another cookie.

Knowing she was on borrowed time, Leanne brought up the idea for the wedding. "What do you think about paying for the Irish guests to come over?" she asked. "We have the money." "Why not," Mr. D said. "It will be a nice gesture." "There are the Sean's Parents, Liam (best man) and family (5) and Liam's parents who are Bernie and Big Sean's friends." "That's only nine people, possibly an infant, depending on when the wedding is. They would stay up to three weeks and we could set up sightseeing for them."

"Sounds good to me," Mr. D said. "Now, can we watch a show?"

They spent the evening watching their shows. The storm howled outside, but the electricity stayed on. Peeking out the window at bed time, Leanne noted at least 6 inches was already on the ground. News casters were reporting multiple storms rolling in. It snowed for six days. Everything was shut down. No school, work or driving. The world was at a winter shutdown. Luckily, everyone had food and for the most part the electricity had stayed on. The Estates were plowed and shoveled out and all the children visited back and forth. On February 5th, everything went back to normal. School reopened, Sean went back to his apartment. Rayna was sorry to see him go. They had been a good team. She enjoyed his company and they had talked about everything while caring for babies. She felt good getting to know about him. They shared lots of stories about growing up. He told her about his Parents and best friend. The twins bonded with him as well. Joannie and Joey gave their seal of approval. Today, the Quads were two months old. They would see the Doctor for a checkup. They had sent the DNA tests in and waited for the results. They had decided to test the babies and both Sean and Rayna. It would be interesting to see if there were relatives out there.

They had decided on a Spring Equinox Wedding. New beginnings would be the theme. They did not want to wait too long. It was enough time for the Irish group to plan. It would be on Leanne's birthday which seemed fitting. Rayna would have still been lost if Leanne hadn't found her only last year.

Rayna had picked out a dress. It was a "princess" style. The bodice was fitted with glittering jewels. A full skirt with the hint of pastel colors sparkled as she moved. The sleeves were three quarter length in case it was cold. She was also having a cape made of satin with a hood. Joannie and Nora were wearing similar dresses with pastel rainbow sparkled tulle. They would wear a ring of flowers in their hair. Joey would be dressed like Sean in a matching tux. The quads would all be in Christening outfits. Though they weren't Catholic, Sean and Rayna had decided to have the babies "welcomed" into the family. Hopefully that would appease Sean's parents. Everything was coming together nicely. Rayna asked Marie, James's partner, to be her Maid of honor. She asked James to walk her down the aisle. She wanted to honor the fact that both had cared so lovingly for the twins. She knew the value of their time all those years. Of course, Leanne and Mr. D were her honorary parents. The ceremony would be right here at the Estates.

Chapter 26: February 2026-Meadow

In the mist of all the preparations, Rayna and Leanne had driven to the Meadow. Driving into the forest, the roads were still pretty snowy. Parking at the caretakers, they almost got stuck. Grabbing their coats, Leanne saw the fairies coming. Aine flew to the side window. Leanne rolled it down. Aine flew in and lit on the dashboard. "I wanted to catch you before you started walking," she said. "The snow is deep and slippery. We have no news yet. Our scouts in both this world and the other world have no information yet. After the Equinox we should have collected enough evidence. I have been watching, your wedding will be soon." Rayna laughed, I can't wait," she said. "It will be an outdoor ceremony in the club house garden. Feel free to bring lots of friends. The butterflies will fit into the spring theme. Those who have "changed" their eyes will see fairy friends. I would be honored to see you there." Aine smiled. "I will see you then," she said. In the meantime, we will keep looking for information." "Sounds good," Rayna answered.

Time flew by. They skyped on Sundays with both Sean's Parents and Liam and his family. Everybody's papers were in order and the trip booked. They would arrive on March 12th, a Thursday. The wedding was set for March 20th, a Friday. They would return on April 2nd. Egobail Enterprises had offered the apartments on site. Everything was moving along.

The plane landed at 4pm. Sean had driven in the company van to pick them up. His parents were thrilled to be meeting their new Grandchildren, daughter-in- law to be and the twins. Dierdre, Danny, Liam and his family, were all excited to meet everyone. "Uncle Sean," 4-year-old Liam shouted, as they cleared customs. Hugging everyone, Sean showed them to the car. The Estates had purchased 3 car seats for the children, and the adults fit around them. Loading the suitcases, Sean and Liam discussed the living arrangements. His family would have their own apartment. The parents would share the second apartment. There was plenty of room for everyone. Bernie could barely contain her excitement. Finally, she would hold her Grand babies. She had been feverishly knitting since Sean's visit and had a separate suitcase of just those items. They never stopped talking the entire 2-hour ride. The family were waiting at the clubhouse. Everyone was there. A buffet was set up. Joey and Joannie were thrilled to meet the babies Grandparents. They had seen them on the computer, but were excited to actually meet them. As the van pulled up the three children, Nora, Joey and Joannie ran out to meet them.

Opening the door Sean helped his mom step down. Rayna stood with the big kids. Big Sean stepped down next. "Mom, Dad, this is Rayna." Stepping forward Rayna hugged both. "And these are the twins, Joey, Joannie and cousin Nora.

Bernie hugged everyone. Big Sean followed suit. The rest of the travelers piled out of the van. The children started into the building and adults welcomed each other. Just inside the room, Rayna had the infants sleeping in their strollers. Bernie stood looking down. She could not believe it; they were finally here. Not wanting to wake them, she sat at the table next to them. Sean moved everyone into the room and started the introductions. The children were a little shy. Danny held Orla, Patrick and Young Liam stood next to him. "Granddad, who are all these people?" the boys asked. "They're your Uncle Sean's new family," he replied. Mary and Liam shook hands with everyone. Rayna and the twins were last. Sean introduced Mary first. Hugging her, Rayna said, "I'm so glad to finally meet you. Sean has told me so much about you." Mary smiled, "He never stopped thinking about you. I am glad to meet you." "These are my older children, Joey and Joannie," Rayna said. Both children shook Mary's hand. "Your babies are coming soon!" Joannie said. Looking down at Joannie, Mary said, "not until the end of April." "Only one baby, not babies. See that baby?" She pointed to Orla. "She's mine and those are her brothers." "Maybe," Joannie said. "Can the boys eat at the kids table?" "Sure," Mary said, "if they want." Liam smiled, "nice to meet you both. You can call me Uncle Liam." "We will," they said running to get Nora and the cousins.

It was a wonderful welcoming for the Irish group. Everyone ate and talked. The infants were held by their Grandparents most of the night. At 11pm the young families started packing up. Children bundled up in jackets and hats, babies in strollers.

They all decided a nighttime walk home would be fun. Each child had a lantern flashlight to guide the way. They insisted on singing as they went. The new Irish friends got right into it and skipped along singing as well. Liam carried Orla; Mary walked with Nora's Mom. They had hit it off right away. Nora's little brother Charlie had made friends with Patrick and wanted to point out his house. Even the dogs ran around. Lulu, Teddie and Fy brought up the back. It was quite the parade.

Sean kissed Rayna at the door. He wanted to get the guests settled in. He promised to be back at breakfast. Leanne brought the children in and sent the Twins to get ready for bed. The babies were all changed and fed. She pushed the stroller in, and carried each to bed. Everyone was tucked in within a half hour. She went to tuck in Joey first. "That was so much fun," he whispered. "I like these Irish people. The boy Liam was fun." Leaning down to hug him, Rayna smiled and said, "Sometimes it's nice to have a boy to play with." "Could I have a sleepover with him?" Joey asked sitting up. "We will see," Rayna answered. "Awesome," Joey lay back down. "What about Uncle Liam," he asked. "Is he my real uncle?" "No honey, just Sean's good friend." "I think he's really fun, I want to call Liam my cousin." "You can honey, now go to sleep." Stepping over Fy, she went to Joannie's room. That was so fun," Joannie said. "I know, they are nice people, right?" answered Rayna. "Do you think we can call the babies grandparents Grandda and Granny?" "I bet they would love that honey. You can ask them; I am sure it will be grand as they say." "Awesome, I like Uncle Liam too. His kids will be our cousins, right?" "Well, he is not really your Uncle, just Sean's best friend." "I am going to call him Uncle," Joannie said. "I can't wait for tomorrow." Giving her a big hug Joannie whispered in Rayna's ear, "and there is more than one baby coming." "We will see, now go to sleep. Love you guys." Stepping around Fy she whispered, "good lord."

She knew better than to doubt them but really, more twins! They can't be right every time, she thought. "I am keeping this to myself." She washed her face and climbed into bed. It was already Midnight. Who knew how early the babies would be up? It was actually seven when they woke up.

Everyone was fed, dressed and waiting for company by 10 AM. The Grandparents arrived at right at 10 AM and settled down with Irish bread Bernie had baked at the condo. She made enough for an army and suggested they invite Leanne and Mr. D. Leanne walked right over and Mr. D would arrive later. He was not a morning person. The twins greeted everyone with hugs. Bernie had carried in a large suitcase. Pulling it over, she pulled out four knitted blankets. Each one was monogrammed with a baby name. The girls had rainbow pastel colors. The boys had rainbow blues and greens. There were matching hats and booties to go with them. Next, she pulled out four little white sweaters. "These," she said, "can be worn at the ceremony in case its chilly." The twins took and covered the appropriate baby with their blanket. Bernie took two more blankets out of the suitcase. "These," she said handing one to each of the twins, "are for you. You should consider Big Sean and I your Grandparents." "What will we call you?" Joey asked. "Granny and Granddad," she replied. They both hugged her and then Big Sean as well. Just then, Mr. D arrived with Lulu. Joannie and Joey greeted him with their blankets wrapped around them. "Look Grandfather," they cried, "Granny O Sullivan made us these." "Well, well," Mr. D smiled, "Now you will have lots of Grandparents, lucky kids." "We are lucky," they shouted.

"Can we call Nora, Mom?" "Sure," Rayna answered invite her over." The rest of the weekend flew by. There was a trip into Boston to sight-see. The

Grandparents had stayed to babysit the quads. Then a separate trip for adults on Saturday night for a show. Again, the younger crowd went for that. Bernie, Big Sean, Dierdre, Danny, Mr. D and Leanne, kept the littles. Anyone under 3. Cousins I and TY and their girlfriends kept the older kids for pizza and a movie at Nora's house. It was a busy week.

On Tuesday, March 17th they had a rehearsal/St Patrick's Day party. They had the hall set up with the indoor ceremony stage. Catered with a corn beef and cabbage dinner as well as cold-cuts and condiments. The Irish group laughed at the corn beef and cabbage. Only Americans think this is the meal for Ireland. There was Irish bread, scones and brown bread with Irish butter and marmalade. There was a large cake, green with shamrocks, and every table held shamrock plants. They had hired Irish step dancers and an Irish band. Everyone had a wonderful time.

The whole Estate showed up by the end of the night. The wedding party had arrived a half hour before everyone else. They practiced outside and again inside just in case. The weather was predicted to be beautiful, and they hoped for the outside ceremony. At 9 PM all the families with children packed up and headed home. The older cousins and Uncles stayed for a while, somewhat of a bachelor party. The women were happy to help settle down the littles. It had been a great night. The caterers had cleaned up leaving leftovers wrapped in the fridge. The women planned a get together on Thursday night. They had hired a group of manicurists to come and do everyone's nails for the wedding. Then, they were having a "proper" tea. The men would hold down the fort at home. The women had a wonderful time. Joannie and Nora were allowed to have their nails done first. Then, they went home to stay with the men. The women had a great time, lots of stories and laughs. Leanne felt it was a great way to get the families to know each other. Having money really did make things easier. Rayna was overcome with joy at sharing her special day. She did miss Joan, her stepmother, but felt truly loved by Leanne and the others. It was a wonderful evening.

Chapter 27: Wedding Day March 20th

Spring Equinox

The wedding was planned for 4 PM. A warm wind blew and temperatures reached 70 degrees at 2 PM. The flowers were set up outside lining the aisle. They covered the bridal archway with spring flowers as well. Already, many butterflies filled the air flitting from flower to flower and everything looked like a fairy-tale and beautiful. Marie was at Rayna's house all afternoon. As the Maid of Honor, she took her duties seriously. They had hired two hairdressers to fix the bridal parties' hair.

Leanne had hired a hairdresser for the three Grandmothers. It was her birthday, and she wanted to look nice for both Rayna and herself. She always joked that these pictures would be in her "death "collage and she wanted to look her best. Mr. D took the afternoon to visit Sean and the other Grandfathers. They had a nice lunch and played cards. They didn't understand why the women fussed so much. They thought they looked good already.

Mr. D had bought a beautiful necklace for Leanne's birthday. He would give it to her before the wedding. It was emeralds and matched her dress. The morning flew by and at 3 PM, everyone except Marie had gone home to finish dressing. The babies were bathed and napping. Joannie and Joey were ready and watching Cinderella with Nora downstairs. Rayna only had to slip her dress on and dress the babies.

She took a minute and sat with Marie. Marie asked "are you nervous?" Rayna took a deep breath.

"Not really," she answered. I love Sean, I just hope all this won't be too much for him." Marie nodded, "Well, he seems to know what he's getting into, right?" "Yes, he has been here often and knows how crazy it can be," Rayna laughed. "I just want him to be happy," she added. They fed the babies at 3:15 PM and dressed them in their "welcoming -wedding" outfits.

The photographer was back, and shot some adorable pictures of them. At 3:45 PM I and Ty showed up to push them in their stroller to the clubhouse. Once there, Leanne and Mr. D would sit with them for the ceremony. Everything went like clockwork. Rayna looked like a princess; her dress was perfect. They decided to walk with the three attendants, (Joannie, Joey, and Nora). Marie and Rayna carried their bouquets, and the girls carried a basket of petals. As they walked towards the venue, they were surrounded by butterflies. The photographer couldn't get enough photos. It was exactly 4 PM as they stood at the back of the garden. The chairs were full of guests.

Rayna could hardly believe all these people cared about her. She tried not to ruin her makeup with tears. Joannie was concerned. "Mumma, its ok. He loves us all," she said. "I know honey, I am just so happy." She took a big breath. James stepped forward, giving his arm. Joey started down the aisle. He went to Sean's side. He carried the ring on a pillow. Next, the girls started down the aisle. They carefully dropped the flower petals. They had been practicing all week. Marie was next. She walked slowly down the aisle. Then, the harpist started the wedding march. James smiled at Rayna. "Come on, after all you've been through?" he said. "You got this." They started forward. At that moment, the entire garden was full of butterflies. They surrounded Rayna as if they were escorts. The sight was mesmerizing. The photographer shot away. That helped Rayna to relax. James handed her to Sean and sat down.

The ceremony was beautiful. The guests were mesmerized by the butterflies, flowers, and of course the couple. They were pronounced husband and wife. Sean kissed Rayna, then the Officiant called for the babies. Bernie carried Patricia, Leanne carried Annie, Big Sean carried Sean and James carried baby James. Mr. D rode his scooter to the front and sitting next to Leanne, he was handed James.

The Officiant welcomed each baby to the family and called on everyone to accept them. Then Joannie and Joey were called forward. James pushed the stroller down and each baby was placed in it. The twins had decorated it earlier and it was quite festive. The Grandparents went back to their seats. James and Marie and Liam and Mary were asked to come forward. "Will you two couples' step in to care for this family of children if their parents need you." "We will," all four answered. The Officiant looked out towards the family. "Will this family help these parents." They answered, "We will." "Thank you, please be seated." Then, turning to Sean and Rayna he asked, "Do you want this family to be as one?" "Will you love and care for each other?" he added. "We will," they answered. "Then I pronounce you a new family."

Everyone clapped, quite a few tears were shed. Just as the twins went to push the stroller down the aisle, the butterflies took flight. They circled the Newlyweds and children. If you looked closely, you would see Fairy dust being sprinkled over them.

Non-believers thought it was pollen. The photographer got beautiful pictures regardless.

Most guests went in for the cocktail hour. The bridal party had pictures taken. Grandparents, Aunts, Uncles and all the children's pictures were taken. The reception started at 6 PM. The babies were taken care of and set up downstairs. They had hired two Daycare Teachers to watch them so the family could eat and dance. Most of the littles after dinner went down for a movie and snacks. That way, parents could enjoy the Evening. It was a fun wedding. After dinner and dancing, they brought a cake out for Leanne. They served both birthday and wedding cake for dessert. The babysitters were on until midnight, so the last dance was at 11:30. The couple danced and everyone blew bubbles. It was a nice ending to a great day.

The couple had decided to not go away. The weekend after everyone goes back to Ireland, they planned, they would take a quick trip to Cape Cod. Gathering up the new family, they kissed the Grandparents and guest's goodbye. They all walked home together. The babies went right to bed. The twins wanted Sean to read them a story. Rayna took her time to get out of the wedding gown. She had a beautiful Nightgown and robe set to wear. After all, it was her wedding night. She tucked in the twins. They were almost asleep. Everybody slept late, even the babies. It was close to 8:30 when they wanted feeding.

The rest of the weekend was pretty low key. They visited with the Irish group. The children had a ball with their "cousins." No matter how many times they tried to explain it, Joannie and Joey would not believe they weren't really cousins. They called Uncle Liam their Real Uncle. The adults stopped correcting them and went along with it. Leanne and Mr. D hosted a goodbye barbecue at the club house. All the kids wanted to play and swim. Why not, the Grown-ups agreed.

Everyone was going to the indoor pool first. The older men wanted to soak in the hot tub. The three older women were content to keep infants happy. Everyone else put suits on regardless of whether they would get wet or not. It was loud in the pool area.

The children were having a blast. The moms were all sitting together on chaise lounges talking and laughing. Leanne was happy to see her children relaxing a little. Sean and Liam were playing with the kids in the pool. Half splashing, half lifeguard. Swimming up to the side, Sean asked Rayna what time dinner was. "I think we'll have them serve it at 5 PM," Rayna replied. "Why?" Liam swam up beside him. "He's always hungry," he said splashing Sean. Mary looked on. "Boys, stop it, you're getting us wet." Though they were in suits, the moms preferred to stay dry. Purposely splashing his wife, Liam laughed. "Come get me," he said smiling. "Ah, no!" she said, rubbing her tummy. "You OK honey?" he asked. "Just a little tired," she replied. Liam jumped out and took Orla from her. "I'll let her swim; you take a break."

He sat on the edge with the baby. "You're not in labor, are you?" asked Rayna. "No, it's too early Mary answered. "Rest, you have been busy since you've come," Rayna replied. Mary sat and closed her eyes. Liam turned and watched her. "Hey," he said to Rayna, "is that a bruise on your foot." "What?" Rayna asked. "The sole of your foot," he replied. Sitting up, Rayna pulled her foot towards her. "Oh that, no I always have had it. It's a birth mark." "Wow that's funny." "Well, I don't think so," Rayna answered, I am glad it's on the bottom of my foot. Some people have marks on their face." "No, no, that's not what I mean. Mary opened her eyes. "Let me see Rayna," she said. Rayna lifted her foot. "It's funny because he has the same mark on the other foot." "Are you kidding me?" Rayna laughed. "Nope!" Liam came out of the water, putting Orla down, he lifted the opposite foot and sure enough an identical mark was on his foot. Joannie was skipping by to get to the hot tub. Glancing from one to the other she said "told ya so," skipping on by. "What a coincidence!" Mary said, picking Orla up to dry and change her. Leanne called out to everyone "dinner served in 45 minutes."

The parents took turns changing and then dressing the kids. It was a "country" themed dinner. Barbecue everything. The Irish group loved it. Strawberry shortcake was dessert and everyone was stuffed. Another great night.

This night ended a little earlier. Mary was still feeling under the weather. Nora's mom offered to take the boys to her place for a sleepover. Bernie and Big Sean took Orla. They wanted to give Mary and Liam the night off. Nora stayed at Rayna's with Joey, Joannie and young Liam. Liam's parents went with Leanne and Mr. D. They were going to visit for a bit. Everyone went on their way just after 8 pm.

Leanne put the kettle on, Dierdre helped set the table. They talked as they worked. Dierdre was very excited and talked of the new baby Mary was expecting. "We're so happy to have so many Grandchildren, aren't you?" she asked Leanne. "I am thrilled, and the Estates has been wonderful. Even when I just get to say hello in passing, I feel good. My

Grandsons actually stop by for a visit," she added. "We are hoping Mary has a little girl. That would be perfect. Two of each." "It is nice to have a sister and brothers, that's for sure," Leanne said.

Lulu ran into the room barking to be let out. Leanne hooked her to the run. The teapot whistled and she called to the men. Everyone was still pretty full from the dinner. Both Danny and Mr. D had "a bit of room for a cookie." So, cookies it was. Lulu came back in and slept in the corner. The four sat down for a chat. "Tell us how you met Big Sean and Bernie?" Leanne asked.

Chapter 28: Dierdre and Bernie, 1997

"Well, we had been married awhile and just bought the house nearby. We didn't have our Liam yet and I worked at the local shop," Dierdre said. "Aye, it was a lovely neighborhood," Danny added. "Up until then, we had lived with me Ma. Since my Da passed, she needed help. Dierdre was lovely to her. Helped her dress, cooked, cleaned and made a lovely home for us. When she passed, we decided to live in a newer neighborhood. We bought in the area we worked, happened to be right near Bernie and Big Sean. We moved just three doors down from them. We met them on the first Sunday, walking to Mass. We all hit it off wonderfully. Little Sean was just 3 months old that first day. It was a warm day for Ireland in August. We decided to stop for lunch that first meeting. We have been best friends ever since. Sean was a delightful infant, always happy and good as gold." Leanne chuckled, "I cared for Rayna in Family Daycare. She too was a good little thing."

Mr. D finished his hot cocoa and cookies. "What about Liam?" he asked. "He was 5 months old when we found him," Dierdre said. "He's adopted?" Leanne asked. "Yes, I thought you all knew," Danny answered. "Now there's a story for you, don't you know," Dierdre started.

"Bernie and I decided to take a visit to the Fairy tree. The famous one at the Hill of Tara. People leave trinkets and such to ask favors of the fairies." "I know it well," Leanne said. "Well, we had been trying for a baby of our own since we got married, with no luck.

Then, we met Bernie and Big Sean and we wanted it even more. So, Bernie and I decided to visit the site on the Fall Equinox, September 22 that year. It was a beautiful day and we brought a picnic lunch. We spread a blanket and sat on the ground watching people come and go. It was just past 5 PM when we decided to pack up. I had brought some ribbons and shiny trinkets to hang. Bernie stayed back with little Sean watching me. It was kind of a lark, but with a hint of hoping. I climbed over the fence; everyone had gone. A boulder, flat on top, lay at the base of the tree. We had watched other people climb and stretch to the lower branches to hang their offerings."

Dierdre took a breath, "I will never forget this," she said. "Just as I reached on tippy toes, a big wind came. It seemed to grab my offering, blowing it high up on the branches. I turned to call out to Bernie. She stood holding Sean with one hand over her mouth. What's the matter? I shouted to her. She took her free hand and pointed to the top of the tree. I climbed off the boulder and stepped back. You may not believe this, but it's true," Dierdre said. "The tree was covered in butterflies. Every color, kind and all sizes. They flew one way then another. We were mesmerized. Bernie ran over carrying little Sean. They are beautiful aren't they she whispered? They certainly are I whispered back. We looked around and we were alone. No one was there to validate what we were seeing.

As if on cue, every butterfly flew around and away. We looked at each other, and back up to the top of the tree. My trinket was somehow hanging at the very top. What was in those drinks? I asked Bernie. Nothing, she said, just plain Lemonade. Well the husbands are never going to believe this, we said laughing. Just then we heard mewing." "Mewing?" Leanne asked. "You mean like a cat?" "We thought so," Dierdre continued. "We looked at each other and back at the tree. The sound came again a little louder. What did you wish for Dierdre? Bernie asked me. What do you think? I answered. It must have been a cat, Bernie said cause that's what I heard. I did not wish for a cat Bernie, we've got two already, don't you know? Once more, we heard the sound. I think it's coming from around the tree Bernie said. Well let's check it out, I said to her. We looked around and everybody had gone. Bernie handed Sean to me and climbed over to my side of the tree. Handing Sean back, I slowly walked around to the back of the tree. I was cautious in case it was a hurt wild animal," Dierdre continued.

Leanne and Mr. D were engrossed by the story. "What did you see?" Mr. D asked. "Seriously?" Leanne laughed. "You're kidding me, right?" "No, what was it?" Mr. D asked again. Dierdre smiled, "I'll tell you," she said. "Around that tree was a basket." "Basket, basket of what?" Mr. D asked. Leanne said, "Oh just listen Sir, you're killing me." Dierdre said, "It was a baby. The basket held a baby. I called out to Bernie, come see this. I knelt down, looking for a note or something. The baby looked at me. Bernie came running around the tree. What, what is it she whispered? She stopped short and almost dropped Sean. Oh my God a baby she said. Whose is it? I unwrapped the blanket, and there was a cylinder. "Cylinder?" both Leanne and Mr. D said at the same time. "Yes, a cylinder," Dierdre said. "I unscrewed it and a note fell out. It said the baby was a boy born April 12 1997 and that he needed a home. Both Bernie and I looked around to see if anyone was watching. The place was empty. What do you want to do? Bernie asked me. I had wished for a baby of my own, but this way? I didn't know what Danny would do. In that moment, I did know I was taking him home. Bernie was behind it 100%. We wrapped the blanket around both boys and lay them together in the carriage. I slid the basket underneath and we pushed that stroller right across the grass. As we walked off the hill butterflies surrounded us as if to say good job. They flew away as we got to the street."

"Wait, what are you saying? You found Liam?" Mr. D asked. "Yes, he is my adopted son," Danny said.

Leanne clapped. "I always said I wanted to find a baby. I never did and had to settle for Daycare children." Dierdre laughed, "I was petrified someone would come take him away, but they never did. Sean and Liam grew into best friends and so did Bernie and I." "Even the Dads became mates," Danny added. "We spent every Sunday after Mass together and many a Saturday night at the pub," added Danny.

Mr. D said, "Wait, did you adopt him legally? Did you call the authorities?" Dierdre and Danny looked at each other. "Well no." "No?" How could you just keep him?" Mr. D asked. "We checked the papers and watched the news," Dierdre said. There were no babies listed as missing or stolen." "We didn't want to turn him into the system either," Danny added. "What if we weren't allowed to adopt?" Dierdre said. "We decided to claim him as our own. We changed his birthday to May 1st 1997 like Sean's. They could be birthday brothers we thought. Then, we filled out a home birth certificate with our names as parents. Bernie and Big Sean signed off as witnesses to the birth and it was done." "Didn't people notice?" asked Leanne. "Well, a couple were surprised but we were able to convince them there had always been two babies in the carriage. I did hold little Sean often before Liam came along. We dressed them the same sometimes after to collaborate our story. People do see what they want to that's for sure." "I so agree," Leanne added. "I would have done the same."

"Wow just wow," Mr. D said, shaking his head. You missed the boat honey. They got to do what you always wanted to do." Leanne laughed. "Well I am too old for that now," she said. "I did know it could work though."

"We told Liam when he turned 21. We felt he was ready for the story by then. We wanted him to know the truth before he started his own family," Dierdre added. He could have cared less, he assured us his childhood had been complete." "It was a relief to feel we did the right thing," Danny said. "We don't know who his birth parents were, but in every way, we are his parents and I am proud of him."

"I think it's wonderful," Leanne said. "He seems like a great guy." It was going on 10:30 PM and Dierdre offered to help clean up. "Thank you so much for all your hospitality Leanne," she said. "We have had a wonderful vacation." "Us too, it's so nice to see Rayna and Sean so happy." Leanne decided to walk them home and take Lulu for her night time walk as well. As they passed each home, Leanne explained who lived where. The night was beautiful with a star filled sky.

Mr. D was watching the news when Leanne got back. He muted the TV as she sat down. "That was a wild story, wasn't it honey?" he said. "Told you it would work," Leanne said. "Glad you didn't get the chance to try out your theory just the same," Mr. D said.

. . . .

Rayna woke up Sunday with the need to go to the Meadow. She had slept fitfully and hoped to see Aine. Texting Leanne, she said, "Taking a ride to the meadow, want to join me?" "Ready when you are," Leanne replied. They were headed out in 15 minutes. Sean and Liam were taking the children to the playground. Mary was still not feeling well.

Leanne grabbed her jacket and met Rayna at the house. "Everything OK?" she asked. "I guess," Rayna replied. "I just need to see Aine. Hopefully she has news for us." The ride was beautiful. The spring weather brought lots of people and dogs out. The Park was warm and they parked at the Rangers house. As they walked across the bridge the butterflies surrounded them. The meadow was already green and alive with young plants and flowers. Aine sat on the wall waiting for them. "I knew you were coming," she said smiling. It still surprised them that she could be seen as a small woman at times. Other times as a small Fairy. "Magic has a way about it," Leanne said. "Who am I to question anything. Already so much unexplained stuff has happened," she said laughing. "So, what have you found out about my Mother and Grandmother?" Rayna asked sitting down. "Quite a lot Aine replied.

Chapter 29: Spring and Summer, 1997

"We know you were left on the firehouse steps, April 21st 1997," Aine said. "The note said you were born on April 12th 1997. We understand your Mom got you out of New Hampshire. She hitched a ride with an older woman to Quincy MA. We are not sure where she stayed those nine days. She disappeared somewhere after dropping you off. Only recently, have we gotten information on her." "What do you mean," Rayna asked? "Have you found her?" "No, not found, but we did learn she was taken back to the other world."

"Your Grandmother, my sister, made it back to Ireland. We learned she arrived here on June 21st. She was spotted in Belfast at the docks. She carried a baby and disappeared into the crowd when approached. We have no more information about her. A baby was left at the Hill of Tara Fairy Tree on September 21st that year. We have no other information on her whereabouts at this time." Rayna held up her hands. "Wait, are you telling me I am a twin?" she asked? Aine stood up, and taking Rayna's hands said "Yes, you are." Rayna was stunned. "I don't feel like a twin," she said. "Who is it, do you know?" she asked. "We are pretty sure," Aine said. "Who, tell me," Rayna said standing up and pacing. "It's Liam," Aine said. "Sean's Liam?" Rayna asked. "Yes, we believe he is the baby my sister brought back to Ireland. She left him then disappeared. We have no trace of her since."

"How do you know my Mother was taken?" Rayna asked. "Well, the map helped pinpoint the door way North of here. I copied it and we sent scouts out. King Egobail and the Elder Council investigated the information this is what we found out."

Chapter 30: The Project

"Let me start at the beginning," Aine said. "Many tales have been told for centuries. You know because you studied a lot of the Myths and fables in college." Rayna nodded her head. "Well, the Pre-Christian Celtic people of Ireland told a story of a supernatural race. They called it the Tuatha de Danaan. They were said to be Gods of Fertility. They were said to be tall luminous beings who had a highly developed society. Story has it when they lost the battle for the land of Ireland to a band of humans they disappeared. They are said to have gone underground to the otherworld. They are believed to come back up from time to time. Some believe that they cursed the Fairies and others in our group. That's why we have trouble with our offspring and keeping our world separate. We have been cross breeding to strengthen our Genes.

The Project was started 30 years ago. Each of the four groups in the "Otherworld" signed up to the experiment. The goal was healthier groups, still separate, but able to "cross breed" if you will. Your Parents, Rayna, were the third group to participate. They signed on to give us a better chance to have healthy children. Your Parents were given drugs to help them conceive, then to also have a multiple birth. Each Parent took the drugs for three months, then planned on conceiving. The group consisted of three groups of Tuatha's, humans and Fairy folk. Your parents panicked and decided to leave after the wedding. Any first-generation children conceived through that protocol have a birthmark. Interesting both you and Liam have birthmarks." "Yes, on the sole of our foot. I have a half moon and star mark and so does Liam," Rayna said. "Yes, they did not want it visible to just anyone," Aine added. "Anyone in the drug trial is predisposed to multiple births. The trial is far reaching. All the governments had a hand in it. We have found the last laboratory to be situated at Pillsbury State Park. You, Rayna, were left the map and key to get into the main building." "Why me?" Rayna asked. "We believe there is a component in your blood that will save both worlds from extinction. Your twin and children also carry the antibodies.

In order to keep your identity secret, Egobail Enterprises will draw your blood. Then they will send it to the lab at Pillsbury State Park. We are still looking for other first-generation subjects. Some people believe that the Tuatha's are from a different Galaxy. We have no proof. We are looking into whether my sister is being held at Pillsbury State Park and still trying to find your mom. I will reach out with any information as I get it," Aine said. "In the meantime, I think Mary may need you." Leanne looked at Aine. "Really, the baby is coming?" "Pretty sure," Aine said. "Better get on home, we'll be in touch."

Walking back across the meadow, Rayna was quiet. "You OK?" asked Leanne. "I think so," Rayna answered. "It's a lot to take in." "It certainly is," Leanne said. "What's the most troubling, having a brother, not knowing if your mother is alive or becoming an Aunt again any minute?" Leanne asked. "Well, when you put it that way, everything!" Rayna answered. "Let's get going," she said. They hurried to the car. As they pulled up to the Estate gates, Sean met them. He hurried over. "I just left you a message. Mr.

D and my Parents are holding down the fort." "I'm driving Liam and Mary to the hospital. Mary is having the baby. Isaac is driving Liam's parents and meeting us there. I'll call you with an update." Kissing her, he hurried away. "Here we go!" Leanne and Rayna said at once. They drove straight to Rayna's.

Everything was under control. Bernie and Big Sean held a baby each. Mr. D was sitting with Liam's children and the twins. They were engrossed in a movie. Meat sauce cooked on the stove, and the water was set to boil. "We made pasta for dinner," Bernie said. We figured it could feed a lot, once we realized the baby was coming," she added.

Rayna sat and picked up Patricia. Feeding her, she turned to Bernie. "Tell me about Liam," she asked. "What do you mean?" Bernie said. "Tell me about the day you found him," Rayna said. Bernie repeated the story just as Dierdre had told Leanne. Rayna's mind was racing. Could this be true? All her life she had wanted a brother or sister. A twin, and her new husbands' best friend? This was unbelievable. She was having a real hard time wrapping her head around the whole thing. She should have realized it when they had the same birthmark. Joannie and Joey had insisted Liam was their "Real" Uncle from the moment they met him.

Bernie looked concerned. "Are you alright dear?" she asked. Rayna lifted the baby to her shoulder. "Yes, just surprised, I guess. I knew he had a different Birthday, so I would not have guessed we were related." "Well, Dierdre so wanted a baby," Bernie said, she thought it was best. "No one was looking for a baby. She loved him from the moment she found him." Rayna nodded, "I have no doubt about that, she may have saved him." Getting up, Rayna started changing the infants. "Well, we have a new baby on the way and hungry people to feed," Bernie said.

She went to the kitchen to start the pasta. The evening past quickly. The children enjoyed the company. Sean stayed at the hospital for Liam and kept everyone advised of the situation. When the children woke up the next morning, they had two new siblings. "I told you," Joannie said laughing. "Yup," Joey added. "We knew there were two babies."

Liam and Mary were surprised when the twins were born. They had seen Doctors in Ireland. Even had an ultra-sound. No second baby was discovered. Their heart beats were exactly in sync. They were two little girls. No names were chosen as yet. Dierdre and Danny were thrilled everyone was healthy. They stopped to see the Grandchildren and show off pictures of the newest babies. Sean was excited for his friend. The women were already making lists of needed supplies. Leaving the children with Rayna and Leanne, Danny and Dierdre went to the condo to sleep. The older children would visit the babies the next day. Mary needed her rest and Liam was staying with her.

The next afternoon, Rayna and Sean visited the babies. Mary was doing well and Liam was excited to get everyone home and together. The babies were adorable. Two little peanuts wrapped in pink. Rayna asked what they needed. To leave the hospital, they needed car seats and clothes. Sean and Rayna offered to pick everything up on the way home.

Liam and Rayna were trying to get used to being twins themselves. They decided to name the babies Dierdre Anne and Maeve Merena after their Grandmothers.

The new babies would be discharged in two days. The plan was to extend their visit. Liam and Rayna made plans to talk when they were settled at the condo. Stopping on the way back, they picked up all the needed supplies for the homecoming. Rayna thought to herself, "Who says money doesn't matter? It sure makes life easier."

Walking into the house, everyone met them at the door to see pictures of the new babies. At the end of the week, the babies came home to the condo. Liam stopped to see Rayna after settling Mom and babies. They had a lot to discuss.

Chapter 31: Rayna and Liam

Sean took all the children to the playroom. He promised to keep them occupied while Rayna and Liam talked. Setting down a pot of tea and plate of cookies Rayna smiled at Liam. "I'll pour," she said. The tea was poured and she sat down across from him. "Well, what do you think?" she asked. "It's a lot to get used to," Liam replied. "I knew about being found and all, but twins? This is incredible, and what are the odds that my best friend happens to meet and marry my twin." Rayna took a long gulp of her tea and nibbled on a cookie. "You have no idea Liam. Would you like something stronger; you might need it?" "No, I don't dare, I have to help Mary. We surely were not expecting the baby yet, never mind twins." Taking another sip Rayna said, "Liam, I need to tell you a story. It is going to sound a little strange. I need you to listen until the end, then you can ask me anything." Does this sound alright?" she asked. Liam nodded. "Ok, here goes."

Liam took a drink of tea and started to eat a cookie. Rayna began as short a version of the "story" that she could. She told about her twins and the birth. She told about the fairies and then about Ireland. She could see him start to wonder if it was real. She told about meeting Sean 7 years ago. Then she got to the part about the Hill of Tara. She added that it was the same place he had been found. She told about the fairy tree and how she had fallen through. Liam sat straight up at this part. He started to ask her about it. She lifted her hand. "Better to listen till the end. Then, I will try to answer all your questions." Liam nodded and took another sip of tea. Telling him about the other world and her escape back, she teared up. Explaining how it felt like a day to her, but she had lost almost 7 years. Her children were 6. She told him about Leanne and the lottery and how Egobail Enterprises had helped them. She explained the Fairy world as best she could. Telling him about the meadow and Queen Aine. She told him how Sean had found her. He raised an eyebrow at Sean not seeing her in over 7 years. She told him about the babies, how her body felt just one day when it was years. She explained that they did not want the Grandparents concerned. She told him everything. "I only found out about a sibling recently," she said. "Aine gave me pictures of my Mother and Grandmother. Leanne had met them. They had looked into her Daycare. That night she had found an envelope with these letters in them." She lay the letters down on the table. "Can I read them?" Liam asked. Nodding, Rayna picked up her teacup. Watching as Liam read the letters, she was able to see exactly when he believed.

"This is truly unreal," he said, laying them back down. "I know, right?" Rayna answered. "What does it all mean? Is our Mother alive? Where are these Fairies?" "I have been visiting them in the State Park since the twins' birth. They claim to have watched over me through the years," Rayna answered. "Our mother is or was a Faerie. our Father a human. Our blood and children's blood, could save us from extinction." Rayna picked up the teapot. "Would you like some more?" "You know, I think I will take that drink if you don't mind," Liam said. "Alright then," Rayna said. "I'll get it for you." She poured a liberal shot of whiskey and brought it to the table. Placing it in front of Liam, she said, "I don't know about you, but I am thrilled to have a brother and a twin, it's fantastic." Liam gulped his drink. "I am pretty excited as well, just shocked about it all. It is a lot to take in Rayna," he said smiling. "Not to mention you have newborn twins yourself." "Aye, aye, that I do. I am still getting used to being the father of five. Now I'm part Fairy. Mary is going to think we are all daft." They both burst out laughing. Sean knocked at the door. "You guys ok?" he asked, sticking his head in the room. Liam smiled. "Well, I just heard the most fantastical story from your wife here." "Pretty sure it's all true," Sean said, "but right now, the natives are restless.

They called Mary. The infants were handled and she was resting. They decided to feed the children together, then take them home for bed. Leaving, Liam hugged Rayna. "It's lovely having a sister, but I am going to wait for the right time to tell Mary." "Do whatever you think is right Liam. We will take a ride in two days to the Meadow. You may want to meet Aine first. She may have information for us." "Sounds good." He took his three home. Nora and Charlie left for home too. Sean and Rayna fed, changed and got their own 6 children settled for the night. As usual, they both tucked the twins in separately. "I am so happy Liam is our Uncle," Joannie said. "Me too," Rayna answered, "but let's just keep it to ourselves. Uncle Liam needs to talk to Aunt Mary and not everyone believes in magic." "She does," Joannie said. "She will believe, you'll see." Using her hand, Rayna made the locking lip sign. "We will wait, OK?" "Ok Mama, but it will be fine."

Joey was next. "I am so happy Mama." "I know

honey. Their a wonderful family. You have always had Nana and Grandfather and all your cousins you know, Right?" "But this is like the cherry on top," Joey said, rolling over. "Love you Mama." Sean had a nice goodnight too. Everyone was happy.

Leanne called the next morning. "Come on over," Rayna said. "Sean is at work for a few hours. Everyone else is busy changing flights and getting baby things." "OK, I will pick up lunch and be there to help with the babies."

At 10:30 AM, Leanne brought lunch and two ice coffees. The babies were lying on the floor playing, bottles were warmed and waiting. Picking little Jimmy up, she grabbed a bib and a bottle. He was usually the most vocal to be fed. Rayna picked up little Sean. "How did it go?" Leanne asked. "Pretty good," answered Rayna. "He only needed one drink after." "Did he believe it all?" "I think after having twins of his own unexpectedly, he did." "Now, the fun part will be the trip to the meadow tomorrow." "We have set it up for 9 AM. That way he will have time to chill before going to Mary." "It is scary telling people; do you think it will ever be different?" Leanne asked. "Well, you never know," Rayna said lifting the baby to burp. "Let's get these leprechauns fed and napping. That lunch is calling me."

Leanne lay Jimmy back down and picked up Annie next. It took an hour to get them down for naps. Lunch was wonderful. They talked as much as ate. Rayna shared the evening talk with Liam. Leanne could not get over the whole story. She remembered the meeting with Rayna's Mom like it was yesterday. Looking at Liam now, she could definitively see the resemblance. "Weird, isn't it? All these moments alone don't mean much. Then, put together, they really tell a story," Leanne exclaimed. "Do you think Mary will believe?" "What about the parents," Leanne asked? "Liam is telling Mary the story today, we are going to the meadow tomorrow," Rayna added. "I will sit with the kids," Leanne offered. "I asked Bernie and Big Sean. I thought you could come with us; it might help Liam." "Of course, I will," Leanne answered. "What time?" "We will leave at 11AM." "Great, I will walk over.

They finished lunch and made brownies for the kids' afternoon snack. Leanne was still there when they arrived. "Nana," they called out. All three and the two dogs ran into the kitchen. They were full of stories. Leanne enjoyed the visit. At 11 AM the next morning, she sat outside waiting for them.

Chapter 32: The Meadow and Plan

Climbing into the back seat, Leanne buckled her seat belt. "Are you ready for this Liam?" she asked. "Well," he said turning toward her, "it is hard to believe." "That's for sure," Rayna added. The short ride was silent. They were all lost in their own thoughts. Turning into the Park, the car was surrounded by butterflies. Leanne laughed out loud. "I guess they expect us." Nodding, Rayna said, "I wouldn't be surprised if Aine has the tent set up." Leanne pointed out the different areas of the park. Liam seemed to enjoy the distraction. They pulled up to the caretaker's cottage. It was still empty, so they parked in the driveway. "This is where the twins were born," Rayna said. "Wow, that was brave," he turned to Leanne. "You delivered them alone?" he asked. "Well Rayna did all the work," Leanne said laughing. "It was a joint project," Rayna said smiling. "It was awesome," Leanne added, "one of the happiest days of my life."

They climbed out of the car. Leanne grabbed her jacket and bag, and they started towards the bridge. "The meadow is just over this bridge Liam," Rayna said. Liam took a big breath. "I am ready to meet them," he said. The butterflies had followed from the car. Rayna said, "look around, they are here already." Liam turned and looked at the butterflies. He closed his eyes and, mumbling to himself, said words they couldn't hear.

The sun was shining over the meadow. Many butterflies circled the tree. "It's beautiful," Liam whispered. "They sparkle in the light." Just then, Aine, in her more human form, came from behind the tree. She looked beautiful. Her long hair was braided around her head. She stood just about 4 ft tall and wore a flowing gown. No wings were visible but there was an aura about her. Walking to meet her visitors, she out stretched her arms. Liam and Rayna walked forward. Rayna greeted her Aunt.

"Queen Aine, I would like to introduce my brother, Liam." Liam stepped forward. He offered his hand, but Queen Aine hugged him. "I always hoped we would find you both," she said. Tears streamed down her face. "You both look like your Mother." Pulling herself away, she said, "let me tell you what I know."

Walking around the large tree, Aine sat in front of the wall. There were cushions placed on the wall. Aine had a bench in front of the tree. "Sit!" she said, pointing. She sprinkled a vial of fairy dust grinning. "Ready for a bit of magic?" At that, a table appeared with refreshments. To help the magic mood, there were four fairies standing at the corners.

"I know it's hard to believe, but if you see with your own eyes, it might make it easier." Leanne and Rayna giggled. "What do you think Liam?" asked Rayna. "Well, Liam said, "if I didn't know better, I would think I was drunk." "Ahh," Aine said. "That's exactly how we have stayed under the radar so long. Humans are afraid to believe. Help yourselves to some refreshments," she added. "I will start."

"You, by now, know about your birth parents, your ties to the other world and that we exist. Egobail Enterprises has a stake in this story as well. It is no surprise that they are involved. They have people working in both worlds. I know Rayna has filled you in, Liam. You both carry blood, that along with the twins, Joannie and Joeys blood, can save us. The laboratory is in the other world under Pillsbury State Park. The World Wide Center for Disease Control, aka CDC, is well aware of this. The Agency has long studied such things. The National Center for Health Statistics, Pregnancy Risks Assessment Monitoring System (Prams), were helping us 30 years ago. You were the first viable pregnancy. When your Mother ran away, they were very angry. You were our hope for a future. Some people in both our worlds want to stop us. The consensus is, if we are unable to have children, we will die out. They are hoping to take the other world for themselves. Humans have done a lot of damage to their world. They want to come below and live in ours. They do not want to wait; they want to start taking."

Leanne looked from Rayna to Aine. "What can they do?" she asked. "Well," Aine said, "we think they can use their blood to cure others." "How is our blood different?" Rayna asked?" "Well, you are mixed race. Your Mother was full blood Fairy and your Father half human, half fairy." Aine let that sink in before continuing. "Why would our parents leave then?" asked Rayna. "Well, your Father had lived with his Father and wanted a more "normal life" for his child. Your Mother was afraid you would be institutionalized when born. It seemed the Health Organization was more interested in the antibodies in your blood. That's why she separated and hid you both."

Liam rubbed his eyes. "Let me get this straight. Our blood can save the Fairy world from extinction. I am a twin who was experimented on before birth, and my mother was a fairy and father half human." Standing up he started to pace. "Are you kidding me, seriously? This is unbelievable." Getting more agitated, he mumbled faster and faster. Rayna stood and reaching out grabbed him. She hugged him tight. "Calm down," she whispered. "It's a lot. Shhhh!" Rubbing his back, she calmed him. Taking his hand, she led him back to the wall. "Sit!" She handed him a drink. "Deep breaths."

Leanne and Aine quietly watched the two. In no time he had calmed down. Rayna sat next to him. She lay her hand on his knee. "Sorry, Liam said, it's just a lot." Aine smiled, "I know nephew, you have had a wild week. It really makes no difference. Our species are very much alike. We just know how to use our magic," Aine added. Centuries of practice.

"Wait," Leanne asked. "How is Joey and Joannie' s blood helpful?" "Well that's what I was going to share next. We have studied their blood. It seems that the Father from Punta Cana was a fairy as well. We have no way of finding him, but their blood has the antibodies too."

"Our intelligence tells us that we need to go to the laboratory. There, we will find Doctors who can use the blood to cure us. You and your children are all we have found still alive. We need you to go together to Pillsbury State Park. There is a Pond. May Pond. On the island in the middle of the pond is a Hawthorne tree. You will use the key to enter the other world."

"Wait, I don't want to lose any years from my children," Rayna said standing up. "I already lost so much." Liam stood as well. "I have 5 children. I won't leave them." Aine also stood. "I know it is a lot to ask. There is a way you will only lose less than one summer. Your sacrifice will save Fairies and keep the other world safe for the others. I can't promise, but you could possibly meet and rescue your Mother and Grandmother." Rayna and Liam stared at each other. "What do you think?" Liam asked. Turning to Aine, Rayna said, "tell me how we won't lose years.

Aine stood and walked over to Rayna and Liam. "The only way we know is to enter the tree on June 21st the Summer Solstice. You will have until August 12th the total Lunar Eclipse, to come back to this world. That is almost two months your time. Regardless of completing the mission, you need to be on this side of the world by the end of the Eclipse. Otherwise, you will lose 7 years per day spent in the other world. It will be dangerous. The Tuatha De Danaan are the keepers of the Center. We do believe they have kept your Mother and Grandmother all these years. Our spy's have seen them caring for infants and children not of our race. They were not able to rescue them. Go home and talk to your loved ones. Your affairs should be in order if you choose to help. I will continue to collect data. Come back in two weeks with your answer." Hugging both, she kissed them on the cheek. "Do your best, I know this will be hard. See you soon," and she turned and was gone.

Liam sat back down. "What do you think?" he asked Rayna. Sitting down next to him, she sighed. "I want to help, and if there is a chance to see our Mother, a dream come true. I am nervous to involve the twins and scared. I did lose almost 7 years. I almost lost Sean and I now have him and the Quads to think of." Sighing, Rayna said, "I will talk with Sean before making a decision." Liam nodded. "I am not sure Mary will believe any of this, it truly is unbelievable. My Parents are more likely to believe. After all, they did find me at the fairy tree." Leanne laughed at that. "It does take getting used to," she said. "The idea of magic is somewhat born in the Irish." "That is true," Liam nodded. "We are convinced easily." "Well, let's get back. I am sure our babies and spouses need looking after," Rayna said. They walked slowly to the car. Reaching the spring and bridge, they stopped for a moment. "What do you think Nana," Rayna asked. Leanne looked back at the meadow. All trace of their meeting was gone. Many butterflies still flew around them, but Aine had left. "Well, I won't tell you what to do. It could be very dangerous, and you know I love you all like my own, especially the twins. I also have grown to love the Fairies and see value in the other world. Who knows what the future will bring? I read somewhere once, that people are the heroes of their own stories. Is it time to be a hero? I can't tell you what to do. Whatever you choose, make it be right for you. George Elliot said "It's never too late to be the person you were meant to be." Go home, talk to Sean and Mary, then talk to your parents. Tell them everything. If you need back up, I will stand by you. Mr. D was a hard sell, but he believed. We are a village and can help you. You just need to ask." They drove the rest of the way home each lost in thought.

THE END

The Author

A. F. Smith is a first time Author. Writing a Contemporary Romance and Fantasy for her debut novel. Writing has been a longtime passion for her.

Ann is a retired Daycare Provider (Educator). Mother of 4 wonderful children and Grandmother of 3. She has cared for more than 100 children, including her Grandsons in her childcare. She lives with her husband of 46 years, dog Rosie and two sons. Her favorite quote from the book is "The last thing you want to do, is to be at the end, finding you didn't fulfill your destiny".

Ann has already started on a sequel to Equinox. Look for **Solstice,** coming in Fall of 2020. The story continues.

www.ingramcontent.com/pod-product-compliance
Lightning Source LLC
Chambersburg PA
CBHW071149100726
47908CB00002B/310